THIS SIDE OF JORDAN

THIS SIDE OF
JORDAN

A NOVEL
BY MONTE SCHULZ

FANTAGRAPHICS BOOKS | SEATTLE, WA

Fantagraphics Books, 7563 Lake City Way NE, Seattle, Washington 98115 | Edited by Gary
Groth. Designed by Adam Grano. Cover art by Al Columbia. Promoted by Eric Reynolds.
Published by Gary Groth and Kim Thompson. | *This Side of Jordan* is copyright © 2009 Monte
Schulz. Cover art copyright © 2009 Al Columbia. This edition copyright © 2009 Fantagraphics
Books. All rights reserved. Permission to reproduce material must be obtained from the author or
the publisher. | Interior graphics by Rich Tommaso, Zuniga, and Gavin Lees. Additional editor-
ial assistance by Kristy Valenti. | To receive a free full-color catalog of comics, graphic novels,
prose novels, and other related material, call 1-800-657-1100, or visit www.fantagraphics.com
| Distributed in the U.S. by W.W. Norton and Company, Inc. (1-212-354-5000), Distributed in
Canada by the Canadian Manda Group (1-416-516-0911), Distributed in the United Kingdom
by Turnaround Distribution (108-829-3009) | First Fantagraphics Books Edition: October 2009
| ISBN 978-1-60699-296-8 | Printed in China

FOR MY FATHER,
WHOSE PERSISTENT INSPIRATION STILL GUIDES THIS IMPERFECT HAND

WHO HAS DONE HIS DAY'S WORK AND WILL SOONEST BE THROUGH
        WITH HIS SUPPER?
WHO WISHES TO WALK WITH ME?

—WALT WHITMAN

I LOOK TO THE EAST, I LOOK TO THE WEST,
A YOUTH ASKING FAITH TO BE REWARDED.
BUT FORTUNE IS A BLIND GOD, FLYING THROUGH THE CLOUDS
AND FORGETTING ME ON THIS SIDE OF JORDAN.

—TRADITIONAL

AMERICA,
THE MIDDLE BORDER

1929

FARRINGTON, ILLINOIS

ALVIN PENDERGAST STOOD OUTDOORS behind the old Farrington auditorium in an Illinois breeze swollen with fresh crabapple blossoms. The farm boy had a fifty-cent ticket in his hand to see the dance derby, but felt too blue to be inside. Orchestra music filtered out into the motor parking lot and across the spring twilight. He had walked alone three miles from the farm late that afternoon with a meat sandwich and a pocketful of Aunt Hattie's lemon cookies in his jacket and hadn't yet eaten a bite and it was past suppertime now. Tall carbon lamps were lit against the dark and clouds of tiny moths fluttered in and out of the pale light. Leaning against a thick maple tree a dozen yards from the back door, Alvin watched a pair of Model A Ford automobiles rattle into the side parking lot where a crowd his own age got out laughing. The pretty bobbed-haired girls were wearing short skirts and sparkling jewelry, while the boys dressed in white flannel, straw hats and spats. Some were smoking cigarettes. Coughing into his fist, the farm boy watched them hurry off into the noisy auditorium.

He ate his sandwich and one of the cookies. After a while, a flatbed truck swung into the parking lot and a young man Alvin's age jumped out and hurried to the back porch, shouting, "Patsy! Patsy!"

A stout fellow in suspenders and a straw boater held the door open for an attractive girl in a polka dot dress who came out to greet the young man. Her brown hair looked snarled and her street makeup was smeared with tears.

The young man bounded up the steps, shouting, "I'll kick that god-damned sonofabitch's head off if it's the last thing I ever do!"

Alvin's jaw dropped as he saw the girl slap the young man across the face.

The fellow stumbled back against the railing. "Hey! What's that for?"

The girl took a wad of chewing gum out of her mouth and threw it at him. "Nuts to you, Petey. We're finished!"

"Aw, honey," the youth whined, rubbing his cheek, "I know you're sore, but I swear that no-good guinea sonofabitch told me my house was burning down! No kidding! I had to go clear downtown and tele-phone Elmer to find out it wasn't true!"

"So long, Petey. Lay an egg!" The girl brushed past the stout fellow on her way back indoors.

"Aw, gee whiz, Patsy," the youth called after her. "Can't you see I'm still full of pep? Why, we'll show 'em who can shake a hoof. You bet we will!"

An older fellow in a brown plaid wool worsted suit and a snappy new fedora came out onto the porch, a lit cigar in hand. "Not tonight you won't. I tell you, kid, you're through."

The youth frowned. "Says who?"

"Says I. Now, scram! We don't need any more dumbbells around our derby." He turned to the fellow in the suspenders. "Gus, see that this here lug of Patsy's beats it."

"Yes, sir."

A smart Tiger Rag started up within the auditorium, promoting a raucous cheer from the grandstand audience. The youth spoke up. "Look here, Mister Cheney, let up on that, will you? Me and Patsy'll win the sprint tonight if you'll only give us the chance. We aren't the troublemakers in this derby. We got sponsors, loads of 'em, I tell you, who think we're pretty swell. What do you say?"

Alvin almost laughed out loud when he saw the man in the fedora exhale a cloud of smoke into the youth's face, then follow Patsy back indoors. This was lots better than dancing.

The stout fellow wearing suspenders closed the door, and turned to face the young man. "Sorry, kid, but if the boss says you gotta scram, then you gotta scram."

The youth jerked loose his necktie and flung it off the porch. "It's not fair, Gus! Not fair at all! We'd a won, me and Patsy. Bet your hat on it. I tell you, somebody greased that guinea sonofabitch to gyp us out of our thousand bucks."

"Sure they did, kid, but if you don't shove off now, you'll just queer yourself for the next town."

Alvin edged closer to the rear of the auditorium, hoping like hell to see some fireworks. Why not? Just last week, a shoe salesman from Cleveland had gotten shot four times in the head out behind the smokehouse on Wilson Street. A boy Alvin knew from the high school football team had found the body and told everyone how much blood he'd seen. His name was printed in the morning newspaper.

"Gee whiz, Gus, even if we didn't win, Patsy and me was hoping for a spray that'd get us enough for a ticket to St. Louis."

"Go back to squirting soda."

"Aw, I don't have the poop for that anymore."

"Well, I say a fellow oughtn't to plug himself up for a big shot in a rotten business like this unless he knows he can put it over often enough to eat regular and keep some kale in the bank."

"I know where I stand, Gus," said the youth. "Cheney does, too. I've learned the steps. You bet I have. Two hundred and thirty-six hours of picking 'em up and putting 'em down, and I'm still fresh as a daisy. Never gone squirrely, neither. Not once. And you ought to see the nifty stunt I planned to put over tonight. Why, it's a panic, I tell you. Look here, I'd be a big shot, Gus, if only the derby was fair and square and Cheney did his duty by some of us."

"Keep that under your hat, kid."

Alvin watched the youth stiffen his back, teeth clenched as if he were about to have a fit. Here it comes! Now he'd see something! Every fight started with a mean pose, like dogs and alley cats.

"Don't lecture to me, Gus. By God, if I ever amount to anything it won't be thanks to bums like Cheney."

The fellow in suspenders stepped forward and slugged the youth hard in the mouth, knocking him backwards off the porch into the dirt below. "Who's the bum, now?" roared the fellow in suspenders. "Eh?" Then he went back indoors, slamming the back door closed behind him.

Electrified, Alvin stole to the edge of the shadows, hoping to see the youth get up and start a ruckus. He'd witnessed plenty of school-yard scraps. Nobody really got hurt from a good sock in the head. He walked out from under the maple tree into the pale carbon light where the youth was sobbing like a baby. When Alvin called over to him, the youth lifted his chin a few inches off the ground, face caked with dust like a lump of cookie dough, his bottom lip bleeding into the dirt. He looked like a clown. Alvin stifled a laugh, even as he was trying to be polite. "Say, you ain't hurt there, are you?"

"Huh?"

"I said, that fellow didn't bust your jaw or nothing, did he?"

"Shove it along."

Alvin stopped where he was, his smile fading to a frown. People just weren't friendly anymore. He shot back, "Well, I guess you ain't too handy, are you?"

"You go to hell, too," the youth snarled. He rose up on one elbow and dabbed his lip with the tips of his fingers, tasting blood. "Lousy hick."

"Yeah?" Alvin veered away toward the front of the auditorium. Skipping off backwards, he shouted at the youth, "Well, I ain't the one busted up, neither. Dumbbell!"

Alvin Pendergast had lived all nineteen years of his life on a farm five miles from the Mississippi River in the pasture country of western Illinois. He and his sisters had been born there, and six of his cousins, three uncles, five aunts, his father and grandfather. His mother and most of his other relatives had grown up on farms between Farrington, Illinois and Beldenville, Wisconsin. Only a few lived in towns, and those in and about Farrington came out to the farm after church each Sunday for dinner. That was tradition. Ham, corn and sweet potatoes. Fried chicken, mashed potatoes, gravy and dumplings. Grace recited by Grandpa Pend-

ergast at the long oak table draped in lacy white linen. While eating, Uncle Carl told jokes about drunken Indians. Uncle Rufus argued county politics with Uncle Henry. Alvin's father condemned race music and lantern-slide entertainments, X-ray experiments and the Universal News Weekly. *The women at the table chattered among themselves concerning Sabbatarians and housework, charity bureaus, fussy neighbors, mail-order houses, and the evils of inebriety. Children invented paragrams and tittered laughter and received scoldings every few minutes or so. After dinner, the men snuck down into the basement to smoke cigars and sip bourbon, while the women gathered in the kitchen for dishwashing and more earnest gossip. Unless it was storming, the children were sent outdoors to play by the creek until sundown. Too young for the basement and too old for run-sheep-run, Alvin had no part in any of it except eating, and believed therefore that not one single Pendergast, Hamill, Chamberlain, Rutledge, Halverson or Gallup cared less for tradition than did he.*

Farm life was a drudgery of frost and manure. Boys wore the stink of it to school. By horse and walking plow, acres of wild grass became cornrows and hayfields. Corncribs and chicken coops were built with hand-sawed lumber. Cookstoves heated the kitchen at dawn. Nobody got rich nor went to the County Home. Some girls slung grain and mended petticoats, others got knocked up in the rafters of a barn. George Pendergast lost a leg in the mechanical reaper. Cousin Oscar went crazy from a pig-bite and chased possums at night for the Morris widow down on Greenfield Road. Snowdrifts buried old Harold Mitchener's duck pond one dark Christmas and Roy Gallup lost three fingers on his right hand to frostbite when he fell through the ice chasing a buck across the fenceline. His brother Rudy drowned. Spring floods stole Auntie Ella's porch and a basketful of kittens. Drought took the field crops a year later and Alvin's father sold his Ford. Uncle Carl became a barber and bought a house on Maple Avenue in Farrington. Aunt Marie married a salesman from Texas and raised her children on Cedar Street two blocks from a trolley stop uptown. Most of the family stayed on. Who else would mend the fences and curry the horses, asked Granny Chamberlain? A leatherbound Bible inscribed with five generations of family history sat on a walnut shelf above Aurora Pendergast's piano, which Alvin passed by in the dark each cold morning before breakfast on his way to the barn Grandpa Harlan had constructed from timber felled himself three years after the Civil War. Both the Bible and the barn smelled ancient.

Four years ago, a week before his fifteenth birthday, Alvin Pendergast developed consumption. It came upon him like a change of seasons, a vague malaise that mimicked nothing worse than a persistent cold, unrelenting fatigue in the mornings, a low fever at night. His family thought he had contracted the lazy habits of adolescence and disregarded his complaints. If he worked hard enough, put his heart into the farm like everyone else, the backache he worried about would soon go away. Keep the old beak against the grindstone, Uncle Henry told him, you'll get somewhere. His father growled at him for chores completed too slowly, his mother and sisters pointed out how skinny he looked. Alvin lost ten pounds to a diminished appetite and could no longer lift Aunt Hattie's bushel basket of peaches. His night-sweats worsened and his skin became sallow and waxen and he caught a cough that troubled him for weeks. One morning after a spell of hacking and violent expectoration, he noticed streaks of blood in his handkerchief. Then the doctors came to the farm and diagnosed him as consumptive, infected with pulmonary tuberculosis. They put Alvin on a train and sent him away to a sanitarium. He wept the first week from fear and loneliness. His ward smelled of feces and formaldehyde. He hardly ate at all and had a bellyache for a month. His breathing was so shallow and labored he often thought he was suffocating. He coughed up blood. He was given cold sponge baths and rubbed with alcohol and taken out of doors to sit in the sunlight when the weather permitted. He consumed milk and eggs and calomel and saline laxatives every few days to aid his digestion. He lost another twenty-five pounds. The nurses brought creosote in hot water for his cough and syrup of iodid for his anemia and hypophosphites of lime and soda to reduce his expectorations, and every day cod liver oil, cod liver oil, cod liver oil. The doctors took X-ray photographs of his lungs and pronounced his condition curable. Still, he grew melancholy and refused to speak to his nurses for a month after enduring the artificial pneumothorax treatments. Then his throat became ulcerous and he suffered horrible headaches and sat in bed for another eight weeks and needed the commode and utter silence and nearly forgot who he was or where he had come from. Only his mother was permitted a visit and he scarcely remembered seeing her, though he was told she came often. Finally he began to walk again and converse with his fellow patients out of doors. He learned pottery and basket-making and how to say a few words in French, and eventually his cough went away with the fever as the tubercles dried up, and his breathing returned to normal, and a year after entering the sanitarium, Alvin was put back on a train one morning and sent home.

With the orchestra gone downtown to a late supper, an amplified radio console was broadcasting a lively Turkey Trot when Alvin climbed the wooden bleachers to the circus seats with a bag of hot popcorn. A stinking gray haze of cigarette smoke drifted above the dance floor, obscuring the lettered banners suspended across the upper auditorium.

FARRINGTON DANCE DERBY — 24 HOURS DAILY!!!

DANCING, MUSIC, & SURPRISE ENTERTAINMENTS

WARNING!!! THIS IS A PLACE OF REFINED AMUSEMENT:

NO WHISTLING, STOMPING, CATCALLS!

DO NOT TOUCH CONTESTANTS!

TWO SPRINTS TONIGHT!!

GENTLEMEN: REMOVE YOUR HATS!!!

Alvin hurried to find a seat as a bell rang, ending the rest period. Last night a dancer from Knoxville had gone nuts and tried to strangle a floor judge after being disqualified during a pop-the-whip. Maybe somebody would get shot tonight. Down on the parquet floor, the surviving dancers were barely hanging onto their partners, shuffling disconsolately about in a dreamy rhythm. Behind the orchestra stage, a large scoreboard read:

COUPLES REMAINING: 13
DAYS DANCED: 9
HOURS DANCED: 237

Alvin and Cousin Frenchy had attended the start of the dance derby when the floor was still jammed with fresh contestants. That night all the dancers had kicked up their heels and twirled around and yelled and laughed and danced like crazy while the hot-eyed spectators in the bleachers cheered and cheered, and the master of ceremonies in a red polka dot tie announced that this would be the greatest dance derby of the year and anyone in town who didn't buy a ticket would be missing something pretty swell. Straight away, a pretty redhead wearing a green plaid skirt and shoes dyed gold caught Alvin's eye. She had lovely painted eyelashes and a tiny rosebud mouth whose smile gave him the flutters. Her dance partner was skinny as a candlestick and had oily hair. They did the Charleston and Lindy Hop like a pair of whirly-gigs and won a sprint and took a bow to a fine applause and earned a spray of silver coins from the dollar loge seats. The girl's name was Dorothy Louise Ellison, and she was from Topeka, Kansas. This was her fifth marathon and she'd hoped to win the grand prize in order to go to college out in California where her aunt and uncle owned a lemon grove. Her partner was a homely plumber from Kentucky by the name of Joe Norton. Alvin desperately wanted to take Joe's part with Dorothy. Trouble was, he could hardly dance a two-step without a manual and lacked the stamina in his lungs, and if Dorothy truly needed to win the contest to attend college, she'd want a better partner than a sickly farm boy with two left feet. So Alvin sat under the **NO SPITTING!!!** sign for more than eight hours watching Dorothy and Joe waltz about the dance floor with fifty-six other couples. When Alvin left with Frenchy at half past three in the morning, Dorothy and Joe were still arm-in-arm, dancing a drowsy Fox Trot, and feigning youthful romance for smiling patrons seated on pillows in the loge seats.

Tonight she was gone.

Sitting up in the sweltering grandstand high above the orchestra, Alvin had a good view of the entire auditorium, dancers and spectators alike. He watched Joe Norton come out of a dressing room hallway late from the break with Patsy on his arm and looked at the scoreboard and counted thirteen couples and noticed that all the other dancers were paired up and Dorothy wasn't on the floor. *That plumber sonofabitch got rid of her,* Alvin imagined as his heart sank. *She was probably too good-looking for him.* He considered leaving, but didn't have the pep for much more walking tonight. Besides, where would he go?

The radio program changed to a cheerful waltz.

Most of the dancers were too hot and exhausted to pick up the new rhythm. A floor judge in a referee's pinstripe shirt clapped his hands to speed them up. Behind the loge seats on the far end of the floor, a large hillbilly family stood up to leave, carrying picnic baskets and milk bottles.

Alvin slid down the plank row behind a pair of fat Chevrolet salesmen eating cold fried chicken out of a metal lunch bucket. They smelled like grease. Alvin watched intently as the master of ceremonies, dressed in black top hat and tails, strode onto the orchestra platform and grabbed the microphone. He had a pencil-thin moustache and slicked-backed hair. His assistant, a slinky blonde dressed up in a cowboy hat and spangles, switched off the radio. Behind the emcee, Jimmy Turkel's five-piece orchestra, back from supper break, filed onto the stage. The drummer performed a brief introduction as the lethargic dancers slowed to a shuffle. Applause erupted from the grandstand. Alvin glared at Joe Norton and worried that maybe Dorothy had been injured or taken seriously ill during the week he'd been away at the farm. Why had she chosen that dumbbell Norton in the first place?

"LADIES AND GENTLEMEN! HOW ABOUT A BREAK FOR THESE COURAGEOUS KIDS! AREN'T THEY SWELL?"

The audience cheered loudly.

An elderly man tossed a handful of coins onto the floor from the side railing. A young dance pair dressed in matching blue sailor suits scrambled over to collect it all up while a crowd of college-age fellows gave them a boisterous hip-hip-hurrah.

More people cheered.

The emcee waved his arms to get everyone's attention again. At the rear of the stage stood Arthur Cheney, the derby promoter from Omaha Alvin had seen on the back porch, still puffing on a fat cigar. *Why hadn't Petey taken a poke at him,* Alvin wondered, digging again into his bag of popcorn. *A fellow who blows smoke in your face is just asking for a good crack in the jaw.*

"LADIES AND GENTLEMEN! LADIES AND GENTLEMEN!"

The thirteen dance couples milled about together in the middle of the floor, hardly moving now. The farm boy watched one of the collegiate fellows giving advice over the railing to a blonde in worn-out slippers whose hollow-eyed partner was sagging off her torso.

The emcee tapped the microphone with his fist. "LADIES AND GENTLEMEN! THESE KIDS ARE SO COURAGEOUS, AREN'T THEY? HEROES, EVERY LAST ONE OF THEM! RIGHT OUT OF THE TOP DRAWER! AND THEY AREN'T DONE YET, ARE THEY? YOU BET THEY AREN'T! NO SIRREE! THEY KNOW HOW HARD YOU'RE PULLING FOR THEM AND THEY'LL DO THEIR BEST TO SEE THEY DON'T LET YOU DOWN! YOU CAN COUNT ON IT!"

Spectators in the grandstand rose to give the dancers a big ovation, several of whom appeared bewildered by the cheering. Since Dorothy was gone, Alvin hardly clapped at all. He didn't much care who won now.

The emcee grinned brightly as he spoke into the microphone again. "WHY, THEY'VE SURE GOT A LOT OF GUTS, ALL RIGHT, THESE KIDS OF OURS, DON'T THEY?"

Alvin felt the wooden planks rumble under his feet from the roar that swept the auditorium as the orchestra struck up a boisterous "Yankee Doodle Dandy." The emcee raised his voice. "BUT HONESTLY, LADIES AND GENTLEMEN, HOW LONG CAN THEY LAST? I ASK YOU, HOW-LONG-CAN-THEY-LAST?"

Across the floor, a knot of people in the loge seats began clapping. More coins showered the sluggish dancers. Alvin watched a homely nurse come out from the dressing room with a bottle of smelling salts. The orchestra played a couple bars of "Dixie."

"NOW, LADIES AND GENTLEMEN, WE PROMISED YOU THESE KIDS WOULD DO THEIR BEST ON THE FLOOR, AND BELIEVE YOU ME, LADIES AND GENTLEMEN, THEY HAVE. OH, YOU BET THEY HAVE! NINE DAYS, LADIES AND GENTLEMEN, NINE DAYS, THEY'VE BATTLED NOT ONLY EACH OTHER, BUT FATHER TIME HIMSELF TO KEEP GOING BECAUSE, WHY, THEY JUST KNOW YOU'RE ALL BEHIND THEM! SURE, THEY'VE GOT BUNIONS AND

BLISTERS, BUT OH, THEY'VE GOT MORE THAN ENOUGH GUTS, TOO, TO STICK IT OUT TO THE VERY END AND WIN THIS GREAT DANCE DERBY FAIR AND SQUARE FOR THOSE OF YOU WHO REALLY CARE TO SEE 'EM DO IT! WHAT DO YOU SAY ABOUT THAT?"

The farm boy almost toppled over as the old bleachers shook under the ovation.

"WELL, LADIES AND GENTLEMEN, IT'S TIME TO TURN ON THE HEAT AGAIN, SO PICK OUT YOUR FAVORITE COUPLE AND GIVE 'EM A BREAK BECAUSE THEY'LL NEED ALL THE BOOST THEY CAN GET!"

The emcee motioned to another heat judge waiting just off the platform. More people were crowding into the next row above, shoving along toward the center of the bleachers. Alvin felt like a sardine in his own row and considered switching seats to somewhere higher up.

"MISTER CLARK, ARE YOU READY?"

The bald heat judge nodded.

A buzz swept through the audience.

The emcee drew the microphone close while raising his right hand into the smoky air. "LADIES AND GENTLEMEN, ARE YOU READY?"

A further deafening cheer shook the building. Alvin craned his neck to see through the pack in front of him. A stout woman to his left jammed her elbow into his ribs to make room. He pushed back as the emcee announced to the auditorium spectators, "WELL, THEN, LADIES AND GENTLEMEN, LET'S SEE HOW LONG THESE BRAVE KIDS CAN LAST! MISTER CLARK, HOW ABOUT A SPRINT?" He turned to Turkel. "MAESTRO, GET READY TO GIVE!"

The heat judge walked into the middle of the dance floor where a painted oval marked off a racetrack for the competitors. Alvin felt someone shove roughly into the row beside him.

"Sorry, kid," the fellow said, as he wedged down between Alvin and the stout woman. He was wearing a felt fedora and a smart blue cassimere suit. "Some local yokel kept stepping on my foot up there."

He smelled like whiskey and hair tonic.

"Ain't a lot of room here, neither," Alvin muttered, watching the dance couples tie together for the sprint. He hated getting shoved, particularly when he didn't feel well.

"You got a favorite?"

"Huh?"

"This derby's hired some real cutie pies, don't you agree?"

Alvin shrugged. "I seen a doll last week, but she ain't here no more." He watched Joe Norton fasten a belt onto Patsy's waist for the sprint and give her a kiss on the cheek. Alvin hoped they'd both trip and break their necks.

"Maybe some fellow bought her off the floor and married her afterward. What was her name?"

"I don't know," he lied, figuring this fellow probably didn't care, anyhow. Besides, he thought of Dorothy as his girl and that wasn't anybody's business but his own.

The dancers were packed together behind a white ribbon at the starting line, jostling for position. Another trio of floor judges came out from behind the grandstand. All three looked like sourpusses. Some people booed and hissed when these judges took their places on the dance floor.

After the emcee backed away from the microphone, Turkel's orchestra struck up a rousing "Stars and Stripes Forever" as the audience stood to watch the sprint. Joe Norton and Patsy were tucked so far back now Alvin could hardly see them, but in front of the pack were a sweetheart couple from Ohio lots of people seemed to be boosting and a slick pair of Mexican dancers nobody much cared for at all.

The fellow spoke into the farm boy's ear, "I got a sawbuck says I can predict which couple's out after this sprint."

"Oh yeah?" said Alvin, his attention fixed on the heat judge whose arm was raised at the starting line. *If Dorothy'd been in this sprint,* he thought, *she'd be out front where everyone could see how swell she looked.*

The fellow dropped his voice. "Don't you know most of these marathons are a slice of tripe? Why, oiling one of the floor judges'll give you the dope on who wins and who gets the air any night of the week."

"Says who?" Alvin growled. He wanted the sprint to start so he could watch Joe Norton and Patsy fail miserably before the whole auditorium. Maybe somebody would even throw a tomato at 'em.

"Says I."

"Yeah, how do you know?"

The fellow laughed. "Well, for starters, I've seen a million of them, that's how. Why, marathon dances were standing them up in Chicago all last summer."

The heat judge's whistle shrieked and the sprint began, thirteen dance couples galloping through the ribbon like the start of a horse race. Spectators howled with excitement. Six couples hit the first turn in a thick pack, scrambling for the lead. Turkel's orchestra played a fast and spirited "California, Here I Come," while the audience down by the floor urged their favorite couples to greater speed. Tied together with a belt, whichever partner had the most pluck and fortitude after nine days of dancing dragged the other around the oval, panicked and invigorated by the knowledge that the team finishing last would be cut out of the derby. All about the auditorium, people screamed and shouted for their favorite contestants to go faster and faster, and razzing those they didn't like. Couples stumbled and fought to regain balance. Those who fell hurried to get back on their feet again. Round and round they went, faces horrid with agony. Alvin rooted for Patsy to take a spill or Joe Norton to drop dead. One athletic-looking boy got wobbly-knee'd on the far turn and his partner, a tiny brunette, jammed her shoulder underneath his arm and began dragging him onward, screaming in his ear while the spectators roared for them to keep up. The parquet dance floor became slick with sweat. Desperate couples skidded and slipped. Turkel's orchestra played a fast Peabody and the emcee grabbed the microphone and exhorted the beleaguered dancers to "HURRY! HURRY! HURRY! TIME'S RUNNING OUT, KIDS! DON'T FALL BEHIND! DON'T FALL BEHIND!"

Alvin felt an elbow nudge him in the ribs. His new friend leaned over close to his ear and said, "See those two in the blue sailor suits?"

The farm boy nodded. Those were the Italians from Indiana. "What of it?"

The emcee announced with undisguised glee, "THREE MINUTES

TO GO, KIDS! THREE MINUTES! HURRY, HURRY, HURRY!"

"Well, they're getting the air."

"Says who?"

"One of Cheney's stooges caught 'em having a lay under the bleachers. I hear the birdie had a flask of gin in her skirt. Some dick from town wanted to prefer charges."

"That's a good laugh," Alvin said, as Joe Norton and Patsy lunged past a couple wearing athletic shirts and shorts soaked in sweat. The dance floor was a frenzy of roughhousing competitors pushing and shoving, male and female alike, battling frantically for position on the final few laps of the sprint. All the spectators were standing now and Alvin found the clamor deafening. He was getting a headache.

The fellow beside him raised his voice above the racket. "You just watch and see if I'm not right."

"Sure I will."

The buoyant emcee cried into the microphone, "ONE MIN-UTE TO GO, KIDS! ONLY ONE MORE MINUTE! HOLD ON! DON'T QUIT NOW! HURRY, HURRY, HURRY!"

Around the track went all thirteen dance couples, struggling to keep upright, racing desperately for the finish. Joe and Patsy were in the middle of the pack just behind the sweetheart couple, but Alvin didn't know how many laps they'd taken. That's what mattered. Whichever team did the most laps won. Fewest laps meant disqualification. Falls earned deductions, too. Joe and Patsy'd had two, but some of the other couples had more than that. All were badly played out. "THIRTY SECONDS, KIDS! ONLY THIRTY SECONDS! HURRY NOW! HURRY!"

Alvin looked for the Italian dance pair wearing sailor suits and saw they were far ahead of Joe and Patsy, just three couples off the lead and heading around the near turn. The oily Mexican pair were dead last and fading, but nobody had sponsored them, anyhow. From where Alvin was standing, it seemed that the sweetheart couple were set to win if they didn't trip up.

Turkel's orchestra finished playing just as the heat judge blew his whistle, ending the sprint. Half of the couples on the dance floor collapsed. Spectators cheered wildly with appreciation while a crew of trainers in white hospital dress rushed out of the dressing rooms, dragging several iron cots for those competitors most badly stricken with exhaustion. Alvin saw Patsy and Joe sitting on the railing near the orchestra platform. Patsy hung her head on Joe's sweaty shoulder. The skinny plumber's eyes were shut. A smartly-dressed Negro sitting just behind them in the loge seats was patting Joe on the back. Alvin guessed he didn't know about Dorothy.

A crowd was gathering near the microphone. The bald heat judge had climbed up from the dance floor and met Cheney and the emcee. Turkel watched for his cue to begin the music that would announce the winners of the sprint.

"Now you'll see," said the fellow beside Alvin. He snuck a silver hipflask from his jacket and enjoyed a quick nip. Then he chuckled and hid it away again. "Why, I doubt any of these marathons are on the up-and-up."

Alvin frowned. "Go on, tell me some more."

"Fact is, the dance derby's just another dirty goldbrick game."

"Oh yeah?"

The fellow took out his bag of peanuts. "I tell you, it's crooked as all hell."

"Says you," Alvin growled. He hated hearing bunk like this. Uncle Henry knocked the derby himself all through dinner last Sunday and he'd never been to one in his life.

The fellow grinned. "You think I'm a joykiller, huh?"

"You said it." *Why didn't this fellow go take a hike?*

"Well," the fellow replied, eating a handful of peanuts, "it wouldn't bust me up to be wrong, but if I am, I'll eat your hat."

The emcee took the microphone in hand. "LADIES AND GEN-TLEMEN!"

A big cheer went up from the grandstand.

He raised a hand to quiet the audience. Cheney stood in close behind him with the contingent of derby sponsors flanking both men. "LADIES AND GENTLEMEN! PLEASE!"

Alvin saw Joe Norton shaking hands with the Negro at the loge seats. Patsy was moving forward to the orchestra platform. Joe Norton followed her past the iron cots. Elrod Tarwater, a policemen Alvin knew from downtown, stood at the corner of the orchestra next to that stout fellow Gus who'd punched Petey in the mouth out back.

"LADIES AND GENTLEMEN, AREN'T THESE KIDS WONDERFUL?"

Another big cheer jolted the auditorium.

"YOU BET THEY ARE! AND WE'RE NOT FINISHED YET! NO SIRREE! NOT BY A LONG SHOT! THESE KIDS HAVE PLEDGED TO KEEP ON GOING SO LONG AS YOU COME OUT AND PULL FOR 'EM JUST AS HARD AS YOU'VE BEEN DOING ALL THIS WEEK! LADIES AND GENTLEMEN, WHAT DO YOU HAVE TO SAY ABOUT THAT?"

The audience thundered their approval.

"NOW, OUR FINE TEAM OF FLOOR JUDGES ... "

A flurry of boos cascaded down from the upper bleachers.

" ... HAVE TABULATED THE OFFICIAL LAP RESULTS OF THIS EVENING'S SPRINT AND I MUST TELL YOU I'VE NEVER WITNESSED A TRUER EXAMPLE OF COURAGE AND PERSEVERANCE! THESE KIDS CERTAINLY PUT IT OVER FOR US, AND I TAKE NO JOY IN HAVING TO ELIMINATE ONE OF THESE BRAVE TEAMS, BUT, LADIES AND GENTLEMEN, RULES ARE RULES. THEREFORE ... " The emcee reached into his vest pocket and withdrew a small white card. "FOLKS, LET'S GIVE A HEARTY FAREWELL TO OUR LOVELY FRIENDS FROM THE GREAT STATE OF INDIANA ... BUDDY AND EILEEN ROMERO!"

Alvin sucked in his breath as a spotlight from the rafters high above the platform flashed down through the smoky haze to illuminate two contestants wearing blue navy sailor suits.

"Ha!" Alvin's friend cried. Wadding up his empty peanut bag, he began clapping with the rest of the auditorium. "Well, kid, can you feature that?"

Buddy and Eileen Romero looked shocked, tears falling now.

"Aw, what do you know?" Alvin mumbled, both angry and mystified. *Who got this wiseacre told the derby wasn't on the level?*

From the platform, the emcee called down to them. "COME ON UP HERE, KIDS! TAKE A BOW FOR ALL YOUR FRIENDS!"

Buddy Romero barked at a floor judge who quickly turned his back. Eileen Romero stumbled into one of the iron cots. Loud applause from the grandstand persisted. Both were showered with silver from the best-dressed people in the loge seats. Neither seemed to notice and continued forward without stopping to retrieve the coins.

Still clapping, the fellow told Alvin, "See, it really gets me how these sapheads won't play the game fair and square."

Gus came to the front of the platform with another pair of trainers and helped Buddy and Eileen Romero up from the dance floor. A spray of coins greeted them there. The emcee waved to Turkel whose orchestra struck up a lively few bars of "Blue Skies."

Alvin saw Buddy Romero receive a certificate and a handshake from Cheney while Eileen Romero wept. Gus escorted them to the back of the platform to a loud ovation. Then the emcee signaled Turkel for a drum roll. Cheney lit up a fat cigar. Those dance couples not passed out on iron cots milled about looking flummoxed and wan.

"Sorry, kid," said the fellow beside Alvin, dumping the empty peanut bag under his bench seat. "I told you, it ain't copacetic."

"Aw, phooey on you, too." He was feeling sick again. His head hurt and his stomach was queasy.

Now the emcee spoke into the microphone with a big grin on his face. "LADIES AND GENTLEMEN! LADIES AND GENTLEMEN!"

Alvin saw Petey in a crouch next to the platform bunting. What was he doing there?

"WELL, WE'VE HAD A REAL SURPRISE TONIGHT! THAT SPRINT WAS QUITE A GRIND, WASN'T IT?"

Joe Norton and Patsy were on the far side of the platform now. Alvin watched a photographer take a flash picture of them with one of the businessmen from downtown.

"YOU SEE, ALL OF OUR KIDS PROVED THEY'VE GOT THE PLUCK TO EARN A PRIZE IN THIS DERBY, BUT LADIES AND GENTLEMEN, TONIGHT ONE TEAM REALLY SHOWED THEIR TRUE COLORS WHEN WE TURNED ON

THE HEAT!'"

The popular sweetheart couple stood arm-in-arm on the dance floor directly in front of the platform, all pep and smiles.

"LADIES AND GENTLEMEN, LET'S MEET OUR WINNERS … "

Another drum roll was summoned from Turkel's orchestra as a shower of silver coins rained over the beaming sweetheart couple.

" … FROM LEXINGTON, KENTUCKY AND JOHNSTOWN, PENNSYLVANIA … JOE NORTON AND PATSY McCARDLE!"

The audience roared with delight. A cloud of balloons was released from the rafters. Firecrackers exploded here and there.

"Hey, they didn't win!" Alvin shouted. "That ain't fair! I tell you, they didn't win!"

"What'd I say?" The fellow beside him laughed aloud.

Down on the littered parquet dance floor, the sweetheart couple was still smiling for their sponsors, displaying the good sportsmanship and sunny dispositions they knew paid dividends in the long run. A woman wearing a gingham apron dress rose and blew them a kiss. Maybe they didn't win tonight, but the marathon was far from over, so the couple from Ohio persisted in waving brightly to their staunchest supporters. Alvin saw Petey sneak up onto the platform while everyone else's attention was drawn to Joe and Patsy crossing the stage past Elrod Tarwater under a blazing spotlight to the microphone where Arthur Cheney stood with his master of ceremonies and a shiny gold trophy. Alvin thought there must have been two dozen people up on the platform now, crowding closer and closer to the microphone, swarming about Joe and Patsy and Arthur Cheney and his emcee. People around the auditorium were shouting and whistling and stamping their feet as Joe raised the trophy high over his head and Patsy gave him a kiss for the cameras and Cheney lifted his own cigar in triumph. Through the crush of celebrants under the hot lights of the auditorium, Alvin saw Petey shove close enough to swing a small pocketknife in a balled-up fist hard down onto the back of Arthur Cheney's neck. Both Cheney and Petey disappeared into the crowd as the promoter fell. Tarwater knocked over the microphone. Alvin thought he heard Patsy scream.

More policemen and trainers rushed forward from backstage.

Then the platform collapsed and the rest was pandemonium.

The evening breeze carried a honey scent of fresh blossoms from a shady home orchard in the next lot as Alvin watched ambulance attendants carry the injured on stretchers from the auditorium while dozens of police and firemen and newspaper reporters and derby patrons milled about.

The smart-mouthed fellow in the blue cassimere suit lit a cigarette in the shadows. He and Alvin had departed the auditorium together through a side door under the old bleachers just ahead of a panicked crowd. Alvin held onto his sack of popcorn and ate a salty handful as his new friend tossed the dead match away into the scruffy grass. *Maybe this fellow ain't half bad,* he thought. *He didn't charge me a dime to find out the derby was a cheat. Now I got something to tell Frenchy he probably don't even know.*

Cousin Frenchy.

He'd slipped Alvin the dope about Doc Hartley coming out to the farm for a chat with Alvin's mom and pop. *Everyone knew Alvin didn't look too good. He'd lost weight and color, and wasn't he coughing again? He couldn't work hardly at all in the fields, got tired too soon, wasn't even strong enough to push a loaded wheelbarrow from one end of the yard to another. He needed treatments again. He was having a relapse. If he didn't go back into the sanitarium, he might not be around for Christmas.* Alvin had no intention of returning to the sanitarium, even though when he woke during the night, his bed sheets were damp with sweat and sometimes he coughed so hard he choked. But the sanitarium doctors had promised him he was cured, that all he needed was lots of sunshine and fresh air and a little rest from time to time. They had lied to him, so he didn't trust them any longer, and if he was going to croak, he didn't want it to be in one of those cold wards that had already stolen a year of his life.

Alvin watched as one of the ambulances left the auditorium for Mercy Hospital downtown. A gust of wind rippled through the dark maples overhead. More people came outdoors.

"That was a close shave," his new friend said, flicking ash off his cigarette.

"That kid Petey's off his head."

"They're all cuckoo, if you ask me."

"You ain't by yourself."

The fellow approached him with a smile. "Say, we haven't really met, have we? My name's Chester Burke."

He offered a firm handshake, which Alvin accepted.

"Alvin Pendergast, sir. Pleased to know you." That was sincere, too. He liked this fellow because he'd been friendly, unlike most people Alvin knew.

"I guess you're local, aren't you? Live in town?"

Alvin nodded. "We got a farm three miles north of here off Wasson Road. It ain't that far."

"Gee, I'll bet that's hard work," Chester said, after a drag off his cigarette. Another ambulance arrived.

"Sure it is," Alvin replied, watching several attendants hurry out to meet it. They reminded him of those fellows who helped carry the dead out of the consumption wards in the sanitarium.

"My uncle hired me onto his hog farm one summer when I was about your age, but I funked it after a month and went home."

"Slopping hogs don't stir you up much."

A tiny woman in a net frock stood behind the attendants as another of the injured was hoisted into the ambulance.

Chester chuckled. "You aren't sore on farming, are you?"

"Naw, it's a panic." Of course he hated it, and everyone in the family knew it, too. They said he was just lazy even when he wasn't sick, which was sort of true, but who's got a smile and a jump in his step for something he can't stand?

"Well, I learned myself a long time ago that it can go pretty hard with a fellow who supplies the sweat on somebody else's safety valve."

Alvin watched Chester take out the silver hip flask again, unscrew it and tip it toward his mouth. Nothing came out. Chester frowned and shook it over the grass and saw it was empty. Then he grinned at Alvin. "Say, is there any place a fellow can get a drink around here?"

Another loaded ambulance left the auditorium, siren wailing across the windy night. Looking over his shoulder, Alvin told Chester, "See this road here?"

"Sure."

"Well, if you follow it down two blocks to an alleyway just past a big blackberry patch, you'll see the old Wickland house on the corner there. Go past it all the way to the end of the alley where you'll find a little gray shack under a big hackberry tree. It belongs to a lady named Marge Bradford, and it's the only place you *can't* get a drink in this town."

Then Alvin laughed.

So did Chester. "That's a swell joke, kid. I like you. I suppose not all farmers are hicks, are they?"

"My uncle Rufus says farmers raise corn, corn makes whiskey, whiskey makes Prohibition agents, and Prohibition agents raise hell."

Chester laughed again. "Why, that's a good one, too."

Alvin grinned, starting to feel better somehow. "He's a jokey old bird."

The thick maples swayed in a cold wind gust. Chester asked, "Have you had any supper tonight, kid?"

"I ate a sandwich." He didn't have much appetite today.

"Well, are you still hungry a little? Reason I ask is, I thought maybe you and me'd find a night lunchroom somewhere and have ourselves something to eat. If you've already had your supper, I'll set you up to a piece of pie. What do you say? I haven't eaten since noon and I'm getting an awful bellyache."

Alvin smiled. "I like pie."

"Well, then, let's shoot the works," Chester said, disposing of his cigarette. "Follow me."

He had parked under a ragged oak at the upper corner of the parking lot. Alvin saw a shiny tan Packard Six hidden in the shadows.

"Gee, this is a pretty swell auto."

Alvin had never seen a Six in the flesh before, only a magazine advertisement that named Packards *"The supreme combination of all that is fine in motor cars. Ask the man who owns one."*

"It's nifty, all right," Chester said, unlocking the door. He climbed into the driver's seat, and reached across to open the passenger door. "Come on, kid. Hop in."

"Sure."

The farm boy climbed into the car as Chester fired up the engine. The interior smelled like cigarettes and gin. A pair of old leather valises were jammed in front of a bunch of boxes in the backseat. Alvin had never been inside of a fine motorcar. He liked it.

At the stop sign on the corner, Chester asked, "Where should we eat?"

"Well, tell the truth," Alvin confessed, "there ain't really nothing open 'round here after dark." Where was he going, anyhow? It'd be a hell of a long walk home by moonlight and he had already begun to feel weak. He sure didn't want to come home wheezing and have everyone in the family see how bad off he was.

"How about the other side of the river?" Chester asked, letting another automobile pass by before he went right.

"I guess so. There's a flock of hotels."

"Should we drive over?"

Alvin shrugged. "All right."

Chester turned at the stop sign, then drove quickly west along Buchanon Street. Most of the framehouses still had lights on, but the sidewalks were empty and the neighborhood was quiet. Alvin knew he had to feed the dairy cows in the morning and replace the floorboards in one of Uncle Henry's barn stalls and help fix his old disc harrow. He also knew Doc Hartley was coming out to the farm tomorrow afternoon to give him another once-over and maybe decide it was time for Alvin's folks to buy another train ticket on the Limited back to the sanitarium. That spooked him something fierce.

Chester asked, "Ever been across the Mississippi this time of night?"

"Not by motor."

"Well, you see, I've got appointments in Hannibal and New London tomorrow. Maybe we ought to hire a couple of rooms, stay over a night or so. What do you think?"

"I ain't got any money."

"We can tackle that tomorrow," Chester said, steering around another corner. The bridge was up ahead, rising out of a cypress grove. "Say, maybe you can help me out in New London. I could sure use a partner who's willing to put in an honest day's work."

"What would I have to do?"

Chester laughed. "Well, you wouldn't be slopping hogs."

Alvin felt his face flush. Now he was really scared. This fellow was asking him to quit the farm, which he hated, without letting anyone know about it, and by noon everyone in the family would say that poor sick Alvin was too dumb to understand just how important it was that he begin his pneumothorax treatments all over again.

Chester swung the Packard onto the bridge that led west across the Mississippi River. Both windows were open and a draft swirled through, cold and nightdamp.

"Well, what do you say, kid? I won't kick about it if you say no, but you have to choose now. I got supper waiting for me on the other side of this bridge."

Life was strange, Alvin thought, as a sort of weary exhilaration came over him. He had walked three miles to the derby and that was a long haul when he lived on the farm, but last week his only true ambition had been to go fishing Saturday morning with Frenchy, maybe lie on a summer hammock afterward by a hackberry grove near the creek. So he said to this fellow he hadn't even known an hour ago, "I guess I'll take that pie."

Chester put the Packard back into gear. "You sure you're not going to pull out of it? It's pretty easy to get bitter if somebody goes back on you."

"No, sir."

"You're a brick, kid."

"Thanks."

HADLEYVILLE, MISSOURI

WHEN ALVIN PENDERGAST WAS THIRTEEN, *two years before the consumption, he and Cousin Frenchy sneaked a ride one Saturday night on a melon truck driving south to market in Macomb. They figured on traveling a while before jumping off in the next county and hitching a ride back on Sunday. It was summer and the night was warm, so they just lay back and counted stars and gabbed about girls and fishing until they got sleepy and nodded off for a few hours. When they woke up, they found themselves parked behind a blacksmith shop next to a backhouse and a chicken coop full of squawking hens and a pack of children collecting eggs for breakfast. Alvin and Frenchy crawled down off the melon truck and walked out in front of the store to have a look-see, take the "lay of the land" as Frenchy put it. Not that there was all that much to see: a long dirt street, all the buildings on one side, shade trees and huge blackberry bushes on the other. Men sitting in chairs out front of the stores. Wagons parked at the curb. Horses reined to hitching posts. No automobiles anywhere. One sign on a post draped in trumpet vines across the road leading into town told them where they were:* Hiram, Ky. Pop. 132. *If they hadn't just recently gorged themselves on melon, they'd have been in trouble because neither possessed more than sixteen cents in his pockets. Alvin had a peculiar feeling, walking down the middle of Hiram's main street with Frenchy, trying to ignore the thought burning in his brain that he might never see home in Illinois again — an awfully black thought* *for a thirteen-year-old. Men stared at them from the storefronts clear down to the end of the road leading out of town. Alvin didn't see any women at all. The heels of the shoes Frenchy wore kicked up a trail of dust behind him, disturbing swarms of black flies off the horse apples in the dirt. Past a livery stable, the road bent left and went up a hill lined with more blackberry bushes. The boys followed it, hoping to find a county highway and another truck driving north to Illinois. Coming down the slope toward them was a preacher dressed all in black and carrying a leatherbound Bible. Back in Illinois, Alvin's mother attended church every Sunday, but his father never went, claiming the Lord knew how he felt about Him and didn't require a weekly recitation of those affections. Sunday School was where Alvin learned all about slingshots and miracles, which he preferred to sitting with the adults where everybody talked about loving the gospel while they farted all morning. Church was fine so long as it didn't last more than a couple hours and Momma cooked dinner afterward, but this particular Sunday in Hiram was different. The preacher had a little boy alongside dressed just the same as he was: black frock coat and suit, wide-brimmed hat, leatherbound Bible and comfort shoes. He had eyes like a crow and a face white as a spook. Man and boy shared the same gait, a purposeful stride that brought them straight down the road to Alvin and Frenchy. Probably they'd have walked right on by had Frenchy not whistled at the boy once they passed. Both preacher and disciple came about together just a few yards past Frenchy and Alvin. The boy wore a scowl like a wolverine. The preacher's face was mild but stiff. Alvin was terrified. Frenchy whistled again.*

"You mock those bringing the Lord's word," said the little boy in a fluty voice, "and He'll see a visitation upon your house. Ask old Pharaoh if that ain't so."

"I ain't got no house," replied Frenchy, puffing out his chest, "and I ain't got no silly-looking hat like yours, neither. And I wouldn't wear one if I did." Alvin smiled. Frenchy hardly ever showed much respect for anyone smaller than himself. He was always puffed up about all sorts of things and let you know about it, too.

"Blasphemer!" said the boy, eyes narrowed in fury. "Jesus'll burn you up! You just — "

The preacher cuffed the boy, knocking his hat off. "You hush now. The Lord's got no tolerance for curses spoken in His name."

Then he walked on up to Frenchy, his face hardened, while the boy bent down to pick up his hat. Tears filled his black crow's eyes, and the little one bowed his head.

The preacher looked down at Frenchy. "You boys look lost." His voice was thick and hoarse, like he'd swallowed gravel for breakfast.

Frenchy shrugged. "We're just walking."

The preacher held a firm countenance. "The road to the Lord is long and confusing. We all need a guide to take us to its proper end."

Frenchy shuffled his feet in the dirt. Alvin hadn't the guts to look the preacher in the eye, nor did he know just what he and Frenchy were supposed to say.

"The Lord provides in Jesus a road map for all our lives," the preacher continued. "Did you know that?"

"Jesus can see into your heart," barked the little boy. "You can't lie to Jesus."

"Hush up."

"They're sinners, Papa," the boy said, backing up. Tears streaked his cheeks and his lips quivered, but he spoke firmly. "Liars and sinners, both. I reckon I smelled 'em when I got up this morning. I know I did."

In the blackberry bushes, birds twittered and squawked. The sun was rising quickly on the morning sky. It would be a hot day.

"The Lord offers salvation in multitudinous forms," said the preacher, "and He does so without want of recompense or gratitude. It's His gracious heart that redeems us. Without our Lord's guiding hand, we'd all walk in constant night, utterly lost and confused."

"We ain't lost," said Frenchy, hardly a quiver in his voice. "We're just going fishing, is all. We like to start early."

Alvin always admired Frenchy's talent for smart-mouthing, another one of the reasons Alvin liked knocking around with him. Also, Frenchy rowed the boat whenever they went fishing and didn't complain about it.

"I don't see no fishing poles," said the little boy, sounding somewhat bolder himself. "Hard to catch fish without no poles." He stepped closer to Frenchy and shook his Bible at him. "Jesus was a fisher of men, but I expect He'd just throw you two back."

Before the boy could crack a grin at the joke he'd made, the preacher backhanded him across the face, knocking him down again into the dust.

The boy lay there whimpering as the preacher looked Frenchy square in the eye. Scared, Alvin backed up some, keeping one eye on the preacher and the other on the boy who lay flat in the dust, hat off, blood trickling from his nose. Alvin thought maybe he and Frenchy would have been better off staying in the melon truck.

"I ought to take you both home with me," the preacher said to Frenchy, "set you

to work learning about the Redeemer and the path He walked. I know you boys are lost. There's no sin in that. We all find ourselves lost now and again. Jesus Himself spent forty days in the wilderness. His suffering lent salvation to all men."

"I told you," said Frenchy, narrowing his eyes to meet those of the preacher, "we ain't lost. We're just going fishing, is all."

The preacher's boy was on his knees now, grabbing his hat and fixing the brim. Tears and blood mixed in the dust. Flies buzzed across the road.

"The path to righteousness is the Lord's inspiration. You boys ought to study on that before you commence to walking any further. There's only one road worth following, and it's the Lord's. You remember that now."

With those words, the preacher strode past Frenchy and Alvin, scooped the little boy up by the crook of his arm, and headed on down the road. Alvin watched them go, his knees shaking.

"Amen," Frenchy said, and gave them one more whistle. Neither preacher nor little disciple looked back. Near the curve at the bottom, they passed out of sight.

Alvin swatted a fly off his face. Frenchy tossed a stone into the blackberry bushes, stirring up some bees. It was a long walk up the road, but Alvin was so afraid to follow the preacher back into Hiram they headed off just the same, deciding to walk home to Illinois if need be. Five hours later, God rewarded them with a ride north courtesy of a businessman from Galesburg, who had been visiting an acquaintance down in Bowling Green. When they reached Farrington, both boys received an enthusiastic whipping with a hickory rod in the tackroom of Uncle Henry's barn, followed by a lecture whose chief message was that life's highway holds extremes of danger and delight and only sinners and fools tempt its fancy.

Chester Burke's tan Packard Six was parked in a grove of old oak and black walnut trees on a shady bluff above the Missouri River a couple of miles from a small town called Hadleyville. Chester sat behind the steering wheel, reading a morning newspaper whose pages riffled in the morning breeze. Alvin Pendergast stood a few yards off in the sunlight, combing his hair and studying his look in a small hand-mirror. His face was sallow and thin, and he had a cough and a slight fever. Back home, he'd be in bed, sweating up the sheets, or maybe riding a train to the sanitarium. Far below to the east, a steamboat plied the wide green swirling current upriver.

Chester called over to him. "Look here, kid: the Babe hit another one. Rupert's gold mine. Greatest drawing card the game's ever had. I tell you, nobody stands 'em up like the Bambino. I saw him at Comiskey last year, swaggering around outside the clubhouse with a bottle of beer in each hand and it wasn't yet breakfast. Well, wouldn't you know it, he hit about a hundred balls out of the park in batting practice, went three-for-four in the game, then left with a dame on both arms! Can you feature that? Of course, Cobb was the real showman — get a hit, swipe a base, knock some poor dumb bastard on his keester. A genuine sonofabitch. My kind of ballplayer." Chester folded the paper to read the next page. He looked back over his shoulder. "Not much of a baseball fan, are you?"

Alvin stuck the comb and mirror into his shirt pocket. "I don't like games at all. They're for babies." Also, he hated getting sweaty from running about in the hot sun. Sports were for dumbbells.

"Don't be a philistine, kid. Baseball's great for the country. Keeps us square and healthy."

"Sure it does."

"You're smart, kid. Anyone tell you that before?"

"Nope."

"Well, it's true. Stick with me, you'll go far."

"Thanks."

"You sick or something?" Chester asked, looking Alvin in the eye with a worried frown.

The farm boy turned away, scared of being found out. "No, sir."

"Got the Heebie-Jeebies?"

"Maybe a little."

"Don't let it stir you up too much."

"I won't," Alvin said, strolling off to the edge of the river bluff. At home, he might have been finishing up with his chores right about now, getting ready to go fishing with Frenchy. They had a spot all picked out for springtime, a little shelter dug into the riverbank by the winter storms on the Mississippi where they could sit in the shade with a tree branch dangling trotlines in the current. Frenchy had been collecting bait for a couple of months, ten dozen nightcrawlers in one gallon fruit jar alone. Frenchy hated fishing alone, so without Alvin there he'd call on Herbert Muller who didn't know a catfish from a groundhog, but who wanted to pal around with Frenchy, hoping to line up some work in the summer. If Alvin ever went home, he planned on crowning Herbert Muller with a rock.

Looking downriver, he thought about Doc Hartley coming out to the farm to see if the consumption had returned. He hadn't traveled to the sanitarium with Alvin, nor had he ever visited. He hadn't told Alvin or his folks about the artificial pneumothorax treatments or how the wards smelled of formaldehyde and death. During that first month at the sanitarium, Alvin watched two brothers no more than nine or ten years old die in the ward together, side by side, like two little pasty white ghosts, hacking their tiny lungs out. Alvin had expected to die himself. He'd thought that's why he had been sent away: to spare his sisters the pain of seeing him croak at home. He saw sixteen people die in his ward during the year he spent at the sanitarium. How could his folks think he'd ever go back there? He'd rather jump off a bridge or dive under a train. If they were intending to send him back to the sanitarium, maybe he wouldn't ever go home again at all.

Chester honked the motor horn.

Alvin spat over the bluff, then returned to the auto and climbed in. Man-sized sunflowers flanked the ditches on both sides of the road and swayed in the draft of the Packard as Chester sped off toward town. There was no traffic for miles. Nobody on the highway at all. It was a funny day, Alvin thought. Not even many birds whizzing through the air. After a while, they ran by the Hadleyville city limits sign. It was almost noon. Shade trees lined the road that led through the back neighborhoods. Flowers bloomed on the white fencelines that marked a few dooryards. A sign read: **Lots for Sale — Easy Terms.** Chester kept the automobile in low as they motored toward the center of town. The quiet sidewalks shimmered in the heat. A couple of blocks farther on, Chester pulled the car over into a Dixie filling station under the shade of a huge weeping willow and let the motor idle. Alvin looked around. Storefronts and flags. Leo Brooks Boots & Shoes, Franklin Bogart's Grocery Emporium, Barton Brothers Clothing and

Furnishings, a Ford agency and repair garage, and a furniture store with a fluttering advertising banner: ***Let us feather your nest with a little down!*** Half a dozen automobiles were parked across the street, a few pedestrians strolling about. It was a nice town.

"Why're we stopping here?" asked Alvin, watching a small hound dog chase a bird across the street. He was feeling jumpy all of a sudden.

Chester shut the engine off and climbed out. "You thirsty, kid? There's a lunchroom right around the corner. Come on, I'll set you up to an ice cold dope."

Alvin grabbed his cap and stepped out of the car. The sun was warmer than ever. Most of his family had the constitution for heat; his sisters sat indoors in the kitchen until high noon, then went out past the barn to play dolls in the tall grass meadows while he'd be hiding under an old shagbark hickory whenever he wasn't working, keeping to the shade. The family said it was his red hair that made him burn. Fishing at the river with Frenchy, he had to wear a floppy hat and a long-sleeved shirt buttoned to the collar. The hat made the girls along the shore think he was bald. He already suffered his affliction; now he had the hat, too. It was humiliating. *My dear son, we all have our crosses to bear,* his mother told him, but what did she know? She worked in her garden everyday and hardly ever needed a sunbonnet.

The attendant came out of the filling station, a freckle-faced towhead hardly older than Alvin himself. "What'll it be, fellows?"

"Shoot some gasoline into our tank," Chester said, handing the boy a couple of dollar bills.

"Yes, sir."

"We'll be back in about ten minutes."

"Yes, sir."

Chester gave Alvin a nudge. "Let's go, kid."

They entered a narrow one-room building across the street where three men in suspenders and blue overalls sat hunched over a game of checkers at a table by the front window. The one kibitzing was smoking a three-for-a-nickel stogie and held a punchboard on his lap. Except for the old fellow in the white chef's hat, reading box scores from the morning sport sheets beside the cash register, they were the only people in the building. Six empty tables were arranged along one wall parallel to a short order counter that ran from the front of the building to the rear. Chester chose a seat at the table next to the back door. Alvin took the chair across from him and studied the lunch program hung on the wall behind the cash register: meatloaf, lamb, beefsteak, roasted chicken, baked ham and tomato soup — each dinner for 50¢.

"Do we have time to eat?" he asked, feeling a queasiness in his stomach that was either nervousness or hunger, probably both. He'd crammed down five hardboiled eggs, smoked bacon, a plate of toast and three cups of coffee for breakfast, but was already hungry again. His appetite was strange since he had gotten sick. Some days he never felt like eating a bite; the next day he couldn't keep his belly quiet.

"Nope." Chester took a package of Camel cigarettes from his vest pocket. He called to the man at the cash register. "Say, dad, how about a couple of Coca-Colas?"

The old fellow nodded and went to get the drinks from an icebox under the counter. They had drawn the attention of the men playing checkers. Chester lit his cigarette and gave them a friendly wave. The old fellow in the chef's hat brought two opened bottles of Coca-Cola and set them down in front of Chester. "That'll be ten cents, please."

Chester dug into his trousers and came up with a nickel and a handful of pennies which he sprinkled out onto the counter. "Take your pick."

After the fellow had gone, Chester took a sip from one of the Coke bottles. "See those three onionheads over there by the window?"

Alvin nodded. In fact, he had been trying to ignore them. He didn't know much about folks in Missouri and what they thought of strangers. Were they friendly here?

"Well, I'll lay they're trying to figure out whether we're bootleggers or drugstore cowboys," Chester continued, "and we both know they couldn't tell a bootlegger from Hoover's grandmother. But what they're worried about are their birdies. That is, whose we'll be loving up this afternoon and whose we'll be ignoring. Trust me, kid. Losing their dames is the first thing folks get muddleheaded over when fellows like us come into town. We could go out and rob them blind, and while they'll be plenty sore, they'll start forgetting about it in a month or so. But if we were to drive off into the sunset with a couple of Hadleyville's sweeties, they'd hunt us down like animals, shoot us full of holes, and cut our carcasses up for the hogs."

Four more men wearing denim overalls came into the lunchroom and said hello to the old fellow at the cash register and took the table beside the checker players. One of them looked over at Alvin and Chester, and murmured a few words to the fellow beside him. The others seated at the table began talking among themselves.

Chester leaned across to the next table and grabbed an ashtray for his cigarette. Alvin felt a bellyache coming on. Chester had brought him here to Hadleyville to help him take some money out of the First Commerce Bank on Third Street. He'd told him so just after breakfast when he paid the bill. *"It'll be easy as pie," Chester said, handing Alvin a note that read:*

To whom it may Concern: My nephew here is come to get his inheritance which is one Thousand dollars. Please let him have it.

Signed, Hazel Reese

"You're going to present this to one of the tellers," he said.

"Don't joke me," Alvin replied.

Chester laughed and told him to get into the car because they had to reach Hadleyville by noon. "Don't worry, kid," Chester said, while they were driving along the highway. "You'll make the grade, all right."

Alvin asked, "You sure we ain't got time for a couple of pork chop sandwiches? I'm awful hungry."

Chester took a quick drag off the cigarette. "I'm sure."

His eyes were bluer than any Alvin had ever seen. He shaved each morning. Smelled like cologne. Wore fresh collars and a swell suit. Had his shoes shined before breakfast. Smiled at everyone he met. Never seemed scared, neither, Alvin thought. Now that was something worth learning. He could do a lot worse than taking after a smart fellow like Chester Burke.

A raucous cheer came from the checker game as somebody won. The old fellow at the cash register clapped. Out on the sidewalk, two rag-tag boys on bicycles rode past carrying fishing poles. Alvin felt envious; that's where he ought to be going. He could probably show 'em a good thing or two. The twelve o'clock whistle at the shingle mill across town shrieked, signaling the noon hour.

Chester snuffed out his cigarette, then drained the last of his Coca-Cola. "Let's go, kid."

Alvin studied the men at the checker game. Did they have any suspicions? Before today, he hadn't done more than carry Chester's suitcases for him and sit around the hotel lobby in New London while Chester finished his appointments; after changing a flat tire at Hannibal, Alvin didn't even have to leave his room. Ten dollars a day he'd earned, seventy dollars since the dance derby, more dough than he'd had in his hand all year. Once he hit a thousand dollars, he could buy his own motor and get a shoeshine every morning, too.

Out on the sidewalk, Alvin asked Chester, "You ain't going to cut me out, are you?"

A black Essex sedan rushed by toward the downtown.

Chester smiled. "Of course not, kid. I'm a square shooter. Trust me. There'll be kale enough for the both of us, you'll see." He stared up the street toward the middle of town while lighting another cigarette.

Alvin watched a group of women come out of Bogart's Grocery Emporium, burdened with packages. They were smiling brightly. Another automobile went by and a dog chased across the street, barking in its dusty wake.

The farm boy followed Chester back up the sidewalk to the Dixie filling station where he bought a stick of chewing gum to settle his stomach. When he came out again, Chester reached into the backseat of the Packard for a gray brim hat and gave it to Alvin. "Here, put this on."

Alvin frowned, but took off his checked cap and tried the hat on. It felt tight. He looked across at the garage window to see his reflection. He shook his head. "It don't fit. I prefer my own better."

He took it off.

Chester said, "Put it back on. You'll wear it to the bank. Throw the other one in the car."

"Well, what's it all about?"

"It's part of the gag."

"Oh."

Chester grabbed Alvin's cap and tossed it into the Packard, then climbed in behind the wheel. Before Alvin could get around to the passenger side, Chester stopped him. "You're going to have to walk there. It's only a few blocks or so. This is First Street. Follow it to Chapman, take a left, go to Sixth, take another left. You'll see it on the corner by the town square. First Commerce Bank. You can't miss it." He checked his pocketwatch. "We'll meet inside at a quarter till. Don't be late."

Then Chester put the car into gear and drove off.

The freckle-faced towhead inside the filling station watched through the plate glass. Alvin gave him the bad eye so he would mind his own business. He hated people staring at him. For half a year after Alvin had come back from the sanitarium, he'd felt like a sideshow freak, people looking at him wherever he went like they'd never seen someone return from the dead. When the towhead pulled a linen shade down against the sun, Alvin really felt alone, so he began walking down the sidewalk past the corner of the lunchroom and across the intersection into the next block of shade trees and modest lumber houses and smaller shanties of corrugated iron that looked more like fancy car garages. He took the stick of gum out of his shirt pocket and stuck it into his mouth. A couple of Fords rattled by. People across the street walked in and out of stores. He ignored them all, pretending like he walked down that sidewalk each day of his life and had every right in the world to be there. *Don't act like a hick that ain't never been to town,* he reminded himself. *Folks notice that. They can tell when you're somewhere you never been before and don't belong.* He chewed vigorously while he walked and held his head up so nobody would think he was timid. He smelled the blossoming home orchards behind the houses and spring flowers that grew beneath butterbean vine along picket fencelines in the shade where the dark earth was damp from recent rainshowers. The concrete sidewalk was cracked here and there, and tufts of grass grew in the fractures.

Towering elm trees and poplars and cottonwoods arched overhead. More motorcars passed and the I.G.A. store across the street gave way at Williams Street to a neighborhood of elegantly fretted wood houses and gardens. Alvin heard hose nozzles hissing, piano scales from sunlit parlors, a hammerfall on steel echoing across the warm noon air. *It ain't so bad,* he thought. *Why, a fellow could get used to a new place like this in a hurry if he needed to.* To hell with the farm and everybody treating him like an invalid. He'd thrown all of that over and was done with it. His confidence growing by the minute, the farm boy walked ahead with a fresh bounce in his step.

Two blocks on, Alvin paused in front of a large two-story frame-house whose dry, ratty lawn covered most of the square lot. A lovely magnolia out front, a thick white oak in the side yard, and two black cherry trees toward the back fence provided shade for a lot where nearly everything had died from neglect. Even the paint on the fence pickets out front had peeled and vanished in a drier season, some-body's initials carved into the wood. The place looked abandoned and it wasn't only the lawn. Nearer the house, just under the shade of the magnolia, dozens of children's toys lay broken and scattered in the scruffy weeds — alphabet building blocks, tin bugles, wooden soldiers, wingless aeroplanes. Back along the side of the house where coralberry grew beneath the window boxes, an old tire hung down from the branch of the oak tree on a short length of rope. When they were kids, Alvin and Frenchy would go twirling in a tire they had hung inside Uncle Henry's barn. The stunt was to get as dizzy as possible, then play wirewalker along the tops of the stalls from one end of the barn to the other without falling off. Strolling out of the barn without stinking head to foot from horse manure was considered the game's supreme merit badge.

Feeling adventurous, Alvin opened the gate, keeping an eye on the front door whose screen was still closed, and crossed into the yard, staying under the overlapping shade of the blooming magnolia and the old oak. As he moved along the fence to the rear of the house, the farm boy saw more junk thrown about: cushions, shoes, an old lamp, a wicker chair without its seat, a rusted bed frame, torn pillows.

He decided that either somebody had been doing spring-cleaning and had forgotten to bring everything back inside or the people living in the house were hillbillies. He came up to the swing and gave it a shove. The rope curled above the tire and twisted into a mean knot where it looped over the branch. Alvin stared at the house. Lace curtains were hung in the window frames, hiding the interior like a shroud. Back of the house, the trashcan had fallen over, spilling its contents all over the walkway between a tool shed and a weed-eaten vegetable patch.

Now he was curious what the indoors looked like, how high the garbage was piled elsewhere throughout the house. A short porch led up to the back door. If it wasn't locked, well, he might just take a quick peek inside. He walked up to the door and reached for the knob, then stopped to reconsider. If someone came to the door, how would he explain his presence in the back yard? Thinking on his feet was not one of Alvin's greatest strengths. All he could say was that he was lost and needed a drink of water and he'd already tried the front door and nobody had answered so he had come around back. Who could get bitter about a fellow asking for help? Alvin reached for the knob again.

"BOO!"

He stumbled backward and nearly fell over. Somebody laughed. Alvin hurried down off the porch, took a few steps backward, and stared up at the kitchen window. He listened for half a minute or so, then took half a stride toward the porch.

"BOO!"

More laughter.

The voice hadn't come from the kitchen, after all. The farm boy stepped back a few feet further and craned his neck upward to a second story window.

The voice, in a guttural whisper, said, *"No! Not there, either!"*

"I see you!" Alvin called out.

"No, you don't!"

Alvin hurried over to the swing and faced the window there above the thick coralberry. Imagining he saw the curtains move, he took a few steps closer. Was that a shadow there behind the glass? He walked close to the side of the house and got up on his tiptoes to see inside.

"You're in there, ain't you? I just seen you!"

Laughter echoed into the yard. *"Nope!"*

"I'm going to come in there and clean you out!"

"No, you won't!"

"How about I give you a good pop in the nose?"

"All right, you win," the voice sagged. *"I'm down here."*

Along the foundation below the window box, a patch of coralberry parted, revealing a narrow crawlspace covered by a lattice grate propped open now. Alvin knelt for a look. Divided from the glare of the noon sunlight, the entry was black as cellar pitch. He'd sooner dive headfirst into a brick well than crawl through that hole. As a kid, Alvin'd had a nightmarish fear of the old boogey-man his sister Mary Ann told him lived in the dirt crawlspace beneath his bedroom floor. She said it snuck in out of a storm one night and favored the house so much it decided to stay. *It ain't no wild beast, neither. It's smart. Real smart. And patient. Boogey-man'll camp out down there for years, eating bugs and mice, stray cats, biding its time till it gets what it come for: a nice fresh little boy. Boogey-man'll wait till some poor little boy walks past by hisself and then it'll snatch him. Take him way down into the earth, so far no human being'll ever see him again, and make him a slave, or eat him, depending on how hard the boy works. You be careful, now. Wouldn't surprise me at all to find it's been working on them boards below your bed, trying to loosen 'em up, so's it can sneak in one night and snatch you while you're sleeping!*

"Hello, hello, hello!" the voice called out to him. "You're not afraid of the dark, are you?"

" 'Course not."

"Well then, come on in!"

A pair of hands and arms became visible in the gloom, small and frail, like a child's, followed by a large head wearing a smiling face that was not a child's at all, but in fact a dwarf's.

"Don't be a dilly-dog," the dwarf urged as pleasantly as possible. "Come on in. It's nice and cool."

Alvin stared at the dwarf, utterly unprepared for this encounter. The only such creature he had ever seen away from a circus was at the sanitarium, a diminutive juggler in clown paint who turned somersaults and chased the nurses about with a wooden paddle. He was shocked. It never occurred to him their sort lived in houses like regular folks.

The dwarf smiled up at him. "I won't bite you. I swear."

Alvin hesitated, preferring to remain out in the sunlight where it was safe.

"Oh please," the dwarf begged. "It's not half as dark as it seems. Why, I'm blind as a tick and I don't have any trouble at all getting about down here. What do you say?"

Alvin looked back across the yard to the street. Except for a pair of birds chirping somewhere up in the magnolia branches, the yard was dead quiet in the early afternoon.

"How about it?" Squinting in the sunlight, the dwarf thrust his head out of the coralberry. His hair was thin as cobwebs and nearly as white. "We'd have an awful lot of fun."

"I ain't sure I'd fit."

"Oh, sure you will. If you don't mind me saying, you're awfully skinny. You're not sick, are you?"

"Hell, no."

"Please?"

Alvin shrugged. "All right."

What did he have to be scared about? This little fellow was only half his size. If need be, he could probably throw him down in a second.

"Wonderful!"

The dwarf backed out of the opening, pushing the tiny grate aside as he went. Leaving Chester's hat behind in the grass, Alvin got down on his knees and pointed himself toward the dark square in the side of the house. Shoving the bushy coralberry apart with his hands, he crawled forward into the shadows.

It was a tight fit. His trousers threatened to catch on the latticework frame as he slithered by, while his knees scraped the foundation and his back struck the upper edge of the grate. Once in, though, he was able to sit up without much trouble. A crawlspace roughly four feet high separated the dirt foundation from the floor of the house above him. Plenty of room.

"Name's Rascal," said the dwarf, scrambling over beside him. "What's yours?"

"Alvin."

"Glad to know you, Alvin." Rascal sat down in the dirt and crossed his legs. He was dressed in a small boy's blue one-piece romper with black button shoes. Alvin had never seen anyone like him before in his life, but tried not to stare.

Ducking a spider web, the farm boy asked, "How long you been under here?"

"Since I lost my marbles last Saturday," said Rascal, drawing closer. "It's black as sin, isn't it? No trouble at all cracking your head open. Don't worry, you get used to it. Actually, I think it suits me. I find myself perspiring less down here."

"What's that smell?" asked Alvin, noticing for the first time a distinctly unpleasant odor, sort of fruity and damp, rotting. He thought he might gag from the stink.

Rascal sniffed the air. "Hmm. My guess would be honeydew melon. Sorry, I've been burying the rinds under the porch over there," Rascal gestured in the direction of the front of the house, "but some nocturnal creature keeps digging them up when I'm in bed. Very troublesome situation. Unsanitary to say the least."

"Maybe you ought to put them out with the garbage."

"Oh, except for collecting my groceries, I rarely go outdoors anymore." The dwarf jumped up, his head stopping just short of the support beams. "Do you care to play some marbles? I found a few of my aggies this morning. There's a place all smoothed out under the kitchen." Rascal grabbed Alvin by the wrist. "Come on, I'll show you."

"I can't. Got an appointment downtown in half an hour. Sorry." He wondered what Chester was doing just then, where he'd gone off to. He never saw fit to tell Alvin anything that mattered.

The dwarf tugged. "Please? It'll only take a minute."

"Oh, all right. But I ain't got all day." Reluctantly, Alvin rose as high as he could without hitting his head, and followed the dwarf on a crooked path between the support pillars and foundation blocks from one end of the house to the other, dodging clots of spider web and gunny sacks stuffed with dirt and assorted broken toys like those lying about in the grass outside. The stink under the house worsened the

farther in they went. More than rotted fruit, the stench of a summer
outhouse whose wooden walls and damp soil collected and preserved
the odor. Alvin shuffled behind Rascal until they came to a narrow
hole crudely hacked out of the floor overhead.

The dwarf stopped and smiled. "That's my bedroom up there.
Would you like to see?" He pulled himself up into the opening and disappeared. Alvin heard his footsteps scrambling across the floorboards.
A drawer opened and shut. Something heavy was dragged across the
floor. Trying to follow Rascal up into the hole, Alvin only managed to
get his head through. He saw Rascal staring at him.

"Aren't you coming?"

"I can't fit."

"How come?"

"My shoulders are too wide."

Alvin swiveled his head to get a better look at the room. It had no
window and only two doors, one of which opened to a small closet.
There was a small iron bed, a common oak dresser, and a low nightstand with a kerosene lamp. Clothes were jumbled up at the foot of
the bed, Post Toasties cereal boxes stacked together beside the dresser,
fruit jars filled with preserves on top, six water jugs next to the closet,
Big Little books piled on the nightstand. Odds and ends collected beneath the bed: rubber galoshes, mousetraps, used-up pencil tablets,
a shoe stretcher, and a pocket spyglass. Rascal dove into the shallow
closet and began rummaging through the clothes and assorted junk
that had piled up, tossing things out onto the floor behind him. After a
couple of minutes, he came out dragging a little old leather suitcase.

"Maybe you ought to go open the back door," said Alvin, "so's I
can come in and sit down. This ain't all that comfortable."

Rascal played with the latches on the suitcase, trying to flip them
up. "Door's locked."

Alvin bent his knees slightly to ease the pressure on his shoulders. If
he were a foot shorter, he could have been standing straight up with his
head in the hole. "I know, I tried it. Just go open it from the inside."

"I mean, my bedroom door's locked, too," said Rascal, pointing
over his back. "That's why I had to pry a hole in the floorboards with a

butter knife. Auntie locked me in and took the key before she left. This used to be a pantry until my behavior last year apparently warranted a change of scenery." The dwarf banged the suitcase hard on the floor. "Dammit!"

"Can't you force it open?"

"I'm trying," said Rascal, banging the suitcase a second time even harder. The latches appeared jammed shut with rust.

"I mean your door."

"Nope." Rascal dropped the suitcase and scuttled back across the floor into the closet. More clothes came flying out behind him: shirts, stockings, a fancy pair of riding boots and a big white ten-gallon William S. Hart cowboy hat. Rascal slid out on his hands and knees carrying a pair of pliers. "She's padlocked all the doors in the house, front to back. So I'm stuck here."

"You could crawl out and bust a window," Alvin told him. "That's what I'd do if I was you. It's your house, too, ain't it?"

"You mean throw a rock?"

"Or use a stick. It don't matter which if you got to get inside."

The dwarf shook his head. "No, I'd feel like a crook and there'd be glass everywhere. What if it rained? I'd have an awful mess to clean up and when Auntie returned, she'd throw a fit."

"Well, suit yourself." Alvin shrugged. "But why'd she lock you in here, anyhow?"

"Doesn't trust me," said Rascal, attacking the suitcase latches with a vengeance, using the pliers to tear out the mountings. His face reddened with the effort.

"Where'd she go?"

One latch broke and popped free. "To a medicine show in Dayton, Ohio. She's addicted to brain tonics."

Rascal worked the pliers on the other, tugging furiously at the lock.

"How long's she supposed to be gone?"

"Three weeks." The pliers snapped and fell apart at the joint. "Oh, for the love of Pete!"

The dwarf spun around and hurled the broken pliers under the bed, then got up and kicked the suitcase against the dresser. When it still didn't open, he ran back into the closet and began digging through his collection of junk again.

Alvin let his head drop out of the room and squatted in the dirt. Sunlight flickered into the shadows through the baseboards that encircled the house, but the only genuine entry was the small lattice grate. Listening to Rascal bang on the suitcase latch, Alvin admired the extensive junkyard the dwarf had created within the crawlspace. Whether from anger or boredom, he had strewn garbage into every corner of the underside of the house; a family of raccoons couldn't have done a better job. It'd take days to clean it all out, digging up what scraps he'd buried and carting it off with the rest of the trash. Alvin wondered what Rascal's aunt would think when she discovered all he had done in her absence. Maybe that's why she didn't trust him alone with the run of the house.

The dwarf quit hacking at the suitcase. Hearing the latches snap open, Alvin stuck his head back up through the hole in the floor just in time to witness the dwarf tip the suitcase upside down and spill a huge stack of papers out onto the floor. Ignoring the loose sheets, Rascal dug hurriedly into the larger pile, sifting to the bottom. When he came up with a thick stack of postcards bound in string, he leaped to his feet. "Aha! Found 'em!"

"Found what?"

"Let me by," said Rascal, straddling the hole. Alvin slipped back down under the house again and the dwarf dropped through the hole, carrying the postcards. He sat in the dirt and handed half of the postcards over to Alvin. "My Uncle Augustus mailed these back to himself from France during the war. When he died, I inherited them with a box of his old correspondences."

"Naked ladies," said Alvin, shuffling through the cards one by one. He'd had no idea this is what the dwarf had busted open his suitcase to retrieve.

Rascal giggled. "Grand, aren't they? If Auntie knew I had them, oh boy!"

Every card featured a different woman, a different pose. More than a couple gave Alvin that hot feeling down below his stomach. Frenchy had these sorts of photographs once when he was living out back of the barn. Some were belly-dancing girls in lacy get-ups with funny tassels on their tits and belly-buttons showing. Others had colored women from Dixie lying on metal cots, posing without smiles or clothes of any kind, completely naked, hair between the legs and all. Frenchy charged his cousins a penny a peek, nickel for half an hour, and bought a bottle of liquor every Saturday night with the earnings.

Alvin shuffled through the cards, the stick in his pants getting bigger by the second. Hurried by the dwarf's stupid grin, he zipped to the bottom of the stack and handed the French postcards back to their owner.

"You like them, don't you?" said the dwarf. "Me, too." Rascal stuck the cards up through the hole and laid them on his bedroom floor. "I used to take them out every so often. Not every day, of course, but I'd have to say three or four times a week. Auntie would say I'm sinning, but what does she know? She's never married."

Feeling an attack of claustrophobia coming on, Alvin looked away from the dwarf toward the exit framed in sunlight across the dark underside of the house. He coughed, and his ears rang.

"I suppose you're late for your appointment," the dwarf remarked, sounding disconsolate. "I'd sure hate you to get in trouble for visiting me."

Through the grate in the crawlspace, Alvin watched the bottom branches of the white oak swaying in the afternoon breeze. "Yeah, I guess I ought to get along pretty soon."

"I wish I had a job," said the dwarf, sitting down against one of the support pillars. "Something stimulating, yet profitable. Perhaps in a department store or a rollercoaster park. Do you know of anything fitting that description?"

"Not today."

"I suppose I should study the newspapers, prowl the pavement, ring doorbells. How else can I expect to gain employment? Can you read?"

"Sure." Scarcely more than labels and street signs, if truth be told, but Alvin didn't feel like admitting one of his worst shortcomings to a stranger. The year of school he had missed being sick set him back so far that he never caught up and didn't care any longer. He hated reading.

"I try to study ten thousand words a day. That's in addition to the fifteen new ones I memorize out of Webster's every night before I go to bed. I also read philosophy and the natural sciences. I've always believed in bettering myself through learning. 'Education has for its object the formation of character.' That's a credo of mine. Do you have one?"

Before Alvin was forced to embarrass himself by asking what exactly a credo was, Rascal leaped up and ran across the dirt to a small hiding space under the veranda where the slats between the front steps afforded a discreet view of the sidewalk.

"Do you see this fellow out here?"

Alvin crab-walked to the steps, then knelt down and angled for a look. He saw a tall man in a gray suit pacing the sidewalk in front of the dwarf's house. "What of it?"

"Well, I'm convinced he's either one of Auntie's gigolos or a cat burglar planning to rob us. I've seen him out there now three days in a row and I confess it's beginning to spook me. Last night, I actually slept with a candle lit. It was quite humiliating."

Alvin didn't think that was anything to get cut up about. Men like him came out to the farm all the time, mostly to take a look at the girls and talk up some bargain that didn't amount to nothing. "Maybe he's just one of those fellows selling soap flakes."

"Oh, I don't know. He doesn't seem very friendly."

They both watched the man, who did nothing but pace up and down. Alvin had no opinion about his character, so he kept quiet. What could he say? The dwarf studied the fellow with a persistent frown. Then the guy broke one of the old fence pickets with a hard kick and walked off.

When he had gone, the dwarf slid away from the steps. "I'm sure he'll be back."

Alvin crept out from under the steps behind him. "If he's a regular burglar, it'll be a knock if he don't."

"Well, I won't stand it. I have a pistol, you know."

"Don't blow off your toe."

"Oh, I'm a sure-shot," the dwarf boasted. "When I was younger, I used to practice on Auntie's empty Cascara bottles nearly once a month."

Alvin remembered his appointment at the bank. "I ought to go."

"Do you have to? Really, entertaining is so much fun. If only I had more room."

"I don't want to be late." In fact, he was afraid of what Chester might do if he didn't show up on time. He had a temper that didn't need showing to be taken account of. Alvin saw it in his eyes. He could be mean if he had to, and Alvin knew it.

"Where are you going? If I may ask."

"First Commerce Bank downtown. Do you know where that is?"

"Of course, I do. It's at Sixth and Calhoun," the dwarf replied. "Why, that's where Mr. Sinclair works."

"Who?"

"Harrison B. Sinclair. An old friend of the family. He and Auntie are quite close. You'll like him a lot. He can be a very pleasant fellow, particularly if you have any money to invest."

"Well, I ain't never been there before."

"Oh, it's only a short walk from here," the dwarf explained, "I could take you, if you like. I really haven't been out of doors in almost a week. I miss the air. A good walk now and then makes for a fine constitutional, don't you agree?"

Alvin thought about that, bringing the dwarf with him. He imagined Chester standing outside even now, checking his watch. How sore would he be if he saw the dwarf? Alvin told Rascal, "I ain't sure I can take you along. It's private business."

"Oh, I wouldn't be a bother. What sort of business?"

"I ain't supposed to say."

"Is it a secret?" The dwarf broke a sly grin. "I adore secrets."

"Sure it is."

"Well, I wouldn't tell anyone. Cross my heart."

Alvin took the note out of his shirt pocket and showed it to the dwarf, figuring it didn't give away much. Besides, he thought, the note's a lie, ain't it?

Rascal laughed when he finished reading. He said, "This is very clever."

"That ain't my real uncle."

The dwarf smiled. "Did you compose this yourself?"

"My partner did," Alvin told him. "He's pretty smart."

"How long've you been in cahoots with this fellow?" the dwarf asked, as he read over the note again.

"Well, I ain't saying."

Rascal looked up. "Beg your pardon?"

"We ain't in cahoots," Alvin said, feeling somewhat awkward now. Maybe he shouldn't have shared Chester's note. Deciding he ought to put the dwarf off the track, Alvin told him, "He's just a fellow I met to do some business with. See, he owns a box factory in Kenosha that makes a new sort of pasteboard and he's looking for folks to work there. I seen his ad in the *Daily News* when I was up north to a show at the Chez Paree, so I sent him a telegram with all the dope about myself, and here we are."

The dwarf laughed. "Oh, I hardly think so. Truth is, you're both here to rob the First Commerce Bank, aren't you?"

Alvin frowned. "Quit your kidding."

"Look, any fool can see this is a decoy note," Rascal said, enthused with discovery, "and not a very persuasive one, either. If you give this to any of Mr. Sinclair's tellers, you'll be a jailbird by suppertime. Let me help you write another."

"Huh?"

"Wait here." The dwarf straightened up, his head still easily below the floorboards. "I've just had the most marvelous idea!"

He dashed off toward his bedroom.

"Hey there!" Alvin called after him. "I got to get along!"

But the dwarf had already climbed up through the hole and disappeared. Alvin crawled under the house toward Rascal's bedroom, afraid he was going to be late now to the bank. He heard the dwarf rummaging through his closet, tossing more things about. It occurred to Alvin that the dwarf bore his cross better than anyone he'd ever known in his life. Had anybody else come to visit Rascal beneath the house in the time he'd been locked indoors? Did he have any friends? Alvin promised himself that if he ever came back through Hadleyville again, why, he'd take Rascal out fishing. The poor little fellow had probably never even been in a boat before.

After a few minutes, the dwarf dropped down through the hole in his bedroom floor, carrying a small black leather doctor's bag. He took a slip of paper from the pocket of his romper and gave it to the farm boy to read.

"This is a much grander plan," Rascal assured him, as he put down the doctor's bag. He wore a big grin. The note read:

> *Gentlemen: The bearer of this letter has a dynamite bomb in his satchel. Please deliver into his possession the amount of two thousand dollars or he will fix this bank of yours for good!*
>
> *Signed, Al Capone*

The dwarf said, "We might've asked for more money, but then they'd have to count it out by hand and that could take more time than we'd want. The police station is only four blocks away."

Alvin was flabbergasted. He knew he shouldn't have said anything about his appointment at the bank. Now what was he supposed to do? If the dwarf was right about Chester intending a stick-up, wouldn't changing the plan now make things even worse? He was scared and confused, and felt his bellyache returning. He coughed again and his eyes watered.

He told Rascal, "Look, I ain't asked for your help. What if they got a bank dick? I could get shot in the head."

"They do and his name's Elmer Gleason and he's only got one eye. He lost the other fighting with Stonewall Jackson at Chancellorsville. If he draws his revolver, just remember to keep to his left."

The dwarf laughed.

Alvin scowled. "That ain't so funny."

"Nobody'll shoot you. I promise."

The farm boy grew more desperate. "What if my partner ain't

robbing the bank, after all? I'll look like a damned fool."

"Oh, there's no mistake, I assure you. I've read more accounts of bank robberies than you can shake a stick at and anyone who'd deliberately choose to hand your partner's note to one of Mr. Sinclair's tellers, well, I'd have to say he hasn't got the sense God gave an oyster. Now, tell me this: what sort of motor car did you fellows drive to town?"

Feeling resigned to the dwarf's intentions, Alvin said, "It's a Packard Six. Sort of straw-colored."

"All right, listen," Rascal said, unfastening the latches to the doctor's bag. He handed it to Alvin so he could see what was inside. "This is what we'll do."

Downtown Hadleyville felt quiet in the noon hour. Motor traffic was intermittent. Birds flew noiselessly from treetop to flagpole. Children and mothers sat together picnicking on the summer grass. Dogs chased after fluttering leaves.

Alvin waited across the street from the bank. A clock tower on the square indicated he still had a few minutes to run off and avoid the necktie party when the dwarf's plan went on the bum. Chester was inside the bank already, his automobile parked in the alleyway behind Orrey's jewelry shop. Frenchy told Alvin once that *"It ain't what you got, it's what you can get away with,"* but everyone in the family knew he was kind of a half-crook and nearly always in trouble. Frenchy couldn't drive through downtown traffic without skipping a light or two, and always thought it was a swell gag to walk out of a five-and-dime with some hot stuff in his pocket. Just last summer, in fact, he'd been to jail for stealing watermelons from a Mormon market down in Nauvoo. He spent six weeks there mopping floors and scrubbing toilets. One night, the convict he shared a cell with popped him in the mouth and knocked Frenchy's tooth out. When Alvin was younger, before the consumption, he had given hell himself to truant officers and gotten sick on corn liquor and stolen molasses candy and penny chocolate drops every so often from Smead's drugstore, but he had been afraid of the punishment for getting caught to do anything much worse. Robbing a bank was different, more than a germ of youthful anarchy or a one-horse beer racket. This would put a smut on his life. Yet when the clock struck a quarter till, Alvin Pendergast carried the small doctor's bag across Third Street and entered the First Commerce Bank of Hadleyville, Missouri.

It was stuffy indoors, a musty odor of perspiration and dried-out leather. Electric fans suspended from a plaster Greek Revival ceiling high overhead spun dust motes lazily through the sunlight. The wood floor creaked underfoot. Chester stood by the wall opposite the merchants' window, scribbling on a sheet of paper and chatting up a pretty girl in a yellow bloomer dress. Seated in a white wicker chair beside a potted palm was an old man wearing a faded butternut gray Civil War uniform with a navy Colt .44 revolver hanging off his belt. He was sound asleep. Three clerks worked behind the cage. A door leading to offices on the second story was open and voices echoed in the stairwell. Except for the rhythmic tapping of a Monroe adding calculator downstairs and a typewriter clacking upstairs, it was even quieter than outdoors.

Remembering his instructions from Rascal, Alvin went to stand in line behind the other customers at the teller's window. He made eye contact with the young man at the adding calculator and nodded a greeting. Chester and the girl stepped into line behind him. One of the bank officers went upstairs carrying a large sack of coins that chinked with every step he took. The elderly bank guard began to snore.

As the first customer in line finished his business, Chester tapped Alvin on the shoulder. "Pardon me."

The farm boy turned around. "Yes, sir?"

"Would it be too great an inconvenience for you to allow this young lady to go ahead? She's in an awful rush."

Blushing, Alvin looked at the girl behind Chester. Her brown eyes were wide and glossy, and Chester gave him a look that told him to let her past, so Alvin nodded. "All right."

He stepped aside to allow her through to the teller's window. She offered a pleasant smile. "Much obliged." A keen scent of Violet perfume trailed behind her.

"Sure."

"That's a swell valise you got there, " Chester remarked, clapping him on the shoulder.

Alvin mumbled, "It's my daddy's."

"Well, it's a knockout."

"Thanks."

Chester smiled and stepped forward to stand with the slender girl. Alvin had to admit he was slick. Chester hadn't shown the slightest recognition when they'd greeted each other. Presumably, he'd done this so often that fooling people had become natural to him.

Nervous as hell now, Alvin watched a pack of young loafers outdoors, lagging along the sidewalk by the barbershop. A paneled cargo truck drove past in a cloud of exhaust smoke. His bellyache worsened. Alvin stood three customers from the window now and the doctor's bag felt heavy in his hand. He tried to concentrate on fishing to calm his gut. Instead, he recalled an old saw Grandpa Louis used to quote whenever the subject of life and labor arose: *"Get the money — honestly if you can."*

When the girl arrived at the head of the line, Chester stepped off to one side to let her do her business. He winked at Alvin. A pair of fellows in striped brown suits came into the bank and went straight for the executive offices at the rear where one of the fine walnut desks had a tall brass spittoon beside it. The prim bank officer wore pince-nez and a fresh blood carnation on his lapel. Alvin wished he could get a glass of water. His knees felt weak. The pretty girl finished her business at the teller's window and stepped aside. She smiled at Chester. He tipped his fedora as she walked past him out of the bank.

Dropping his voice, Chester murmured to Alvin, "Use your noodle, kid."

Then he, too, walked off, farther down the counter to the merchants' window where a notice from the Advertising Association was hung on the back wall.

"May I help you, sir?"

The farm boy stepped up to the teller and set down the black doctor's bag, scared half out of his wits now. The teller was a fellow maybe Chester's age with oil-slicked hair and a gray wool suit that was probably from Montgomery Ward & Co. He looked drowsy. Alvin handed him the note.

A cool draft swept into the bank from the corridor leading to the rear entrance. Somebody had just walked in through the door leading out to the alley. Voices from the stairwell went silent. The back door swung closed with a bang.

The teller looked confused. "What is this?"

Alvin narrowed his eyes, trying to stave off panic. He kept his voice low. "Can't you read?"

"You have a bomb?"

Alvin picked up the doctor's bag. "Right in this here satchel. Just like it says in the letter."

The teller's face flushed. "Is this some sort of joke?"

"I ain't laughing, am I?" Alvin replied, utterly numb below his neck.

He heard murmuring behind him from a man and a woman waiting in line.

"This is against the law," the teller offered, trying to sound calm while his chin trembled.

"What of it?" Alvin replied, annoyed now. Somehow, fear and fever emboldened him. He raised his voice. "I ain't feeling too good and I might be contagious, so give me the money, you dumbbell, or I'll blow us all up."

"Oh, my Lord!" the woman behind him cried. "He's got a bomb!"

"A bomb!" somebody else shouted. "That boy there's got a bomb!"

When Alvin turned to address the commotion, his teller disappeared beneath the counter. Two men ran out of the bank. Another woman by the bank guard fainted. Old Elmer Gleason still hadn't awakened. The bank officers were staring at Alvin. Unsure of what to do, he opened the doctor's bag and stuck his hand inside. "I ain't joking you. I'll blow us all up. I swear it!"

"Somebody please do something!" another woman cried. "He'll kill us all!"

"Not unless I tell him to!" a voice called out from the rear of the bank. The dwarf emerged from the back door hall dressed in a gray single-breasted boy's corduroy knickerbocker suit that looked spick and span after his grimy under-the-house attire. Even his cornsilk hair was combed and his shoes polished. "Mr. Sinclair! May I see you a moment?"

Another fellow in the teller's line behind Alvin snuck out of the bank and ran off. The bank officers who had been hiding in the stairwell came down into the lobby behind the dwarf who marched over to the cages and got up on his tiptoes to counter level. "How's my money doing?"

The prim fellow in pince-nez left his desk. Keeping an eye on Alvin, he asked, "What's this all about? Do you know that young man over there?"

"Of course," the dwarf replied, steely-eyed. "He's an anarchist I hired to bring that bomb here this afternoon."

Alvin felt everyone staring at him. His bellyache had gone, but his knees still rattled. The handle of the bag was damp from his sweaty palms. He considered running away.

"I don't understand," Mr. Sinclair said to the dwarf. "Where's your Aunt Esther?"

"She's in Dayton on business. I'm in charge of things while she's away. Is my money still here?"

The bank officers looked at each other, surprised by the question. "Of course it is," replied Harrison B. Sinclair. "Why, your aunt is one of our most valued customers."

Alvin saw Chester mumbling to the teller at the merchants' window. The teller nodded and began opening the stack of drawers just beneath the counter.

"Sure she is," replied the dwarf, "but it's not her money. It's mine. May I see it?" The dwarf pulled himself up onto the edge of the counter. "I've decided to take some of it with me today."

The merchants' teller in front of Chester had a large sack open and was shoveling money into it. Alvin glanced at the street outside. Sidewalks were mostly empty, no motor traffic.

The bank officer told the dwarf, "That's not possible without your aunt's approval."

"Why not?"

"Well, she's your legal guardian. Her power-of-attorney in this case extends to withdrawal of funds from the trust your late parents, God rest their souls, set up on your behalf."

Rascal looked briefly in Alvin's direction and frowned. Was he really surprised to hear this, Alvin wondered. "That doesn't seem fair," the dwarf said. "Is it legal?"

"Perfectly."

Both bank officers smiled.

"So, even though it's my money, I can't have any of it."

"Not without your aunt's signature," said Mr. Sinclair. "I can show you the figures, if you like."

"Figures don't lie," the dwarf remarked, "but liars can figure. I'd prefer to see my money."

"Look, son," Sinclair said, confidently, "I'm not sure why you came down here today. It's always been my understanding that you were perfectly aware of this financial arrangement, and that it was quite acceptable to you. Now you're asking us to remove a considerable sum of money from our vault just so you can see that it's there. If you'll pardon my being blunt, but that seems a little childish, don't you agree?"

The dwarf slipped down off the counter and shook his head, looking hangdog. "I thought we were pals, Mr. Sinclair. At least, you said we were. Remember when you told me that? It was on my twenty-first birthday, and you and Auntie were up in her bedroom and I was hiding in the closet, spying on you two? Remember? And afterward, you said if there was anything I ever needed, I could come right down here and ask, and you'd do whatever I wanted, no matter what. You said that! Remember? Anything!"

Harrison B. Sinclair's face became a deep crimson, both angered and embarrassed. "I have no idea what you're talking about."

The dwarf turned to Alvin. "Tommy, please bring me the satchel."

The farm boy carried the doctor's bag over to the dwarf. He could barely walk and wondered when this would all be over. He noticed the bank guard was just waking up. Keep to his left, Alvin reminded himself.

"Thanks," Rascal said, a grave expression on his moony face. "You can run along now."

Chester snatched a sack from the teller and whispered something else to him. As discreetly as possible, Alvin walked back across the bank lobby. Chester left the merchants' window and headed for the door. Mr. Sinclair asked the dwarf, "What are you intending to do?"

"Well," Rascal replied, reaching into the doctor's bag, "I ask myself just that question everyday." He drew out a handful of rocket-sticks, tied together and painted up to resemble dynamite.

"Good grief!" one of the bank officers shouted. "He's really going to blow us up! For Christsakes, Harry! Do something!"

The dwarf took out a match and lit the fuse attached to the stack of rocket-sticks. "If I can't have my inheritance, then nobody can!"

Alvin slipped out the front door of the First Commerce Bank.

Inside, a woman screamed and a huge BANG! echoed throughout the building.

His heart thumping wildly, Alvin hurried down the sidewalk to the corner and around back to the alleyway behind the jewelry store where Chester's Packard was parked beside a board fence swarmed with hollyhocks and sunflowers. He threw his hat into a rubbage barrel, and climbed into the automobile. There, he watched Chester rush up the alley, carrying the sack of money. "Here, kid, stick this in the backseat."

Alvin grabbed the sack and tossed it into the car.

Chester asked, "How'd you come across that bomb idea?"

"Me and that little fellow. We thought it up together."

"Where'd you bump into a nut like that?" Chester asked, as he went around to the trunk. "He's bugs."

"I don't know," Alvin lied, feeling confused now and dizzy from his sudden adventure.

Chester removed his hat and brown coat and threw both into the trunk, then grabbed a new blue coat and hat from his valise. "Well, you put it over just swell. They lapped it up."

Thrilled by the adventure of it all, Alvin felt brave enough to smile. "We gave 'em the works, didn't we?"

"You sure did." Chester put on the blue coat and hat, then handed Alvin the keys to the Packard. "I'll meet you on the sidewalk next to

Lowe's furniture store. Don't be late."

"I won't."

Once Chester had gone off down the alley again, Alvin reached back into the Packard and shoved the sack of money under a pile of clothes in the rear seat, then got in and started the motor. Before he could put it in gear, the dwarf came out the rear of Orrey's jewelry store with an old leather suitcase in hand.

"Wait!" he yelled, struggling to reach the car. "Don't go yet!"

"What do you want?"

"Take me along!"

Alvin let his foot slip off the gas pedal and the dwarf dropped the suitcase into the dirt beside the Packard.

"Everything I said went," the dwarf told Alvin, opening the passenger door. "Now they want to kill me. You have to take me with you."

"It ain't my motor."

"Please? I won't be any trouble at all. You have my word."

What was he supposed to say? Without the dwarf, he might be in jail now. Alvin shrugged. Chester could decide what to do with him once they got out of town. "All right, get in."

The farm boy put on his old cap and drove out of the alley and turned left on Fourth Street past the Postal Telegraph office. It was a short run to Main Street at the end of the block. Rolling toward the town square, Alvin's stomach flip-flopped. The sidewalks on both sides of the street adjacent to First Commerce Bank were crowded with people milling about and gesturing in every direction. Alvin slumped low in the seat and drove by without slowing. Both bank officers were outside talking to a local policeman who had just arrived. Elmer Gleason was also out on the sidewalk, lying with his back against a lamppost and receiving treatment from a nurse. His revolver had been drawn and lay next to his leg on the pavement.

A muffled voice from the rear seat mumbled, "Where are we?"

"Hush up," said Alvin, driving now down to the end of the town square.

A strong breeze rippled the flags on the storefronts. Slowing further, Alvin drove by Chase Esquire's Insurance, the Palace movie house, and Johnson Murray's Hardware. As he passed Lowe's furniture, he saw Chester stroll out of M. K. McDonald's wallpaper emporium. Alvin stopped the Packard at the curb just long enough for Chester to come around and jump into the passenger seat. A young woman wearing a rosy porch dress and a straw-bonnet tied with a pink bow under her chin leaned out the store's front door and shouted, "Eight o'clock sharp now!"

Chester waved with a grin. "You said it, sweetheart!"

Alvin checked the mirror. Nobody was coming yet, but he held the Packard in gear just in case.

"Don't be late!" She fluttered her eyelids.

"Oh, I won't!" Chester said, waving to her again, the smile frozen on his face. Then he turned to Alvin and growled. "Step on it."

The woman blew Chester a kiss, "Bye-bye, Charley!"

Alvin accelerated up the street toward the town limits. The road was clear in both directions. No flags or stores. Just a broken-down harness maker and a closed berry crate factory. Hazel bushes and zig-zag rail fences and nanny goats in a small old cornfield. Passing a farm tractor parked on the outskirts of town, he asked Chester, "Who was that lady?"

"Just a dame."

"She invite you to supper?"

"You bet she did. I honeyed her up for almost an hour."

"What for?"

Chester laughed out loud. "What for? The old haha, kid. If I got pinched back there, she'd have sworn on a stack of Holy Bibles I was sitting in her lap the whole afternoon."

"Oh."

After crossing over a plank bridge, they drove past a square wooden sign reading **Come back soon to HADLEYVILLE, MO.** Ahead stretched the road west to Kansas or Oklahoma or wherever they chose to go. The afternoon sky overhead was blue clear up to heaven. Alvin slipped the Packard into high gear and leaned back. How far away was Farrington, Illinois now? Farther than yesterday.

As the farm boy drove up the highway between the vast wheat

fields, he asked, "Where're we headed?"

Chester laughed again. "Where do you want to go, kid? Name your poison."

Just then the dwarf popped up from beneath the coats and suitcases in the rear seat and leaned his gnarled elbows on the leather seatback. There he announced, "Well, fellows, I don't know where we're going, but we're on our way."

HARRISON, KANSAS

A SEA OF PORCUPINE GRASS, tall and golden in the mid-afternoon sun, surrounded a small white farmhouse and a ramshackle barn. Parked in back of the farmhouse was a tan Packard Six, deliberately hidden from the road. Alvin Pendergast stood by the iron pump watching the dwarf bathe in a water trough. Rascal had just dropped his knickers and kicked them aside, then stripped off his union suit and jumped in. He sank himself up to his chin and splashed water at Alvin.

"Why, it's not so bad," the dwarf remarked. "Hardly smells at all."

"Horses drink out of it," the farm boy said, plugging his nose. "You could get a disease."

Rascal dunked his head. Water stopped splashing over the sides of the trough. Submerged, the dwarf freed small air bubbles from his nose. Then a single finger broke the surface like a periscope, made a circle, and disappeared. All about the farm, wild grass in the empty fields swayed lazily. Crows yakked on the fence-posts. Alvin listened to bedsprings squeaking behind the window at the middle of the house where Chester entertained a girl from town. Every so often, Chester's head bobbed up into view, a nasty grin stuck on his face. The brown-haired girl beneath him squealed off and on while a portable Victrola that Chester had dug out of a closet played "Waiting on the Robert E. Lee."

With a great splash soaking Alvin's shirt and pants, the dwarf emerged from the depths of the trough. He leaned forward, both arms hung over the wood.

"Do you have any soap?" he asked. "I still feel grimy."

Alvin looked at the water stains on his shirt and pants. "You got me all wet."

"Maybe you ought to climb in here and wash off."

"I guess I'm washed enough already."

The farm boy watched Rascal rub his scalp with the tips of his fingers, scrubbing diligently. The old pump filled the wooden trough to three-quarters full, but nobody had bothered to clean it out in a while. Horsehair floated on the surface of the water and stuck to Rascal's upper arms and chest. It looked filthy. Not a hundred dollars could get him swimming in there alive and willing.

"Of course, a sugar bath would be much more refreshing."

Alvin frowned. "A what?"

"Sugar bath."

"What's that?"

The dwarf wore an expression of incredulity. "You've never had a sugar bath?"

Alvin shook his head. "Never even heard of such a thing. Are you joking me again?"

The girl under Chester shrieked as the iron bed frame slammed against the back wall, rattling the window. Chester grunted a response, then laughed out loud. The song quit and he replaced the needle. *Way down on the levee in old Alabamee ...*

"They sound like dogs," said Alvin, trying unsuccessfully not to listen to Chester rutting with his honey pie fifteen yards away. "I bet she's hating every minute of it."

"I bet she's not," the dwarf replied, continuing his scrubbing. His white hair was plastered flat on his scalp, almost invisible in the bright sunlight. The thick blue veins on his chest and skull made the skin look translucent. If Rascal had been outdoors at all since winter, Alvin thought, it must have been on a cloudy day. The dwarf dunked his head again, while the farm boy's ears went back to the window and the sassy girl squealing beneath Chester.

Half a day's drive from Hadleyville had led them across the Missouri border into Kansas where, after nightfall, Chester drove to the outskirts of a small town named Gridley and sent Alvin on foot to buy the three of them some supper. The road into town was dark and muddy and twice he tripped, negotiating the sinkholes between ditches. The sole restaurant in Gridley offered steak and onion dinners for forty cents, including tapioca pudding. They ate on a blanket in the wet grass under a sky threatening rain, then drove on to a tourist camp north of Abilene. Only Chester got much sleep those first few nights out of Hadleyville, taking his own cabin and staying to himself, as usual, and not being too talkative, as if something had put him in a foul mood. Meanwhile, Rascal kept Alvin up for hours, chattering endlessly about famous individuals he'd met: Lincoln's bastard nephew, Napoleon's barber's granddaughter, Teddy Roosevelt's wet nurse. Each episode ended with somebody offering Rascal a trip to Egypt or Norway or full-shares in a new railway venture financed by J.P. Morgan, rejected by the dwarf in favor of tending his award-winning vegetable garden in Hadleyville. Whether the dwarf actually believed his own stories Alvin didn't know, and once he had heard them each a dozen times, he didn't care much, either.

After twelve days of eating from paper sacks, they decided to stop for breakfast at Charlie Harper's Restaurant & Glassware Emporium in a little town called Harrison. Cheap soda glasses etched and fluted to resemble expensive Viennese crystal were mounted high on the walls with calligraphic tags beneath each one describing its stylistic lineage. Only the crudest hicks from the sticks could have been fooled, but Alvin managed to embarrass himself by asking how long it took to ship glasses like that across the ocean. The dwarf laughed so loudly the manager came out of the back room carrying a club. After eating, Alvin and Rascal went outdoors. Chester followed a few minutes later hand in hand with the darling brunette waitress and announced she'd be spending the afternoon with him. Her name was Rose, and her recently deceased Uncle Edgar owned a farm five miles south of Harrison. Since the day he'd gone into the ground, Edgar's house had sat empty, so they would all be more than welcome to sleep there overnight. She looked only slightly older than Alvin's sister Mary Ann who had her fourteenth birthday the week before Easter, but

Chester didn't seem to care in the least. He told her his name was Calvin Coolidge III and that he'd made packs of dough in the oil game. After giving Alvin and Rascal a few dollars to buy groceries, he swept Rose off her feet and deposited her into the front seat until it was time to head out to the farm. Once there, they retired to Uncle Edgar's bedroom where they remained for the rest of the day, playing records, sipping gin from a hipflask and rolling in bed.

Rascal stood up in the trough and splashed water on his waist and legs. Out of modesty, he kept his back to the bedroom window. He told the farm boy, "A pound of powdered sugar mixed into a bath nourishes the skin. I try to take a sugar bath at least once a month."

The dwarf climbed out of the trough. His splashing had made a muddy quagmire of the immediate area. He grabbed his white union suit and tiny brown knickers and put them back on.

"Sounds dumb to me," said Alvin, keeping out of the mud. He heard the girl giggling now. What the hell was Chester doing to her? The farm boy hadn't taken that girl for a floosie when they first met.

Rascal wrestled his cotton shirt and red suspenders over the damp skin of his upper body. "That's just because you've never tried one."

"I wouldn't want to. Sugar's for eating, not washing."

The dwarf worked the pump to clean off his hands. "Don't be so sure. Sugar's just another one of God's gifts we're to use as we see fit."

"Then I'll stick to sprinkling mine on hotcakes, thank you very much."

The iron bed stopped squeaking. Rascal put on his black button shoes and slicked his hair with the wet palms of his hands. He smiled at Alvin. "That was thoroughly refreshing."

The record ended as Chester raised the bedroom window and stuck his sweaty face out into the afternoon air. Alvin saw Rose get up off the bed behind him bare-naked and head for the bathroom. Seeing her lolling breasts got him going again and he tried to put her out of his mind, doubting that Chester would share her with his partners.

Chester called out, "Anybody hungry?"

"I am," replied Alvin. "I'm starving." That was a fact, too. His stomach was rumbling fierce.

"What do you want to eat?"

"Anything."

"All we have are eggs and potatoes," the dwarf announced. "Have either of you ever tried an Idaho soufflé?"

Chester disappeared from the window. Alvin could hear him talking to Rose about cooking. He didn't usually consult with them about meals. They ate where he chose and did what he said. That was swell with Alvin who didn't have many ideas these days, but Rascal voiced his opinion on everything from filling stations to petting parties. When Chester had first seen the dwarf in the backseat of the Packard, he hadn't raised his voice at all in ordering Rascal to get the hell out of his motorcar. Nor had he started shouting when the dwarf refused to do so on account of having planned and executed the better part of the bank robbery all by himself without even asking for so much as a red cent in profit. Chester kept driving, and after the argument quit a dozen miles down the road, he made it clear that Rascal would be allowed to ride along and take part if he was able to prove his worth in one fashion or another. This suited Rascal just fine. He had plenty of helpful ideas. Bootleggers and cutters and hold-up men intrigued him, and whenever Chester was off somewhere, the dwarf would philosophize about the nature and purpose of criminal behavior in modern society. Little of this discourse made sense to Alvin, though Rascal's enthusiasm for their adventure was infectious. For his own part, Alvin avoided Chester as much as possible, afraid of getting the bad eye, or a bawling out for having invited the dwarf along. Mostly, Chester had been pretty swell to Alvin, picking him up a sturdy old Montgomery Ward suitcase and a fresh pair of shoes as if they were best pals for no reason the farm boy could figure. After all, he wasn't doing anything special, just lugging trunks and looking after the auto. Anybody could have done that. What did Chester have him along for, anyhow? Maybe he'd gotten sick of driving around on his own. He had a smile for every occasion and treated Alvin better than anyone else ever had. But one evening when Alvin tried asking Chester where he grew up, he got told in just such a voice to mind his own business, and that was that. Besides which, later on that same night, Alvin's night sweats returned and his breathing became labored and he knew he was getting sicker again, and didn't want Chester to know it for fear of being put out on the road himself. So far, he was content to ride along a while further, if for no other reason than to see where they might end up. And where else did he really have to go besides back into the sanitarium?

"Do you prefer your boiled eggs with pepper or salt?" Rascal inquired of Alvin. "I ask this because I've become quite fond of pepper recently, much more so than when I was younger. I just used to detest it, while Auntie would sprinkle it on practically everything she served, even pie and puddings. One of her more despicable habits."

"I hate boiled eggs," said Alvin, stepping over to the pump. His hands were as dusty as his shoes. If it weren't for Rose, he might have stripped down and jumped into the trough himself. All the driving they'd done the past two days had made him feel smutty as hell. No doubt he stunk pretty badly, too. He drew water from the pump and splashed it onto his bare arms and face, ladling water onto the back of his neck and letting it run down his shirt. That felt good. Rascal headed for the barn while Alvin finished washing off. Indoors, Chester's voice carried across the farmhouse as he and Rose walked in one room and out another discussing supper. Hoping to avoid being dragged into the debate, Alvin followed Rascal into the barn. Chester had told them to sleep in the stalls in order to keep an eye on the Packard after dark. The dwarf had quickly made a bed of moldy straw and left Alvin wondering whether sleeping in the hayloft violated Chester's instructions. All the livestock were long since gone, and dried rat dung littered the floor. Wasn't there any room at the farmhouse?

Alvin called for Rascal. When he didn't hear back, the farm boy went looking for him out behind the barn where the fence was broken down. It had been some time since a plow had entered the field and the grass had grown tall. Maybe a dozen yards beyond the rail fence, the tips of the grass rustled, indicating where Rascal had gone tramping about. Sparrows sailed by overhead, darting high and low. Insects buzzed in the grass. Rascal giggled. Alvin lay down and closed his eyes and listened to the insects and the birds and the dwarf. When he and Frenchy were kids, they were always running out into the cornrows at twilight and playing hider-seeker with big sticks, which they used to slap the stalks and taunt each other. After dark, they'd huddle together with a kerosene lantern and dig for fishing worms in the black loam.

Alvin heard the grass rustle nearby. The dwarf sat down next to his shoulder and asked, "When's supper? I'm famished."

"I hope soon. I'm hungry as a horse."

A door slammed shut back at the farmhouse.

Rascal sighed. "I wish I were a farmer. I love animals."

"You love spreading manure, too?"

"If need be. I'm not afraid of work."

Alvin rolled onto his shoulder and spat in the grass. "You think you know what farm life's all about, but you're just a dumbbell. There ain't nothing swell about it at all, and if you grew up on a farm like I did, you'd hate it like the dickens, and that's a fact."

"I doubt that very much," the dwarf replied. "One man's cross is another man's lintel. You ought to try locking yourself in a closet for a couple of weeks if you don't think that's so. See how that suits your fancy."

"Well, I'd rather live underneath that ugly old house of yours for twenty years than spend another day shoveling chicken shit."

Rascal plucked a stem of grass and stuck it in his mouth to chew on. "When I was young, I had a chicken named Evelyn. Auntie sewed her a dress to wear when she went outdoors. I made her a bonnet with a red bow. She'd fetch buttons and thimbles all day long if you coated them with maple syrup or peppermint."

"A chicken?"

"Yes."

"Fetching like a dog?"

"Yes."

"I don't believe you."

"Well, it's true. She was the cutest thing you ever saw, all fancied up like a society lady out for a stroll. I'd hoped to have her taken to a taxidermist when she died, but that ugly dog from next door, Mr. Bowser, cornered Evelyn under the porch and chewed her up so badly we couldn't find enough of her to stitch together. It was very sad."

Alvin looked the dwarf straight in the eye, astonished at his story-telling audacity. "You are the goddamnedest liar."

"I am not!"

"You are so!"

Chester called out across the grassy fields. Alvin picked himself up and headed for the farmhouse. He found Chester standing by the water pump, ladling water into his hands which he used to slick his hair back just as Rascal had done. He was dressed handsomely for town: blue jacket and trousers, a new felt hat. His shoes looked newly polished and spit-shined. Rose sat on the raised windowsill, her legs hanging down, bare feet swinging above the dirt. All she wore was a white silk envelope chemise. Her hair was damp and stringy with sweat, her blue eyes dark and hollow.

"I've got some business to put over in town for a few hours," said Chester, eyeing the young farm boy. "I'll be back later on. Rose'll fix some supper for you and the midget if you like. She's a swell cook."

"I'd rather go with you into town, if that's all right."

"Well, it isn't. You're staying here until I get back."

"There ain't nothing to do."

Chester worked the pump once more, drew a handkerchief from his back pocket, and dried his hands. He told Alvin, "Another hour or so, the sun'll be down. Nobody's supposed to know we're staying here, so keep the lights out. Don't go running around, either. If someone sees you, they're likely to come give us a once-over. I won't be gone too long, so be a sport and keep your eyes peeled. Get some sleep, too. We'll be driving out of here at dawn." Chester lowered his voice. "Keep an eye on this birdie for me, will you? She'll do anything you tell her to do, just make sure she doesn't try to go anywhere until I get back." He looked over at her, still sitting motionless on the windowsill, her brown curls fluttering in the breeze. "She'll be coming with us tomorrow."

Rose smiled.

Alvin gave her a small wave.

Chester walked over to the window, kissed Rose once on the mouth, ran his hand through her hair, then walked over to the Packard and climbed in. As the engine started up, Alvin saw Rascal standing by the barn door, nearly invisible in the shadow. The tan Packard rolled out from behind the farmhouse and down the dirt road leading to the highway. Chester beeped the horn twice as he turned in the direction of Harrison.

They sat in the kitchen, watching Rose fry up the eggs and potatoes on an old wood-burning stove. Outdoors, the sundown sky cast burnt shadows all across the dusty yard. Rascal had removed a stuffed pillow from the front room sofa and used it to raise the level of his seat at the table. Alvin played with the tarnished silverware Rose had dug out of her uncle's boxes in the cellar. He also had his eye on Rose in her white chemise. Something inside him stirred when he studied the curves of her body and the milky-white skin of her neck and shoulders. Her dark hair was long and curly, fussy from her afternoon under the sheets with Chester. She had a musky odor, too, not entirely unpleasant. When she looked at him, he could hardly breathe. Maybe he loved her. Back at the restaurant when they were all hungry and tired from traveling, Alvin wondered why Chester had invited her out. Now, alone with her in the kitchen, he knew clear as a bell that if he had the guts Chester had, he would date her up himself. If he had the guts.

"I can still scramble 'em if you'd prefer," Rose said, turning from the stove. Her face was sweaty from the heat and it made her even prettier. "You just tell me what you like."

"If they're not boiled, I don't care how you fix them," replied Rascal, rubbing one eye.

"Can't boil an egg without a pot," Rose said. "You didn't see one out in the barn, did you?"

"No, I didn't."

"Then, there you go. No boiled eggs."

"Fried eggs are swell, too," said Alvin, feeling like a hick all of a sudden. "If I was cooking, that's how I'd fix them." Why couldn't he spit out a quick word or two to catch her eye? A fellow can't expect much if he won't deliver nothing. Frenchy always told him that and he was right.

Soon enough, Rose slid the fried eggs and potatoes onto three plates and sat down at the table with Alvin and Rascal.

"Shall we say grace?" the dwarf asked.

Rose looked over at Alvin who shrugged, wholly ignorant of the topic. She told the dwarf, "Go on, if you like. I don't trust God. He don't listen to me much."

"All right." The dwarf bowed his head. "O merciful Father who hath turned our dearth and scarcity into plenty, we give Thee humble thanks for this Thy special bounty, beseeching Thee to continue Thy loving kindness unto us, to Thy glory and our comfort, through Jesus Christ our Lord. Amen."

His stomach grumbling, Alvin picked up his fork. "Let's eat."

"You said it," added Rose.

"Is there anything to drink?" the dwarf asked Rose, as he dug into the fried potatoes.

"Icebox's dry as a bone, but there's water in the well."

"Are there any glasses?"

"Not anymore," replied Rose. "Just some tin cups in the cabinet back there." She motioned toward the pantry.

The dwarf shoved his chair back from the table.

"Bring me one, too," Alvin said, his mouth drier than a hole in the ground.

"If I get you a cup, will you pump the water?" asked Rascal. "I have an awful pain in my shoulder."

"Nope, I ain't that thirsty." Why the hell should he do all the work? Chester wasn't here.

"Thank you very much."

Rascal glared at Alvin and headed for the pantry. After a few minutes of rummaging around, he came out with a tin cup and crossed through the kitchen and out the back door. The screen slammed shut behind him. Alvin listened to him trotting across the yard to the trough pump. It was dark out now. Crickets sang in the bushes by the rear porch. The pump creaked as Rascal drew water from the well. Alvin stuck a forkful of eggs into his mouth and tried his best not to stare at Rose's titties. Her knife scratched the plate as she scooped some eggs onto her fork. While the dwarf worked the pump over and over, the farm boy felt his passion coming back again.

"You come out here very often?" he asked Rose.

"Only when I need a fellow."

She said this without changing expression, still shoving eggs and potato into her mouth. It stabbed at Alvin's heart. His face flushed and his own appetite faded.

"You got a girl back home?" Rose asked, setting her fork down for a moment.

Alvin swallowed a chunk of fried potato and shook his head. The truth embarrassed him. "None in particular. How come you ask?"

"My daddy thinks I'm a whore."

He stopped chewing. "Is that so?"

She leaned close, her eyes sparkling. "Do you think I'm a whore?"

What was he supposed to say? He shrugged. "How should I know?"

"When we met back in my daddy's restaurant, and you first saw me, did you think to yourself, 'She sure looks like a whore'?"

Alvin felt his face redden deeper. Rose's attention was fixed hard on him. He was sure he smelled Chester's gin on her breath. "I thought you were pretty swell-looking."

"Are you jealous of Calvin?"

"Huh?"

The pump stopped outdoors and the dwarf's footsteps scurried back through the dirt toward the house. Rose said, "Me lying down with him, instead of with you? Are you jealous?"

Alvin shrugged. "Sort of, I guess." Sure, he was jealous as hell, but what could he do about it? He didn't hardly smile at her in town. Who knows what she thought of him back there?

"Don't be," she said. "It ain't account of you that I'm with him. It's 'cause of my daddy. He's scared of Calvin. The second he laid eyes on him, he told me to stay away from him."

Rose put down her fork and napkin.

"Do you love him?" Alvin asked, afraid of her reply. If she said yes, he'd likely throw up.

"Who?"

"Calvin."

"Of course not. I don't lie down with fellows I'm in love with. I don't flirt with them, neither, though I have to say I'd rather be thought of as a whore than a flirt. But this's got nothing to do with love. No girl with half a brain and an ounce of self-respect would consider it."

"I ain't following you."

"That's 'cause you're not a girl, and you don't know my daddy, neither."

The back door opened and Rascal came inside with his tin cup in one hand and a small brown feather in the other. Quietly, he sat down at the table, took a drink from the cup, laid the feather on the side of his plate, and began eating once again. Alvin watched how the dwarf held his fork funny, twisted nearly backward in his hand, making him bring food to his mouth in a strange looping motion. The farm boy wondered who taught him that.

Rose got up from the table and went to the back door. She opened it and tossed her leftover eggs and potatoes out into the yard. "My cooking stinks."

Then she laid her empty plate on the counter and walked out of the kitchen. Rascal continued eating. Alvin listened for Rose. She had gone into the bedroom. The bedsprings squeaked as she plunked herself down onto the mattress. Alvin finished his own food and got up, setting his plate on the counter next to Rose's. The dwarf had his head down, methodically shoveling egg and potato into his mouth, one forkful after another. Alvin went outdoors to relieve himself.

A cool wind had come up in the past hour, blowing dirty feathers off a mud hen carcass all over the yard. A dozen or so floated in the water trough. A sweet hay smell filled the evening air. The farm boy walked across the yard to the edge of the field by the barn and unfastened his pants. He was feeling a little better. The summer grass rustled and swayed before him as he pissed into the dirt and stared out across the prairie. Farrington was not so flat, so vast and empty. Here in Kansas, the wind played through the grass like the fingers of God. In the daylight, every contour of the prairie justified property lines divided according to high ground and low. Sunlight made visible the particulars of slope and expanse. Darkness erased them, creating an endless flatland beneath the tips of the tall prairie grass. The wind in

Alvin's face blew across a hundred miles of fields.

The back door banged in the wind. Alvin finished pissing and buttoned up. Rascal appeared in the doorframe, staring off into the dark. A moment later, the light went out in the kitchen. Rose had assured Chester that the farm still had electricity, but the only room with working electric lights was the kitchen. All the others required kerosene lamps after sundown. A yellow glow behind the window shade in the main bedroom indicated that Rose had lighted hers already. A small shadow moved in front of the shade, the dwarf visiting her for conversation. Rather than going back indoors, Alvin decided to eavesdrop at the window, hoping he'd overhear some conversation concerning himself. Nobody ever spoke honestly in the presence of the person they were discussing. When Alvin was a boy, Granny Chamberlain had told him that any fly on the wall hears more truth spoken in half a minute than any man in his lifetime. She said this with the conviction of a woman who had held secrets deep in her heart for more years than her family had been alive.

He crouched beneath Rose's window. The dwarf was speaking, his hushed voice barely carrying past the glass. Alvin peeked over the windowsill and saw Rascal seated on the bed beside Rose, holding her hand in his. Alvin sank back down again, astonished. Was Rose allowing herself to be wooed by the dwarf? Maybe that silver tongue of his made up for the peculiarities of his appearance. Rose giggled loudly. Rascal's voice became slightly louder, enthusiastic, chirping like a bird. It was too much for Alvin to bear outdoors, so he crawled along the side of the house to the kitchen door and slipped inside.

With the lights out in the kitchen, he had a difficult time negotiating his way from the back door to the hallway dividing the bedroom from the front of the house. Once there, however, the lamp Rose had lighted guided him in her direction. The door was partway open. He tiptoed up to it and craned his neck around the edge to have a look inside. She and the dwarf were still sitting side by side in the middle of the bed, her hand in his, both smiling. Chester's hipflask was on the nightstand.

"I don't believe a word you're saying," Rose giggled. "It's a lie, all a lie!"

"Palmistry is one of the ancient sciences. I learned it from my Uncle Augustus who was taught by a lovely Egyptian woman at Alexandria where it's been practiced for thousands of years. I've been fascinated by mysteries of the occult since I was a child. I intend to see the famous oracle at Delphi one day before I die."

"My daddy got his fortune read once by a gypsy who told him he'd die a rich man. He says it's all hokum."

Rascal ran the tip of his forefinger down the middle of her palm and across to the base of her thumb. "Belief, like beauty," the dwarf replied, in a solemn voice, "exists in the eye of the beholder. Truth, on the other hand, is unwavering and eternal. Your own flesh reveals it. Doubt not that which you know to be true."

Then Rascal giggled, too.

The bedroom stunk of liquor and sweat.

Alvin walked in. A flickering yellow light from the single kerosene lamp danced lazily on the bare walls. The portable Victrola sat mute on a wooden chest by the footboard. Rose and the dwarf ignored Alvin completely. He cleared his throat to get their attention, but Rascal continued to chatter on as he stroked the palm of Rose's left hand with his forefinger, tracing a circuitous pattern between her thumb and little finger.

" ... and so your children from this marriage will be lost in a ballooning accident in the Congo only to be captured by a tribe of pygmies and ransomed for a herd of goats to a family of Quakers and returned a year later to America where they'll become doctors, healing the poor and destitute of Philadelphia."

Rose laughed and withdrew her hand from Rascal's. She fell back onto the pillow behind her head. She winked at Alvin. "Will they remember their dear old mother every Christmas?"

"No," replied the dwarf. "In fact, the ballooning accident will cause a rare form of amnesia that destroys all memory of their former lives. It's very tragic."

"Are you sure?"

Rascal nodded. "I'm sorry."

"Then I'll need to have more children."

"And so you shall," said the dwarf, a moony smile on his face.

Rose jumped up off the bed. "Oh, goody!"

She took the hipflask and had a sip, then wiped her mouth with the back of her hand. She crawled back across the bed to open the window on the yard and stuck her head out for a look. "I think it might rain tonight. I hope you'll be all right in the barn. My uncle had trouble with the roof leaking. It can get awfully wet and cold out there."

"Maybe we ought to stay in here," said Alvin, looking at himself in the silvered mirror over the dresser. "We could throw down some blankets and sleep on the floor."

Her eyes looking boozy now, Rose replied, "I don't guess Calvin'd appreciate that much company tonight."

"Well, that's fine," said Rascal. "Actually, I prefer the outdoors. There's nothing like fresh air, I always say."

"It's freezing in the barn," said Alvin, sitting down on the bed next to Rascal. "Probably catch cold out there if we don't get our toes chewed off first by the rats."

The dwarf stiffened. "Rats?"

"There's always rats in an old barn, crawling around in the hay. I saw one this afternoon, in fact."

Rose twisted her head back toward the dwarf. "This boy's just pulling your leg. Ain't no rats in my uncle's barn."

"You calling me a liar?" said Alvin. Of course, he hadn't really seen a rat, but then again who was to say there weren't any hiding in the straw? Frenchy was always finding rats up in Uncle Henry's hayloft. He'd kill them, and cut off their tails for fish bait. Frenchy said, "*The fish ain't been born who can tell the difference between a rat's tail and a fat worm flopping off a hook.*" And he was right, too, because they caught a lot of catfish using rat tails.

"Although I am not afraid of rats," said the dwarf, "it is a well-known fact that they carried the Black Plague throughout Europe in the Middle Ages and were nearly responsible for the destruction of our entire species. They're very dirty creatures. I wouldn't care to be bitten by one while I'm sleeping. Rabies, I hear, is a dreadful disease."

"It kills you in a day or so," Alvin said. "You choke to death from foaming out of your own mouth, like a sick dog."

"There ain't no rats in the barn!" Rose repeated. "I swear I'd sleep out there with you myself if it wasn't for Calvin. And I wouldn't be scared at all, so don't you be."

She sat down on the bed, sipped again from Chester's flask, and curled up with her back against the headboard. Rascal gently slid over beside her and took her right hand and traced his forefinger once more across the middle of her palm. Feeling a little queasy, Alvin got up off the bed and went to the open window, prepared to lean outside and upchuck if necessary. His forehead felt slightly feverish and he guessed another sweat was coming on. Turning about, he found Rose staring at him while the dwarf stroked her palm. What kind of girl was she? Could he yet kiss her?

"Where're y'all headed from here?" she asked.

Alvin shrugged. "Maybe the Dakotas, California. Who knows?"

"You go where Calvin tells you to go, don't you?"

"Only when there's money involved."

"Oh yeah?" Her eyebrows arched in surprise at his answer. "What made you decide to stop in Harrison?"

He felt insulted again. "Why are you such a busybody? Who told you to come out here and lie around in this bed all afternoon, huh? Something tells me you take orders pretty damn well yourself."

Rose grinned. "Well, of course I do, sweetie pie. Been doing it my whole life. Daddy tells me to clean out my closet and throw away my old dolls, I go do it. He tells me to shine his shoes and wash his shorts, I do it. He tells me to sit in his lap and sing 'Good-bye Liza Jane,' I sit there and sing till he tells me to stop. Nobody in Kansas takes orders better than Rosa Jean Harper."

"Aw, quit your sniveling," said Alvin, shaking his head. His opinion of her was diminishing by the minute. "I ain't never got a break from my daddy, neither, but it don't bust me up none."

"Did he tan you?" Rose asked, after sipping again from the hipflask.

" 'Course he did. What of it?"

"My daddy calls me his little princess whenever he's squiffy."

"Your lifeline indicates royalty in a previous lifetime," said Rascal, taking her free hand once again. "Perhaps the servitude you provide in this life offers atonement for sins of indulgence committed in another."

"Probably," said Rose. "Some days, I feel awful bossy. It's just that I can't seem to find anyone to boss around in Harrison, is all."

"I'll be your slave," offered Rascal. "Command me!"

"All right," said Alvin, his fever rising now, "choke it. She knows you ain't on the level." He walked over to look in the closet. Maybe there was something he could steal.

"Envy doesn't become you," replied the dwarf, putting his back to the farm boy.

"I told you both, it's Calvin my daddy don't trust," Rose said, re-adjusting the pillow at her back. "Says he's a shady character. But I think he's just more polished than people around here, and I like that. Makes me feel polished, too. Like a real lady. My daddy'd like his daughter on a leash that's just long enough to wait on his customers and get the cleaning done upstairs and down. He's scared of somebody like Calvin coming along and sneaking off with his little girl."

"Where's your momma?" Alvin asked, kicking over a stack of empty hat boxes.

"She run off with a shoe salesman when I was four. Daddy called her every name in the book. Of course, I say if it makes him feel better to think of her as a whore, so be it, but I guess he's still plenty sad about her. Every one of us got feelings, and when you get treated bad, it hurts, no matter how much you go around telling people it don't."

The dwarf said to Rose, "Did you know that once you were a hand-maiden to Cleopatra, serving her in a slave barge on the Nile after being led into captivity from Babylon the Great where you had been a queen?" His eyes were wide as saucers. "It's truly amazing to chart your palm. An honor, if I do say so myself."

"Calvin wants to bring me with him when y'all go tomorrow," said Rose, closing the hipflask. "He knows my daddy's giving me hell. Said if I go with you, I'll eat steak every night of the week. You think I ought to believe him?"

Alvin was beginning to feel sick and stupid. Rose and the dwarf talking like they were stuck on each other didn't seem right, like they were lying about things and spreading gossip. Aunt Hattie told him once that talking behind people's backs was like whispering secrets in the devil's ear.

"Is Calvin Coolidge III a gentleman, in your opinion?" asked the dwarf, releasing Rose's hand. "Is he honorable?"

"Well, he kissed my hand before lying down here next to me. He even asked permission to take his clothes off. I liked that. It shows class."

"A man well-bred is rarely ill-led," said Rascal.

"Pardon me?"

"Don't pay him no mind," said Alvin, frowning at the dwarf. He went over to the Victrola and spun the record. "He's just spouting off."

Rose shrugged. "Well, I just wish my daddy understood that a girl can't spend her whole life washing floors and sewing on buttons." She straightened up. "Do either of you fellows know how to dance?"

Alvin wandered back over to the window for some fresh air. "Dancing's for sissies," he said, sticking his head outside. The stuffy room made him feel faint. He needed to lie down.

"I had lessons when I was six," said Rascal. "Miss Angelina taught me all sorts of fancy steps. I was her star pupil. I believe I even won an award once."

"I can do a swell Charleston," said Rose. "Watch!" She hopped off the bed and began dancing furiously in the middle of the room. In mid-step, her stocking feet slipped on the throw rug and she tumbled forward, landing on her face and slamming her chin hard on the wood floor. "Oww!"

She rolled over, bleeding from a gash on the jawline. "Goddammit!"

Rascal slid down beside her and cupped his hand over the wound. Alvin remained at the window, more amused than worried by her injury. The dwarf reached back and dragged a corner of the sheet off the bed to use as a compress against Rose's bleeding chin. "Hold it here."

After placing Rose's hand on the sheet covering the cut, Rascal dashed out of the bedroom. His tiny footsteps pattered through the house into the kitchen. The screen door swung open and closed with a bang. Alvin shifted his position to catch sight of the dwarf at the pump, working it quickly, a long white rag wadded up beneath the spout. Water gushed out onto the rag, soaking both it and Rascal.

The dwarf stopped pumping and ran back toward the house. Then the door opened and shut with another bang and a moment later the dwarf burst into the room, dripping water all over the floor.

"Here," he said, removing the sheet from Rose's chin and replacing it with the wet rag. The girl moaned in pain. Rascal said, "We have to get you cleaned up. Infection is an ugly consideration with any injury. I once got lockjaw from a rusty nail in my closet and couldn't speak for a month."

"Who was sorry about that?" asked Alvin, feeling nasty now.

"It hurts," Rose moaned, as the dwarf swabbed the wound and the skin surrounding it. "Oww!"

"Be brave," Rascal said, wiping off the blood that had trickled down her neck. "Is there any alcohol in the house?"

"Of course not," Rose answered. "Kansas's as dry as Arabia these days."

"No hootch in the cellar?" asked Alvin. "You sure about that?"

"My uncle never touched liquor in his life. He didn't hold with drinking. He was a good Christian gentleman until the day he died."

"A regular flat tire, huh?" Alvin said, the smirk on his face growing minute by minute. Realizing there wasn't a chance in hell of bedding down with her allowed him to say whatever he felt. He liked that. Speaking his true thoughts for once made him giddy. Love was for the birds.

"Liquor leads men to ruin," said Rascal, fashioning Rose a bandage wrap from the rag. "It lies at the heart of all our foibles."

"Women, too," replied Alvin, "but at least the bottle won't chew your ears off."

Rose said, "My uncle maintained that liquor was evil and he'd rather burn in hellfire than allow even a drop of the contentious fluid to touch his lips."

"Good for him," said Alvin. He watched Rascal wrap the bandage around Rose's jaw from ear to ear and pull it tight. Maybe he ought to choke her next.

"Oww!"

The dwarf tied it with a bow at the back of her head. "I'm sorry."

"I feel stupid," said Rose. She stood up and checked herself in the mirror. "It looks like my jaw's wrapped for a toothache."

"Vanity must always follow utility in the world of medicine," the dwarf explained. "Have you a needle and thread handy? We ought to properly close that wound. Otherwise, you'll have a scar for a souvenir."

"No, thanks," said Rose. She took a step back from Rascal and covered her chin with the palm of one hand. "I don't mind scars. I got plenty of them already. One more won't spoil my beauty."

"Of course not," said the dwarf, and he gave her arm a light pat.

"I'm going to bed," Alvin said, sliding off the window frame. "This is just too damned much excitement for one day."

"Calvin'll be back soon," said Rose. "Don't you want to sit up a while?"

"What for?"

"I'm staying," said Rascal. "Rose says I can hide under her bed and listen to the fireworks so long as I keep quiet."

"Calvin'll break your neck."

"He won't know I'm here. I won't make a sound. I can play dead better than a dog if I have to. Ask Auntie. She called the funeral parlor one afternoon when I pretended to have a stroke. I held my breath for three minutes and made my face turn blue. She got so scared, I thought she'd have a stroke of her own."

Looking at Rose, Alvin said, "Well, then maybe I'll join you under the bed and we'll both spy on Calvin. I can keep pretty quiet myself."

"Nobody's hiding under my bed," Rose said. "I'd never allow it. Privacy's important to a girl. Being men, you can't understand that because y'all got to boast about what you do and who you done it to. We girls got too much dignity to go around sharing our most intimate, private activities with the whole world."

"You'll get no argument from me," said Rascal. "I wouldn't think of intruding on your privacy."

"You little two-faced Judas!" Alvin growled. "Why, you just said you were going to hide under the bed and listen to everything she did."

"Only if I were invited to do so," replied the dwarf, showing Rose his broadest smile, "and seeing as I'm not," he got to his feet, "I'll be on my way to the barn." He took Rose's hand and planted a kiss on the knuckle of her wedding finger. "I thank you for the opportunity of reading your fortune. Good night."

Then he walked out of the bedroom.

Rose crawled up onto the bed and stretched her legs. Alvin heard the kitchen door open and close again. He looked over at Rose. She smiled. "Nighty-night."

He nodded.

She whispered, "Don't tell him I said so, but I think your pal's the cutest little fellow I ever saw. If he were another foot taller, I'd bed down with him in a minute."

Stopping at the water trough to wash his face, Alvin worked the pump, studying the horizon for headlights. Chester had been gone quite a while now. Whatever business he had was keeping him longer than Alvin had expected. Of course, he'd probably eaten supper in Harrison, maybe steak and potatoes, pie for dessert, a beer in the basement of a scratch house downtown, afterward. Why the hell had he gone alone?

Alvin stopped pumping and wiped his hands dry on the tails of his shirt. A wind swept out across the fields of grass and chilled the skin on the back of his neck. He felt a peculiar vibration in his bones, but it wasn't fever. Kansas spooked him. The wind carried a smell with it, musty, dry, dead. A spook's breath, stale and dirty. Older than dirt itself. Without a doubt, Alvin believed Kansas was populated by ghosts and haunted like a vast grassy cemetery. He was scared that if he stayed too long, somehow he'd become fertilizer for the same grasses that whispered to him now in the windy darkness.

The farm boy walked to the barn. He heard Rascal singing up in the hayloft. The dwarf loved music, although he could barely carry a tune. The top of his head bobbed just above a bale of hay where he danced in time to his own song.

> *I found a horseshoe, I found a horseshoe.*
> *I picked it up and nailed it on the door;*
> *And it was rusty and full of nail holes,*
> *Good luck 'twill bring to you forevermore.*

It was an old railroad song Uncle Harlow used to sing whenever he came back from the depot. Rascal had mangled the tune such that he'd probably helped chase out the spooks. Alvin headed for the ladder to the loft. If not for the lamp hung there, the interior of the barn would have been black as pitch. The dwarf was on his hands and knees, digging into a moldy old bale of hay with a rusty screwdriver.

"What're you doing there?" Alvin asked, looking around. The wood at the dwarf's feet was crisscrossed in scratches made by the screwdriver he was holding.

"Hunting."

"What for?"

"Rats." Rascal jabbed at the bale of hay, stabbing randomly here and there. "They make nests in the hay. I have to flush them out and kick them in the head." The dwarf stood up over the bale and jabbed furiously down into the top of it, zigzagging his attack from one end to the other. His tiny hand was a blur above the hay.

"Get any of 'em yet?" the farm boy asked. He had never heard of anyone hunting rats with a screwdriver. Uncle Henry stuck them with his pitchfork and Frenchy shot one with a pistol after it chewed up his boot. Best was to smoke them out and club them when they ran for it.

"I'd appreciate some help," said Rascal, jabbing at the sides of the bale now. Sweat dripped off his forehead. "After all, they'll bite you, too."

"There ain't no rats in here."

The dwarf quit chopping at the hay. He twisted the screwdriver in his fist and looked up at Alvin. "You lied?"

"Sure I did."

The dwarf sat back against the bale. "Why did you lie?"

Alvin shrugged. "I didn't care none for how you were whooping it up with Rose, telling those stories and getting her going. It made us both look like dumbbells."

"The fool and the wise man often reflect a common image."

"Huh?"

"Envy doesn't become you," said the dwarf, poking the screwdriver into the bale of hay. "Rose appreciated our attention. She's sad and lonely. We made her smile."

"She's just joking us, is all. I didn't care for that, neither."

"Joy has its own rainbow. I'm satisfied that, however we did it, tonight was quite special for her."

"Says you."

"I do."

"I'm going to bed," the farm boy said, with a yawn. He was sick of jawing over that girl.

"You're not planning to wait up for Chester? I'll bet he has a story of his own to tell. Do you know why he went back into town?"

"No, do you?"

"Yes, but I'll wait for him to tell you all about it. I'm sure it was very exciting."

"What if he don't come back here at all? What if he throws us over and goes off by hisself?"

"We'll buy a train ticket to Wichita."

Now that was a spooky thought. A shiver ran through Alvin's heart. "I ain't never been there before. What would we do?"

"I'm sure we could hire a decent flat in a roominghouse and find ourselves work with the cattle trade, no trouble at all. Uncle Augustus brought me out to the Dakotas one summer when I was a boy and I learned all about working on a ranch."

"Sure you did."

"Well, it's the truth."

"You think Chester robbed the bank?" By now, of course, the farm boy knew his boss was some sort of gangster, because of the associations he seemed to have wherever they went. Alvin just wasn't sure what all Chester did at night while they were sleeping.

"Of course not. There's much more profit today in booze-traffic. Every town in this great republic of ours has its own speakeasy. Who do you think keeps them stocked with demon rum?"

"I never seen a drunkard or a saloon downtown this morning."

"Did you notice the soda fountains and drugstores?"

"What of it?"

"Well, they're selling more than soda pop these days. Why, I'd wager you'll find overnight liquor in milk bottles on half the stoops in

Kansas tomorrow morning."

Alvin mulled that over. Cousin Frenchy kept quart bottles of whiskey hidden in Uncle Roy's root cellar and had a drink habit he couldn't crack. Uncle Cy believed half the population of Farrington was misusing liquor. "You think Chester's a rumrunner?"

The dwarf replied, "He's no snooper."

"Well, I ain't for squealing on nobody, neither, but I'll bet you there's plenty of homebrew outfits in these parts. I seen empty gallon jugs packed in straw and sodden boxes in that kitchen cellar. I smelled kerosene and molasses down there, too. Don't tell me that uncle of hers wasn't an old soak."

"Auntie imbibed Coca Cordials while she was sending dollar bills through the mail to the Reverend Dr. Wilson in support of National Prohibition, and seeing a revenue officer from Peoria, too."

"Well, my Aunt Clara makes cider with a kick, but it ain't kitchen brew."

"Laws are made for men," said the dwarf, "not men for the law. Who can be made moral by legislation? Persecution causes a crime to spread. *This ought ye to have done, and not to leave the other undone.* I'm sure there are temperate uses of alcoholic drink, but until they're commonly understood, gangsters like Chester are certain to knock heads with the Volsteadites, leaving the rest of us caught in the middle."

"Well, I ain't interested in getting pinched over some stall to sell a few bottles of hootch."

Rascal got up and walked to the ladder. He put the screwdriver aside and went backwards down the first few rungs. Stopping halfway to the barn floor, the dwarf said, "These are dangerous times, my friend. Very dangerous. We must keep our wits about us, if we wish to survive."

Alvin got up, too, and followed the dwarf to the ladder. "What's that supposed to mean?"

"The heart of the adventurer is sly," Rascal said, as he descended to the floor of the barn. Stepping away from the ladder, he looked back up at Alvin. "Even in his dreams, he is alert."

Rascal disappeared into one of the stalls directly beneath the hayloft.

Alvin sat down on the ledge beside the ladder. He felt drowsy and ill. Below him, the dwarf shuffled about in the dark, fixing his bed for the night. After a few minutes, Alvin climbed down the ladder and looked in on the dwarf. He was hard to see, buried in the straw with only the bald top of his head visible in the yellow lamplight. With each breath, little puffs of dust blew free from his mouth. Alvin noticed the light in Rose's bedroom was extinguished. She, too, had given up on Chester, and had gone to sleep. The farm boy took the lantern off the ladder and walked to the back of the barn where he had chosen his own stall. He hung the lamp on a post nail. The night wind hissed in the long dry grass. Trying to ignore the fever chill in his bones, Alvin spread his bedroll out over the straw and lay down on his back. If anyone was worrying about him at home tonight, he was sorry, but they'd intended to send him back to the sanitarium, and that was a lot meaner than him running off. Like his own daddy used to say, *"A man finds his own road one day and starts walking. He don't argue an east fork into a west one, and he don't set hisself facing backwards, neither."*

After ten minutes or so of looking for bats in the upper rafters of the barn, Alvin fell asleep. *Out on the Mississippi with Frenchy, fly casting into a swift green current, sunlight on the water, catfish tapping at the underside of the skiff, inviting themselves to get caught and fried up for supper. Frenchy had trotlines baited with rat tails. The skiff had a hole in it, leaking water in at Alvin's feet. Baling with his right shoe wasn't working, so he removed his left and used that, too. A catfish as big as a pig flew into the boat, landing in Alvin's lap, knocking him over. The skiff capsized. Swimming underwater, Alvin found himself caught in Frenchy's trotlines. Freeing himself just before drowning, he rose to the surface. The river was black. Stars flickered overhead while upstream, fireworks exploded in the night sky above the Illiniwek Bridge where a crowd had gathered to witness another suicide like Mable Stephenson, jilted by her college geography teacher, who did her lover's leap at high noon on Christmas Day in front of a hundred people, landing headfirst on a frozen log and breaking her neck. Alvin swam in that direction. All along the shoreline, giggling voices rang in the bushes. Rose was atop the bridge, her arms spread wide, the hem of her white chemise blowing wildly in the wind. As Alvin swam close, she leaped away from the bridge and* something blunt struck Alvin between the eyes, waking him, and a voice he didn't recognize, ordered, "Get up, you little sonofabitch!"

Alvin felt cold steel pressed to his forehead and opened his eyes. A dark figure stood over him. A rifle barrel extended from Alvin's forehead to the hands of the man standing in front of him. "Nobody robs Charlie Harper, you little double-crossing sonofabitch!"

"Huh?"

"You think I couldn'ta guessed who done it?"

The barrel dug into the skin between Alvin's eyes, hurting more now that he was waking up.

The man yelled, "ROSA JEAN!"

Off to Alvin's left across the barn, a small shadow darted through the railing of the last stall and slipped outdoors.

"Get up," said Harper, nudging Alvin in the butt with the toe of his boot. He pulled the old Sharp's rifle back a few inches from Alvin's face. "ROSA JEAN!"

The farm boy climbed to his feet as slowly as possible while searching the barn for something to use as a club if the opportunity to fight presented itself. His head spun with vertigo. A cough rattled out of his chest. With the lamp extinguished, most of the barn was black.

"ROSA JEAN!" Harper poked Alvin in the ribs with the rifle, directing him out the barn door toward the farmhouse. "Get on out there, and don't try nothing, you little shit-heel!"

They walked out of the barn in tandem, connected by the length of rifle. A cold wind swirled in the yard, sweeping dust about and scattering stems of dried grass from the empty fields beyond.

"ROSA JEAN!"

The back screen door banged open and shut in the wind. Rose's bedroom window was raised an inch or so, the drapes closed. Nearing the trough, Alvin wondered if she was watching.

Charlie Harper prodded Alvin in the back with the rifle and shouted again. "ROSA JEAN!" Water dripped from the pump. The kitchen door banged hard. Alvin took three more steps, and Harper called out, "ROSA JEAN!"

Then another voice, just off Alvin's right shoulder, said, "Stop right there."

Harper stopped, and the rifle barrel left Alvin's back.

Chester's voice spoke once again, "Go on, dad. Put that rifle down."

Alvin swiveled his head to see Chester, rising from a hiding place beside the trough. His .38 revolver was held at arm's length and pointed directly at Charlie Harper's head. Chester cocked the hammer back. "No cause for trouble now. Just do like I say."

The kitchen door flung open and Rose came out into the yard. Her hair blew wildly in the wind, her white chemise billowing up. Alvin's hands and feet felt cold. He studied Rose's face for indications of fear or surprise or anger, and saw none. He was terrified himself.

"They robbed us, Rosa Jean," said Harper, whose attention was not on Chester at all, but rather on his daughter. "They snuck in after closing and robbed us blind."

"I don't want to shoot you, old man, but I surely will if you don't set that rifle down."

"They're crooks, Rosa Jean. Scoundrels. They took every last cent in that safe."

Rose stood perfectly still, maybe thirty or forty feet from Alvin, teary-eyed in the wind and dust, staring past her father toward Chester who began slowly to circle behind the old man.

"They don't care nothing about people like us, Rosa Jean," said Harper. "They come here to hurt us, is all. They're nothing but goddamned liars and cheats."

"Come on, dad, put the rifle down," Chester said, his voice flat and nerveless. "Let's be friendly here. What do you say? No sense in getting hurt over a little misapprehension."

"Daddy," said Rose, walking now toward him, hair blowing across her face. "Please put the gun down."

"They're thieves, Rosa Jean. Don't trust them."

Chester had circled clear around Harper, standing just behind his right shoulder. Harper's rifle still pointed toward Alvin's back. Rose stopped fifteen feet from the water trough, her arms held out imploringly to her father. "Daddy, please!"

Out of the corner of his eye, Alvin caught a glimpse of Rascal standing motionless by the rear corner of the house, watching from the shadow of the eaves. Then he heard Harper release the hammer, and a moment later the barrel of the Sharp's rifle struck the dirt behind his feet.

"Goddamned sonsofbitches!" said the old man, and sunk backward to sit down on the trough. Rose walked forward another three steps, muttering something under her breath indistinguishable in the wind, and got close enough to her father to have her dress sprayed with blood an instant after Chester placed his pistol against the back of Harper's head and pulled the trigger.

The blast echo circled the yard and chased out across the fields. Charlie Harper's body lurched into the trough with a large splash. Stink of gunsmoke filled the dark.

Paralyzed with shock, Alvin found himself utterly transfixed by the sight of Charlie Harper bobbing in the black water. As Rose drew near, she whispered, "Daddy?" and leaned over the trough.

"Well, I guess that plan was a dud," said Chester, his gun still held out in the air where Harper's head had just been. "A fellow really ought to cut out boozing after work."

Dust stung Alvin's face, forcing him to look away from Rose and the water trough. He sought out the dwarf by the north side of the farmhouse and found that Rascal was gone. Chester jammed the pistol back into his waistband. He grabbed the handle of the pump and jerked it twice to draw fresh water from the well. As Chester ladled it into his cupped palms, sucking a drink, Rose grabbed up her father's rifle from the dirt beside the trough. Cocking the hammer, she swung the barrel around to Chester's direction, but he had already drawn his revolver again.

Alvin watched dumbfounded as Chester calmly took aim and shot Rose through the chest.

She fell away from the trough, landing flat on her back, a small black stain from the wound soaking the hole in the front of her chemise. Her eyes were wide open, staring up into the night sky. Her left foot twitched for a couple more seconds, then stopped altogether.

Another gunshot echo faded across the dark.

Chester stared at her a little while, revolver drawn and pointed, then shook his head, put the gun away again, and washed his hands clean under the pump spout. He rubbed them hard, scraping and scrubbing with his thumbs and fingertips.

Alvin had lost all feeling in his limbs.

The rising water floated Harper's body to the rim so that his hands appeared determined to try and grip the edges. A vile taste crept up into the back of Alvin's throat and he coughed harshly. Vertigo came and went. That section of Charlie Harper's face disintegrated by the exit wound remained underwater.

Chester let go of the pump handle before the trough could over-flow. He took a handkerchief out of his breast pocket and used it to dry off his hands. Then he told Alvin, "She'd have killed us both. We're lucky I saw her."

Alvin stared at Rose, lying just below him. The dead held no par-ticular fascination for him, having seen over the years his Uncle Otis, old Grandpa Chamberlain, his second-cousin Leroy, and a traveling salesman give up the ghost right before his eyes on the farm in Far-rington. Funerals followed harvest celebrations as the most popularly attended ceremonies in the county. None of the casket dead resem-bled themselves. Faces all waxy and pale. Lips and brows painted. Eyes stitched shut. That was the difference. Here, Rose looked prettier in death's shadow than she had sitting on the bed indoors. It spooked Alvin. If he leaned over her, she'd be looking him right in the eye. The stain had quit, just a damp soiled patch on the fabric, requiring only a good scrubbing with soap and vinegar. Her eyes needed clos-ing, though. Otherwise, she wouldn't get her reward. At every wake, Granny Chamberlain said, *God's sweet smile is too glorious to behold with white eyes revealed.*

As Alvin bent down to close Rose's eyes, Chester leaned forward and grabbed him by the wrist. "Don't touch her. Don't touch either of them. Just leave them where they are."

Then Chester walked off toward the back door, his blue suit jacket fluttering in the wind. Thoroughly terrified, Alvin looked once again for Rascal. The dwarf had been by the rear of the farmhouse, watch-ing everything. Afterward, he had run off like a scared rabbit. Alvin went over to the rail fence for a look into the fields. It seemed even darker now than when Harper had led him out of the barn. Trees only a few dozen yards away were all but invisible, just big hazy shadows somewhere out beyond the fence. Alvin stopped breathing and listened to the wind hissing through the grass on the dark Kansas prairie.

The back door slammed shut and Chester came out into the yard, carrying the thirty-dollar Victrola under one arm and a flat piece of wood under the other, a narrow shelf from one of the white kitchen cabinets. He walked over to the trough and placed the wood upright against the pump. Then he took a pocketwatch out of his vest, checked the hour, and headed to the Packard, announcing that they had to go. Rascal walked out of the barn loaded up and ready to depart, his wool blanket in one hand, Alvin's bedroll in the other. He went only as far as the middle of the yard, where he stopped and waited for Alvin to pay his last respects at the trough. Back around the rear of the house, Chester started up the car.

Both bodies looked like genuine Farrington farm corpses now, dead as yesterday. Wind had partially covered Rose's hair and fingers in dust, and clouded her eyes. If she hadn't yet beheld the Lord, she surely would in the next hour or so. Alvin came around the trough and found himself facing the board Chester had laid up against the pump. It was a message scribbled in charcoal, intended for whoever found Rose and Charlie Harper. It read:

We was attacked by a band of wild niggers. They killd this poor man and his little girl. Im chasin them to Missouri. Send help

Signed Calvin Coolidge

STANTONSBURG, NEBRASKA

THE DWARF WADED AT THE SHADY CREEK BOTTOM in cold water up to his kneecaps, the suspender straps to his short denim overalls hanging loosely at his side, insects buzzing about his sunburned ears. Overhead, cottonwoods rustled and shook, fluttering leaves and dry bunchgrass down into the creek bed behind a narrow two-story framehouse on the great Nebraska prairie. Alvin Pendergast tossed his cap and farm shoes and socks underneath a fallen cottonwood log, then rolled up the cuffs of his work trousers and dangled his feet off the log into the narrow stream. Cold water numbed his toes and they tingled when he withdrew them from the current. Brushing a shock of hair off his forehead, he watched Rascal squat in the creek like a duck and fish the sand with his fingers, sloshing in quick circles, making paddling motions and humming to himself. Chester had taken the Packard and headed back up the highway to Stantonsburg: pop. 1328. He had told them to wait down in the creek bed until he came back. By Alvin's guess, that was two hours ago. Feeling a little better today than he had all week, Alvin wanted to go over town himself, buy a soda pop and have a look around, maybe find a pretty girl to jolly at the sweetshop, get her going with a nifty Ford joke or two

("Why is a Ford like a bathtub? Because you hate to be seen in one!"). He liked that idea. What was the use of traveling around, he thought, if you don't go nowhere?

"The flora and fauna of our Republic," said the dwarf, "are quite fascinating when one takes care to observe them in their natural habitat. I once kept a grand collection of lady bugs in a Mason jar for a season of breeding." He bent further and sunk his elbows into the water, dredging a trench in the creek bottom and rising up with two handfuls of mud. "Creatures of a lower order have always been a great interest of mine."

"My cousin Frenchy eats crawdads cold," said Alvin, dunking his toes again. "Don't ask me why."

The water felt better now, less icy. The farm boy sunk his legs in up to his calves and sloshed around. It was hot out. The creek bed was cooler than up on the prairie, but Alvin still found it generally stifling. If the water had been deeper, he'd have already dived in and had himself a swim. He splashed lightly with his feet, watched the ripples expand. He liked fooling around in the middle of the day. Work was for saps. Water bugs skittered across the surface. A moldy odor of decaying vegetation on the muddy banks floated in the air. He asked the dwarf, "Can you swim?"

"Actually, I've never tried."

"Scared of drowning, huh?" Alvin smirked, picturing the dwarf flailing his arms and sinking like a rock. Alvin himself had learned to swim when he was three, taught by old Uncle Henry who couldn't swim a lap in a bathtub anymore.

"Of course not. In fact, I'm sure I could manage quite well. My Uncle Augustus once swam across Lake Michigan in a rainstorm. He assured me buoyancy runs in the family."

"I didn't ask if you float or not," Alvin said. "I asked if you ever been swimming."

The dwarf's hand shot down into the water. "Ahhh … there … devil, devil, devil!" It came up empty, three tiny streams of soggy sand leaking between his fingers. He looked over at Alvin. "Do you suppose there are any snapping turtles hereabouts?"

"I never met nobody before who couldn't swim," Alvin remarked, letting his legs slide down a bit further off the mossy log. Sunlight sparkled on the current. Maybe he'd just go ahead and jump in. His cotton shirt and brown trousers were filthy, and needed washing. "Seems like something everybody ought to be able to do. Like walking, or riding a horse."

"When I was a child," replied Rascal, "we owned a stable of race horses down in Kentucky. People came from as far away as India to buy them from us for all the great competitions around the world. I believe we won the Queen's Steeplechase on more than one occasion."

"I'd go swimming everyday in the summer if I didn't have chores to do," said Alvin. He splashed water in the dwarf's direction, hoping to soak him. Half the time he and Frenchy went fishing, they wound up giving each other the works and riding home in Uncle Henry's Chevrolet dripping wet. "My cousin and me'd go swimming in the Mississippi Saturday mornings and be back home for supper. Swam all the way across once, like Johnny Weissmuller. Dove off the Illiniwek Bridge, too. Just to scare people who never seen someone do it before."

Rascal waded across the creek to study a pool worn by erosion into the far bank. "Do you see these bugs here?" He flicked his fingers lightly on the murky water lapping against the bank. "If I had a jar, I'd collect some and take them with us. Do you know, none of them have ever been more than a foot or so from this spot in their entire lives? It's a fact. They're born, grow up, mate and perish right here in the mud by this little creek. What do you suppose they know about life?"

"They're bugs. They don't have a need to know nothing."

"So you say."

"So I know." Alvin dropped off the log into the cold creek water, making a big splash. He really wished Chester had taken him into town for a hotdog and a soda pop.

Plucking violets off the embankment farther downstream, the dwarf remarked, "Are you aware that amphibians are the precursors of modern man?" He dipped his hands into the stream, letting the current wash over the pretty wildflowers.

Alvin began kicking about, digging his feet in the sand. "Pardon?"

"Well, millions of years ago, we crawled out of the primordial swamp to establish civilization, while our cousins, the amphibians, remained behind."

The dwarf released the wild violets into the stream and saw them float away into the splintered shadows. Alvin watched Rascal wade off down the creek, exploring the bank as he went, dipping his hands into the water when he saw something of interest, letting the sluggish current wash over his bare legs.

His own two legs growing numb from the cold, Alvin sloshed his way back to the damp sedge and climbed up onto the grass. Threads of sunlight like silver spider webs shone through white poplar leaves. He felt drowsy now, and hungry. All he'd eaten were buns for lunch. Chester had refused to let them visit a café. Clearing a place to sit amid leafless stems of scouringrush, the farm boy told the dwarf, "I guess I wouldn't mind lying in the mud all day. What makes us so smart? Maybe we ought to've stayed right where we were. Been better off. Most of us, anyhow."

"Evolution is not a matter of choice." Rascal refastened the shoulder buttons on his romper. "Rather, I believe, it's a form of destiny."

"Favoring frogs and salamanders, huh?" Alvin laughed. Aunt Hattie had always maintained that evolution was a hokum which denied God's bitter miracle of life. She believed Noah strolled out of the ark on December 18th, 2348 B.C. and that's when the modern world began. Who's to say she wasn't right? Nobody had even half the answers. Life was too damned confusing.

"I collect them, of course," said the dwarf, wading back toward the shore. "Studying one's past is invaluable for understanding one's place in the world. Do you think we'll eat soon?"

A dozen yards downstream, Rascal sat down in the soggy sedge and rinsed the mud from between his toes. Alvin climbed back up onto the rotting log. Balancing on one foot, the farm boy picked his nose. Meadowlarks chattered in the cottonwoods. Leaves fluttered down into the creek bed. Alvin walked to the end of the log and balanced above the stream. His sister Mary Ann could turn a cartwheel on a worm fence without falling off. Alvin searched for stream minnies in the creek bed. He watched the dwarf scramble up from the water and sit down in a pretty patch of blue verbena that grew near a thicket of sandbar willows where he put his shoes back on. Rascal said, "If I lived around here, I'd want to have lots of neighbors close by."

"You mean, shouting distance?"

"If you will. Only through a life of society do men truly flourish."

"Not me," said Alvin, turning a circle on the log, careful not to slip off. His bare feet didn't offer much purchase on the damp moss. "I'd keep people about a mile off, so's I wouldn't have to hear 'em yammering all day long. Most folks talk too much."

"I can recite by heart the inaugural addresses of nine Presidents of the United States. Uncle Augustus taught me when I was only six."

"That'll earn you a living."

The dwarf pulled his legs up under his chin and rocked backward. "I've often thought I ought to be a newspaper man, perhaps a city editor. I'm sure I have many of the correct qualifications. I can read quick as the wind and my grammar is excellent."

"Why not just be President?"

"I've considered it."

"You'd have to wear one of those tall black Lincoln stovepipes, you know? Think they got one big enough for that head of yours?" His laughter echoed loudly down the creek. He liked joking the dwarf. It passed the time.

Rascal frowned. "There's no cause to be cruel."

Tired of the creek, the farm boy paced to the end of the cottonwood log and hopped off into the long grass. He picked up his cap and went to put on his shoes. "I'm going up to the house and have myself a glass of lemonade."

"Wait for me!"

Up on the Nebraska prairie, a light wind pushed across dry fields of Indian grass and flowering thimbleweed and bush clover, trading hay scents and dust. Overhead, the summer sky was blue and clear. The old gray framehouse was sheltered by a dense grove of common hack-berry trees and a thick bur oak in the front yard. Red berries of a bittersweet vine draped the downstairs sleeping porch, and the back-house under white poplars by the creek was shrouded at its rear in wild grape and poison ivy. A one-horse shovel plow and a Mayflower cultivator lay beside a dusty tractor near the barn, and a collection of milk pails and peach baskets were piled like junk next to a perforated bee-smoker beneath an old plum tree. Alvin thought maybe the fellow who owned the farm used to be more prosperous. Maybe life had given up on him.

The gravel driveway out to the county road was empty.

The farm boy listened to the bleating of sheep from somewhere across the fields. He walked under a sagging laundry line to the rear of the house where the kitchen door had been left ajar. His shoes kicked up dust wherever he strode. A familiar stink like rotten crabapples trav-eled here and there on the breeze. He brushed a curious bumblebee off his forehead and went over to study a tall wire birdcage framed in wood planks that stood almost as high as Alvin himself. There were still piles of dried shit on the dirt floor, but a foot-long section of chicken wire was ripped away near the bottom and he guessed some slick old fox had torn into it one night and had himself a snack.

Chester had told them the fellow who occupied this house was an old pal of his from Black Jack Pershing's army, but he also made them promise to stay hidden until he got back from town, so Alvin guessed it was another lie. Chester had driven the Packard up to the front door and invited himself inside for a drink of water. Hadn't bothered to knock or call out. Just went in like that. He came out five minutes later, rolling a Walking Liberty half-dollar over his knuckles and whistling a tune. He said he was going downtown to fix himself up with a shampoo and shave, then settle some business arrange-ments for the afternoon. *"It's the roving bee that gathers the honey,"* Chester had told Alvin as he got back into the Packard. Then he had driven off and left them.

To Alvin's eye, the house looked poor, or maybe the owner was just tired. Then again, maybe he was occupied most of the day smuggling corn whiskey and Chester had come to help him out of a fix. But if Chester had a plan doped out, he wasn't sharing it yet. Since Kansas, he'd just driven them around, visiting storehouses in small towns, cutting hootch in swill tubs, selling Scotch whiskey through the backrooms of pool parlors in old beer-jugs, and joyriding through the countryside in a hired liquor truck. For helping with the loading and unloading of whiskey barrels, and changing a flat tire now and then, he had paid Alvin fifteen dollars a week, and given the dwarf another thirty dollars for putting over a pretty fair applejack recipe and devising a scheme that involved the construction of pineapple bombs. There hadn't been any further talk of bank robbery since Kansas. Chester hadn't allowed it and both the farm boy and the dwarf knew how to hush up. None of them mentioned Charlie and Rose Harper at all. Lately, though, Alvin had been having bad dreams, and they weren't just fever.

The narrow sleeping porch was screened-in, but the back door leading to the kitchen was flimsy and rattled loose when the wind gusted. Alvin heard the dwarf thrashing up through the leafy milkweed above the creek, so he went inside.

The house was dark and cool. He listened to a mantel clock ticking in another room. Floorboards creaked underfoot. The pale lime-green kitchen smelled of coffee grounds and pipe tobacco. The latest issue of *Farm & Fireside* lay open on the table in the middle of the room. Filthy plates and cups were stacked in the sink. The ceiling was cracked and water-spotted. Window curtains were soiled. He looked in the icebox and saw only a bottle of milk and a chunk of cheese. Not much to eat. Except for a few canned goods and cornmeal, most of the pantry shelves were empty, too. Didn't this fellow ever go to the grocery store? Probably he was a bachelor, or a widower like Uncle Boyd, Alvin thought, as he opened a cupboard next to the cook stove in search of a clean glass. No woman would let her kitchen look this sore. He found a glass and brought it to the sink and ran cold water from the tap, then had a drink. He felt strange being indoors without having been invited. He had already been partner to a bank robbery and the killing of a fellow and his daughter, and he felt sick and lousy about it. He hadn't known any of that was going to happen. Over and over Rascal said it wasn't their fault, yet even though Charlie Harper had stuck a rifle in his face, Alvin still felt awful guilty. If the Bible was true like Aunt Hattie claimed, then he was probably going straight to hell when all he had wanted to do was stay out of the sanitarium. He might've jumped off a train and joined some workers at a tent colony or hired himself a cheap boardinghouse room and slung hash in a buffet flat. It needn't have amounted to much. Trouble was, he was getting sicker now and worried that sooner or later he'd have to see a doctor for the consumption, and he knew what that would mean. He supposed his daddy was burned up about him skipping out on his chores and all, while his momma sobbed after supper now and then. Alvin presumed his sisters were probably fighting over who'd be getting his room. He hadn't meant to run off for good. That was certainly a mistake, but what was done was done. Now he wished somebody would come along and tell him what he ought to do next.

He drank another glass of water, and belched.

The dwarf was in the yard outdoors, fooling with the birdcage. Alvin could hardly see through the dirt-smudged windows, but he heard him plain as day. Rascal had crawled into the cage where the fox had torn a hole and was fiddling with the dangling perch, making it swing.

A small door just outside the kitchen pantry led down to the basement and a quick peek from atop the stairs showed it was darker than a cow's innards, so Alvin left the kitchen for the dining room, telling himself again there wasn't no harm done just looking around. He wasn't a thief. One day if he ever got healthy enough to work again, he'd own a house of his own, and if somebody ran in while he was away and didn't do nothing except have himself a glass of cold water, why, that'd be all right. A mahogany sideboard across from the dining room table displayed a set of small porcelain jars with flowers painted under the rims and a silver tea service beside the jars. Dust covered everything and Alvin guessed the fellow didn't drink much tea, nor had any use for little jars with flowers on them. He opened the top drawers to the sideboard and found white lace table covers and linen napkins neatly folded one on top of the other. He saw a fine set of silverware, too, then shut the drawer to prove he wasn't tempted. He listened briefly to a pair of catbirds chirping in the hackberry. Wind clattered at the backyard door. The interior of the house smelled musty. Alvin went into the front room where the mantel clock was ticking.

This reminded him of Uncle Henry's parlor on the farm: a couple of shaded table lamps, two easy chairs and a fancy green velour Morris chair, an old phonograph console beside a long sofa, a Windsor upright piano, a blue Axminster rug in the middle of the floor, and a crystal set on an oak Bible stand near the fireplace. Alvin considered switching on the radio, but thought better of it. His sisters did nothing except listen to radio shows, hour after hour at home. They favored those fellows that sang and played the ukulele and cracked jokes. He didn't care for none of that. He and his daddy and Uncle Henry only tuned in when there was a horse race or a boxing match. One night they heard Jack Dempsey knock a fellow out quicker'n lightning. Uncle Henry jumped up out of his chair and shook a fist at Alvin and his daddy, cackling, *"Now you see it, now you don't! Now you see it, now you don't!"* Alvin's daddy had bet fifty cents on the other guy.

He picked up one of the magazines piled on a walnut table and riffled through it. He stopped at a lingerie advertisement for Hickory Shadow Skirts and gave a good once-over to the smiling girl posed in her undergarments. *"Begin to know the comfort, beauty, and style of Hickory. Ask for Personal Necessities by Hickory. At your favorite notion department."* Almost before he knew it, he'd torn the page out of the magazine, folded it up, and stuck it into his shirt pocket. Then he slipped the magazine under the bottom of the pile and pretended he hadn't noticed it was there at all.

He went over to the staircase. There was a cob pipe left on the newel post, half-full of tobacco as if its owner had intended to bring it with him, but had forgotten. Alvin could hear a shade flapping at an open window upstairs. Family photographs decorated the stairwell, rising to a stained glass window at the top of the steps. As the farm boy mounted the staircase to study the portraits, he heard a squirrel land on the rooftop from one of the shady hackberry trees. Then the dwarf came into the house through the kitchen, letting the screen door bang closed behind him. When Rascal called out, Alvin went upstairs.

At home, his bedroom was in the rear attic with a window facing over his mama's vegetable garden toward the pinewoods north of York's peacock farm. He'd painted a sign that ordered his sisters to keep out. Though Alvin protected his own privacy, an irresistible curiosity sent him up these stairs to the top where a short hallway led to three bedrooms and a toilet closet. He felt jittery. It was scorching under the eaves, airless and humid. Wind had sucked the bedroom doors shut, so the hall was dusky beyond the stained glass window. He paused outside the nearest door and listened to the window shade flapping in the draft. Downstairs, the dwarf was wandering room-to-room, calling out Alvin's name as if they both belonged in the house. The radio came on, spilling orchestra music into the silence, then switched off again. Alvin opened the door in front of him and peeked inside. It was a young boy's room, cluttered with cowboy paraphernalia and wooden aeroplanes and toy soldiers. There was a single bed and a nightstand and a writing desk beneath the window. On the wall above his bed was a large movie photograph of Tim McCoy from *War Paint* and several others of Douglas Fairbanks and Rod La Rocque and Rin-Tin-Tin and Mickey Mouse. The boy's writing desk was covered with paper thumbnail sketches of automobiles. His bed was carelessly made and a pair of denim overalls lay on the floor by the closet. Alvin went to the open window and lifted the shade and took a look outdoors where he could see clear to the grassy horizon, miles and miles away. Nebraska seemed almost as lonesome as Kansas. Old farmhouses. Silos and barns. Dirt and sky. Wind probably most days. On the way here, he had seen a remarkable sight: fields of cornhusks unattended to, stalks wilting, wildrye and hound dogs chasing through the empty rows, ash barrels stuffed with fodder, the dust of wheel-worn roads blowing to heaven. *No point in owning the land,* his daddy once told him, *if you aren't willing to do nothing with it. Work it, or it'll go tired on you. Won't grow nothing, won't feed your children. A man who won't work his own land, deserves to live in a house built by strangers.*

Alvin heard the dwarf at the bottom of the stairwell, so he went back out into the hall. He knew it was wrong sneaking around like this, yet he couldn't help himself. At least he hadn't stolen nothing. Chester hadn't told them not to go indoors. Besides, they'd gotten thirsty sitting in the creek bed and it was hot as blazes out. What did he expect? Alvin went down to the room at the end of the hall. Inside was nothing but a common iron bed with brass knobs and a mattress with a green blanket and a feather pillow, a plain oak bureau, and a small chamberset table and lamp. No rug on the floor. Bare walls painted white. Like living in a stall, Alvin reflected, without the straw. There ought to at least be a pretty picture or two on the walls. He had a few swell boat pictures in his attic room and a racy tabloid photograph of Peaches on her honeymoon that Frenchy had gotten for him in Chicago. Alvin didn't hold much for decorating, but he knew what he liked.

Stifling a cough, the farm boy went back across the hall to the next room just as the dwarf arrived on the second floor landing. From the door, a smothering odor of sweet lilac filled Alvin's nostrils. Inside, he found a shade-drawn bedroom jammed with lavender draperies and gilt curtain bands, a grand chamber suite in carved black walnut: bed, chiffonier, dresser, washstand and mirrored wardrobe, a marble top center table with an ormolu kerosene lamp, brass cameo miniatures, and a blue china vase stuffed with frayed peacock feathers. The bedroom walls were adorned with wire-hung paintings and floral lithographs and the floor covered by a crimson tapestry rug. Velvet pincushions and stuffed pillows were piled upon the bed under a fringed gauze turnover canopy. Awed by the elegant clutter, Alvin wasn't sure he ought to go in. He'd never seen such a pretty bedroom in his whole life. Aunt Emeline had some fancy stuff all right, and so did Granny Chamberlain with her porcelain dolls and papier-mâché, but how a lady in a house as plain as this could fix out her room so swell, he couldn't figure. No doubt somebody had some pretty high coin.

Promising himself not to bust anything, Alvin walked into the middle of the bedroom. The ceiling overhead was painted like the summer sky outdoors, fluffy clouds drifting about here and there, tiny swallows on the wing. A vine of stenciled ivy encircled the outer border. If he hadn't known better, he'd have thought the lady who slept in here was a queen. On the dresser were Ivorette hairbrushes, and hair combs and tuck combs, nail files, lingerie clasps, perfume bottles, skin lotions, Pompeian night cream, a powder puff box, a pair of bevel glass bonnet mirrors, and a Mavis 3-piece set. How could anyone on earth ever use all that?

The dwarf came into the bedroom behind him, holding a cloudy glass of lemonade.

Alvin frowned. He hadn't seen any lemons in the kitchen.

The dwarf asked, "Why didn't you answer when I called?"

"I didn't hear you," Alvin lied, checking his look in the dresser mirror. His freckles were nearly hidden under the dust on his face. He felt hot and grimy and knew he needed a bath. Maybe Chester would hire a couple of rooms in a hotel later on after supper.

"Wasn't the creek refreshing?" the dwarf asked, strolling across the rug, a dreamy look of contentment on his misshapen face. He sipped from his glass of lemonade.

"It ought to be," the farm boy replied, as he sorted through a pearl button collection in a corner of the dresser top. "That water's cold enough to freeze the whiskers off a brass monkey." He stared at the dwarf's drinking glass. "Say, how come you didn't fix me up with a lemonade?"

"You didn't wait for me," Rascal said, walking over to the dresser. He plucked a Japanese fan from a dry rosewater and glycerine bottle, and carefully unfolded it. "He's a widower, you know."

"Who?"

"The fellow who lives here."

"How do you know that?"

"I read a note of bereavement downstairs," the dwarf explained, replacing the fan. "His wife Annabelle passed away a year ago Christmas. Apparently it was quite unexpected." He put down his lemonade and opened a top drawer, rummaged around a little, then took out a jewelry box and sprung the clasp, revealing a splendid assortment of scarf pins, rings, lavallieres, necklaces and silver thimbles.

"Don't steal nothing," Alvin warned, suddenly protective of the late woman's possessions, though he had no idea why. He didn't even know what she looked like.

"Do you think I'm a thief?" Rascal drew out a gold Daughters of Rebekah pin. "Why, I've never stolen anything in my life. I couldn't imagine stooping so low."

"Says you."

The dwarf returned the enameled pin to the jewelry box. "What in the dickens are you talking about?"

Alvin found a matchstick in a silver child's cup and stuck it in his mouth to chew on. He smirked at Rascal, and gave him the bad eye.

That prompted the dwarf to grouse, "I suppose this is what I deserve for traveling with a no-good like you."

Alvin shut the jewelry box drawer. "Lay off the wisecracks."

The dwarf picked up a brown bottle containing pure sweet spirits of nitre. "Here, try some of this. It'll fix you up all right."

Alvin scowled, sure this was a gag. He grabbed the bottle, anyhow. "What's it good for?" Reading the label didn't offer much instruction. He didn't recognize half the words.

The dwarf giggled. "Whatever ails you, and if nothing ails you, it's good for that, too."

"Aw, cut that stuff," Alvin growled, putting the bottle of nitre back on the dresser top. The heat upstairs had begun to irritate him. "If you weren't so cuckoo, I'd take out my cast-iron knucks and knock you flat."

Rascal smiled. "There's no need to offer alibis. Why, I'm more than willing to rough it up a bit. Uncle Augustus taught me several nifty wrestling holds when I was younger. If I were you, I'd think twice about who you'd be scrapping with."

Alvin heard a motorcar coming up from the county road. He went across the hall into the plain room to look out the window, and saw Chester's tan Packard Six rolling to a stop by the front of the house. "He's back."

The dwarf darted out of the woman's bedroom, and hurried off to the stairwell.

"Hey!" Alvin shouted, rushing after him.

The dwarf bounded down the stairs.

Alvin followed him to the first floor and went outside through the kitchen door, while Rascal left the house by the front porch. Wind kicked up in the driveway, sweeping leaves from the hackberry trees and stirring dust about the yard. Chester stood beside the automobile, his foot on the runningboard as he lit up a cigarette. The dwarf had engaged him in conversation before Alvin reached the plum tree on the side of the house. Chester flicked the burnt match away. His eyes were bright blue in the sunlight. Alvin guessed his pow-wow in Stantonsburg had come off all right. Maybe he'd even found another girl downtown to play post office with.

When Chester noticed the farm boy, he smiled and called across the wind, "Well, we made a ten-strike today, kid!"

"How's that?"

"It's like I've been telling you right along. Some fellows furnish the manure while others grow the flowers. They tried to cut in on us, but I wouldn't let 'em because they're all a lot of damn four flushers and they know it."

Alvin hadn't any idea what Chester was talking about. He coughed into his fist.

"Well, they weren't half through before I gave 'em the raspberry and put on my hat. That's when one of them got the big idea that we were all set to throw everything over and go home unless they came around pretty damn quick."

Chester opened the passenger door and took out a small black traveling bag. Then he slung it through the air over to Alvin. The cowhide bag skidded in the dirt at the farm boy's feet. "Go on, see for yourself."

Rascal scampered over as Alvin undid the latches. Inside, the bag looked stuffed with greenback bills.

Chester told the farm boy, "With what we got there, you could buy that whole hick town of yours and make yourself mayor."

"Like Al Capone!" the dwarf enthused, reaching in and riffling through a handful of bills.

Chester frowned. "Don't be a wiseacre."

Alvin just stared at the dough. Chester had told them if he cashed-in downtown, they'd be able to settle some obligations. He hadn't said anything about striking oil. Too scared to touch it, the farm boy stepped back from the bag.

Holding up a fistful of bills, the dwarf grinned. "This is quite a fortune!"

Chester tapped ash off his cigarette into the dirt. "It'll make out all right."

Rascal stuffed the cash back into the bag. "May I ask you a great favor?"

"What's that?"

"Well, I'd like to have a photograph taken of myself in bed with this money that I could mail to Auntie in Hadleyville."

Chester shook his head. "Just bring the dough back over here."

Alvin saw a small truck out on the county road coming from the east, lifting clouds of dust on the blue summer sky. Rascal closed the leather bag and lugged it over to the Packard where Chester stuck it into the rear seat once again. He told them, "Keep this under your hat. We need to beat it up to Des Moines without giving anyone the dope on how big we put it over. You get me?"

The dwarf nodded. "Of course."

"You fellows stay out here. I need a drink." Chester looked Alvin in the eye. "All right, kid?"

"Sure."

Chester flicked his cigarette into the dirt and went inside by the front porch. After the door closed, Rascal walked down to the small barn where the farm tractor was parked.

Looking back out to the county road, Alvin noticed the small truck slow at the approach to the driveway. Butterflies churned in his belly. Every so often, he'd heard about trespassers getting shot in Illinois. He considered hurrying indoors to fetch Chester, but decided against it. Maybe he was expecting this fellow and just get sore that Alvin had come into the house when he had already been told not to. On the other hand, maybe this fellow wasn't expecting to find a pack of strangers at his door at all.

Alvin had an idea.

He went over to the Packard and undid the radiator filler cap and raised the hood.

By then, the dwarf had noticed the truck, too, and gone to hide inside the barn. Alvin knelt behind the Packard until he heard a noisy truck motor drawing near and the crunching of tires on the dusty gravel. Chester still hadn't come out of the house. When the truck rolled to a stop half a dozen yards away, Alvin rose from his hiding place, hands apart. A cloud of dust stirred up from the driveway swept over him. He coughed harshly and waved it out of his face as a tall scrawny man in work overalls and an army-style hat climbed out of the driver's door. A small boy seated on the passenger side remained in the truck. The man said, "Who are you?"

Alvin shuffled his feet in the dirt, mute.

A wary frown on his brow, the man studied the farm boy up and down and gave the Packard a quick once-over, too. He asked, "You broke down?"

Alvin forced a nod.

"Radiator?"

He nodded again.

"There's water in the pump and a iron pail." The man gestured toward the other side of the house, well shaded in hackberry. He added, "It'll pay you to use a spout. I got a can back over yonder in the barn by the feed cutter."

Alvin mumbled a thank you, still scared enough to faint.

The man turned his attention to the boy seated quietly in the truck. "Arnie, get along into the house."

The boy climbed out of the truck, holding a tiny jackknife. He was wearing a pair of denim trousers and a red-checkered shirt and black cowboy boots. His light hair was freshly combed with a well-oiled cowlick that resisted the wind. He stared at Alvin, eyes clear and curious.

"Go on now," the man told him.

The boy walked past Alvin without a word, up the steps and into the house. Alvin guessed the kid was just as scared as he was. Then he remembered who was still indoors and his belly went cold. Why had Chester chosen this fellow's house? It didn't make sense.

"It's my son's birthday today," the man told Alvin. "I just brought him into town for a haircut and a root beer."

Urging himself to speak up, the farm boy said, "He's a swell kid."

"What're you doing out here?"

His brain gone dead as wax, Alvin persisted with the same lie, "We're broke down."

The man fixed him hard with a stare.

He's no dumbbell, Alvin thought. *He knows I ain't being square with him. If he had a shotgun handy, he'd probably knock me out of my shoes.*

The man walked over toward the porch and found a stick in the dirt and brought it back to the Packard. Keeping an eye on Alvin, he poked the stick down into the radiator, then drew it out again. Wet.

He said, "Where's the other fellow?"

Alvin didn't know how to answer that. He felt like a dirty crook and knew he wasn't smart enough to make up another lie. A warm gust of wind kicked up dust and left grit in his eyes. As he rubbed them clear with one hand, he heard the man hurry away toward the house where his boy was calling from indoors.

Alvin saw the dwarf emerge from the corner of the small barn and walk up as far as the tractor.

The front screen door swung shut with a bang.

He had no idea what to do now. He felt rotten as hell. He thought if he wasn't such a coward, he'd probably run off down to the county road and hike back to Illinois. He heard voices briefly inside the house. Alvin closed the hood of the Packard and put the radiator filler cap back on.

Then he waited.

Several minutes went by. The dwarf left the farm tractor and crossed the yard to the side of the house near the plum tree. Dust swirled about. Then the screen door swung open and Chester walked out onto the porch carrying a box of glass canning jars. He paused at the top of the steps and called down to Alvin, "Do you like peach preserves? I just found these down in the cellar."

Alvin shrugged. "I ain't all that fond of 'em."

"No?"

"Nope."

Chester smiled. "Me neither."

Then he threw the box off the porch upside down.

The din of glass shattering brought Rascal from around the side of the house.

Chester was already down the steps by then, striding toward the Packard. He motioned Alvin to get into the automobile, and slid in behind the wheel. When he started the engine, the dwarf rushed over and climbed into the backseat. Then Chester put the Packard into gear and quickly steered the motorcar around in a circle, aiming it back down the gravel drive. Just before mashing his foot on the gas pedal, he said, "Let me tell you, boys. Hospitality's not what it used to be."

Then they were hurtling down the road toward Stantonsburg, a great hot cloud of dust trailing in their wake. Part of Chester's morning newspaper billowed up and out of the backseat of the Packard. It alighted once in the middle of the road, and flew off like a kite into the fields. Along the roadside, switchgrass stood taller than the Packard and swayed in the draft as the automobile sped by. Alvin saw dozens of sparrows perched on telegraph wires, crowding one another for room, hardly paying notice to the roaring motor. Only a few people were about anywhere he looked: a man on a tractor off in a cornfield to the east; three women standing under the porch eaves of a tall white farmhouse to the west; and outside a small house next to the road, a little girl with pigtails chasing a black Labrador through billowing laundry in a windy yard.

After driving about three miles, Chester spoke up again. "Listen up, kid, here's how I've doped this out. I arranged a four o'clock appointment at the Union Bank over in Stantonsburg. We'll be meeting a fellow there named Jerome. When I telephoned this morning, I told him about a young pal of mine whose uncle just kicked off and left him a load of dough and that he'd like to start up a bank account."

"Who's that?" Alvin said, somewhat desultorily. He felt thoroughly demoralized over what had just happened back at the farmhouse, and thought if he weren't such a yellow-bellied coward, he'd jump out of the auto right now and kill himself. That'd cure his cough for good and all, and who'd miss him, anyhow? Nobody, that's who.

"You."

"Huh?"

"Your name's Buddy McCoy and you just inherited a bag of money from your dear old Uncle Homer. You're rich now, see, you're getting up in the world, and you want your dough in a safe place, so you asked me to set you up with a bank downtown. You heard they're a fine lot at Union, and you're sure they'll give you a square deal, but you want it to be confidential. That's why you came up with the big idea of running in after hours. If they want to take charge of your money, it'll have to be at your convenience. When I had him on the wire, Jerome told me he'd be delighted to have you call today at four if that'd make you happy. He seems like a swell fellow. Of course, once he lets us in, we'll clean 'em out. Swell gag, isn't it?"

"It's a wonderful plan," the dwarf acknowledged from behind a Texaco road map he was studying. Alvin glared at him. Chester drove faster, bouncing across the dips in the road, swerving here and there to avoid sinkholes. A quarter mile farther on, he ran the Packard straight over a dead fox.

The whole idea scared the hell out of Alvin. He didn't want to go inside another bank at all. If he were lucky, he'd get shot and it'd be over and done with. Hanging his arm out the window into the hot draft, he said, "Maybe I ain't made for this sort of thing. I hate lying and I ain't very good at it, neither."

"Nobody lies better than I do," the dwarf remarked.

The farm boy agreed. "You're a bag of wind, all right."

"Perhaps I ought to play the role of the wealthy nephew," Rascal argued, ignoring the jibe. "All you'd need to do is give me my lines. I'm a whiz at memorization, and I can be utterly convincing."

Chester shook his head. "Not on your life. We couldn't put that over in a bughouse. Who'd leave his fortune to a midget?"

The Packard struck a sharp dip in the dusty road, jolting the dwarf off-balance, bouncing him backward into the seat.

"I'd rather stay with the car," Alvin persisted, worried like the devil now. "I ain't cut out for selling this stuff. It gives me a big bellyache and I ain't ashamed to tell you."

"I don't need you in the car," Chester barked. "I need you in the bank acting like a lucky plowboy whose rich uncle just fell down a well. So stop squawking. You can put it over, all right. Just don't act nervous. Remember, they got to listen when they know who you are."

Stantonsburg was shady and quiet in the afternoon, sidewalks mostly empty, shops all closing up in the four o'clock hour, both roads leading out of town clear of traffic.

"They're having a rutabaga festival today over at a fairgrounds across town," Chester said, as they rolled through the center of Stantonsburg. "What the hell's a rutabaga?"

"The rutabaga is a large turnip with an edible yellow root," the dwarf explained. "Auntie and I once grew them in our garden. One year, we even won a blue ribbon at the Hadleyville Fair for best of show. Rutabagas are quite tasty if you know how to prepare them."

"Momma used to cook them on Sundays after church whenever Reverend Tyler'd come for dinner," Alvin added.

"Aren't they swell?" said the dwarf, smiling.

"No," Alvin replied. "They taste like boiled shoes."

"Cut the chatter," Chester interrupted. "Fact is, thanks to the festival, downtown's closing early today, so we'll be the last customers doing business at the bank. They'll lock the doors behind us and we'll have all the time we need. You just keep your mouth shut and let me do the talking, we won't have any trouble."

Chester steered over to the curb between Rexall Drugs and Foote's hardware, a block and a half from the Union Bank. He stopped the car and turned off the motor. The air was dry and smelled of cornfields. Chester climbed out of the Packard, stretched and yawned. Alvin got out, too, then jerked his thumb in the dwarf's direction. "What about him? What's his job?"

Without looking at Rascal, Chester replied, "He's staying in the car, and keeping his mug out of sight. I doubt they have a lot of midgets around here and if they see him with us, you can be sure they'll remember."

"I could disguise myself," said the dwarf, still sitting low with his Texaco map in the backseat. "I was in a play once."

"Well, that won't go around here. You're sticking with the car, see?" Chester added, "We'll be back in about twenty minutes, so I'm telling you straight: no monkey business. After this, we're pulling out."

He reached back into the Packard and grabbed the black leather bag. He handed it to Alvin. "All right, kid, let's go."

They headed up the sidewalk toward the Union Bank. Most of the blinds in the upper windows on Omaha Street were shut. Birds perched on the rooftops surveyed the empty sidewalks below. Already, the hair on the back of Alvin's neck bristled. He searched the elm trees for black crows, a sure omen of death. Probably he ought to have borrowed Granny Chamberlain's corncob Cross of Jesus out of Momma's chifforobe and brought it west with him. That old crucifix, his momma had maintained, held sway against all manner of jinxes and evil. Granny Chamberlain lived to be eighty-nine so far just by hanging it on a nail over her bed and whispering the Lord's Prayer before sleeping every night. She prayed for Alvin when he was in the sanitarium and he came home cured, so everybody knew its power was genuine. Of course, he had also gotten sick again, which just proved nothing was on the level anymore.

As they came up to the Union Bank, Alvin saw a fellow in a blue pinstriped suit with a white carnation on his lapel waiting behind the glass at the front door. He dangled a set of keys on a large iron ring in his left hand and cracked a big smile as he stepped outside to greet his new customers.

Chester tipped his hat to the guy. "Afternoon, sir. Are you Jerome?"

"Indeed, I am. And you're Mr. Wells, I assume?"

"Yes, sir."

They shook hands.

"Well, did y'all have a nice lunch?"

"We sure did."

The fellow stuck his hand out to Alvin. "My name's Walter Jerome. You're Buddy, I presume."

Alvin nodded, the phony greeting stuck in his throat. He coughed and turned away.

"He's a little nervous," Chester explained. "First time in town and all. Forgets himself with excitement. You know how it is."

"I surely do," said Mr. Jerome, and offered his hand again to Alvin.

Alvin's arm began quivering, and he felt like a dumbbell. "Glad to know you, sir," he mumbled, eyes watering as they shook hands. He hated fibbing like this.

"Glad to know you, too, Buddy. Quite glad, in fact." He took Alvin by the crook of the arm. "Come on in out of the sun."

Jerome led Alvin and Chester into the shadowy interior of the bank whose dark wood and fabrics lent a somber tone to daily financial transactions. There were no windows, except for those facing out on Omaha Street. The large safe sat against the rear wall behind the teller stations. Beside it on both sides were the bank officers' desks and a small door leading to the president's office. It was closed. Only Mr. Jerome and a single bank clerk were still working.

"Let me take that for you," Mr. Jerome said, reaching for Alvin's bag. "Howard! We have a deposit to make. Could you give us some help?"

The clerk behind the teller's window got up from his desk and came around to the gate dividing the lobby from the offices and unlocked it. Mr. Jerome walked through with the black bag, which he handed to the clerk. Then he turned back to Alvin and Chester with a smile. "Howard here'll take good care of you."

"This is a straight deposit, I assume," said the clerk, adjusting his eyeglasses.

"Yes, it is. We'll be watching over this young man's fortune until he decides what investments he'd like us to make for him."

Having no idea what they were talking about, Alvin smiled and pretended to be content with the arrangement. The clerk reminded him of a chemistry teacher he had at Farrington High School, Mr. Fisher. Both wore old-fashioned bowties and striped suspenders and were skinnier than matchsticks.

Chester asked, "I assume the rate of interest he's receiving will be commensurate with the amount of cash we're leaving off today."

"Of course."

The clerk set the bag onto the desk behind him. Mr. Jerome twirled the ring of keys on his forefinger and smiled at Alvin. "This is the best decision you've ever made in your life, young man."

The farm boy mumbled, "I sure hope so."

"Now, if you two gents'll excuse me," said Mr. Jerome, "I have to be running along to the fair. My son's showing the biggest rutabaga this county's seen in forty years."

Walter Jerome stared at Alvin a moment, as if studying on something in his mind. Then he switched his attention over to Chester. "A thought just occurred to me. Do you two have any plans for supper? I ask because my wife's planning a feast this afternoon in celebration of the blue ribbon we're certain Jonathan'll be bringing home from the fair and, well, you'd be more than welcome to join us, if you'd like. We'd be dining at half past five."

Alvin nodded his approval, hoping that eating a meal would make him feel better.

Chester agreed. "That's swell of you. We'd be pleased to join you and your family. Thanks a lot."

"Well, we live out on Route Four, north of town. Just drive in that direction three miles or so and you'll see us up on a rise to your left. Big white house and a red barn next to it."

"I'm sure we'll find it."

"Wonderful!" Mr. Jerome took Alvin's hand and gave it another shake. "Thank you again, Buddy, and we'll see you soon."

Alvin nodded. "Sure."

Then Mr. Jerome shook hands with Chester and headed for the door. Before stepping out into the street, he called back to the clerk, "Howard, be sure they get the proper papers and all that, will you? Receipts and such?" He winked at Alvin. "I wouldn't want young Buddy here forgetting where he put his money." Then he laughed and wandered out into the sunlight.

The clerk took the bag over to a desk beside the safe. Chester strolled through the teller's gate behind him. "You'll be keeping the money here, is that right? In case he wants to pay it a visit one of these days?"

"A visit?" the clerk asked, somewhat startled by Chester's presence in the office area. "I'm not sure I know what you mean by that."

Chester put his hand on top of the cowhide bag, preventing the clerk from opening it just yet. "What I mean to say is, you keep your money right here in this safe, don't you? It's not all sent away somewhere a fellow can't get to it if he chooses."

Still waiting on the public side of the teller's window, Alvin watched the clerk wipe his forehead with the back of his hand. It was hot inside the bank, stuffy and humid. The clerk said, "Of course, we invest some of what's deposited here, but our customers always retain adequate means to withdraw their funds. Certainly."

The wall clock above the safe chimed four o'clock.

Waiting until it finished, the clerk said to Chester, "Excuse me a moment," and went over to his desk, pulling open the top drawer and taking out a ring of keys similar to Jerome's. "It's that time of day," he said, smiling at Alvin as he passed through the teller's gate. Chester sat down at the desk beside the safe and unfastened the latches of the black bag while the clerk locked the front door.

"Now, ordinarily," the clerk called from over by the front door, "we don't allow anyone inside the bank after hours, but seeing as this is a unique circumstance, Mr. Jerome thought it best that ... "

The clerk's voice trailed off as he saw Chester counting a stack of bills he had taken out of the bag. He finished locking the front door. "Perhaps you ought to allow me to ... " The clerk jammed the key ring into his pants pocket and hurried back into the teller's cage. Before he could get there, Chester had already stuck the money back into the black bag and closed it again.

"This is a lot of kale," said Chester.

"Yes, it is," said the clerk, taking the bag off the desk. "But it's in good hands here with us. You can be sure of that."

"Oh, I am."

"Great! Then let's just take this." The clerk unlocked the back office.

"Say, what are you doing?" Chester interjected, as the clerk opened the door.

Pausing in the doorway, the clerk looked back. "Pardon me?"

"Well, shouldn't that go into the safe?"

The clerk shook his head. "Opening the safe after hours is strictly forbidden. Therefore, I have to put this in Mr. Jerome's office overnight. Rules, you know?"

Chester frowned. "So that's your racket, eh? Why, young Buddy here brought that money a long way today to see it put in your safe. If you're telling us now it'll be spending the night in some desk drawer, well, I guess we'll just have to take it back home, maybe find another bank for it."

"I assure you it'll be perfectly secure in Mr. Jerome's desk."

"No, I think we might have to take it with us. Sorry."

Chester stared the clerk in the eye. It was a standoff. Alvin studied the clerk's face, indecision apparent in his eyes. He had a twitch in one of his eyebrows and sweat beading on his upper-lip. What would he do? And what did Chester have in mind? His plan sounded fishy.

"Oh my," said the clerk, glancing at the black leather bag. "I don't know."

"Why not just open the safe and put the money away," said Chester, "Nobody'll get wise to you and it'd make us happy."

"I can't do that."

"Why not?"

"Bank regulations."

"They're for hicks."

"Pardon me?"

Chester glanced up at the clock. His expression was changing now, the sunny disposition he had worn into the bank dimming as quickly as the light outside. Alvin watched him unbutton his coat and look the clerk straight in the eye with the same expression he had shown Charlie Harper that night by the water trough in Kansas. "Open the safe."

"I've already told you, I can't do that."

"Sure you can."

The frail clerk shrunk back into the office doorway. "I'd lose my job."

"Well, here's the lowdown," Chester said, exposing the revolver tucked into his waistband. He offered the clerk a big smile. "I'll kill you if you don't."

The clerk looked at the gun, then quickly over at Alvin, himself surprised by Chester's sudden abandonment of the stunt they'd been putting on. "I don't understand."

"Sure you do, pal," Chester growled. "And don't kid yourself. I've taken care of plenty of birds like you. Now, open the safe."

"I can't," the clerk whined. "I tell you, I'll lose my job."

Chester lunged forward and grabbed the clerk's left hand and forced his three middle fingers backward until the clerk's knees buckled and he tumbled into the doorframe. Chester urged the clerk's fingers back further until they fractured with a loud crack. As the clerk slumped to the floor, eyes bulging from pain and shock, Chester seized him by the collar. Then he jerked the .38 revolver out of his waistband and pushed the barrel up under the clerk's chin. "You're not the brainiest fellow in the world, are you? Snap out of it and open the safe, or I'll take this gat and blow your brains out!"

Too scared to move, Alvin watched Chester drag the clerk over to the safe, then pick up the black bag, set it on the desk again and flip open the latches. With his left hand firmly planted on the clerk's collar, he began tossing the neatly stacked greenback bills out of the bag with his right, dumping them onto the desktop. When he finished, Chester balled the clerk's collar up in his fist, and rammed the man face first into the safe, shattering the clerk's nose on the steel door. Then Chester jerked the sobbing clerk by the collar again, and positioned him eye level with the big combination lock on the front of the safe. Chester jammed the revolver into his ear. He dropped his voice. "Well, sweetheart, this is your last chance. What'll it be?"

Simultaneously moaning and mumbling, the clerk raised his good hand and began dialing the combination. Keeping an eye on him, Chester called over to the Alvin, "Come over here, kid, and help me stack the cash."

His legs trembling, Alvin took another look out into windy Omaha Street. It was still mostly empty, although here and there, a few people passed in or out of those shops not yet closed up for the day. Hoping the Stantonsburg police had gone off to the rutabaga festival with everyone else, the farm boy walked around to the teller's gate and let himself into the office area.

Chester yelled, "Come on, make it snappy!"

The safe swung open. Chester shoved the sobbing clerk aside and began grabbing stacks of orangeback bills piled up on the middle shelves. Trying to keep his eyes off the clerk, Alvin hurried over to the desk and picked up the bag and held it open for Chester to shovel the money into. The clerk crawled off toward the back office doorway and lay on his side against the frame, cradling his fractured fingers in his lap while blood streamed from his broken nose. By now, his face had swollen grotesquely and the odd, mewling noise that came from his lips gave Alvin the chills.

"Let's go, kid. Hop to it," Chester urged, trying to fill the black bag as fast as possible.

There were bonds and safe deposit boxes lining the top and bottom shelves, but Chester ignored them in favor of several smaller stacks of large-denomination bills. Besides, the leather bag had only so much space in it and his plan had been for ironmen, nothing else. Alvin stacked the bills as fast as he could, filling the bag to the rim. He was scared to death, but tried not to let on. For all he knew, Chester might crack him in the skull, too.

"All right," Chester said, straightening up. "We're done. No sense being greedy."

The farm boy closed the black bag and refastened the latches. The clerk was watching him with squinty eyes, puffy and black. Alvin felt guilty as all hell and pretended not to notice. Chester looked around, searching the office area for something. Then he grabbed Alvin by the sleeve.

"Say, slip me that cushion over there," he told Alvin, pointing to one of the teller's stools that had a small blue cushion on the seat. The farm boy went over and fetched it off the stool. "All right, now beat it out of here. Wait for me down on the corner. I won't be long."

Alvin stole one more look at the clerk who had lapsed into shock. The swelling had changed his features so much that Alvin had a hard time recalling exactly what his face had looked like when they had entered the bank a quarter of an hour ago. He felt awful enough for him, all right, but what could he do?

"Wait a minute, kid!" Chester shouted. "Here." He threw Alvin the key ring. It flew past the farm boy's head and slid into the door. "Just go ahead and leave the keys in the lock. I'll take care of them when I go."

Alvin picked up the key ring and unlocked the door, leaving the keys hanging from the cylinder, and hurried out of the bank into the late afternoon sunlight. The wind had risen outdoors now, sweeping dust along Omaha Street, flapping through the store awnings. Alvin hurried down to the corner by the lamppost and waited there while a man and a woman came along the block toward him, heading in the direction of the bank. The farm boy felt lightheaded from fear and guilt, shocked at Chester's viciousness, and ashamed of his own culpability. He felt short of breath and dizzy, barely able to walk a straight line. He was afraid he might keel over right there on the sidewalk. The man nodded a greeting that Alvin ignored. After they passed, the farm boy walked down the sidewalk another dozen yards and got sick in the gutter.

An amber sunset reflected in the crystal glassware of the dining room facing west through a bay window. Streams of patterned color washed intermittently on the floral wallpaper of the room and across the ivory-hued linen tablecloth and porcelain china. Steam from the kitchen clouded the mirrors behind the sideboard while a breeze from an adjoining foyer cooled the front of the room where the diners sat.

The teenage girl was both fascinated and appalled by the dwarf. It was clear she had never encountered such a creature and found his presence at her supper table intriguing. They sat across from each other, beside Alvin and May Jerome's father, catty-corner to her mother, and Chester Burke. Pork roast and sweet corn, mashed potatoes, brown gravy, rutabaga and biscuits occupied the center of the table.

Rascal talked and ate simultaneously, half a biscuit in one hand, a silver fork in the other. "Well then, after he showed me the medal he won at San Juan Hill, I brought him into my bedroom and took out my collection of Indian arrowheads dug up at camp one summer on the shores of the Belle Fourche River. He was so impressed, he shook my hand and promised me a certificate of merit if I ever visited Washington."

"How wonderful!" said Mr. Jerome, a big cigar in his hand. "Your family must've been very proud. I hear Teddy cut quite a figure in his day."

Rascal nodded. "Yes, indeed. In truth, he and I got along famously. Had he lived longer, I'm certain we'd have become great friends. We had so much in common."

The dwarf took a sip of lemonade and chewed off another piece of biscuit. He smiled at May Jerome, and she blushed. Alvin listened, but he had no appetite of his own. The dwarf didn't know yet what had occurred inside the bank. Alvin did, and it made him sick and desolate, afraid even to speak for fear of revealing his revulsion over what he had witnessed. He had let Chester bully and beat that poor clerk without offering a word in the fellow's defense. He had proven himself gutless and was thoroughly ashamed. If God worsened the consumption for his complicity, Alvin wouldn't kick about it. Even coughing his guts out would be less than he deserved.

"You must tell your Teddy Roosevelt story to our boy when he gets home," Mr. Jerome said to Rascal. "When Jonathan was growing up, the president was one of his heroes. I remember when he was about six or so, he cut a section of tail off my wife's favorite roan to fashion a mustache, which he glued to his upper lip. Naturally, she did not find it amusing," he smiled at Mrs. Jerome, "but the rest of us were in hysterics for a week. Jonathan looked so darling."

Rascal leaned forward and snatched another biscuit off the serving plate and put it on his plate. Buttering it, he offered another anecdote similar to Mrs. Jerome's, substituting Teddy Roosevelt's mustache for Kaiser Wilhelm's. Everybody laughed but Alvin who had already heard the story twice before. Instead, his interest was distracted now by May whose olive-green eyes bored holes in his heart. The late sunlight sparkled in them, and glowed on her pale skin. Even riddled with guilt, he thought he might be falling in love.

"Look here, Buddy," Mr. Jerome began, looking Alvin in the eye, "I must say, the idea of you working that farm by yourself does my heart good. The pioneer spirit's in some decline today, but a young fellow like yourself taking on that sort of responsibility makes me feel mighty encouraged."

The farm boy barely mumbled, "Thank you, sir." His enthusiasm for prolonging Chester's gag had evaporated and he wished Jerome would forget they had ever met. In fact, he'd rather not say another word about that bank business for the rest of his life, however brief that might be.

Mr. Jerome puffed at his cigar. "No, I thank you, young man. Pride's a divisible commodity, isn't it? I like to think that your good fortune's an inspiration we can all share."

Buttering his biscuit, Rascal added, "A man is more fairly measured by his efforts than his accomplishments." Then he stuffed the biscuit into his mouth.

"Well spoken," replied Mr. Jerome, flicking the ash off his cigar onto a small dish beside his dinner plate.

"Actually, Buddy plans on selling if he gets a good price," Chester said, removing the cloth napkin from his lap and dumping it on his supper plate. "Fact is, the boy's sick of farming, but didn't want his uncle to know it. Now that the old fellow's dead, what Buddy'd like to do is move off the farm to the Big Town while he can still wash the smell of chicken shit off himself. Pardon my French."

"My goodness," Mrs. Jerome muttered, clearly shocked at Chester's language. May averted her eyes while suppressing a grin with her napkin. Rascal winked at her and swallowed his fifth biscuit. Staring out into the backyard where a chicken strutted about in the dirt, Alvin considered excusing himself to go outdoors. He needed to piss.

Chester eased his chair back from the table.

"Is that true, Buddy?" said Mr. Jerome, putting his cigar down, "You're planning to sell? Why, I wouldn't advise — "

The doorbell rang.

"Excuse me," May said, then leaped up and hurried out of the room through the folds of the crimson portière.

"Are we expecting someone, dear?" Mr. Jerome asked his wife.

She shook her head. "No, I don't believe so."

At the window, a string of crystal prisms suspended in front of the glass clinked lazily together in the draft from the hallway. Rascal grabbed another biscuit and buttered it. Chester took the watch out of his pocket, flipped it open, and checked it against the wall clock. Alvin played nervously with his soupspoon, tapping it softly on his plate. His heart was thumping and he felt vaguely feverish and wanted to lie down. He muffled a rattling cough with the cloth napkin. Maybe he'd die tonight.

The tasseled portière divided and May walked back into the room. "Daddy," she said, "Mr. Hancock's here to see you. Shall I ask him in?"

"Certainly."

She left again.

"George Hancock's got an insurance business down the block from your new bank," Mr. Jerome told Alvin. "He's a swell fellow. I'll introduce you."

"Why would he come all the way out here so late in the day?" Mrs. Jerome asked her husband. She still looked disturbed by Chester's remark.

"If you'll sit there a moment, dear, I expect we'll find out."

"These insurance fellows," Chester chuckled, looking Mrs. Jerome straight in the eye. "You sure got to hand it to 'em. They get their split, all right, though it beats me how they do it. Maybe I'm stepping in too deep, but when I look at their rake-off at the end of the month, sometimes I think I'm in the wrong racket."

He checked his watch again as May was followed into the dining room by a thin, balding man wearing a striped-brown worsted suit. Mr. Jerome shoved his chair back and stood up. So did Chester. The dwarf whispered something to himself, and set his butter knife down.

"Hancock!" Mr. Jerome said, grabbing the man's hand and shaking it. "What brings you out here tonight?"

"Perhaps you ought to introduce our guests, dear?" his wife suggested. She smiled at Rascal, and sipped from her water glass. The dwarf had sliced his last biscuit into five identically sized triangles and arranged them on his plate in the shape of a star.

"Of course. Hancock, this young man here," said Mr. Jerome, pointing to Alvin, "is Buddy McCoy, our newest customer, and his business associates Mr. Wells, and, uh, — "

"Name's Rascal," said the dwarf, bouncing up. He stood on his chair and reached forward across the table to shake hands with Hancock. "Pleased to meet you, sir."

"Likewise," replied Hancock, disconcerted somewhat by Rascal's odd choice of clothes and general appearance. He looked back at Mr. Jerome. "Wally, I'm afraid I've got some terrible news."

"Oh?"

"Your bank was held up this afternoon," Hancock glanced at the women, then lowered his voice, "and whoever did it killed Howard, shot him in the head."

"Good God!"

Mrs. Jerome let out a gasp and sank into her chair. May, who'd been whispering with Rascal, went silent. Alvin felt the blood drain out of his face. His eyes watered and he stared down at his plate. He thought he might puke again. Chester lifted a toothpick from a vest pocket.

Hancock said, "The safe was cleaned out of cash. All they left were stocks and bonds."

Chester jumped up. "Good grief, that's Buddy's inheritance! Five thousand dollars!"

"Now, wait just a minute!" Mr. Jerome said, confusion on his face, "Let me think a minute here. When did this happen?"

"We were there until a quarter past four," said Chester, "and we didn't see anybody at all. Your fellow locked up after we left."

"The back door wasn't locked," Hancock countered. "Edna was supposed to meet Howard outside at four-thirty. When he wasn't there, she tried knocking, then found the back door unlocked and went right in. He was in your office, face down, a pillow covering his head, blood all over the floor."

"Lord Almighty!"

Alvin felt like choking now. His fingerprints were all over Chester's crime. This was the end of him, for sure, and he deserved it.

Hancock said to Mr. Jerome, "The marshals are driving over from

Kelsey. Meanwhile, we're advising folks to stay indoors and keep an eye out for strangers riding around."

"We're expected in Norman by noon tomorrow," said Chester, sliding the toothpick into his mouth. "We've got a business appointment at National Bank. A late arrival would put us in a jam."

"Howard's dead?" asked Mr. Jerome, apparently the fact of it not yet settled in his brain. He looked at Alvin, who lowered his eyes and looked away. The farm boy felt like a snake in the grass.

"Shot in the head," Hancock affirmed. "Killed like an animal on the floor of the bank."

Mrs. Jerome excused herself from the table and left the room, her daughter in tow. At the supper table, Chester complained about the lack of security at the bank and the loss of "Buddy's" family's hard-earned funds. Rascal offered to send a telegraph back to New York City for summoning detectives from the Pinkerton Agency, men with whom his family had dealt for years on a variety of secret cases. Then he left the table and disappeared into the rear of the house, presumably to the water closet behind the kitchen.

Alvin slipped away outdoors.

It was almost pleasant now. Along the prairie horizon, twilight darkened the Nebraska sky. A barking Irish setter chased a chicken into the barn and shot away again, on the run elsewhere. May came out onto the porch and sat in a wooden swing, looking west toward the prairie. Alvin walked over toward her and stared across the yard. This ruse was cruel and he felt ashamed to be part of it, but was too afraid to admit his guilt, so he said nothing.

"I'm sorry you lost your money," May told him as she swayed gently in the swing. Her eyes were soft with tears. "I'm sure my father will do everything he can to get it back for you."

Alvin nodded and leaned against the porch railing. The sky was a reddish-purple on its western edge, lingering color before the dark. In the distance, a flock of sparrows soared over the prairie toward a grain silo on the next farm.

"I think stealing is awful," May continued, "particularly when it's from people who've worked their whole lives to save up. My father says those aren't men at all, but mad dogs who ought to be rounded up and hung like horse thieves. He says violence is all their kind understand. Fight fire with fire."

Alvin nodded again, having no real idea what to say. He watched the dusk-wind flutter in her hair, saw the sunlight at the end of the day glisten in her eyes. The Irish setter barked out back of the barn, howling at drifting shadows in the empty fields.

May got up off the swing and went forward to the railing just away from Alvin. She watched her dog cross under the fence and romp into the wheat. She shouted to him, "Max! Maximilian!" Hunting in the wild fields, the setter ignored her, preferring to run.

"I got a dog at home," said Alvin, after May stopped calling.

"You do?"

"He's a bloodhound, chases squirrels and rabbits. Or at least, he used to. He can barely shuffle down off the porch nowadays. He's getting on, I guess."

"What's his name?"

"Red."

"That's nice."

"My daddy picked it out, on account of Red's got big old red eyes."

May nodded and looked back out to the west. "I love animals. Mother and Father do, too. That's why we moved out here from town. I wanted to have a horse, so Father bought me Tillie. She was a Paint. I rode her everywhere — to town and back, over to my friend Nellie's, everywhere. She just died last year. We buried her over there behind the barn."

"I seen men riding horses across the Mississippi in the dark once."

"How cruel!"

"Pardon?"

"I mean, those poor animals. They must've been terrified."

"I don't know." Alvin shrugged, feeling a strange chill. "It was dark."

Both May and Alvin put their backs to the wind. When Alvin turned his head again to cough, Rascal was walking out from behind the house with a chicken in his arms. The dwarf was humming to himself while scratching the chicken's beak with his right forefinger. Just outside the barn door, the chicken leaped from the dwarf's grasp and ran for the fence. Rascal gave chase. Scared by his pursuit, the chicken changed direction and flew back into the middle of the yard. Rascal ran hard after it, knees bent almost to the dirt, arms outstretched wide, clucking with his tongue, acting crazy. He dove at the chicken and missed. It scurried across the yard and up onto a fencepost, screeching with fright.

The screen door opened and Chester came out, followed by Hancock and Mr. Jerome. He put his hat on while surveying the yard out front and told the farm boy, "We're leaving."

Hancock drew a pocketwatch from his vest, checked the hour, and mumbled something to Mr. Jerome that Alvin was unable to hear. Chester turned back to the other men and shook hands with both of them. He flicked the toothpick away and walked down the steps and headed for the Packard.

"I guess I got to get along," Alvin said to May, reluctant to leave. He decided she was the prettiest girl he had ever met. He tipped his cap. "Pleased to have made your acquaintance."

"Nice meeting you, too."

"Well, so long now."

"So long."

Alvin swung his legs over the railing and dropped down into the yard. A breeze gusted again, sweeping up clouds of dust, forcing Alvin to cover his face as he followed Chester to the automobile. The dwarf was already there, perched up in the backseat, a long chicken feather stuck in the thinning white hair behind his ear. Back on the porch, May leaned forward, her elbows on the railing. Mr. Jerome stood side by side at the top of the stairs with Hancock, both staring west into the late sunset. Chester steered the Packard out of the yard.

They drove about four miles along the narrow highway to the west, riding in silence through the warm evening. Alvin sat back in the seat, one arm out the window, and daydreamed about going fishing with May. *She'd have hold of his hand, her tiny fingers entwined in his, sitting on the riverbank, maybe whistling an Irish folk tune or two. She'd be quiet and listen while he talked about working with Frenchy on his daddy's farm, riding to dances on a buckboard and home again by moonlight. He'd tell her about the consumption and she'd take him in her arms and tell him how badly she felt about his sickness, her skin milky white in the darkness under the cottonwoods, her young eyes reflecting starlight, her lips redder than —*

The dwarf poked him in the back of the head. "Someone's coming after us."

"Huh?"

Alvin twisted in the seat to get a better look as Chester checked the mirror. About a quarter mile back, an automobile, headlamps glowing bright, raced toward the Packard.

"He's driving like a rocket," observed the dwarf. "He'll catch us in a minute."

"Can we outrun him?" Alvin asked Chester, certain it was federal marshals the instant he saw the approaching headlights. Instead of speeding up, however, Chester slowed the Packard to less than twenty miles an hour. The other automobile roared up from behind, closing until its headlamps illuminated every strand of white hair on Rascal's head. Its horn beeped twice and Chester ran the Packard over to the side of the road. A blue Nash "400" sedan pulled up alongside, George Hancock behind the wheel. He sat there a few seconds, staring at Chester and his two traveling companions. Then he eased back on the throttle, quieting the motor.

"I know what you fellows did," said Hancock, hands falling to his lap. His eyes met Alvin's for a moment, and moved on to the dwarf and back to Chester, fixing each as if for memory's sake. "We're not all hicks from the sticks out here."

Chester fidgeted with the gear lever and the button at the bottom of his shirt. Alvin tried to slow his racing heart by taking measured breaths, in and out, in and out. The dwarf sat rock-still just back of his shoulder. Chester squinted his eyes and looked across at Hancock. "What's your game, mister?"

Dry stalks of corn on both sides of the road shook as a breeze gusted and dust blew up over the hoods of both cars in its draft. No one blinked.

His face to the wind, Hancock said, "I saw you and that kid there go into the Union Bank this afternoon. I saw you both come out again, one after the other a quarter of an hour past closing time. I also saw Edna Evans go around back, looking for her husband at four-thirty. I never saw anyone else. Before or after."

Chester steeled his gaze at Hancock. "Is that so?"

The wind gusted again in the cornrows and rained dust across the windshields of both vehicles.

"I'll shoot square with you, Wells, or whatever your name is," Hancock said. "I didn't care for you from the moment I laid eyes on you. Oh, I've been to Chicago, all right, and I've seen plenty fresh fellows of your kind, swaggering through fancy restaurants, throwing money around like Carnegie, pretending to be respectable. You might've fooled Walter, but you didn't fool me. I know what you are. I didn't say so back at Jerome's out of fear for his family's lives, but I'm saying it now because I'm not afraid of you. Not one iota. Oh, I guess you're pretty tough when you've got the upper hand on somebody who's — "

"Look here, Hancock," Chester interrupted. "I'm afraid what we're having is a case of misapprehension."

"You're a liar, too."

"No, sir," Chester replied, "Not at all, and I'll prove it to you. Let me ride with you back into Stantonsburg. We'll put everything square."

Chester smiled at Hancock who eyed him back in return, clearly taken off guard by Chester's offer. Warily, Hancock asked, "Yeah? What about these two fellows?"

Chester shrugged. "Buddy here and the midget can drive on alone to Norman tonight. I'll worry about catching up to them once you and I've worked out our little misunderstanding."

Hancock studied him. "The marshals'll be at Stantonsburg in half an hour. I plan on driving straight into town to take it up with them. What do you say to that?"

"I'd say that'd be swell by me. I'd like to get this baloney cleared up in a hurry."

Chester opened the door and stepped out into the road. Only the irregular humming of twin automobile motors disturbed the quiet.

"All right, get in the car," Hancock said, flipping open the passenger door. "And don't try pulling anything. I know a few tricks of my own." He folded his jacket open to show a revolver in the waistband.

Chester smirked. "I'm sure you do. Just let me get my hat." Reaching into the foot-well of the backseat beside the dwarf, he murmured to Alvin, "Forget Norman. You boys drive on through to Council Bluffs and hire us a couple rooms at the Dakota Hotel. I'll meet you there at eight in the morning."

Then Chester snatched his hat up and crossed the road, jumping into the seat next to Hancock. He gave Alvin a wave and shouted, "Take care of my auto, kid!"

A moment later, George Hancock spun the blue Nash around in a half circle and accelerated back down the long empty road toward Stantonsburg. Alvin and the dwarf watched until the exhaust cloud spun into ether and the red taillights were swallowed up in the broadening dark.

ALLENVILLE, IOWA

SIX MILES EAST OF ALLENVILLE, an hour toward twilight, the farm boy and the dwarf found matching headstones beneath a shady oak tree in an old pioneer cemetery and sat down to watch the sunset on the prairie horizon. The plots were laid out on a mound, rising thirty feet or so above the great expanse of grass and wildflowers that led to the edges of the sky. Below the mound, down a path that wound through an old stand of white oaks and bitternut hickory and across a narrow creek bed, was a ramshackle house facing a road that ran east, perhaps even as far as the Mississippi River. The August sky was windless, stems of surrounding grass and leaves of the trees under which the dwarf and the farm boy sat were quiet in the soft roselight at the end of the day. The dwarf curled his legs under himself and leaned back against the tombstone while the farm boy stretched out his own legs through white larkspur almost to the next headstone. No one had been buried on the mound in many years and the wooden gravemarkers scattered haphazardly about the finer granite tombstones were weathered nearly blank, their testimony and witness to the dead long worn off by wind and sun.

"I, myself," said the dwarf, "would prefer a simple grave, perhaps in my garden beneath the pear tree, there where another child might till the earth above my corpse and plant tomatoes in my belly, let my legacy be quickened fertilizer come season." He frowned. "Of course, Auntie would never permit it. We're all to be entombed together in a great marble cenotaph overlooking the Missouri River by a grove of willows where everyone who passes by will comment on how pompous our family must have been. I've often considered an anonymous death, perhaps being run down by a train out of state somewhere, in hope of avoiding an eternity of humiliation."

The dwarf played his fingers through the petals of purple morning glory between his knees. Sunlight, reddened by the hour, shone on the pallid skin of his face and lit his eyes as he stared directly into the sunset, smiling an unspoken thought. The farm boy had rolled over onto his belly and traced the carving on the tombstone in front of him with a forefinger, scratching flecks of dirt away with an overgrown nail, slowly marking by touch the immutable dates of birth and death.

OLIVER HEDDISON HENDRICK
BORN
JAN. 23 1853
DIED
JUNE 8 1877
NATIVE OF OHIO
AGED 24 YR'S SIX MO'S 15 DA'S

In this green land, his heart found peace,
In God's sweet arms, his soul now sleeps.

The farm boy said, "It don't matter much to me at all where I go afterward. Once I'm dead, I'm dead, and I don't figure I'll be caring all that much."

"Oh, I disagree," replied the dwarf. "In truth, Auntie assured me long ago that as we're all signed and sealed over to the afterlife, the choices we make in the here-and-now bear directly upon how much we'll enjoy God's offerings in the Great Reward."

"Huh?"

"Whose day our Lord saw fit to bless, receives at dusk a finer rest."

"Well then, I guess you and me got things all twisted up, don't we?"

The farm boy stood and took a long look into the west, shading his eyes against the sun, and spat. On this mound, the long prairie grasses grew fully and wildflowers bloomed free of plow and scythe. Tall soft tails of switchgrass leaned up just slightly higher than the lanky farm boy's belt buckle. Below the mound, a soft breeze swept across the fields like the gentle swells of a sundown sea. If he looked far enough into the west, he could glimpse the painted grain silos of the farms encircling Allenville where boys like himself labored in the day's end, counting the minutes down to supper and then maybe a few hours of freedom afterward in the dark.

The dwarf got up, too, wandering across the cemetery to another plot of headstones, these ringed in ornamental wrought iron and set upon by weeds and stems of yellow goatsbeard. The gate to the plot was missing and the surrounding rail had rusted and broken in several places and the headstones themselves were fractured by intruding vegetation both crossways and up from the gravesites. Although the dates of birth and death were yet legible on the old granite, the names were gone, weathered into anonymity by sixty long seasons.

The dwarf murmured, "In daydream we recall what our hearts thought buried."

His thin white hair glistened in the sunlight and his skin appeared almost limpid. He turned to the farm boy. "Are you much disposed toward recollection?"

Ignoring the dwarf's question, the farm boy strolled over to a wood marker stuck in the dirt within a patch of prairie rose and knelt down for a closer look.

Shielding his eyes with the back of one hand, the dwarf walked toward the western edge of the mound, parallel to the farm boy, staying within earshot for conversation sake. Just ahead, a small stone angel was posed in shawl and rose wreath atop a granite block, eyes gazing south, look of contentment carved onto a cherubic face.

Staring up at the statue, the dwarf recited another old rhyme, "When a mother dies, young forth to bring, her soul is borne on angel's wings."

Now the farm boy came up behind him to have his own look at the stone angel. "That thing must've cost some high coin." He circled it slowly, looking for an inscription that was absent. "Spend all that money, you'd think they'd include a name or something to let folks know who they're looking at and all."

When he came around to the front again, the farm boy noticed the dwarf was rocking back and forth on his heels like he did when he was occupied with himself. His eyes were glassy, a half-smile of sorts on his lips, arms akimbo.

"Does she look like some person you been acquainted with?" asked the farm boy. He took another look at the stone angel. "I guess she's sort of pretty."

The dwarf stopped rocking and coughed once. His eyes watered from the effort and he shook. After clearing his throat of the dust they had both been inhaling on a dozen back roads leading out of Nebraska, the dwarf drew a clean breath and remarked, "My mother passed away granting me life. Auntie said she suffered greatly giving birth to me, but refused to cease her struggle until I came forth. She lost consciousness an instant after I drew my first breath in this world and her valiant heart stopped before she ever saw my face. Auntie told me the midwife heard a faint flutter of wings above my dear mother's bed as she died." The dwarf looked up at the farm boy. "Do you believe in the unseen?"

Having no answer for the dwarf's question, the farm boy shrugged and studied instead the stone angel whose expression seemed to change ever so slightly in the angle of the sun's path across the sky. In Farrington, he had witnessed a cow choke to death trying to swallow an apple whole, witnessed a hound dog get his rib cage crushed running blind under the iron wheels of a loaded hay wagon. He had seen a stroke take a traveling salesman on Uncle Henry's front porch and a heart attack steal away Grandpa Chamberlain, interrupting him at Sunday dinner with his mouth full of sweet potatoes, and how Uncle Otis's eyes twitched and his tongue lolled about when he broke his neck falling drunk off the barn on the Fourth of July in the summer of 1921. The only wings Alvin had ever heard during the dying were those belonging to his momma's chickens flapping in the yard out of doors. In his experience, when God came for you, be it quick or be it slow, it was done in silence. One moment you're here, the next you're gone. Wink of an eye. Neither was it wondrous or beautiful. Dead squirrels smelled up the woods in summer. Cows and dogs stunk, too, even worse if they weren't gotten rid of soon enough. Grandpa Chamberlain owned a particular odor in the casket he never had in life. The consumption wards at the sanitarium reeked of antiseptics and gloom. Death drew a peculiar shade down on the living, not just putting out the light, but changing the color, too, into something waxy and pale. Something ugly.

"My mother had eyes blue as the sea," the dwarf told him. "She played the piano and sang after supper for people passing by out of doors. Auntie said she danced on the front porch in the dark before bedtime and wrote poems to everyone she knew. I'm told they were quite beautiful."

"When I get the call," the farm boy muttered, "I hope they nail the casket shut and not let anyone have a look-see at all. I'd like to be recollected as a living person, not some hollowed-out scarecrow in a black box."

Now late sunlight gave the stone angel a pink hue as a cool breeze swept slowly through the grass. Insects tossed and spun in its wake. Below the cemetery, a solitary flock of sparrows sailed east across the prairie.

"Sacred is the breath of life in our lungs," the dwarf recited, "God's precious gift by death now undone."

The farm boy sat down in the grass beside a patch of black-eyed susan. He pulled his knees up to his chest and lowered his eyes. The dwarf walked around back of the stone angel so that the statue blocked the last rays of sunlight from the red west. Then, in the shadow of the angel, he whispered a prayer for himself and the farm boy, and waited for evening to fall.

Along the road to Allenville was a tourist camp in a sheltering wood of black walnut and sycamore trees. Alvin Pendergast sat on a narrow spring-cot in one of the small cabins, listening to rain and thunder in the summer dark. He had just awakened from a nap and was alone. The one-room cabin was drafty and his cotton mattress smelled moldy and worn out. Next to the camp was a roadside stand popular with motorists. Because it was a weekend, plenty of automobiles were parked out front. Alvin heard a couple of fellows slosh past through the mud singing, *"How pleasant is Saturday night when you've tried all the week to be good."* Both were drunk.

From his cot, Alvin stared out into the dark where a gust rippled through the leafy sycamores. Water leaked into a corner of the cabin, dripping steadily into a pot they had borrowed from a family traveling to the Badlands. Dampness clouded his lungs. Alvin grabbed his shoes from beside the iron cot and put them on. He felt rheumy and vaguely depressed. The dwarf had gone out at twilight, just before the rain began, and left him alone to sleep. A round of thunder had awakened him from a fitful dream in which he had been cornered behind a downtown show window by federal marshals and shot down mercilessly like a dog. His mother had been there, too, and he had cried for her to hold him as he bled. He had such dreams often in the sanitarium, cloudy black nightmares of drowning and doctors dressed as undertakers pushing squeaky-wheeled gurneys through unlit wards.

He coughed harshly and put his cap on and went outdoors into the drizzling rain. There were people all about, some sitting on the stoops of the small cabins, others crowded into touring tents or huddled under blankets in automobile beds. Across the camp, Alvin saw a pack of grimy children splashing gleefully in the mud and wondered where their folks were. He smelled wood smoke on the humid rain-washed air and a chicken roasting on a barbecue spit nearby. Electric lights glowed on a tall wire from one end of the camp to the other. He heard a concertina playing and walked in that direction. Rain dripped from the sycamores. Voices rose and echoed across the darkness like the ceaseless chatter of the sanitarium hallways that had kept him awake night after night when he was his sickest. A motor horn beeped and Alvin looked just quickly enough to see a liquor bottle shatter against a thick black walnut tree. A lucifer match flared and a woman laughed from the rainy shadows behind one of the cabins. She called out and the farm boy stopped and stared into the dark and a big derby-hatted man came forth soaking wet and stared back at him. Alvin almost gave him the raspberry, but knew he wasn't fit enough to scrap with a fellow that husky. The cabin door opened and a woman in curlpapers stuck her head out, saw the derby-hatted man, and shouted a dirty word at him. Alvin watched him zip open his trousers and piss across the mud toward the cabin door as it slammed shut again. Then the man closed his trousers and barked his own filthy obscenity and Alvin went off into the dark without looking back.

He sloshed past the middle of the auto camp where the sewer on the other side of the registration hut smelled ugly and foul. When the gang of soggy children ran by, Alvin kicked mud at them and they squealed with laughter. Rain poured down harder and a gusting breeze shook the wire of lights. Somewhere ahead, a pitchman called numbers for a beano game. Then Alvin saw a tent ringed with electric lanterns and picnic tables under the canvas roof and a crowd bigger than ever, the dwarf among them.

"93, LADIES AND GENTS, 93!"

The caller stood atop a makeshift podium with a megaphone, drawing game numbers scribbled on small wooden disks from a cigar box. The dwarf was sitting at a table with five other tourists: a ruddy-faced man in a squam hat and a slicker coat, and four women Alvin's mother's age in rainproof cotton or gabardine twill coats and hats. Each had a game card and a pile of dried beans beside it.

"Come in out of the rain, young fellow!" the ruddy fellow called out. "Pull up a chair!" He held a cheap stogie cigar between his teeth.

"Is this him?" one of the women in gabardine asked the dwarf. She wore a mesh net in her hair and a stick of punk behind one ear.

Rascal fiddled with his beans, then looked up with a smile. "Why, yes it is. Although I didn't think he'd ever wake up."

Still muddleheaded from his nap, Alvin walked in under the tent covering while the pitchman called out another beano number.

"15, LADIES AND GENTS, 15!"

Water dripped on the table from his cap as Alvin shuffled himself into a folding chair. He felt as if everybody at the beano game had their eye on him and worried what the dwarf had told them. Alvin was used to keeping things confidential himself and didn't trust the dwarf not to feed them the wrong dope. He knew Rascal would tell a lie for a piece of toast.

"Want a card?" the older fellow asked him. "We'll get you one up front."

Alvin coughed again and shook his head, not feeling much like playing games tonight. He hated beano, anyhow. His aunts played it at the Farrington auditorium once a month for a nickel a card and Uncle Henry thought it was a smart racket, even though Aunt Clara told Hattie that beans were for eating, which Alvin thought was pretty funny.

"We're from Ashtabula," said the woman with the punk in her hair. Did she just give Alvin the glad eye? "My name's Margaret and these are my friends Alice, Hazel and Bertha. We're Couéists on a pilgrimage."

"*Day by day, in every way, I'm getting better and better,*" the dwarf chirped, quoting Émile Coué's famous auto-suggestion.

"Indeed, we are," Margaret enthused.

"Glad to know you," Alvin said, politely, although truthfully he didn't really care one way or another. He had met quite a lot of people on the road since Easter and could just as soon have given them all the raspberry. He felt his forehead for a fever and found it warm. He knew he ought to go back to the cabin and lie down again, but he also wanted to see what sort of stunt the dwarf was putting over on these dumbbells.

"I told you, this ain't no roadside pulpit," said the man with the cigar. "How about we just play the game and let this little fellow finish his story."

"Certainly," Margaret agreed.

The other three women smiled sweetly at the farm boy. One of them down at the end of the table wearing ear puffs gave him a wink. She reminded him of the old nurses he knew at the sanitarium who fed him cod liver oil five times a day and made him walk up and down the halls with his bottom showing and joked about it when they thought he was asleep.

Thunder rumbled in the rainy distance and Alvin saw lightning flash. He sniffed the damp air and decided it was warmer than before he had taken his nap, which meant a thunderstorm rising. Alvin wondered what everyone was doing out here playing beano under a tent in this weather. If a tornado blew through this tourist camp, that'd be it.

"42, LADIES AND GENTS, 42!"

"Where was I?" the dwarf asked, sliding a bean onto his card. He seemed preoccupied, distracted by an errant thought. Alvin wondered if Rascal had a worry in the world besides where his next meal was coming from. Not a damned thing since Hadleyville had seemed to trouble him.

"Mosquitoes of the foreign tropics," the ruddy fellow said, tapping ash off his cigar into the mud behind him. He smiled at Alvin and gave him a friendly nod. The farm boy looked away.

Margaret interjected, "Speaking of which, I've been bitten so often this summer I feel like a dartboard. Isn't that true, Alice? Our tourist sleeper hasn't proven to be bug-proof at all, has it?"

"No, dear," the woman seated across from Margaret replied. "Not at all. We need a shower of Flit."

She wore eyeglasses that had fogged up in the rainy air. How she could see her card well enough to play was a mystery.

"You ought to've bought a good wall tent like I suggested," said the woman with ear puffs. Alvin noticed that her card already had three beans horizontal on the middle row. "You know, Hazel and I haven't had any bother whatsoever with mosquitoes."

"Well, Bertha, I should say you've been very fortunate, indeed," Margaret remarked, forcing a smile. "They've given us thunder this entire trip."

"Yes, but Hazel and I also prepared well."

"I tell you," Alice insisted, "we ought to have brought along some Flit."

"9, LADIES AND GENTS, 9!"

"Actually, my mother's used oil of cloves for years," said Hazel, fixing her own elastic hair net, "and she's never been mosquito bit. Not once."

That explained the spicy odor Alvin had smelled when he sat down at the table.

Putting a bean on his card, the ruddy-faced fellow said, "When I was with the First Nebraska at Manila in '98, we seen mosquitoes the size of hummingbirds. If you got bit by one of them, you were finished. It's the sickliest place on earth."

"I detest mosquitoes of all sorts," Margaret said, with a shiver. "They're despicable pests."

"Well, thanks to the mosquito," the dwarf said, trying to maneuver himself back into the conversation, "poor Uncle Augustus was virtually addicted to quinine for the final thirty-three years of his life. He never recovered from the recurring spells of malaria he contracted on a secret mission for Queen Victoria to Java."

"Where?" the farm boy asked, hoping to get under his skin. Whenever Alvin felt sick, he enjoyed sharing his misery with others. Easiest was making his sisters cry. Mary Ann acted like a baby whenever she got teased. Everyone in the family hated that.

"The Dutch East Indies."

"Never heard of it," Alvin said, with a practiced sneer and a fake giggle.

The dwarf clucked his tongue. "Well, it's very far away in the Java Sea, south of Borneo. You know, you really ought to consider studying geography some day."

"Says you."

"44, LADIES AND GENTS, 44."

Margaret shifted a bean onto her card, then told the dwarf, "My friends and I hope to travel around the world one day."

"We believe all roads lead to Rome," said Bertha, winking again at Alvin.

"You ever been to Borneo?" the ruddy fellow asked Rascal after a puff on his cigar.

The dwarf shook his head. "No, but twice dear old Uncle Augustus circumnavigated the globe. He was the bravest man I ever knew. His photograph was taken on six continents and I saw each of them on the walls of his library when I was a boy. At every supper, he led us in a toast to the seven seas, '*Sail and sail, with unshut eye / Round the world for ever and aye.*'"

"He ought to've been with me and Dewey at Manila in '98. Now, there was something to sing about."

"I want to hear this little fellow's story about Queen Victoria," Bertha said, playing with her beans.

"Yes," Margaret agreed. "Let's hear his story."

"Are you certain?" the dwarf asked. "It's quite frightening."

"Are there ghosts involved?" asked Hazel, a slight tremble in her voice. Alvin almost laughed aloud. Now he knew these folks were dumbbells.

"No," Rascal replied, "but there'll be many horrible deaths. I had nightmares for a month after I first heard the story myself."

"Oh, I adore a good nightmare!" said Alice. "Do tell your story."

"Sure, go ahead," the ruddy fellow agreed.

"All right." The dwarf smiled. "Well, in April of 1883, my Uncle Augustus and a fellow from Stepney by the name of Louis Hurlburt hired onto a tramp steamer as firemen sailing to Java. Apparently, the Queen was quite worried about Dutch intentions concerning Singapore and wished to discover how earnest its colonial regents had become. Uncle Augustus said Java was a wonderful paradise of the most lovely orchids and ancient temples, yet also terribly dangerous in those years. Why, a grown man might be gored to death by a wild ox, drown into a dark mangrove swamp, or earn his fortune in oil and rubber according to the whims of fate."

"Gee, maybe I'd ought to go hunting there one day," Alvin interrupted, as thunder rumbled in the distance. The rain had lightened to a steady drizzle, hissing in the cottonwoods nearby.

"Oh, I should think you'd be fortunate not to be eaten by a royal tiger. It's one of the most perilous jungles on earth."

"36, LADIES AND GENTS, 36!"

"I wouldn't be at all ascared. I shot a bear once from my bedroom window."

"Now, that takes some doing," the ruddy fellow remarked, placing a bean on his card.

"Sure it does."

"Well, having devoted considerable study of my own to the Dutch East Indies," the dwarf continued, "I've always been astonished by the course Mother Nature took in that strange corner of the earth. Did you know there are wild fig trees in the forests of Java whose branches droop downward to become roots for even more trees? Its leaves are so large, the Javanese natives use them as plates for their meat. And there are great bats with wings five feet or more across. I've read authentic reports of sleeping babies snatched from their bamboo cradles and whisked away into the dark by those infernal creatures."

"My goodness!" Margaret exclaimed. "That isn't true, is it?"

Alvin shook his head. " 'Course it ain't. He's just pulling your leg."

"Look it up in the *Geographic*," Rascal said. "Only a month after sailing into Bantam Bay, Uncle Augustus saw lemurs hunting birds at night with eyes that glowed red as coals. Why, he personally killed a wild hog and six Java musks for food when he became lost in the jungle by the Vale of Poison at Butar, where he nearly perished in a fog of deadly carbonic acid gas after rescuing two hundred Javanese native children from Dutch slavery inside a secret diamond mine."

"Well, I'll be switched," said the ruddy fellow.

"What a marvelous story!" Alice remarked.

"56, LADIES AND GENTS, 56!"

The dwarf studied his card for a moment. "Oh, it's only the beginning. You see, Java is called the 'Land of Fire' because of its many volcanoes. Above the blue sea, in the Straits of Sunda, one of these fire towers, Mount Perboewatan on Krakatau, began spewing smoke and steam. Naturally, my uncle and Mr. Hurlburt were somewhat concerned, but after the Queen wired a secret message ordering them both to remain in Java, there could be no thought of departing. Posing as Pieter Van Dijk, a coffee and tobacco grader from Amsterdam, Uncle Augustus traveled all summer from port to port within the Straits, while hot volcanic ash rained down upon the sea and a huge black thundercloud of smoke spread out from Krakatau. In the meantime,

Louis Hurlburt had secured a position as a stoker aboard the Dutch mail steamer *Governor General Loudon*, which was ferrying interested parties back and forth to the volcanic island for scientific observation. Uncle Augustus sailed there in late May and was quite astounded by the smoke clouds and the constant hail of stones and fire. He went ashore with a crew of engineers. The wide beach was buried under a foot of thick pumice and two feet of ash. All vegetation on Krakatau had disappeared, only bare stumps and a few leafless trees remained and the air smelled of sulfuric acid. Uncle Augustus gathered up a small collection of black pitchstones when he left Krakatau. In fact, I have one of them in my bedroom at home. It's a wonderful souvenir."

"19, LADIES AND GENTS, 19!"

"Oh, I'd love to see it one day," Bertha said, then checked her card. She sighed.

The dwarf smiled at her. "Perhaps you shall."

At another table, a woman rose with a child in her arms and walked off into the rainy dark toward the roadside stand. She was crying. Alvin saw a fellow in suspenders and a felt hat jump up and start after her. The pitchman left the podium and caught the fellow at the edge of the tent and had a few words with him. Some people at another table began hooting for the pitchman to go back to the podium.

The dwarf said, "Well, by August, Mount Danan on Krakatau had also erupted and all the Straits were cast into utter darkness. On Sunday the twenty-sixth, Uncle Augustus crossed from Prinsen Island north to Telok Betong at Sumatra where he had a dinner appointment with a Dutch admiral who much admired good cigars. The admiral's daughter, Elise Van Leeuwen, who also attended, negotiated a trade with my uncle involving a crate of South American coffee for a collection of lovely Java sparrows Miss Van Leeuwen had recently purchased at Katimbang. By now, ships had arrived from all over the world, maneuvering in the Straits to witness the great paroxysm. Lightning flashed in the black clouds over Krakatau. Earthquakes rumbled across the islands. The admiral's daughter grew fearful and left dinner early for a steamer heading back east across the Straits to

Anjer. After she had gone, Uncle Augustus began proposing a toast
to the glory of Dutch rule in the East Indies when a tremendous explosion thundered across the Straits. Uncle Augustus rushed from the
saloon with the admiral to watch a great black cloud rise into the dark
heavens from Krakatau. He knew he ought to quit the port, as well, but
a morning telegraph from Anjer had stated that the *Loudon* was already
en route to Telok Betong, and Uncle Augustus felt duty bound to wait
for Mr. Hurlburt. The admiral, however, decided to leave immediately
aboard the gunboat *Berouw* to evacuate both his wife and daughter for
Batavia on the northwestern coast of Java. After saying good-bye to his
worried host, Uncle Augustus went to have one last glass of whiskey at
the Bergen Hotel near the River Koeripan."

The pitchman quit arguing with the fellow in the felt hat and went
back to the podium where he grabbed another disk. "71, LADIES
AND GENTS, 71!"

"An old soak, was he?" said the ruddy fellow, leaning back in his
chair. He laughed out loud.

Alvin saw a woman wearing a cotton dress and a blue Sunday bonnet
join the pitchman at the podium. She spoke in his ear, which appeared
to upset him, because he spilled the cigar box of disks into the mud.

Rascal frowned. "I beg your pardon? Misusing liquor was very
common in those days and I'm sure the volcanic rain had quite a lot to
do with his intemperance that dark afternoon."

"You said it."

The pitchman climbed down off the podium to retrieve the disks
while the woman in the Sunday bonnet shook a finger at him. A gust
of wind rippled the string of lights.

The dwarf scowled. "Look here, none of us can imagine in the
least what it must've been like to feel the very earth tremble underfoot like Judgment Day. Now, as I was saying, when Uncle Augustus
finally left the hotel, he found people dashing here and there, carrying
their children and valuables away from the port. Another infernal blast
thundered across the black waters from Krakatau and within the hour
a rain of ash and stones began to fall. The wind was blowing fiercely
from the northwest when Uncle Augustus stood on the pier looking

across Lampong Bay for the *Loudon* and saw the first volcanic waves approaching from Krakatau. They rose from the sea much too quickly to permit escape by anyone on the shore. Having nowhere to go, Uncle Augustus ran to the end of the pier and dove into the bay just ahead of the first big sea wave. When he rose again from the deep, he saw the waves had swamped the pier and poured across the postal road into town, destroying the government offices and all the other buildings at sea level and chasing the survivors up to the District Hall on higher ground. The crew of a pilot boat that had ridden out the danger in deeper water found Uncle Augustus grasping a wooden crate. He was given dry clothing and a cup of hot tea and a biscuit and told to stay off the decks as large stones from Krakatau were falling now all across the Straits. Soon, the salt ship *Marie* anchored nearby and signaled the arrival of the *Loudon* from Anjer, and Uncle Augustus persuaded the captain of the pilot boat to ferry him over to the mail steamer."

Once the pitchman had collected the muddy disks, he climbed back up onto the podium and called out the next number: "18, LADIES AND GENTS, 18!" The woman in the Sunday bonnet scowled behind his back.

"Oh, your uncle must've been awfully brave," Bertha remarked. She found a place for another bean on her card. Alvin saw she had three now in a vertical column.

"Of course he was," Margaret said, clearly disgusted with her own card that had no more than two beans side by side anywhere across its surface. "Now, stop interrupting!"

Suddenly, the woman in the Sunday bonnet snatched a handful of disks from the cigar box. The pitchman reached for them, but the woman refused to give them back. As the caller grabbed at them again, she backed away. Alvin heard cackling from another table.

"The sea was rising and falling almost by the minute now. Lightning glowed in the smoke over the volcano and warm pumice littered the water. Aboard the *Loudon*, Uncle Augustus inquired as to Louis Hurlburt and was told he'd left the steamship at Anjer. His companion apparently intended to row north to a secret telegraph station in a sugar mill near the port of Merak to send a message to the

Queen, informing her of the great cataclysm. However, the *Loudon* had already heard from the telegraph master at Anjer, reporting damage at the drawbridge there, boats smashed everywhere, and word that high waves had entirely destroyed the Chinese camp at Merak. Sometime after midnight, Uncle Augustus and the crew of the *Loudon* saw another great wave rise from Lampong Bay and sweep toward the port, destroying the harbor light and the warehouse and a coal storage on the pier and briefly capsizing the *Marie*, throwing the admiral's gunboat *Berouw* from the east side of the pier clear over to the other."

Still lacking a handful of disks, the caller took one from the cigar box. "64, LADIES AND GENTS, 64!"

Margaret scowled over her card. "Oh, fiddle-faddle!"

Shuffling another bean onto his card, the ruddy fellow tapped ash off his cigar, then asked, "Didn't no one there know how to drop an anchor?"

"Yeah, how about that?" Alvin agreed, hoping to see Rascal squirm over this dumbbell story of his.

"Of course," the dwarf replied, adding another bean to his own card, "but the volcanic waves were so enormous, not even an anchor could hold the ships against their fury. Why, Uncle Augustus said he'd never been so frightened in all his life. Blue flames of St. Elmo's fire flew about the sky and the wind that swept over the *Loudon* smelled of hot sulphur like Hades itself. The sea was so rough, Uncle Augustus was obliged to remain aboard the mail steamer until dawn, listening all night long to the explosions from Krakatau becoming louder and louder until half past five when a blast unlike anything Uncle Augustus had heard on this earth shook the *Loudon* and knocked out the ear drums on half the members of the ship's crew. He saw the admiral's gunboat beached high up on the shore and insisted the ship's boat take him back across the bay to the *Berouw* to help his old Dutch friend. Well, of course, the journey was trying beyond faith. The sea was filled with masses of floating pumice, and lightning struck the mast conductor repeatedly, and a furious wind tore at the decks. When the first mate refused to bring the boat any closer than a quarter mile from the port, Uncle Augustus dove into the bay once again and swam alone to shore through the dangerous surf. All was chaos aboard the stranded *Berouw*. Several members of the gunboat's crew had been swept overboard by the wave that had carried them onto the beach and the admiral had been struck in the head by a fallen cocoa-nut tree and knocked unconscious."

Alvin asked, "Were there any wild monkeys in the tree that hit him?"

Bertha and Hazel both giggled.

A scowl on his face, the pitchman took two disks from the cigar box. "58, LADIES AND GENTS, 58! DO WE HAVE A WINNER YET?"

"No, I don't believe so," replied the dwarf, sounding testy now. "Would you mind awfully not interrupting? Poor Uncle Augustus was in a terrible scrape. Why, it's one of God's greatest miracles that he came out alive."

"When does he get the malaria?" Alvin asked.

"Soon!" growled the dwarf. "For heaven sakes, will you please keep quiet?"

"Go on," said the ruddy fellow, "finish the story."

"Thank you, sir. Now, where were we?"

"A scrape in a cocoa-nut tree."

"17, LADIES AND GENTS, 17!"

The dwarf shifted a bean onto the middle of his card, and continued with his story. "Oh, yes. Well, those fortunate souls at Telok Betong who survived the initial sea-waves returned to the village again to gather up their remaining possessions while Uncle Augustus labored furiously with the crew of the *Berouw* to get her back into the bay. More boats were washed ashore from the harbor and Uncle Augustus said the sky was blacker than the blackest night and hot pumice big as pumpkins rained down upon them as they worked. Of course, the effort was hopeless. Within the hour, four more volcanic waves rolled over the port, stranding the *Berouw* farther up on the beach and drowning another half-dozen members of the crew, including the poor old admiral, the captain, and his first navigating officer. Uncle Augustus felt quite terrible. He advised everyone to abandon the gunboat and find safe shelter from the waves and the mud rains and the furious wind. The *Marie* had already pulled up anchor and left for deeper waters. Then came a sound Uncle Augustus described as God Himself clapping His hands together, and the black smoke clouds brightened to a fearsome crimson over Krakatau as the volcano gave a mighty roar and blew itself to heaven with the greatest explosion ever witnessed by mortal man! Within minutes, Uncle Augustus saw a gigantic wave emerge from the briny deep and rush toward the shore. Most of the crew ran in panic for the jungle. Knowing he had no chance to escape on foot, Uncle Augustus hid down alone in the captain's cabin, closing himself in and awaiting his fate in the dark. When the huge sea wave struck the *Berouw*, Uncle Augustus was praying to the Lord for deliverance from the tempest. It washed completely over Telok Betong, leaving nothing but rough seas in its frightful wake."

"47, LADIES AND GENTS, 47!"

"My heavens!" Alice cried. "How dreadful!"

"Everybody was killed, weren't they?" the ruddy fellow asked, looking over his card.

The dwarf nodded, his voice somber now. "Nothing survived. Uncle Augustus recalled the gunboat tumbling over and over in the roaring water, himself hurled about the small cabin like a child's toy until at last he lost consciousness. When he awoke, all was quiet. The great wave had receded, leaving the battered gunboat perched thirty-feet above sea level on the River Koeripan, more than a mile and a half inland. Uncle Augustus crawled from his hiding place and used a rope to climb down off the gunboat. Hot ash still rained from the dark sky. Where once fields of rice had grown, Uncle Augustus saw nothing but mud and boulders. So, too, had all the lovely Javanese villages been washed away. Not even the paroquets cackled in the jungle. When Uncle Augustus called out for help, no one answered. He was quite alone. Having little idea where he was, Uncle Augustus determined to stay put until the clouds broke, so he climbed back up onto the gunboat."

"87, LADIES AND GENTS, 87!"

Hazel added a bean to her card. Bertha frowned at hers.

"The next morning he built a fire, then killed a wild hog and ate it with crackers from the crew's rations. Not until the moon lit the night sky nearly two days later, was he able to see Lampong Bay and walk out of the jungle along the Koeripan to the appalling ruin of Telok Betong. At the first of September, Uncle Augustus took a ferry across the Straits of Sunda to locate Louis Hurlburt. The volcanic island of Krakatau had mostly disappeared, as had the seaports of Anjer and Merak, along with the Dutch admiral's pretty daughter, her collection of Java sparrows, and more than thirty thousand poor souls. Though Uncle Augustus searched the west coast of Java for a month from Tjeringen to Bantam Bay, he never found his companion, and the malaria he contracted from tramping through those damp jungles of paradise remained with him for the rest of his days."

"12, LADIES AND GENTS, 12!"

Nobody spoke at the table. Rain dribbled off the tent sides, and the electric lanterns shook in the damp breeze. Then the ruddy fellow shoved his chair back and stood up. He tossed his burnt cigar out into the mud and stared the dwarf in the eye and began clapping. The four ladies remained seating, but they joined in, too, with a fine round of applause. Rascal acknowledged their admiration with a stiff bow from his seat.

When they were through clapping, the farm boy remarked, "Well, that's a swell story. Was any part of it true?"

"Of course," replied the dwarf, sliding a bean to the bottom row of his card. He added, "Uncle Augustus wrote it all down in a private diary which was bequeathed to me after a Prussian sniper took his life at Delville Wood. I value no possession of mine more greatly and it's been immensely instructive these past few years. Dear old Uncle Augustus believed that our lives bear irrefutable testimony to the immortal purpose of character and courage in this world, and he held selflessness as the pinnacle of virtues. Indeed, his epitaph on the family mausoleum at Hannibal reads most eloquently: *We owe respect to the living; to the dead, we owe only truth.*"

"13, LADIES AND GENTS, 13." The pitchman's voice sounded weary.

The dwarf slid another bean across his bottom row, then cried,

"Why, I believe I've won!" He stood and shouted loudly enough for everyone under the tent to hear, "BEANO!"

Alvin got up and walked off into the rainy dark.

The breeze felt warmer somehow, but the drizzle persisted. When he was sickest with consumption, Alvin had dreamt of angels in gauze masks wandering the halls of the sanitarium in search of those whose failing lungs would lead them to God's bright countenance, or eternal night, depending upon whether the Bible was true or not. Now he wondered how it felt to be carried away by a giant sea wave. He imagined a blast of wind and the sky of stars disappearing, his body thrust suddenly upwards like a bird in flight.

Alvin walked out to the front of the muddy camp where the roadside stand was crowded with motorcars and people. He smelled liquor in the dark and burning pipe tobacco. The woman he had seen with the child under the beano tent sat in the rear seat of a brown DeSoto. She held a cup of coffee to her lips, sipping like a cat. A pack of men in suits and neckties stood behind the automobile just under the rear awning, yammering away about Jack Johnson and Kansas blue laws. Another crowd of fellows in a Ford runabout pulled in off the road, soaking wet and singing "Alabamy Bound" at the top of their lungs. Getting to the short order counter ahead of them, Alvin bought a hotdog and a Coca-Cola from the change in his pocket and went off to the side of the building. A large truck roared by on the wet road. Alvin felt the damp draft on his face as it passed. Stifling a cough, he ate the hotdog and drank his soda pop and threw the empty bottle into a thick growth of sumac. An angry voice cursed back at him from the dark and a sturdy-looking man in mudcaked overalls and a denim jacket came out of the bushes, buttoning up his fly. Looking Alvin square in the eye, he produced the empty pop bottle. "Fill this up with corn liquor, young fellow, and I won't crack you in the head like you just done me." Then he bent forward so Alvin could see a bloody laceration at the hairline.

"I didn't even know you was there," the farm boy said, though he might have supposed in a place such as this there would be someone lurking in the bushes.

"You ain't been around all that long, have you?"

"What of it?"

"You been sick, ain't you? Don't lie to me. I can see it in your eyes. You got the cure, but it ain't made you well, so you gone looking for another and all you found is more trouble, and now you're sicker'n you ever been, and that's the plain truth, ain't it?"

Alvin wiped his nose with the back of a sleeve and shook his head as the rain began to fall harder again. "I catched a cold this morning, that's all."

The man took a sniff of the pop bottle. "I had the whooping cough once, and that wasn't nothing but a sidetrack. Am I better off for it? Well, I can still do a pretty fair buck-and-wing when the fiddler plays, and peddle bananas enough for a suit of up-to-the-minute clothes and a swell lay every other week or so with any little slip-shoe lovey I like, if that's 'better off' in your lingo."

"I ain't said nothing about that," Alvin replied, watching another automobile streak past. The man tossed Alvin's empty pop bottle back into the sumac. He smelled like onions when the wet breeze shifted and one of his eyes sagged unnaturally and Alvin guessed he had a kink from too much back-stall booze.

"Who was it that run you off? Your daddy? Is that how come you're looking all blue? He tan your britches once too often?" The man chuckled.

"What's it to you?" the farm boy answered. He didn't care for this fellow and wished he hadn't begun gabbing with him in the first place. He felt his fever coming on, maybe even a coughing fit.

The man stared at Alvin like he had a bug on his face. "Well, don't pay no mind to that. We all done things we ain't proud of. We like to be held up to our better angels, but it ain't always that simple, is it? Why, I seen men so beaten down with shame that life become just a dark cloud they couldn't see out of no more, and I'm here to tell you liquor don't cure it, neither, though some of us surely believed that's so. Truth is, nobody's wise to how cold-blooded and mean this world can be when a fellow's out of sorts with the straight and narrow and can't see his way back and there ain't no forgiveness waiting up the road."

"I ain't asking no one to pass the hat," Alvin said, temper rising. He didn't care for folks feeling sorry him even when he was hid away in the sanitarium, and he surely didn't need no dumbbell's sympathy.

"Is that a fact?"

"You said it."

The wind gusted hard, blowing wet leaves across the rainy night sky. The young bunch in the Ford runabout swung back out into the road and drove off, still singing like melon vendors. Alvin envied them, wished he'd been invited along.

The man said, "I guess you're a pretty tough egg, aren't you?"

Alvin frowned. "How's that?"

"You don't let nothing stir you up, do you?

"Well, I ain't no baby."

"Oh yeah?" The man smirked. "Well, answer me this, sonny boy: who's buying your breakfast?"

The cabin door was ajar when Alvin came back from the roadside stand. He peeked through the window and saw Chester beside one of the camp cots with an electric lantern in hand. His suit was smudged with dirt, his felt hat dripping rainwater. When he noticed the farm boy on the stoop, he said, "I got a job for you boys."

A damp gust of wind shook the walls of the small structure and hundreds of tiny flecks of rotted wood cascaded down from the ceiling. Alvin shielded his eyes from the glow of the lantern. "What's that?"

"I'll show you outside."

"Thunderstorm's coming," Alvin noted after smelling the air. Farm life had taught him how to smell a storm on a night wind, hours before it arrived. It was a dandy skill, but didn't earn him much more than dry clothes on a rainy day.

"We don't have time to worry about rain," Chester replied. "Too much work to do tonight."

The dwarf rose from a dark corner of the cabin, suitcase in hand. Illuminated in lamplight, his eyes glowed yellow and his skin looked waxen and old, his hair white as corn silk. Chester directed the lamp toward him. "You can leave that here. You'll be coming back soon as you're done with the job."

Rascal put down his suitcase. "All right."

"Storm's coming up," Alvin said, tucking his shirt in. "Be here soon. Maybe quicker."

"I heard you the first time," Chester said, bringing the electric lantern back toward Alvin, suspending it in front of his face. "I tell you, don't worry about it. Weather's got nothing to do with your job tonight. A little rain won't bother a thing."

"Be more'n a little, I'd guess."

"No matter, you've got plenty of work to do, rain or no rain."

"There'll be rain," Alvin assured him.

"Swell," said Chester, losing patience. "I'll be waiting by the car. Hop to it."

He walked out.

Alvin went to the cabin door where black droplets swirled about on the wind. Close on the heels of an electric flash in the east, thunder boomed across the dark. He took a hard look at the sky. Lightning could strike a man dead in an instant. On the farm, cows and horses got hit now and again. Fried to the bone, carcass smoking, even in Noah's rain. Alvin felt the dwarf beside him, also studying the clouds with a watchful eye.

"Won't pay to get hit by lightning," the farm boy said, holding a hand out into the rain which was falling harder now. His shoes and socks felt soggy.

"I remember being terrified of it as a child," the dwarf agreed. "Auntie had to close my windows and tie down the shades so that I couldn't see it flash. I'd hide under the bedcovers until the thunder stopped and Auntie told me it was safe to come out."

Alvin shook his head. "That's dumb."

"Oh?"

"Everyone knows you can't hide. If it's got your name, you're fixed, and that's all there is to it."

The dwarf stared up into the dark, rain blowing about overhead. "I don't believe in that sort of silly superstition."

"Don't matter if you believe it or not," Alvin replied, watching sheets of rain drench the tourist camp. "It's a fact, just the same. If you doubt it, go on and take a walk out there. You don't need a lightning rod on your head, neither. Just remember: it's not in God's plan to have everybody check out in their sleep."

He smiled, hoping he'd gotten under Rascal's skin a little, stirred him up some.

Another lightning strike lit the sky to the east. The dwarf counted by seconds to nine, then the thunder roared across the prairie. As the echo died away, Chester's voice followed from the automobile parked under a black oak by the road. "Hurry up, goddamn it!"

Standing just out of the rain beneath the big oak, Chester held the electric lantern over the rear seat of the Packard for Alvin to see inside. Pale lamplight made visible a youth's face partly wrapped in gunny cloth and shadows. His eyes were shut and his hands folded into the heavy overcoat that covered him up.

"He's out of the game," Chester said, as if it weren't obvious.

Alvin's skin crawled. "You shot him?"

"He slipped on a banana peel and broke his neck."

The dwarf slid quietly into the front seat on the driver's side for a better look.

Alvin stared at him, heart thumping. The boy wasn't much older than himself.

Chester spoke up. "He had more spirit than brains."

"Huh?"

He handed the lantern over to the farm boy whose legs were trembling now.

"He had a set of keys I needed and didn't care to negotiate for them. He was a stubborn little sonofabitch." Chester smiled. "I liked that."

Alvin directed the lantern again toward the rear seat of the Packard. Chester had hiked the boy's collar up higher than normal to hide the bruising about the larynx, but the swelling showed still in his cheeks and eyelids. Alvin found himself transfixed by the boy, slumped in the seat, looking drunk and passed out, yet in fact deader than last November's turkey. The farm boy pressed his face to the glass and watched the dwarf climb into the rear seat beside the dead boy as if they were old friends out for a ride in a motorcar. Alvin shuddered as rain began to fall in earnest.

Chester said, "He's just some hick. Nobody to concern yourselves over. Go on, jump in and get acquainted. We need to beat it out of here before somebody sees him."

"How come you brought him here, anyhow?"

"Well, I thought you boys could give him a swell send-off."

Half a mile or so from the tourist camp, Chester pulled off the highway onto a narrow road that led east through a soggy wheat field to a dilapidated farmhouse and a sagging old barn. He parked next to the storm cellar behind the barn and got out. Both Alvin and the dwarf joined him there in the rain. Chester said, "Come on, get the kid out of the car."

He took the electric lantern off the front seat of the Packard and switched it on. "Look here, boys, I have to be getting along. I've got an appointment in town tonight and it won't pay to be late. There's a shovel and a pickaxe in the cellar." He handed the electric lantern to the farm boy. "When you're done putting this kid in the ground, go back to the camp and get some sleep, then meet me at the Methodist church in the morning. You remember it? That tall skinny white building with the steeple we passed by this afternoon. If you hurry along, it won't take you more than a couple hours. When you get there, don't go in until the service lets out, all right?"

With the rain pouring down harder, Alvin asked, "Where do you want us to bury him?"

"I don't care."

Then Chester got back into the Packard and started the motor. A great cloudy fog of exhaust billowed out of the tailpipes. He told the farm boy, "Go on, get him out of there."

Alvin gave the lamp to the dwarf, then reluctantly leaned inside the Packard and grabbed the dead boy by his shirt collar and pulled him up off the seat. The boy's corpse smelled like fresh shaving soap; Alvin figured it was still a few hours yet from stinking. He tugged it into the doorframe as the dwarf put the lantern down in the mud and took hold of the boy's legs and pulled. Together, they dragged the stiffening body out into the mud beside the rear wheel.

"All right, now close the door," said Chester, lighting a cigarette. He switched on the automobile's headlamps. "I'll see you boys in the morning."

They stepped back as Chester stuck the transmission into gear and rolled away from the barn, and watched as he drove quickly down toward the county road, honking once before he disappeared into the rainy dark. It was a mean and peculiar road they had been following since Hadleyville, Alvin thought, as that awful sinking in his heart began once again, mostly a lot of winding around and doubling back and traveling the old routes nobody else chose to drive. Tonight and tomorrow it'd be Iowa, and a week afterward Oklahoma, or maybe Nebraska again. All summer long, Chester had been sneaking in among these people like some dark angel on Judgment Day, cleansing the scrolls of those whose sad fortune had drawn them across his path. Alvin knew his own soul had been soiled by complicity and no apology made to the families of the murdered would redeem him. Sick in his heart for what he'd seen since Hadleyville, believing that retribution for the guilty was assured, he had ridden quietly these many miles and raised no conflict with Chester for any of it. Why not? If consumption had sealed his fate like the doctors whispered behind his back, how come he lacked the courage to meet God at the Gate of Virtue? What held him back? If he weren't so afraid of Chester, he would have gone to the police and told them everything. That'd fix him, all right. Sure, Alvin knew he'd probably wind up in jail himself, or get shot, but at least he wouldn't be stuck out in the middle of another wheat field, burying a dead body whose killing he didn't have any part of. Why couldn't he just go and do that? Why was he so goddamned yellow?

Alvin picked up the lamp and held it over the dead boy's face pelted now by rain as he lay in the mud. Wind blew open the boy's collar, exposing the fatal bruise to the lamplight. Feeling a sudden touch of nausea, he turned away and headed across the yard toward the storm cellar to get the shovel. One of the doors fell off its hinge as he raised it open. The cellar was black as tar. Nine steps led downward into the dark. Two of the boards were cracked through with splinters. These steps Alvin maneuvered past by clinging to the cellar walls, lamp suspended in front of him. Old webs clouded the stairwell. The floor of the cellar was damp and smelled horrible. Alvin ran the light back and forth, wall to wall. More webs, junk, boxes, tins and bottles. He spied rat droppings atop several of the boxes. Frenchy had been bitten once, hunting through a dank fruit cellar in the dark where he didn't belong. The howl he had made when a nesting rat bit him in the hand carried clear up to the house where Aunt Hattie was hanging out the laundry. His crazy screaming scared the daylights out of her and when she saw his hand and Alvin told her about the rat, she fainted dead away in the dust.

The cellar was leaking. Alvin's shoes sloshed in the mud as he directed the lamp here and there. A dead mouse floated inside a lidless fruit jar. Scores of eviscerated flies and moths lay in ragged webs suspended beneath the support beams. An odor of wet rot persisted even with the cellar door propped open to the storm. The lamp was mostly useless. Alvin kicked at the junk along the walls from one corner to the next until he finally located the shovel alongside a stack of boards. Holding the lantern with one hand, he slid the shovel out with the other, careful not to disturb whatever might be lurking beneath the lumber. He wondered how Chester knew about it. Maybe this was where he had murdered the boy. What had brought him out here? Was it just to kill the kid? Did he give the poor dope some line about bees and honey to string him along? Alvin decided Chester was the evilest fellow he'd ever met. He wished they'd never said hello. What on earth had persuaded him to cross the river with Chester that night? Was he so sick and lonely that he'd needed the company of a fellow who didn't know him from Adam but offered up a slice of pie if Alvin would walk out on his family? Having consumption clouded his judgment back on the farm, made him tie his shoes backwards and forget to water the chickens. Some days he'd walk out of doors with his fly open or leave the keys to Daddy's auto on the fencepost. He grew tired from hardly nothing at all and had to sit down until he got yelled at. All his decisions seemed confused. Then again, choosing right from wrong wasn't so easy when his fever spiked and he spewed blood with a cough. If Alvin hadn't gotten his relapse, he'd have never run off like he did. Now he had traveled so far from home, he doubted he'd ever get back. How could he? After all he'd seen and done, Chester wouldn't ever let him go; Alvin knew that for a fact. And if he snuck out one night? How would he know where to go that hadn't any spotters or gun mates of Chester's just waiting on him to show his face? How far could he get before one of them caught him in an alley somewhere and shot him in the head? He had no auto to drive, and not enough dough for a train ticket. Too sick to walk more than a few miles, too scared to seek help, Alvin felt caught in a trap of his own stupidity. He was doomed and he knew it. All that was left was to see how it played out, in what dark place or gallows he'd meet his just reward.

Rising from the cellar, shovel in hand, Alvin saw the dwarf sitting in the mud beside the dead body. A cold damp wind replaced the steady rainfall again as the storm drifted. The dwarf carefully refastened the boy's collar buttons, and gently combed his wet tussled hair with his fingers. Alvin's own hands were numb from the cold. Hurrying across the yard, he tossed the shovel into the mud beside the dwarf and seized the dead boy by one arm and heaved him upward. Startled by Alvin's urgency, the dwarf fell backward onto the seat of his pants, then scrambled to his feet.

"We ain't got all night, you know," Alvin said, raising the boy halfway up to his feet. "He needs to be put down good in the ground before it really gets to storming. Otherwise, the rain'll wash him out." He looked at the dwarf. "Come on, help me!"

"Where'll we bury him?" asked the dwarf.

"In one of the stalls," Alvin answered, reaching down with his free hand to grab the lantern, "under the dirt and straw where nobody'll find him."

"Oh, that's very clever."

Rascal wrapped both his arms around the boy's thigh and hoisted one whole leg out of the mud. Meanwhile, Alvin tugged the boy's torso up toward his own chest and began hauling the corpse back into the barn. Wind tore at the boy's coat, flinging it open into the dwarf's face. From an inside pocket, a flurry of papers slipped out and blew free into the air.

"Wait!" The dwarf let go of the boy's leg and ran after the papers, scattering now across the yard.

"Leave 'em be!" Alvin shouted, trying in vain to support the boy alone. His weight shifted, tilting the stiff corpse off balance, which caused Alvin's feet to slip in the mud. The boy fell away from him, landing face down in the mud. Alvin coughed harshly and put the lantern down and called for Rascal to help, but by now the dwarf had chased to the end of the rainy yard, collecting soggy papers one after another and stuffing them down the front of his romper. Across the prairie to the east, lightning stitched the night sky. The rumble of thunder reverberated in the yard. Maybe the storm would pass on by, Alvin thought, dumping a few buckets of rain, then hurrying off somewhere else. If a twister hit now, they'd be finished. Aunt Florence had hid herself in a fruit cellar at Gorham when the great spring tornado of '25 blew that town off the face of the earth. Witnessing one up close gave her a fright she had never forgotten. When the cellar doors blew off, she saw a full-grown milk cow fly over a barn upside down, and a row of chicken sheds come apart and vanish into thin air — boards, wire, nails, chickens, all gone in the snap of a finger. If Alvin caught sight of a whirlwind out here tonight, he'd take off running and never look back.

Black droplets struck him on the head as he stood searching into the dark for the dwarf. Down by the fenceline that ran from the ramshackle house on out to the road, Rascal dashed from post to post gathering up the last of the papers. When he was done, he checked the sky for signs of lightning, and dashed back toward the barn.

"What'd you go running off for like that?" Alvin yelled, as the dwarf reappeared out of the dark.

"The wind blew his letters away. I had to recover them."

"What for? He don't have no more need of them."

"They're his, nevertheless. They belong to him. If you'll recall, the Egyptian pharaohs were buried with many earthly possessions."

The farm boy smirked. "You think he's Egyptian?"

"I doubt it, but the principle is the same — honor and duty regarding the dead."

Alvin watched the dwarf begin stuffing the papers back into the boy's inside jacket pocket. "What sort of letters were they?"

"I didn't read them."

"Why not?"

"It's none of our concern."

"Give 'em over," said Alvin. "Let me see."

The dwarf stopped stuffing and held one hand over the coat pocket. "Of course not."

"Huh?"

"I can't let you see them. They're private."

"He's up there pushing the clouds around," Alvin said. "Who's going to pay any mind?"

"It wouldn't be proper."

Rain began falling harder again. If the storm had indeed drifted south, maybe a few straggling thunderheads had found the farm and released their burden.

"Honor is one of the transcendent virtues," Rascal continued, his face solemn and gray. "Our lives are meaningless without it."

Lightning flashed nearby. Thunder cannoned in the sky. Rain cascaded across the yard in cold black sheets.

Drenched, Alvin growled, "Goddamn you." Then he reached down, grabbed under the boy's arm, and lifted. The dwarf stuffed the rest of the letters deep into the boy's pocket and took his other arm to help raise him up.

"Get the lamp!"

Rascal snatched the lantern, shuffling it into the crook of his arm. Together they dragged the dead boy through the barn door. When he was safely out of the rain, they dropped him and stepped back to rest. The body was caked now in mud, head to foot.

"Might I express an opinion here?" Rascal asked.

"No."

The dwarf frowned. "Well, that isn't fair. I've as much a right to a voice in this as you do."

A fierce cough shook Alvin's chest and his eyes watered. "No, you don't. Chester put me in charge of burying the kid. Not you."

"That isn't so. He told us both to bury him."

"He meant me, though. Hell, you can't even lift a shovel, much less bury someone on your own."

"Why, I've buried several persons."

"When?"

"On that expedition into the Black Hills you'll recall I discussed with that banker's family on our visit to Stantonsburg."

"You mean the trip you took with Teddy Roosevelt?"

"I never said the President was there with us, only that he was impressed with the collection of arrowheads I'd brought back from the Belle Fourche River. Why do I bother carrying on a conversation with you? You never listen to anything I say."

Alvin coughed again. "Tell me who you buried."

"Mary Alexandra Foxweather, a fine woman who sadly succumbed to the spotted fever three days' ride out of Fort Dodge. Mary's husband George decided that as it had been Mary's desire to travel out West, she ought to be put to rest in her heart's country. Therefore, we found a restful knoll just across the river from our camp and laid her in the ground. Seeing as how Mary and I had become so close during our journey, and since George suffered greatly from clavicle arthritis and was under his physician's instructions to avoid physical exertion of any sort, I was elected to perform the duties, which I did."

"Was everyone else crippled?"

"Sarcasm is the last resort of the devil's logic."

Alvin shook his head. "Quit your sniveling and let's get this over with. I'll go bring the shovel."

He walked back out into a soft drizzling rain and stood there several minutes, watching for lightning strikes on the cloudy sky. When he fetched the shovel from the mud and brought it back into the barn, he saw the dwarf had taken a bucket full of rainwater and washed most of the mud off the corpse. He had also cleared a space in the second stall for a gravesite — all the old damp straw piled up to one side and an outline drawn in the dirt. Alvin stared at the boy still lying where they'd dragged him, his jacket buttoned, cuffs folded down.

"He looks swell."

"Thank you."

"Like to do some digging?" Alvin asked, walking over to the stall. He felt light-headed with fever and wanted to get this over with so he could go back to bed.

"I'd rather not."

"I thought you were the gravedigger here."

"I never said so."

"Well, that's what I heard."

Rascal averted his eyes. The electric lamp hanging from a nail above the dwarf draped a silhouette across the dead boy beside him. A cold gust of wind shook the roof of the barn, cascading more dirt down off the shingles.

"Well, don't trouble yourself," Alvin said, hoisting the shovel, "I'll do the digging. You'd just be in the way, anyhow."

He entered the stall and jabbed at the ground with the tip of the shovel, testing the firmness of the earth. It was muddy and soft only half a foot down; after that, he'd have to work at it. Maybe the exercise would be good for him.

He dug for half an hour.

By then, the storm had passed, leaving only a cold stiff wind behind to shake the barn roof and bring a draft inside. Alvin's shoulders ached from the effort of his work and his eyes burned with fever. When he had dug four feet down below the level of the dirt floor, he quit and climbed out of the hole and rolled onto his side, thoroughly exhausted. Once Alvin's breathing eased and he quit coughing, he said, "Let's put him in."

The dwarf, who had been sitting quietly holding the boy's hand and whispering to him in the dark, crawled now to the edge of the grave and peered in. "Is it deep enough?"

"For who?"

"To shield the deceased from life's grand and awful misery."

"It's deep as it's gonna get unless you do some of the digging."

"I believe we owe him a decent burial."

"And he'll be getting one," Alvin said, struggling to his feet, "soon as you help me put him in the ground." He tossed the shovel over to the wall and grabbed the lamp and held it over the hole he'd dug. Down at the very bottom, water was seeping in from all sides. "It's flooding."

Rascal leaned into the hole for another look. "You must have dug into a well."

"It ain't that deep," said Alvin. "I'd guess it'd be runoff from the storm."

The dwarf stared hard into the hole. "Perhaps we ought to dig another hole elsewhere."

"We?"

"Well, we can't have him floating out of his own tomb."

"He won't," Alvin assured the dwarf. "We'll just bury him quick before the water gets too deep down there. Come on, help me get him over here."

Together, they dragged the boy's body to the hole and dropped it in. The corpse landed with a muffled splash. Water soaked immediately into the edges of his clothing and Rascal removed the lamp from over the hole.

"Well?"

"Well, what?" Alvin said, wiping his hands dry on the front of his shirt. "It's done. Give me the damned shovel."

"We owe a prayer to the deceased," said the dwarf, placing the lamp in the dirt beside the hole. The electric light seemed to flicker. "For honoring the dead even as we cherish the living."

"I don't know no prayers," Alvin growled. "You say something."

"Are you certain? In the eyes of the Lord, performing a recitation of the common prayer in a burial of someone close is held in the highest esteem."

"I never even seen him before Chester brought him here. You just go ahead and do it. I don't have nothing to say."

"If you wish."

"I do."

Alvin picked up the lamp. He was tired and sore and his throat hurt from coughing.

"All right." The dwarf bowed his head and clasped both hands together at his belt buckle, then drew a long deep breath, shivered once, and began reciting, "Unto Almighty God we commend the soul of our brother departed, and we commit his body to the ground, earth to earth, ashes to ashes, dust to dust; in sure and certain hope of the Resurrection unto eternal life, through our Lord Jesus Christ. Amen."

"Amen."

Then Alvin filled the hole and covered the grave under straw. When he was finished, he returned the shovel to the cellar where he had found it, and followed the dwarf by electric lamplight back through the wet cornfield to the county road. By midnight they were both asleep in the tourist cabin again.

An hour or so after dawn, the farm boy and the dwarf ate meat sandwiches and a pair of mushmelons for breakfast at the roadside stand, then left the auto camp and headed down the county road to Allenville. The skies had cleared and the sun felt warm and dried their clothes as they walked along, suitcases in hand. The dwarf kept to the shoulder of the road, while Alvin strolled down the middle, humming a tune his grandmother had taught him when he was a baby. He'd had sweaty dreams all night long about the kid they had buried, but now that his fever was gone, he was doing his best not to remember. They hadn't seen any traffic since sunup when a truck carrying a load of hay drove by heading away from Allenville. The driver honked and gave a wave as he passed and the dwarf saluted in return. The farm boy just watched. None of the roads near Allenville had been paved yet, so the wheel ruts and damp earth made walking arduous. The dwarf seemed unconcerned. He meandered in and out of the weeds along the shoulder of the road and talked unceasingly about people and places Alvin had never heard of.

"Of course," said the dwarf, "had our guide warned me of the dangers of the cave beforehand, I'd have never dared take such a risk, at least not alone. Fortunately, I was able to keep my wits about me and devise a plan to mark my progress until a solution presented itself. Can you guess what I did?"

"No." Alvin was keeping count of black crows on the fencelines from the tourist camp to Allenville. If he reached a dozen, he would stop and make a cross in the dirt of the road ahead.

"Well, I'm sure you recall how Theseus unraveled a ball of string in the labyrinth of the Minotaur. That was my inspiration, but as I had no string, I was forced to improvise. You see, at such depths within our earth, the stygian darkness evolves creatures whose very skin glows phosphorescent, thereby creating visibility where sunlight never shines."

"Glow-worms," said Alvin. "I seen 'em before. They ain't nothing special." He watched a pair of crows take flight several hundred yards up the road. That made six since breakfast, a bad sign. "Me and Frenchy used to fix lanterns out of fruit jars and fireflies when we were kids so's we could fish in the dark. That's what you ought to've done."

"Perhaps," replied the dwarf, "but seeing as how I had no jars, nor were there any fireflies in the cave, a different solution was required. Nor were the creatures I spoke of glow-worms. Rather, they were a peculiar form of fungus that grew along the cave walls. What I did was to secure great handfuls of them for storage in my haversack and I used them to finger-paint arrows along all the maze of passageways leading to a subterranean river where at last I discovered a secret crevice in the cavern wall underwater and took advantage of a favorable current to float to safety. I emerged less than a mile from our camp. Afterward, I was told by our guide, a full-blooded Shawnee, that my escape was most remarkable and that he'd never before heard of such cleverness."

"So you were made chief of his tribe, right?"

"No, but I did receive a genuine war bonnet with eagle feathers in honor of my achievement, thank you."

"Look, don't tell me another one of them stories," said Alvin, kicking at a clump of dirt. He was tired of the dwarf's claptrappery. It gave him a headache. "I don't want to hear no more."

Rascal set his suitcase down and sat on it to rest. Wisps of his white hair fluttered in the morning breeze as he stared out across the fields. Alvin walked across the road and looked into the ditch where last night's rainwater puddled up under the weeds. He saw his reflection in little pools here and there. He looked filthy. It had been two days now since he'd taken a bath. He probably smelled, too. But what of it? Mostly it was just the dwarf who had to smell him and he wasn't no spring flower himself. Traveling was hard. Somehow Alvin had thought it would be a swell adventure, but he hadn't counted on the miles between towns, the empty roads, hours of boredom, and lonesome feelings that came more and more often, especially when he thought of the killings. If he lived on the farm until he was ninety, he didn't guess he'd see half of what he had witnessed since Hadleyville. If he lived.

Alvin looked across at the dwarf, still perched on his suitcase, eyes focused somewhere down the road ahead. "Tell me something," the farm boy said. "How come you never run off before?"

The dwarf shifted to face Alvin, folding his ankles over one another and clasping his hands together in his lap. "That's a very good question."

Alvin nudged a clump of dirt into the ditchwater and watched it sink. He put his own suitcase down and felt his forehead. Since they'd stopped to rest, Alvin guessed his temperature had gone up a degree or so. He still held out hope his clothes would be dry before he reached the church. Walking around in stinking clothes was bad enough without them being wet, too. One of the nurses at the sanitarium had told him that if he ever caught pneumonia, he'd be done for.

"Did you know that I come from a family of considerable means?" asked the dwarf. He left his suitcase and walked down into the ditch on the other side of the road until only his head showed above the dirt. Rascal began picking wildflowers from the embankment and formed a bouquet, which he clenched in his right hand. When he had gathered as many as he could easily hold, he climbed back up and told Alvin, "Auntie always said flowers gild the heart dearly, and that we ought never to go a day without appreciating their loveliness."

Using the stem of one flower, he bound the bouquet, and recited, *"Wildflowers exhale the gentle fragrance of our Lord's sweet breath."* He held the bouquet out to Alvin. "Would you like one?"

Alvin shook his head. "They give me hayfever."

"How dreadful." Rascal slipped the bouquet into his back pocket. "If I suffered such an affliction, I don't know that I'd survive. How would I be able to work in my garden?"

"I guess you couldn't."

"Have you been feeling homesick lately?" the dwarf asked. "It would be quite understandable, given the circumstances of our journey thus far."

Rascal took his suitcase and began walking down the road again toward Allenville. The farm boy kicked another dirt clod into the muddy ditch, then started walking again, too, keeping to his own half of the road. He lied to the dwarf when he told him, "I ain't homesick."

"I've been worried lately about my garden," Rascal said. "I'm sure it hasn't been watered since I left." He shook his head. "Perhaps there've been rainshowers."

"Maybe you ought've stayed put," Alvin said, "not come along at all. Maybe you made a mistake."

"I'm quite certain that if half of all the decisions we make in our lives prove to be correct, we are indeed fortunate. However, hindsight, Auntie always said, is a cat with his head stuck in a milk bottle. Had I remained in that crawlspace beneath my house much longer, I have no doubt I'd have become quite ill by now, perhaps even deceased. Do you miss your family?"

"I don't know." Alvin shrugged. "Why?" He wondered who missed him. He knew his sisters didn't, but maybe his momma or Aunt Hattie. Daddy'd be too mad at him for running off. Did Frenchy? Who had he found to collect bait and go fishing with? That goddamned Herbert Muller?

"I never really knew my family. Did I tell you that?"

"You said your momma died when you were born."

"Yes, she did, and my father left home when I was seven. That was when Auntie came to take care of me."

"Where'd your daddy go?"

"Out West, so I'm told. Auntie says he went to seek his fortune in gold somewhere in Alaska. By all accounts, he was quite successful, as he sent a great deal of money back to Hadleyville until the day he died in a mine explosion."

From the grassy fields ahead, a flock of sparrows suddenly took flight, angling overhead to the west. Rascal hummed a few notes of a tune he'd been working on since Omaha. After a moment, he stopped and said, matter-of-factly, "Auntie's a very wealthy woman. She's invested quite intelligently for many years and now she's one of the richest women in all of Missouri."

"Sure don't show it much, does she?" said Alvin. A bee buzzed his head and he swatted at it with the back of his hand. It'd be just his luck to get stung.

"I assume you're referring to the dilapidated condition of our house. Well, to be truthful, since it doesn't actually belong to her, Auntie doesn't much care about its appearance. We had a gardener for several years, but Auntie dismissed him last June when she took a summerhouse with friends in Mobile. I tried keeping the yard up by myself, but I fatigue quickly in the heat, and, of course, we had an awful winter, which kept me confined indoors for weeks at a time. I suppose I ought to have hired more help, but … "

The dwarf's voice trailed off as he looked down the narrow dirt road. "Actually, I'm a pathetic little coward."

"Huh?"

"Truth is, Auntie's stolen my inheritance and locked me away. The house in Hadleyville, its contents, the fortune held by the bank, were all kept in trust for me by my mother and father. When I con-tracted scarlet fever several years ago, Auntie had herself appointed executor of my estate in the event I became too ill to manage my own affairs. She's been using my money to finance her investments in expectation of my death which the doctors have always assured her is imminent."

"That don't seem fair." Now he understood why the dwarf had acted so nutty in the bank.

Rascal shrugged. "Since Auntie's my closest living relation, upon my death, everything I now possess, all my estate, becomes hers.

Knowing this, I believe she persuaded Mr. Harrison B. Sinclair to gain the advantage of investing these funds in advance of my demise. He and Auntie are crazy about the stock market. Of course, the house and several other properties are another matter entirely. She cannot touch them until I die and their worth far outweighs the money kept in Mr. Sinclair's bank."

The dwarf walked on quietly for a few minutes, but farther up the road he stopped and told the farm boy, "I lied to you back in Hadleyville when I said Auntie locked me in my room because she didn't trust me alone in the house. Before she left for Dayton, we had an awful fight and called each other names and I told her if she spent one more night there I'd burn us both up. Well, you can just imagine! She grabbed me by the arm and tossed me into my bedroom and locked the door. Sometime in the middle of the night while I was asleep, she stuck some bottles of water, crackers and peach jars in a box, and slipped them into my room. Then she went off to the medicine show. I tried to pick the lock, but she'd also taken my Houdini kit while I was sleeping, so I had to pry up the floorboards with that old butterknife and make my escape. I had no idea I'd offended her that badly. Am I so ugly?"

"Well — " the farm boy paused a second. "I guess I ain't never seen nobody like you before."

Ordinarily, human deformities turned his stomach. He had seen patients at the sanitarium whose faces were so encumbered with what he thought were tubercles that their heads looked like big overripe vegetables. Uncle Truman had a stump for a left arm that always gave Alvin the shivers, and whenever he and Frenchy went to the carnival, Alvin steered clear of the freak pavilion because it scared him so to see people with misshapen heads and no limbs and contorted bones and other oddities of nature.

"You mean, a dwarf."

Alvin nodded.

"Well, I'll tell you, Auntie led me to believe that when my father received word of my affliction, he blamed it for my mother's death. However, in those dear dead days before he left to go out West, he never let on that he felt so. We seemed to be quite close."

"Maybe he didn't blame you at all," Alvin suggested, resisting a cough. "Maybe she just made it up to get under your skin." *Why was everyone so damned mean these days?*

"I've considered that. Auntie raised me, you see, with the help of my Uncle Augustus. After his death, however, I was left permanently in Auntie's charge. She hired tutors to educate me, citing my condition to the Hadleyville schoolboard as part and parcel of a chronic health problem that prevented me from attending school with other children. To me, she said it was necessary that I be educated away from wicked boys and girls who would certainly taunt me and break my heart long before I had the chance to strengthen and bloom. Uncle Augustus provided that part of my education which involved the out of doors by taking me on excursions into the wild, and trips out West where I had the opportunity to ride horses and strike fire from flint in the deep woods. We read *The Strenuous Life* together by firelight on the banks of the Belle Fourche River and fished with our bare hands. I think Uncle Augustus had honest affection for me and I loved him like a second father. When he was killed in the World War, I felt his absence greatly. From then on, I had to remain in Hadleyville, studying piano and literature and tending garden at the rear of our yard where Auntie had granted me the favor of a sunny parcel."

The dwarf set the suitcase down again to catch his breath. A warm wind blew across the wheat fields on both sides of the road. Alvin felt himself wheezing and stopped to rest. His breathing had begun to sound funny. He saw an automobile raising dust on another road in the distance and decided to hitch a ride if the opportunity came along. Whether it was good for him or not, he was tired of walking, and his right instep was throbbing like a bone felon.

"Do you read many books?" the dwarf asked.

"Nope."

"You see, I believe I've learned most of what I know by reading. My mother loved to read, or so Auntie told me. Many of the books we own were hers left to me in her will. And Uncle Augustus had a great library in Hannibal, more than ten thousand volumes containing the collected wisdom of our entire civilization. As a child I was left for hours in that room to browse on my own, which I did quite enthusiastically. Have you read much of Oscar Wilde?"

"Who's that?"

"A writer I much admire."

"I already told you, I don't like books. I quit reading soon as I got out of school."

"Well, that's too bad."

"You can't learn nothing about life from a book. None of those books got you away from your aunt, did they?"

"No."

"They didn't get you that money of yours from your daddy, did they?" Before the dwarf could answer, Alvin asked, "You got any friends back home?"

"Auntie wouldn't let me out of the yard unsupervised, but if by friends you mean — "

Alvin interrupted the dwarf. "You ain't got no friends back there because you don't do nothing but sit in that garden of yours fiddling with flowers like an old lady."

"There's no need to be cruel."

"I ain't being cruel," Alvin shot back. "Just truthful."

"I've already admitted to being a coward."

"It ain't just that," Alvin said, feeling anxious all of a sudden and jittery, and no idea why. "You got nobody yelling in your ear to get out of bed in the morning, no chores between you and fishing whenever you like. What do you have to kick about? You got the swellest life I ever heard of. I'd swap with you in a second. Anybody says they wouldn't's a damned liar."

"If someone offered me a job, I would certainly trade places with him. I believe the discipline of manual labor would be instructive and helpful."

"It'd kill you, is what it'd do."

The dwarf waved off a nosy bee. "Look, I don't expect you to be sympathetic, of course, as I haven't had cause to labor for wages a single day of my life. In terms of basic needs, such as food and clothing and shelter, I've never wanted. Auntie made certain of that. We had a cook, and a delivery boy for groceries, and a woman who came in twice a week to clean. Each was under specific instructions to speak to me only when addressed and never to discuss away from our house what had occurred indoors that day. While the delivery boy had a distinctly unfriendly manner about him, I can say, I think quite confidently, that I made fast friends with Bessie, our cook, and Pleasance, the cleaning lady. In the afternoons, when Auntie was gone visiting friends, the three of us would sit together in the parlor and play whist for lemon candies, and in the evening we'd sip apricot brandy and use Auntie's Ouija board to communicate with the spirit world."

"Why didn't you get yourself a regular job?" Alvin asked, his eyes fixed on a grain silo about half a mile to the east. Not since his year at the sanitarium had he had the opportunity of playing cards in the middle of a workday. Even afterward, when he was still sick, his mother made him clean house and wash windows and follow her around picking up clothes after his sisters. Frenchy laughed at him and said he ought to start wearing an apron dress.

"I was discouraged from even considering it," the dwarf replied. "I'd given thought to writing stories for the *Hadleyville Journal* when I was as young as thirteen, but Auntie told me if I sold even one, my photograph would be published by the paper the next day and she'd become the laughingstock of the community, and might even draw attention from the Eugenics Society. I did grow many wonderful tomatoes and green beans in my garden that Auntie sold at market, but Bessie and Pleasance told me later that she always maintained they'd come down river by steamboat from her cousin Percival J. Miner's garden in Festus. I didn't care. More important to me was that people had actually thought enough of what I had grown to buy it and serve it in their homes. The very idea pleased me no end."

Alvin walked ahead maybe a dozen yards or so, studying the sky for rain clouds and crows, tracing with his shoes wagon ruts in the old dirt road. He figured they had walked a couple miles now since leaving the tourist camp. Though the air was cool in the wake of the storm's passing, the sun was rising higher on the morning sky and before long the road would be warm and the walking more difficult. He was surprised that no truck or automobile or haywagons had come by for so long. He looked back for the dwarf and saw him resting on the suitcase. Rascal wasn't like anyone Alvin had ever met before. He seemed to be some character out of a tall tale spun around a campfire at night when everyone had drank too much corn liquor. Sometimes when they were lying out under a tree in the dark beside Chester's automobile, trying to get a little sleep, Alvin would look over and see the dwarf staring up at the stars, a silly sort of grin on his face, his lips curled back exposing his big teeth, and Alvin would wonder if the dwarf knew more about driving around to strange towns and doing what they were doing than he ever let on.

The farm boy slowed his walking to a casual stroll. Allenville was still a mile or so ahead and the sun was rising higher in the summer sky. He watched the dwarf strain to lift his small suitcase. A day ago, Alvin would have been happy to see him suffer, but this morning he felt sorry for him. He called back to Rascal, "Want me to carry that?"

"No, thank you," the dwarf replied. "It's my responsibility, although I believe I'm developing a blister on my palm."

"Those'll kill you."

"I've had my share, thank you. I'm sure I'll survive."

"Suit yourself."

Half an hour later, the farm boy and the dwarf reached the south side of town. The dirt road gave way to plank sidewalks and tall leafy poplars providing shade. Most of Allenville looked plain and ugly, bleached of life and color by the wind and weather off the Iowa prairie.

"I don't believe I can walk any farther this morning," the dwarf said, dropping his suitcase. His red face was sore with fatigue and sweat beaded up on his brow and stained his romper about the armpits. He looked bedraggled. "Perhaps we ought to rest a while."

Alvin saw a circus poster nailed to a telephone pole across the street in front of a motor garage and a telegraph office, and went over to have a look.

The poster was still grimy and damp from the evening rainstorm and the dates had been torn away, so Alvin was left to guess when the traveling circus had actually made its appearance in Allenville.

"A circus," the dwarf remarked, circling the pole. "How wonderful."

"It ain't here no more," Alvin said, trying to get the poster off the pole. He put his own suitcase down and stuck his fingernails under the wire staples and popped one of them loose.

"I love the circus," Rascal said. "Uncle Augustus took me to Hagenbeck-Wallace when I was young. We were given a tour behind the scenes to see how the performers actually lived while on the road. I remember being quite impressed. Everybody was very kind to me and presented both Uncle Augustus and myself with souvenirs before we left."

"What kind of souvenirs?"

"I don't exactly recall, but I'm sure they were lovely."

"Well, I won me a prize once at a carnival throwing darts when I was six years old," said Alvin, prying free another section of the poster. "I still got it, too. A genuine Injun tomahawk from Custer's Last Stand."

"That's nice," said Rascal, as he bent down to collect one of the staples Alvin had popped off the pole. He stuck it into his romper and snapped the pocket closed. "Actually, now that you mention it, I do recall winning a fine crystal vase on the midway by pitching lead slugs into several open milk bottles. The circus people told me that nobody had ever done so well at that particular game. I might've been given a ribbon as well, but I couldn't say for certain. I felt quite proud, regardless."

"Sure you did," said Alvin, tearing loose the last two corners of the poster from the telephone pole. He read it over carefully once more, then folded the poster into quarters and slipped it under his shirt. "Well, I'd sure like to go see the circus again. I ain't been to one since I was a kid. I remember my daddy telling me how them bearded ladies give you the evil eye if you look at 'em wrong, and once they give it to you, your brains are scrambled the rest of your life and you ain't good for nothing but raking leaves. Maybe we ought to find out where this circus went and follow it down the road. It couldn'ta gone too far."

"Perhaps we could make the suggestion to our companion. Everybody loves a good circus," the dwarf said. "Why, even Auntie shared a belly laugh during the clown act last time we went, and ordinarily she has no sense of humor at all."

"I'd like to go," said the farm boy, growing an enthusiasm for the idea. "I won't deny it."

"Then I vote we ought to. It's settled."

"We'll see."

They headed down to the end of the alley at the fenceline that bordered the fields surrounding Allenville, then turned west and walked on for another quarter of a mile or so down a long country lane until they heard hymns from the church at the crossroads just outside of Allenville. In a bell tower atop the steeple, a flurry of sparrows chattered. Whitewash had flaked away from the siding, and a quarter of the shingles were missing on the main roof. Sections of the stained glass along the upper windows were also cracked and in danger of falling out.

"They ought to at least paint it," Alvin remarked, giving the church a good once-over from across the road. "Don't seem right to let it go like that."

"I suppose they haven't the resources," the dwarf replied. "I paint-ed our back porch one day when Auntie was off on errands and was shocked to discover how much everything cost. Had Auntie seen the bill, I doubt she'd have allowed it."

"I guess a church'd be able to afford it," Alvin said. "They don't do nothing except collect money."

"Do you attend often?"

"Not if I can help it." He hated church and didn't ever read the Bible. It was all baloney.

Alvin listened to the singing.

> *There's a land that is fairer than day, and by faith we can see it afar*
> *For the Father waits over the way, to prepare me a dwelling place there*
> *In the sweet (in the sweet) by and by (by and by)*
> *We shall meet on that beautiful shore (by and by)*

Rascal said, "Auntie and I attended services every Sunday morning together until I turned twenty. We went by hired carriage and greeted each of our fellow Christians by name along the route. It made for quite a spectacle, I must admit."

> *To our bountiful Father above, we will offer our tribute of praise,*
> *For the glorious gift of His love, and the blessings that hallow our days."*

The dwarf added, "It was also one of the few occasions where she allowed herself to be seen with me out of doors. At the church, we had our own special place reserved in the front pew and two fine leather-bound volumes of the hymnal."

> *In the sweet (in the sweet) by and by (by and by)*
> *We shall meet on that beautiful shore (by and by).*
> *In the sweet (in the sweet) by and by, (by and by)*
> *We shall meet on that beautiful shore.*

"Singing's the worst part of going to church," said Alvin, listening to the hymn. "Any old bunch of billygoats'll sound about as good as most folks trying to carry a tune."

"I was elected to the choir," Rascal said, "though, of course, Auntie did not permit me to perform for fear I'd embarrass myself in front of our neighbors."

"I hope you thanked her."

"In fact, her fears were quite unfounded. My voice back then possessed near perfect pitch and I'd long since committed all our hymns to memory. I'm sure my performance would have been memorable."

> *We shall sing on that beautiful shore, the melodious songs of the blest*
> *And our spirits shall sorrow no more, not a sigh for the blessings of rest.*
> *In the sweet (in the sweet) by and by (by and by)*
> *We shall meet on that beautiful shore (by and by).*

Alvin stuck his suitcase in the weeds and crossed the road to the side of the church and looked in through the yellow windowpanes. The pews were packed with people dressed in their Sunday finest. At the pulpit, the preacher was lecturing hellfire and brimstone while the choir behind him nodded grimly. It didn't seem all that different from services Alvin had attended in Farrington. Singing and shouting. Lots of old people acting drowsy, small children getting pinched by their mothers for fidgeting too often. Who paid any mind to what some dumbbell preacher had to say? When Alvin first caught the consumption, Reverend Newbury came to the farm and took his hand and told him Jesus dwelt in his lungs and if he kept faith in the Lord, Jesus would do his breathing for him until the Holy Spirit healed that awful disease. A month later Alvin was in the sanitarium, nearer to heaven than health.

The farm boy stepped down from the window and looked around. He and the dwarf seemed to be the only people nearby not inside the church. Somehow it made him feel truant and guilty, like he ought to go indoors and sit down, maybe sing along for a few minutes or so. Rascal walked along the road a little further, studying a patch of Arkansas rose growing at the foot of the fence that bordered the fields next to the church. Probably the dwarf wouldn't be allowed inside a church with normal folks, Alvin thought, on account of a case like his would make the Lord look bad. Then again, maybe the preacher would just hold Rascal up as an example of what can happen if you don't go to church or say your prayers at bedtime. Being born a dwarf might even be the mark of Cain, for all anyone knew, God's judgment on a wicked man or woman for sins unforgiven. Aunt Hattie always said the Lord worked in sly and secretive ways. He knew everything you ever did, and everything you planned to do, and though you might fool Him now and then, when the last card got thrown down, you'd always know His hand was the strongest. Alvin watched the dwarf pick a handful of purple asters and fold them into his fist for carrying alongside the small suitcase. Somewhere along the line, Rascal's family must have earned the Lord's attention in a powerful way. *How well we bear our burdens*, Aunt Hattie had told Alvin, *marks us in the Lord's countenance, for it was He who bestowed them, after all.*

"It's a beautiful day, don't you agree?" said the dwarf, walking toward Alvin. He offered a wildflower, but the farm boy declined.

"I already told you, I'm allergic."

"Then I'll keep them myself for luck," Rascal said, tucking a blossom into his romper before scattering the remaining handful into the wildrye next to the church. "God smiles on Sundays. I can hardly recall one where it rained."

"Maybe we ought to go inside," Alvin said, tired of waiting around outdoors. He'd like to have been able to stretch out in the back row on a long pew and have a nap. Truth was, he was beginning to think he would have to see a doctor sooner than later.

"Do you think that would be wise? Chester was most specific in his request that we wait until service lets out."

"Well, I ain't standing here all morning."

"I don't mind waiting," the dwarf replied. "Impatience is the devil's lure."

"Shut up."

The dwarf crossed back over the road and picked up his suitcase. Alvin walked around to the rear of the church to look for the back door. Most of the conveyances people had used to travel to the church were parked there, scattered about in no particular order, old buggies and motorcars — including Chester's tan Packard. There was only a short section of fence along the north end of the church separating the lot from the surrounding fields, and most of the horses hitched to the buggies stood in the morning sun, grazing where grass was long enough. As Alvin drew nearer, he saw a homely young girl with stringy brown hair sitting on a wooden fifteen-gallon water bucket, a tattered Bible in her lap. She was fiddling with a partially unraveled ball of lavender yarn, a cat's cradle. The girl's plain thin face was pale as powder and her print dress thread-worn and dull.

"Hey there," said Alvin, easing between two of the horses. The girl looked up, squinting her eyes against the sun. The farm boy asked, "You watching these horses?"

"They ain't watching me."

"How come you ain't in church with them other folks?" Alvin noticed a purple birthmark behind her ear, a sign of misfortune. Also, she had a nose like a russet potato. Poor thing.

She cocked her head. "Why ain't you?"

"I got business out here, that's why." He puffed himself up for her benefit.

"Me, too."

The girl completed the cat's cradle and sat still on the wooden bucket. The morning breeze blew lightly through her hair. Within the church, organ tones accompanied the plaintive voices of men and women joined in song. Alvin studied the girl. She looked drowsy and dim-witted. She was stick thin, but had soft little titties on her chest, so he figured she wasn't more than four or five years younger than himself. Her eyes were cloudy, her face expressionless as a cow's. Maybe she was sick, too. A girl her age had died in the sanitarium the morning Alvin was released, drowned in her own blood. He'd never heard a peep out of her.

"You from around here?" he asked, shuffling his feet in the dust. It was all he could think of to say. For some reason, he grew shy. Maybe she was a little pretty. He'd seen worse.

" 'Course," she replied, fooling with the yarn. "I been adopted by the Lord."

"Where do you live?"

"Inside the church," she said. "Down in the basement."

"You like sleeping in a church?"

"I don't mind. They's worse places."

He nodded. "Yeah, I guess so."

"Jesus didn't never live in any big old mansion," said the girl, unraveling her yarn out through the palm of one hand. "He didn't need all that fanciness to get by."

Inside the church, the organ quit and the singing stopped. Shortly after, Alvin could hear the preacher's voice echoing within, as if everyone listening to him was half-deaf.

"Maybe I ought to go in there and sit down," Alvin said to the girl. "I guess nobody'd mind."

"Don't you love Jesus?" the girl asked, squinting up at Alvin in the glare of the morning sun. Something with her eyes caught Alvin's attention, how they flicked about like squirrels in a tree. *This girl's not right in the head,* Alvin thought. *She's suffered some peculiar condition whereby she can sort of talk all right and even make a little sense now and then, but some part of her is cracked and not even sleeping in a church can fix it.*

"I guess Jesus got enough to worry about." Alvin stroked the mane of the horse harnessed to the buggy. "He probably don't care what I do or where I go. I could get inside there and sit down in a corner somewhere, He might not even notice me."

"His eye is on the sparrow and I know He's watching me," the girl said, quoting from a hymn Aunt Hattie sang in the kitchen on Sundays. "We all been adopted by Jesus, and He loves us no matter what we do 'cause we're His children."

"You get that from a preacher?" Alvin heard the doxology, *Praise God, from Whom all blessings flow,* as the collection plate was being passed through the congregation.

"Nobody had to tell me," said the girl. "I knowed myself it's true. I trust Jesus."

"Good for you."

"You better, too."

"Oh yeah?"

"All sinners need Jesus."

"What would you know about sin? You're just a girl."

He was losing patience now, and decided she wasn't anything worth looking at, after all.

"Why ain't you scared of Jesus?" she asked. "Didn't nobody tell you He's coming soon?"

"Jesus don't scare me as much as some other things," said Alvin, taking a look down the road toward Allenville. He felt a bad cough coming on, maybe even a dizzy fit.

"What other things?" the girl asked.

"That ain't no concern of yours."

"There ain't nobody's business that ain't Jesus'."

"Well, you ain't Jesus now, are you?"

Alvin let go of the horse and walked out toward the edge of the field where the last buggy was parked. Why had he even bothered trying to strike up a conversation with a stupid girl obviously afflicted by some dumbpalsy? He'd just wanted to be a little friendly, and ended hearing another sermon. People weren't nice anywhere these days. He looked for Rascal. Last he had seen him, the dwarf was digging around by the roadside for more wildflowers. The organ had started up again with another hymn.

Alvin walked along the fence until he came around to the church front and climbed the ten steps (one for each of the Lord's Commandments) to the landing and eased open the large wooden door. With the preacher's voice raised once more to his congregation, nobody noticed Alvin slip inside and take a seat by himself on the far end of the rear pew. He removed his cap and looked for Chester and saw him in the front row on the aisle, felt hat in hand, attention rapt and focused on the preacher perched above him. He didn't notice Alvin. The surrounding congregation wasn't much different from those who sat in the pews back in Farrington. The ladies wore the same frilly sunbonnets and the men smelled of Wildroot and Saturday night liquor. Not one of them did anything but sit like boards and listen to a fellow who looked like every country preacher Alvin had seen in his life: stony-faced, a plain black suit that might've been shared with the local undertaker, eyes like hot-fire.

The preacher's voice bellowed between the pitched and narrow walls of the small church, "FRIENDS, YOU MIGHT THINK YOU CAN CHOOSE YOUR RELIGION, BUT IN TRUTH IT ALWAYS CHOOSES YOU. THE LORD *PROVIDES* WHILE SATAN *DIVIDES*. IGNORING THAT FACT CAN BE THE GREATEST MISTAKE OF YOUR LIVES! FRIENDS, I AM NOT HERE TO OFFER YOU SALVATION! ONLY THE LORD CAN DO THAT! I AM NOT HERE TO LEAD YOU PAST WORLDLY TEMPTATIONS! ONLY JESUS CAN DO THAT! ONLY THROUGH HIS EYES WILL YOU BE ABLE TO SEE THE SHADOW THAT'S BEEN STALKING YOU SINCE THE DAY YOU WERE BORN! YOU CANNOT MAKE RESTITUTION TO ME FOR ERRORS OF FAITH OR JUDGMENT! I AM NOT YOUR REDEEMER! JESUS IS! BUT I AM HERE TO WARN YOU TODAY: SINCE THE FALL, OUR HEARTS HAVE BEEN BLACKENED BY SINS CONCEIVED AND CONCEALED! ALONE, WE HAVE NO HOPE OF REDEMPTION! ALONE, WE ARE ALREADY LOST AND GIVEN OVER TO THE FIERY PITS! OUR FATES ARE SEALED, OUR AGONY DELIVERED! THE ROPE ABOVE THE GALLOW SWINGS IN A TROUBLING WIND! *YEA, THE LIGHT OF THE WICKED IS PUT OUT, AND THE FLAME OF HIS FIRE DOES NOT SHINE!* TRUSTING IN THE CERTAINTY OF OUR ANGUISH, WE WALK DEAF, DUMB AND BLIND TOWARD THE PIT! YET, JESUS DOES NOT FORSAKE US! EVEN AS WE HAVE FORSAKEN OURSELVES, HIS GRACIOUS HEART WAITS TO REDEEM US, TO RESTORE OUR SOILED — "

Alvin got up and walked out.

Disgusted with sermons, he sat down on the top step of the porch and watched the breeze wash across the fields of wildrye to the south. The sun was hot now and Alvin unbuttoned his shirt cuffs and rolled up his sleeves. What the hell had Chester brought them here for? What was his plan? The farm boy walked down to the bottom of the steps to look for the dwarf. He guessed that Sunday services were almost done and soon the organ would play its final hymn. He wandered out to the road and discovered Rascal sitting astride the suitcase once again, his bouquet of purple asters in one hand, a black leatherbound Bible in the other.

"What's that you're reading there?"

The dwarf looked up from the page. "The Book of Job. I thought that, as we are not allowed inside the church, and seeing it is Sunday, after all, I ought to study."

"Where'd you get that?" Alvin asked, pointing at Rascal's bible.

"From a thoroughly delightful young lady I just met."

"I hope you don't mean that ugly little thing sitting over there behind the church looking after the horses."

"Oh, did you meet her, as well?"

"Sure," Alvin replied. "She talked my ear off about Jesus. I think she's afflicted."

"Oh? Why, she seemed quite enlightened to me. I was impressed by her command of Scripture."

"She says she been adopted by Jesus," said Alvin, "but she don't hardly know nothing about anything, especially her own self. She thinks she's smart, but she don't begin to fool me."

"I found her quite well-versed in the Scriptures. I wouldn't be surprised if she teaches Sunday school somewhere. She's very bright."

"I think she's dumb as ditchwater," said Alvin. "The day she starts teaching folks about Jesus, Billy Sunday'll be singing polkas with the devil in Hades."

"Well, I wouldn't worry about that," said the dwarf. "Our Lord only calls those He deems most capable."

Inside the church, the organist began playing and Alvin heard the front doors swing open. The dwarf closed the Bible and jumped up, grabbing his suitcase. As the first people flooded the staircase, Alvin followed the dwarf across the road and behind the church where the homely girl was still perched on her wooden water bucket, the cat's cradle yarn in her lap. When she saw Alvin and Rascal, she swiveled on the bucket to face them.

The dwarf gave the Bible back to her. "I'm sorry that I did not get the chance to finish studying Job's plight. I promise to try and locate a Bible of my own very soon and complete my lesson."

The girl smiled. "You been teaching this one here about the Lord?"

Before Rascal could reply, Alvin stepped forward and snatched the Bible out of the girl's hand. "Looky here, sweetheart: he don't need to teach me nothing about nobody! I already learned about Jesus Christ Almighty when I was half this tall, and only dumbbells ever believed there was such a thing, and I don't need no ugly little girl telling me nothing to the contrary! You get me?"

Then Alvin threw the Bible into the dirt and took the dwarf by the crook of his arm and hauled him up to the fenceline on the north side of the church where people filing out to their buggies or automobiles couldn't see them.

"I don't know why you waste your time like that," Alvin said, giving the fence a good shake.

Rascal laid his suitcase against one of the posts and growled back, "I have no idea what you mean."

"That ugly girl."

"Well, you were very rude."

"She wouldn't understand nothing else."

"Nevertheless."

"How long do you figure we're supposed to wait out here?" Alvin asked, taking a look out toward the rear where people were beginning to depart. He felt jittery as hell now. A motor roared to life nearer the road and the backfire caused some commotion with the horses. Alvin heard the girl yapping like a barking dog as she tried to calm them down.

"We just ought to take care not to be seen, I suppose," the dwarf said, down on both knees studying the weeds growing along the rotting plank foundation of the church. "We're to be entirely inconspicuous."

"Pardon?"

Rascal looked up, glee drawn on his face. "I believe there may be field mushrooms growing underneath here!"

"Oh yeah?"

"I tried for so long to grow them under our washroom, but even where our plumbing leaked, the soil conditions were simply unsuited for their purposes. Here, though, even in midsummer, the dirt is moist and sweetened by shadow, ideal for waxy caps." He frowned. "If we only had time to crawl under for a look." Rascal stuck his arm under the foundation.

"You get yourself spider-bit sticking your hand under there like that," Alvin said, having a quick peek of his own. "A black widow'll kill you in nothing flat." He snapped his fingers for emphasis, then coughed.

"I'm quite careful not to disturb their webs."

"That don't matter much to them that like to bite you."

"In fact, most spiders aren't at all aggressive by nature," the dwarf replied. "They're shy to the point of cowardice. They attack only when prodded to action. That includes the black widow. I've never had any trouble."

"Just the same, I wouldn't be poking around underneath there like that, if I was you."

"Well, seeing as you have little or no interest whatsoever in learning about the natural world, I'm sure you wouldn't."

Alvin looked back toward the rear of the church. Buggies and automobiles were rolling off down the road, people heading home for Sunday dinner. Soon, only the homely girl remained out back. While Rascal dug for mushrooms at the north wall, Alvin watched the girl stroll about humming some hymn to herself. After a few minutes, she disappeared. Hearing the door close with a soft thud, Alvin nudged the dwarf with the toe of his boot. "Maybe we ought to go in."

The dwarf swiveled his head to look up. "Pardon me?"

"I think we ought to go inside now."

The dwarf pulled his arm out emptyhanded and wiped the dirt off onto his sleeves. "I'd rather wait out here until we're called."

"I bet he's sticking up the collection plate."

"Oh?" Rascal stopped hunting in the black dirt. "Is that what he told you?"

"He didn't tell me nothing," Alvin replied. "I just figured it out on my own. Why else'd we be here at a church?"

"It doesn't seem to me as though heisting the collection box from a country church would prove all that worthwhile."

"Maybe he knows something we don't."

"I'd assume so," said the dwarf, starting back in again with his one-armed digging. He didn't appear much interested in what was occurring inside the church. Alvin noticed how most of the trip Rascal had been like that, talking about everything under the sun, except what they were doing day after day in these towns they visited. Alvin felt guilt and fear daily, while the dwarf's conscience seemed not to trouble him. It was a plain mystery how Rascal managed to avoid confronting the truth of the crimes they'd helped Chester commit. At night Alvin wondered if perhaps the dwarf actually enjoyed all the misery they'd inflicted, or if everything the dwarf had endured in his former life had frozen his heart to the suffering of others.

A voice echoed across the morning air. "You two there! Come over here!"

Alvin saw the preacher standing down by the corner of the church. The homely girl stood behind him, grinning ear to ear. She pointed a finger at Alvin and raised her voice. "See? That's the skinny one there that don't accept Jesus as fact!"

"How come you two been waiting out here?" the preacher called up to Alvin.

"He's ascared of Jesus, that's why," said the girl, "I believe that's how come he don't want to hear nothing good for him."

"Is that so?" said the preacher, slinging his arm around the girl's shoulder.

"I ain't ascared of Jesus," Alvin called back to the preacher, "and anyone says so's a liar." He glared at the girl. "I just rather be out of doors, is all. I was sick once. That ain't no crime."

Chester came around the corner of the church now, smoking a cigarette. He stopped beside the preacher. "I told them both to wait outside so as not to disturb your service. Truth is, I was afraid the sight of the midget might upset some of the smaller children."

The preacher studied the dwarf, then asked Chester, "You three been traveling together?"

"No, sir, I just happened upon these two young fellows on my way out of Harlan yesterday evening. They were walking alongside the road after sundown, looking all worn out and hungry, so I asked them if they'd like to share a ride. Feeling charitable, I bought them supper. It was clear they hadn't eaten in days. When I asked them where they were headed, they said 'Topeka' where the midget had them hired to a job in a shoe factory. Recalling our Lord's admonition about forsaking our brothers in time of need, I volunteered to drive them. All I asked was that they stay to themselves and be on good Christian behavior when I made my appointments. I'm sorry if this boy here has upset your girl." Chester gestured toward Alvin. "Frankly, he's grown up ignorant his entire life. Ignorant of other people, and ignorant of the Lord. He may even be a trifle slow, if you get my meaning."

The preacher nodded, his face still grim. A gust of wind ruffled his black coat.

Chester added, "I'd be pleased to complete my presentation to you indoors if you'd be so generous as to allow me five more minutes of your time, sir." He pulled out his pocketwatch and checked the hour. "I need to be running along by noontime, anyhow."

"They comin' in?" asked the girl, sneering at Alvin once more. "I could teach this one how to thank Jesus, proper and all."

The dwarf grabbed his suitcase. Alvin decided that if Chester hadn't been there just then, he would have given the girl a good choking.

"Bring them in with you," the preacher told the girl, then walked back around to the rear door, Chester on his heels. The girl stuck her tongue out at Alvin before chasing after the preacher.

The shadowy interior of the church basement served as a rectory, and smelled like rats to Alvin. Rats and mildew and wet rot. He guessed they'd had a little water leakage from the storm last night. There were three sets of shelves on either side of the door with boxes filled with Bibles stacked up on them, and small cartons with what looked to be bookmarks cut to resemble the Savior. Alvin took one and stuffed it into his back pants pocket, then followed the others into an office with a small pine desk, a leatherback swivel chair, and three other caned chairs along one wall. A painting of Jesus suffering on the bitter road to Calvary hung behind the desk.

The preacher was holding a brass candleholder in one hand and a pewter one in the other, rolling them over, examining both with deliberation and care.

"It's a matter of devotion, I'm told," Chester said, matter-of-factly, a salesboard held against his side. "A question of esteem that reflects how you and your congregation feel about the Lord, what He means to you, what place He holds in your hearts."

"Ten dollars is a lot of money," said the preacher. "I could buy a stack of hymnals for that and a new collection plate."

"Sure," Chester replied, "but you've already got songbooks and a fine collection plate that everybody who's sat in here for the last two hundred and fifty Sundays has seen and admired. What I'm offering is something different, something uplifting and beautiful to dress up the altar of the Lord and give your congregation a feeling of wonder and delight."

The preacher cracked half a grin, barely perceptible. "I got to hand it to you, Mr. Harris. You make an awful good pitch."

"Thank you, sir."

Alvin looked over at the dwarf, seated beside the young girl in the caned chairs, suitcase at his feet, sharing a read in one of the hymnals. Alvin caught sight of the safe in one corner behind a painting of Jesus, exposed slightly by the tilt of the gilded picture frame. Probably Chester intended to rob the collection plate, after all.

"Trouble is," said the preacher, "I just can't see how we could possibly afford those candleholders of yours, as much as I'd like to say we can."

"Well, I understand your dilemma," Chester said, affecting a slight drawl. "Times are hard all over these days. Why, just last week I was passing through a town in the Panhandle where the only bank they'd ever had there, only one that'd come to their town, just shut its doors for keeps. Broke my heart to see what it did to those good Christian people. It seems these days, nobody but bankers and bootleggers can afford much of anything at all, doesn't it?"

"We're just a small church and — "

"But it's times like these I find people are most in need of something to help them forget how terrible life can be," Chester persisted, "something to make them feel good inside, something bigger than themselves."

"How's that, Mr. Harris?"

"If you could afford it, you and your congregation would build the biggest, most beautiful church in the state of Iowa, wouldn't you?"

"We think we have ourselves a pretty nice little church, right now."

"Sure you do," said Chester. "It's swell. All I meant to say is that what I'm offering you are some items worthy of what you've already got here, something to point it up a little."

Chester smiled.

The preacher shook his head. "No, sir, I have to tell you I don't believe in dolling up a house of the Lord. And I have to say, sir, that'll need to be my last word. But I do thank you for stopping by."

Chester's smile broadened. "Well, we all make mistakes, don't we?"

The preacher frowned. "Beg your pardon?"

Chester quit smiling and gave Alvin that look he'd been expecting all morning long. "I'm just sorry we couldn't do business, pal. I hate getting up early just to be disappointed."

The preacher walked to the door. "Well, there's nothing to be done about it, but I'm obliged to you for coming to see us, just the same. Let me show you out."

"Why, that'd be swell of you."

As the preacher turned to go, Chester drew his revolver and shot him in the spine.

The preacher struck his head on the doorframe and fell face first to the cement.

Deafened by the revolver's discharge, Alvin couldn't hear what Chester yelled as he grabbed the girl by the collar and shoved her forward into the hall. The dwarf had escaped unseen. Ears ringing, Alvin bolted over the body of the preacher and headed for the back door. Somewhere in the church above, Chester was shouting at the girl who responded with a horrid wail. Alvin looked outside, expecting to see the dwarf running off down the road. Instead, the yard was empty. Filled with confusion, Alvin looked back down the hall toward the preacher where a pool of blood was spreading out from under his black coat. Upstairs, the girl had quit screaming. Alvin wanted to go hide out somewhere. He didn't give a hang about his split or becoming a big shot, nor was he afraid of going back on Chester, because he knew that sooner or later, the cops would get them both, dead sure.

But instead of beating it out of the church, he climbed a narrow paneled oak stairway that brought him up behind the stage backing the empty pulpit where the small church choir had stood during morning service. Only a stack of hymnals remained, and the silence within the building brought a quiver to Alvin's soul. He walked over to the pulpit and gazed out on the quiet rows of pews, and saw the dwarf kneeling in supplication to God, murmuring prayers in a hoarse and worried voice. Somewhere within a room high in the church, a mean thump echoed through the walls.

"How come you run off like that?" Alvin asked, gripping the sides of the pulpit like the preacher himself. His trembling hands rattled the wood. He felt woozy with shock and fear.

"Murder," replied the dwarf, rising to his feet once again. "Despicable and low. Villainous!" He contorted his face to reinforce the words.

"Ain't many killings you can call good," the farm boy said, his legs quivering, too.

"In a house of the Lord!"

"Ain't many good places to get killed, neither." He was becoming sick to his stomach.

"It's so discouraging," the dwarf said, shaking his head. "I'm thoroughly ashamed."

"On what account?"

"I'm sure we oughtn't to have let him do it. His vileness bears witness upon us as well."

"I'd be quiet, if I was you. If we can hear him up there," Alvin said, nodding at the ceiling, "he sure can hear us down here."

"I witnessed the life pass out of a man of God as I stood by in silence."

"You shut your mouth now," said Alvin, fear rising in his gut. Footsteps creaked in the wood overhead as someone crossed from end of the room to the other. Alvin tiptoed away from the pulpit back to a small door behind the choir box. He opened the door as quietly as he could manage and slipped inside another narrow oak staircase, this one leading high into an attic beneath the belltower. Alvin crept up to a landing illuminated by a stained glass window of the Apostles at Galilee. Five steps higher still was another door. Alvin pressed an ear to the wood. When he heard nothing, he nudged the door open a crack and peeked into a small room. Flat on her back in bed, dress hiked up to her chin and naked underneath, lay the young girl. Her eyes were shut tight, face smeared with tears, lips pursed, her arms held rigidly to her sides, legs bent apart and bowed at the knees. Blood from her middle parts stained the sheets. Chester stood at the far window, fastening the buttons of his vest. He was whistling one of those jazz tunes Alvin heard on the radio from Chicago at night. The farm boy eased the door shut and hurried back downstairs where he saw the front door flung open to the sunlight. He went outside and looked around and found the dwarf hurrying away with his suitcase, a quarter of a mile down the road. Was he trying to make a bust for it? Alvin took off after him, yelling for Rascal to stop. Scared of getting left behind, he snatched his own suitcase from the weeds across the road and ran like a bandit to catch up.

It didn't take long. Seeing the farm boy coming, the dwarf quit walking and stared back at the church steeple and the flock of sparrows circling its faded belltower. Still horrified by the shooting, Rascal's eyes were fixed upward, his spirit destitute. As Alvin caught up to him, the dwarf said, "My behavior shames me. I can never go home now."

"Huh?"

"Were my pockets to hold thirty pieces of silver, I could be no less guilty of betrayal."

"What the hell are you talking about?"

"A double-faced Judas is what I am. I ought to have warned the preacher of imminent danger. Because I did not, his death is on my record before the Lord."

Alvin kicked a clod of dirt into the fenceline. "That killing wasn't nobody's fault but his who pulled the trigger. There ain't nothing we could've done." Yet he felt his own eyes filling with tears.

The dwarf began walking again down the road to the south.

"Where the hell do you think you're going?" Alvin called after him. The dwarf walked on. Alvin hurried forward and circled ahead of him and blocked his path. His voice trembling, he said, "I asked you a question. Where the hell you going?"

The dwarf stopped and put his suitcase down in the dust. "I'm not sure."

"You can't run off and leave me out here by myself."

"Of course I can."

"It ain't right!"

"By that I assume you to mean it would be unfair for me to let our collective guilt pass on to you alone. Have no fear. I plan on confessing my own part in this tawdry affair to the proper authorities in due course. And, in any event, I can hardly hide my guilt from the Lord, and it's His judgment, and His alone, we ought properly to fear."

"I don't know no one 'round here, except you and Chester," said Alvin, looking nervously about. He felt scared and cold in the pit of his stomach. "If you run off, what the hell am I going to do? I never been this far from home before, and I don't know if I like it so much."

The dwarf wiped his brow with the back of a sleeve and stared out across the fields to the prairie horizon where the late morning sky was blue and clear. Nearby, in the wildrye beyond the fence, insects buzzed. A warm breeze was on the rise. The dwarf folded his hands together at his waist. In a reverent voice, he said, "Forgiveness is the Lord's, but redemption abides keenly within the guilty and the brave."

Alvin told him, "We got to beat it out of here."

"Would you help me save us both?"

"Huh?"

Hearing the familiar exhaust note of the Packard Six, both the farm boy and the dwarf turned to watch Chester wheel the automobile out of the churchyard and begin driving down the road toward them.

"Yes or no," said the dwarf, picking up his suitcase. "Indecision is itself an act of cowardice."

The motorcar drew near and Chester slowed to pick up his two companions. He wore the identical grin on his face he'd shown just before shooting the preacher in the back. Not a hint of worry at finding his two companions down the road. Before the Packard pulled even with the farm boy and the dwarf, Alvin said, "Just tell me what you want me to do."

Chester stopped the Packard beside him and flung open the passenger door. "Swell weather for a Sunday drive, don't you think? Climb on in and let's go."

The dwarf hoisted his suitcase into the rearseat of the Packard and scrambled in after it. Alvin tossed his own suitcase on top of Rascal's, then slid into the front seat and pulled the door closed.

"What do you say about the three of us getting something to eat?" Chester asked, sticking the Packard back into gear. "I've worked up an awful appetite this morning."

"Sure," Alvin replied, as the automobile sped up. He tried to hide his fear and disgust. "I can always eat." He kicked something in the foot-well and looked down and saw a canvas sack stuffed full of dollar bills.

"What a racket," Chester said, shaking his head. "Why, if I'd had the first idea how much dough these fellows rake in every Sunday, I'd have started my own church years ago. Why bother chasing the saps all over Creation when every Sunday morning they show up on your doorstep, pleased as punch to give you every red cent they own."

"Tithing," remarked the dwarf, "is one part alms and one part penance."

"Where're we headed?" Alvin asked, sticking his arm out into the draft. He felt dizzy.

Chester shrugged as he stepped on the accelerator. "Wherever you like. I'm feeling swell today, so you two go ahead and choose.

Anywhere's fine with me."

Hearing that, the dwarf slipped his hand into the farm boy's shirt and fished out the poster Alvin had torn from the telephone pole back in Allenville. Wind blowing in his hair, he told Chester, "We found a circus."

ICARIA, MISSOURI

AT SUMMER'S END, the farm boy from Illinois stood with a leather trunk and a pile of suitcases under the white arc lights of a small rail station platform in southern Nebraska. It was nearly half past ten and the train was late. A warm evening wind blew through a grove of weeping willows next to the depot and a crowd of young sports from the state college collected about a pair of Ford automobiles, drinking booze from a thermos bottle and joking. Down at the end of the platform beside the ticket office, Chester Burke sat on a wooden bench with a young brunette the farm boy fancied for himself. She was awfully pretty with silver-blue eyes and a melodic laugh that stirred Alvin's heart. She wore thin white muslin and a pink scarf she fiddled with while Chester flirted. Alvin had noticed her first while he and the dwarf were unloading their baggage from the taxicab. When she was alone, waiting by the depot with a brown valise and a hat box, lace hanky in hand and weeping unaccountably, Alvin thought to go up and comfort her, perhaps put his arm around her and listen to her troubles, but he was too shy, so he left her alone. Now all Alvin could do was watch helplessly from across the platform while Chester honeyed her up and made the farm boy feel like a lemon.

The office door opened and the dwarf came out with the station agent, both laughing. A breeze gusted and Alvin brushed a shock of hair from his eyes. Dust kicked up in the oily roadbed. He felt for the ticket in his pants pocket and looked down the tracks again for the late train. He was anxious to leave. He had already snuck out that morning to see a doctor for his aggravating sore throat. Alvin knew he had been getting sicker day by day, but was afraid of mentioning the consumption because he didn't want to be ordered to the hospital, so he said nothing about the persistent cough nor the recurrent night sweats he had endured since Kansas. Still, the doctor detected his anemia and prescribed a dosage of iron and arsenic and ordered him home to bed. Chester had parked the Packard in an old livery stable ten blocks from the depot, hiding it until their return from Missouri where Rascal had found Emmett J. Laswell's Traveling Circus Giganticus in a small town called Icaria. For five weeks now, the dwarf had been hunting Laswell by newspaper and rumor. He had scoured fair bulletins and trade notices, sent off telegraphs, written letters to chambers of commerce by the dozen, encouraged by Chester who paid cash-value for the effort without question. Now, upon the dwarf's recommendation, Chester had purchased train tickets to Missouri because a grimy wagon circus had stopped to put on a show there, though Alvin had no idea why that had him so stewed up.

The farm boy watched Chester take one of the peachy brunette's hands and give it a soft pat as she mooned up at him from the shadows beside the office. Rascal hopped down off the platform to place a nickel on one of the iron rails. The station agent went back indoors to the information desk. In the dark distance, a train whistle sounded. While Chester Burke slipped his arm around the young girl's shoulder and lightly nuzzled her ear, the dwarf hurried from the tracks toward Alvin and the baggage. Clouds of dust moths swarmed the arc light. A family of six dragged suitcases and stuffed burlap sacks up onto the rail platform. Three traveling salesmen in overcoats and felt hats walked up out of the willow shadows past Alvin. A sleepy woman with a small boy holding a hot-water bottle to his ear appeared nearby. The train whistle echoed again, and the blazing electric headlight of the great locomotive flashed down the tracks. The dwarf scrambled back up onto the station platform. Inhaling dust aggravated Alvin's cough and made his head swim. He felt his fever rising and needed to lie down, worrying now that he might not be long for this world.

"I've just spoken with a most remarkable fellow," said Rascal, wiping dirt from the roadbed off his short pants. His blue suspenders were dusty and his white cotton shirt stained by perspiration.

"I ain't carrying your bags no more," Alvin replied, his attention still focused on Chester and the brunette. Seeing them together like that gave him a peculiar bellyache. "It ain't fair."

A man and a woman in evening dress walked toward the station, the man carrying a leather valise and a burning quarter cigar, the woman a longstem red rose.

The dwarf stared intently at the college fellows roughhousing beside their automobiles. Farther down the platform, a baby's fitful squalling was half-drowned out by the station agent announcing the arrival of Union Pacific passenger service to Kearney, Columbus and Omaha. More people crowded the platform, a few casting curious glances at the dwarf in his odd clothing.

Rascal said, "Did I tell you how my Uncle Augustus helped drive the golden spike for the Union Pacific at Promontory, Utah?"

Alvin frowned. "Not yet."

"Well, Dr. Thomas Durant, vice-president of the railroad, had been commissioned to drive the last spike at the grand ceremony, but having been enfeebled the night before by a spoiled bite of mince pie, he directed Uncle Augustus to take his part. I'm told the best engineers were quite impressed by Uncle Augustus' strength and prowess."

"Did he get a medal?"

The dwarf thought for a second. "Why, yes, I believe so."

"Hot diggety."

At last the locomotive arrived in a huge cloud of steam. A conductor and six Negro porters stepped off close to the station agent's office. Alvin looked for Chester through the crowds to get his help with the luggage. A group of college fellows with slicked-back hair and polished spats came onto the platform, reeking of gin.

"I'm very excited," Rascal remarked, watching people getting on and off the train. "Oh, it's been years since I've traveled by Pullman car. Of course, Auntie steadfastly refused to hear of it since Uncle Augustus died, claiming my constitution was entirely too frail for railroad transportation. As often as we fought over this, I was unable to persuade her otherwise. She can be quite stubborn. Did I ever tell you I once operated a locomotive?"

Across the busy platform, Alvin saw Chester draw the brunette toward him and kiss her hard on the lips. When they broke, she was grinning like a spaniel puppy. The farm boy felt ill from fever and nerves. Truth was, he hadn't been on a train since riding back from the sanitarium, another of the reasons he had run off with Chester: to get away from the farm, maybe live it up for once. Frenchy had taken a day-coach to Chicago the day after he graduated Normal School and gotten drunk on Canadian ale at a blind tiger in Cicero and woke up along the windy Lake Michigan shore with only his hat on. When he came home, he told Alvin he'd never had such a high time. Fellows they both knew in Farrington got stewed on hard cider and blackstrap and every so often attended the Odeon picture show after supper or church fairs on Sunday and some got buried in the same old clothes they had worn on their wedding day without ever having left the farmlands of Illinois. *Work and pray, live on hay.* Well, nobody could say that of Alvin, any longer. He had seen a lot of the world this summer, and it wasn't anything to snicker at: roadside stands and barley fields hiding a thousand barrels of hootch, bed-bugs in tourist camps, motor-speeding by moonlight, suitcases full of orangeback bills, girls and killings. Cold-blooded murder. He had seen plenty, all right. Lately, though, he found himself in the middle of the night thinking about Aunt Hattie's hermit cookies and the mullen weeds that grew under his bedroom window.

Two pretty co-eds dressed in chic wool-velour coats and Clara Bow hats stepped off the train into the over-smiling welcome of the college fellows, one of whom planted a wet kiss onto the cheek of the first co-ed. The conductor directed a redcap to help the family of six with their baggage. Chester boarded the train two cars down at a compartment sleeper with the smiling young brunette on his arm. Alvin tugged at the steamer trunk, pulling it upright. He told the dwarf, "Like I said,

I ain't fetchin' yours no more. It ain't fair."

The conductor called out "All aboard," and after another few minutes the train whistle shrieked and sparks flew out of the engine compartment as the fireman, black-faced with coal grime, stoked the furnace. Smoke billowed high into the dark.

"I wouldn't think to ask," the dwarf replied, grabbing two of the smaller suitcases and dragging them toward the train and the nearest redcap. Alvin followed the dwarf through a crowded vestibule on a second-class Pullman sleeper whose berths were already drawn with curtains. The narrow aisle was hectic with people shoving past in both directions. Odors of disinfectant mixed with stale tobacco fumes and sweat. A white-jacketed porter hustled by with dust cloths and fresh bed linen and a portable vacuum cleaner.

"I'll need the lower berth, of course," said the dwarf, stopping at number eight. He tossed his suitcase onto the bed and immediately crawled inside. Alvin frowned as a plump woman with a small child shoved past, grumbling about ill-mannered people crowding the aisles. He looked up at the upper berth and decided it was too cramped. The train whistle screeched.

"I ain't climbing up there," the farm boy said, setting his own leather suitcase down. "You take it. I'll give you a boost."

"No, thank you. I prefer where I am." The dwarf pushed a buzzer next to the window as the Pullman car lurched into motion. The whistle blew again and the locomotive chugged slowly forward along the tracks. Down at one end of the car, the washroom door opened and a fellow in a waistline suit and gray fedora exited, a folded newspaper tucked under one arm.

"Yes, sir?"

Alvin found the Negro porter at his elbow, holding a small step-ladder. Rascal stuck his head out of the lower berth to watch. The farm boy said, "I ain't getting up there. I want this one down here."

The porter said, "Looks to me like it already been spoken for." He picked up Alvin's luggage to be stowed away.

Just down the corridor, a young woman wearing a flamingo pink silk tea gown stepped out into the aisle from number four. "Oh, porter, could you help me, please?'"

"Yes, ma'am." He turned to the farm boy. "Be right back, sir."

Leaving the stepladder at Alvin's berth, the porter moved off down the aisle while the sleeper car swayed gently side to side. One of the conductors entered the Pullman from the front vestibule. Through the window, the last lights of the factory town flickered out of the dark. Rascal rolled over on the bed and closed the curtain.

"May I help you, sir?" the conductor asked Alvin, as he arrived at the berth.

"I ain't sleeping up there," replied the farm boy, coughing into his fist. "It ain't room enough."

"Your ticket, please?"

Alvin handed it over to the conductor who took one quick look and gave the ticket back again. He told the farm boy, "Well, I'm sorry, but there are no other accommodations available on this train tonight. I'm afraid you'll have to make do. Your porter'll help you up. Goodnight."

Tipping his cap, the conductor walked off toward the drawing rooms at the rear of the car.

Rascal stuck his head out through a fold in the curtain. "These berths really are quite comfortable."

"Aw, choke it," Alvin growled, climbing up into his berth.

Soon the electric lights were extinguished and the Pullman car was dark. Across the aisle, Alvin heard a salesman in the upper berth snoring like a sick bear. Half a dozen times, the porter passed by. Twice, the girl in number four summoned his attention. Another short dumpy fellow waddled back from the washroom, stinking of gin and cigars. In his cramped upper berth, Alvin watched the night countryside fly past, lights of scattered farmhouses glowing like tiny stars on the black prairie. He wondered how far east the other passengers were going. St. Louis? Cleveland? Pittsburgh? Washington? All those places he'd likely never live long enough to see. Trains ran all night in America. He wondered what it would be like to get off one in Boston or New York, walk around under a giant skyscraper, eat in a swank restaurant somewhere, attend a movie show with a big crowd, ride a subway car to the waterfront and watch the big ships come in from China, all the ladies of joy flocking to sailors and other young strangers like himself.

Rascal tapped on the underside of the bed. Alvin ignored him. The dwarf tapped again. Somebody passed by in the aisle, scent of bay rum trailing behind. Two men were conversing in low voices at the front of the car with the porter. Rascal tapped again and Alvin stuck his head through his curtain and leaned over the side and pulled open the dwarf's berth. "What're you doing that for?"

The dwarf's smiling face thrust out from the dark. "Shall we play a game of Hearts?"

"Go roll your hoop."

Rascal ducked back into his berth and rang for the porter. The whistle from the locomotive screeched and a few seconds later the clanging of klaxon bells at an empty crossroads echoed briefly through the Pullman car. The porter came down the aisle to Rascal's berth. "Yes, sir?"

"Is there a toilet?"

"At the front of this car."

"Much obliged."

The porter left.

Rascal crawled out of his berth, fully dressed. Peeking out from his own berth, Alvin saw a woman's face and enormous bosom emerge from behind the curtain in number three, curlpapers in her hair. "Good heavens!" She gave a tug on the curtain to the berth above her. "Harold?"

A man's voice answered. "Yes, dear?"

"It's that strange little man again!"

"Close your eyes, honey, he'll go away."

Rascal gave her a polite bow.

The woman shrieked, "Harold!"

Another man stuck his head out of a lower berth. "For crying out loud, would you folks please keep quiet!"

The dwarf closed his curtain and rushed off toward the front of the Pullman. Alvin stretched out. He closed his eyes and tried to forget his bellyache. After a while the salesman in the upper berth across the aisle quit snoring. Alvin listened to the occasional train whistle and thought of the trestle across the Mississippi where he used to fish and swim. *Fact was, nobody knew where he'd gone. Maybe they thought he'd gotten on a truck and ridden to California, or else jumped in the river and drowned. Probably Joe Mitchell would organize a pack of men to drag the current below the trestle and ol' Stewball would throw a couple sticks of dynamite into the water to try and get the body to come up out of the muck, after which they'd go home and eat a chicken dinner and get drunk and probably forget about him in a week or so. Maybe Frenchy would nail up some notices down river and drive Uncle Cy's Chevrolet south to Quincy, but it wouldn't be more than a month before most of them would give up and figure he just bumped off from his consumption somewhere. Poor old Alvin was dead and gone to Jesus. Someone else'll have to feed the cows now and water the chickens. Maybe Mary Ann. She doesn't hardly do nothing around the house but read drugstore magazines and chalk up her face for snooty Jimmy McFarland. If Daddy wasn't feeling stingy, he might order up a nifty stone for the gravesite and maybe Frenchy would get a haircut and wear a suit of black broadcloth and everyone'd come and bawl their eyes out for a couple hours and say a sorrowing word or two about what a fine kid good old Alvin had been when he was alive for tolerating his illness and all, and how much they were going to miss him, and how nobody could ever weed and water a garden as good, and who could forget how he fixed Mrs. Wilkie's worm fence in a day and a half for nothing more'n a jar of watermelon pickles and a glass of cider, and how after hearing that, the preacher might even tell everybody that poor dear departed Alvin Frederick Pendergast was a saint and a credit to his grieving family, after all.*

The train roared past a blackened junction town without stopping. Alvin had finally drifted off to sleep when a woman's voice down the aisle called from the dark, "Good heavens, Harold! He's back!"

Alvin felt the stepladder scrape against the lower berth. The double curtain rustled, and parted briefly, allowing somebody to struggle up onto his bed, nearly pulling the bedlinen off in the process.

"Hey!"

"Shhhh!"

The berth light flashed on and Alvin saw the dwarf propped up near the window-fastenings at the foot of the berth. Rascal held a fistful of bills. "We're rich!"

Feeling wobbly and lightheaded, the farm boy leaned out through the curtain to look down the aisle where the woman from berth three was talking to the porter: "I tell you, he's deliberately spoiling my sleep."

"Yes, ma'am."

"My husband owns fourteen chain stores and I want something done."

"Yes, ma'am."

"Harold!"

Alvin ducked back into his berth. The dwarf had curled up next to the window and spread the bills out on the blanket. The farm boy switched off the berth light, then shushed the dwarf. Somebody grabbed the stepladder. The porter's face thrust into the upper berth. Seeing the two of them together, he smiled. "Why, ain't that something. Looky here."

"Yeah?" Alvin coughed hoarsely. Now he wasn't sure he could get back to sleep.

"I s'pose y'all ain't needing this ladder no more."

"I guess I will tomorrow morning," the farm boy said, rubbing his eyes. He noticed his bedclothes were damp and smelled moldy. "When's breakfast? I'm so hungry I could eat a rubber boot."

"Well, sir, I'd say you're still a few hours shy of a cup of coffee and a doughnut, but I'll come get you, don't you worry. Yes, sir." Then the porter turned to Rascal who was hiding in the corner of the berth at Alvin's feet. "And if I was you, little fellow, I'd keep my eyes peeled. There's a lady we both know who'd like her husband to give you a good old-fashioned lickin'."

"I can't imagine why," Rascal protested. "I haven't done a thing."

"Well, she's awful cranky."

"So I noticed."

"Now, don't say I ain't warned you. 'Night, boys."

"Good night."

When he heard the porter open the washroom door, Alvin switched on the berth light and grabbed a handful of the bills lying on the blanket. He riffled through them, counting haphazardly. "We got better'n two hundred bucks here."

The dwarf switched the light off. "It's three hundred and seventy-three even, and it's not ours, it's mine. I won it fair and square."

"Says you," Alvin replied, still holding a handful of bills. "I ain't had this much cash-money in my whole life. Where'd you steal it?"

"I just told you, I won it playing thirteen unusually trying hands of Fargo Pete with some very sneaky cardsharks back there in the clubcar. In fact, I was fully prepared to be murdered by them when the game was over. A thoroughly nasty fellow named Patch was quite upset with me for emptying his pockets. It's a wonder I survived." The dwarf reached for the money. "Here, give it to me."

Alvin snatched it away. The dwarf lunged across the bed and grabbed at the dollar bills in Alvin's hands, but he was too slow and the farm boy tucked them under his pillow.

"I'll ring for the porter," the dwarf warned.

"Aw, be a sport. Let me have some of it."

"Why should I? You didn't win it, I did."

"Don't be stingy. I ain't feeling good." His pillow was half-drenched in fever sweat.

"Listen here, if you return it to me," the dwarf said, "I'll give you a share."

"Oh yeah?" Alvin coughed. "How much?"

"I won't say until I have it all back."

The train passed a crossroad, bells clanging in the dark. Another prairie town briefly lit the upper berth as the Pullman swayed gently. Reluctantly, the farm boy shoved his handful of bills back to the dwarf. "Well, you better not leave me flat, you old skinflint. Remember, if it wasn't for me, you wouldn't even been on this train tonight."

"Thank you. Now, if you're truly feeling ill, perhaps we ought to call for a doctor."

Alvin shook his head. "There ain't nothing wrong with me. It's just allergies."

"Oh, I doubt that very much. You've been under the weather for weeks now and I'm quite worried. It's obvious you're not well."

"If you say so."

"Look, there's no sense in avoiding a fact of health. You're not afraid of doctors, are you?"

"No!" Alvin scowled. "And there ain't nothing wrong me, neither. So why don't you just tell me how you won that dough?"

Collecting the bills together one by one, the dwarf replied, "I told you, it was Fargo Pete."

"What the hell's that?"

"A card game, you ninny! The rules are quite involved, otherwise I'd teach them to you." Rascal began counting up his money in the dark. "As a child, I used to play for hours on end. I'm an expert Fargo Pete player."

"Maybe we ought to try a hand or two."

The dwarf stifled a laugh. "That's precious."

"Huh?"

"When I was eleven years old, I suffered an awful spell of rheumatism and had to be confined to bed for a week. This was the middle of July, so the upstairs of our house was terribly hot, and, of course, the rheumatism gave me quite a high fever and dreadful sweats and I couldn't move a muscle without enduring the worst pain imaginable. Auntie shifted my bed under the dormer where a breeze provided some comfort. She and Miss Evalena from next door administered salicylate of soda every two or three hours with buttermilk and Dover's powder at night and wrapped up my legs in cotton-batting to ease the horrid inflammation. It was quite hellish, I assure you — that is, until I was paid a visit by the sweetest angel in God's creation. Dear little Betsy Bennett was new to Hadleyville and had no friends before we were introduced to each other by Auntie and Mrs. Bennett, who'd chanced to strike up a conversation at the grocery store. She wore blue gingham and corkscrew curls and a yellow ribbon in her hair and had read every volume of *Chatterbox* I owned, cover to cover. Betsy was the most remarkable child I'd ever met. Naturally, we became great friends. It was she who taught me how to play Fargo Pete, and I must admit that when it came time for Betsy to go home, I was forced to give her my favorite savings bank as penalty for all the tricks I lost. Even so, the very next morning she returned with a basket of hot cinnamon buns and a pair of loaded dice with which she allowed me to reclaim the penny bank. Wasn't that lovely? All week long we shared my buttermilk and told each other riddles and quoted poems and jingles from *St. Nicholas*. She read to me from *Marjorie-Joe* and I read to her out of *Tales of the Days of Chivalry* and *The Little Colonel*. I taught her sailor's knots and Indian cures and she showed me how to darn my own stockings and to say 'Merry Christmas' to the deaf. Why, I believe it may have been the grandest time I ever knew as a child, despite my painful rheumatism. Unfortunately, Mrs. Bennett was called away by relatives to the mines in California. The last I heard from dear Betsy was a Christmas card she mailed from a tiny gold town in the mountains. She wrote that it had been snowing for a week and she'd seen a bear in the woods behind her house that very morning."

Bells clanged at a crossroads and Alvin heard the salesman across the aisle begin snoring once again. In the dark corridor below, the porter passed by whistling to himself. Rascal folded open the curtain to stop him. The dwarf said, "I'm terribly hungry."

The porter cracked a grin. "Don't I know it."

"I'd like a meat sandwich and a glass of lemonade."

"Well, sir, don't know's I could do that. Kitchen's closed for the night, but I believe the candybutcher's catnapping in the dining car right now and I guess he might have you a snack if you can wake him."

"Splendid! How do I get there?"

"Just follow this aisle ahead through the vestibule to the next car." The porter pointed to the rear of the Pullman. "Go through that one, too, and there she'll be."

"Wonderful! Thank you very much."

"Yes, sir."

The porter walked off.

Alvin said, "I ain't a-going with you. I'm waiting for breakfast."

"I don't recall extending the invitation," replied the dwarf, struggling to re-tie his shoes.

Across the aisle, a thin fellow in nightclothes parted his curtain. "Shhhh! Trying to sleep here."

"Sorry," Alvin whispered, as the dwarf jumped down into the aisle and hustled off.

"Harold! It's him again!"

"Who?"

"That awful little man!"

The farm boy quickly tied his shoes and slid down off the upper berth into the darkened aisle, landing with a loud thud. At once, several people rang for the porter. Murmuring apologies as he went along, the farm boy chased after the dwarf.

A crowd of men in gray wool flannel suits stood in the drafty vestibule smoking cigarettes and sharing conversation with a pair of conductors. Alvin nodded as he came through. Before he reached the door to the next Pullman car, one of the conductors grabbed his shoulder. "Hold on there, young fellow."

"Huh?"

"Do you have a ticket for that car?"

Alvin felt his face flush. "No, sir."

"Well, then, you can't go in there. These cars are fully engaged."

Through the glass, Alvin saw somebody come out of the men's smoking room in the next Pullman. The rhythmic click-clack-click-clack of the gently swaying train vibrated underfoot. The farm boy told the conductor, "I ain't feeling too good. I need something to eat."

"Well, son, I'm afraid it's a little late for that. The diner's been closed for hours now."

One of the men piped up, "Oh, Wilbur, don't be a stiff. Let the poor kid through. The swells won't mind. Look how skinny he is. It's obvious he hasn't eaten in a week. Say, I'll bet Ollie'd set him up to a wienie sandwich in half a shake."

The stocky man smoking a cigarette beside him added, "Why, sure he would. And probably throw in a cup of coffee, too, for a folksy young fellow like this."

"I ain't no hick," said Alvin, his blood rising. As the train swayed, everyone in the vestibule steadied his balance and a touch of vertigo chased behind the farm boy's eyes.

"Do you hear that, Wilbur?" a third gentleman chimed in. "This boy's not some sap from blind baggage. He's an earnest young fellow

who won't let you put it all over him just to keep this railroad running on routine lines. If he's sick like he says he is, why not do the fair
square thing and let him by? A fellow shouldn't need a lounge suit to
get a sandwich."

"Let him through, Wilbur," said the other conductor. "The railroad
won't go belly-up on account of a hungry kid."

"Well, I couldn't stand the gaff if it did," Wilbur said, stepping
aside to allow Alvin by. "All right, then. Go ahead, son. Have yourself
a sandwich, but be quick about it. I'll be through that car in another
quarter of a hour, so there'd better not be any monkey business."

"Thanks."

Crossing the threshold, Alvin heard a round of laughter behind
him and felt humiliated. Gasbags! Why had that rattlebrained conductor allowed the dwarf to slip by so easily? It wasn't at all fair. He
entered the men's washroom and used the toilet. Checking himself in
the mirror afterward, his face appeared waxy and sallow. He hadn't
any idea he looked so awful. Alvin felt the train rumble under his feet
and heard the clanging at another crossroad. He washed his hands,
dried them off, and went back out into the empty aisle again in time
to see the lights of a Dixie filling station disappear into the darkness.
Alvin heard laughter from a compartment near the end of the car. He
walked quietly along the aisle to drawing room "A," found the electric
light on and the door cracked open, and stole a peek inside. The brunette from the station platform, now wearing a gold kimono, winked at
him, then called to someone out of Alvin's view, "Oh, Clarence dear,
it seems we have company."

The farm boy backed up into the aisle, flushed with embarrass-
ment. Then the door swung open wide and Chester appeared in a
blue flannel robe, holding a plate with a cheese sandwich and a stack
of crackers. Seeing Alvin, he broke into a wide grin. "Well, what do
you know? Hiya, kid!"

He leaned forward and grabbed Alvin by the elbow and dragged
him into the drawing room and shut the door. "Honey, meet Melvin.
Kid, say hello to Alma."

Gardenia perfume wafted up as the brunette offered Alvin her hand. "Evening, dear."

The farm boy shook her hand politely. "Hello."

Chester grinned. "Melvin's a corking athlete, footballer with the college at Lincoln."

"You don't say?" she giggled, nudging a soft brown curl off her eyebrow. "Why, he doesn't look at all the sort. He seems like an awful softie and those freckles are so boyish."

Alvin blushed to see her study him like she did. He still thought she was swell, and he'd lay her in nothing flat if he had the chance. Chester sat down and took a bite of his sandwich. The green carpet was littered with cracker crumbs and Alvin smelled liquor.

Chester laughed. "Well, I tell you, he's as rough as they come. Aren't you, kid?"

The farm boy shrugged. He knew how haggard and pale he looked, but what could he do about it? Truth was, he felt even worse. God, how he hated being sick.

Chester went on, "You bet he is! Why, the papers in Lincoln say he's another Red Grange, and I don't doubt it for a minute. Anyone who knows his football can tell he's got the stuff."

The brunette slipped a silver hipflask out from the folds of her gold kimono, took a sip, and giggled again. "Well, what's a hero like you doing riding a train in the middle of the night? Shouldn't you be in a gymnasium somewhere doing calisthenics or throwing a medicine ball around with the other boys on the team?"

"Sure, I guess so," Alvin stammered weakly, trying his best to play along. "I just ain't thought that much about it. Nobody told me what to do today, so soon as my feet started itchin', I went and got on the train." He summoned a feeble smile. Lying didn't seem that tough, anymore.

Chester drew a bottle of Canadian whiskey from his handbag and filled a shotglass on the table beside him. "What he means to say, darling, is that he thinks school's for the birds. Melvin's commercial, see, and he's gotten up a meeting to try for a professional team in St. Louis and believes he can cinch a job so long as his mother doesn't find out. She's something of a trueblood Christer from a rock farm down by Abilene, and more than anything in the world she wants Melvin to get ducked before she passes on to her reward. He's still got a raft of faith in the Old Book, of course, and the importance of church fellowship and all, but he can't just chuck everything to take a swim for Jesus. Well, at any rate, as you can see, the poor kid's feeling awful bum about it."

Alvin saw the pretty brunette staring at him, a bright twinkle in her eye as she took another sip from the silver hipflask. He felt a slight chill from his fever and had to steady himself.

Alma said, "Why, I'll bet you a cookie that Melvin's mommy is darned proud of her boy even if he isn't a Sunday School teacher." She offered Alvin her hipflask. "Here, honey, have a jolt. It'll help. Honest."

Chester grabbed her wrist. "Don't tempt him, sweetheart. When I met Melvin in the lunchroom of that rube burg this morning, I could see the poor fellow was already about to crack. Why, he almost fainted in his eggs, didn't you, kid?"

"Sure I did." The farm boy noticed that the brunette's kimono had parted above the waist giving him a discreet peek at one of her pale pink breasts. Suddenly he felt flushed, and stifled a cough even as his peenie stiffened.

Alma frowned. "Gee, honey, that's awful! Maybe you hadn't ought to've taken that church dope so hard. My momma, bless her heart, baked peach pies for twenty-two years at the Methodist fair back in Kimball and never took her eye off the pulpit until Reverend Waller called her down one Sunday evening for sneaking a gallon of sweet-wine into the punch, and him, that mucker, with a cocktail shaker in his office closet and Mabel Hutchins from the choir waiting up in the attic. Poor Momma came home fussing that Reverend Waller didn't have any call to bawl her out like he did, and if the Lord only asked temperance of the congregation, well, forget it! And I tell you, honey, Momma never went back. If you ask me, all religious folks are crabs."

Chester downed his whiskey with a smile. "Gee, that's a swell story, sweetheart, but would you mind awfully taking a smoke in the toilet? Melvin and I have a few things to talk over and that means man to man, darling, get what I mean?" He walked over and opened the door to the washroom annex and jerked his thumb at her to get up.

"Clarence, honey, you know I told you I don't smoke."

"Well, this is as good a time as any to get the habit." He tossed her a package of Chesterfields from the table. "Here, now beat it."

"Hey!"

He grabbed her harshly and gave her a kiss on the lips. When Chester stepped back again, the brunette was smiling. He said to her, "You love me, don't you, darling?"

"Honey, I'd give you a clout in the head if you weren't so nice to pat." She wiggled her fingers at the farm boy. "Toodle-loo, Melvin."

After the toilet door closed, Chester dragged Alvin over to the window and sat down in front of him. "She's a peacherino, isn't she?"

He nodded. "She's slick, all right."

Chester clucked his tongue. "Dumb as a cow, though. For two hours now she's been gassing about some fellow her sister's going with and how he bought her a new electric refrigerator." Chester poured another shot of Canadian whiskey and drank it in one gulp. Then he took a cigarette from his robe and lit up. Flicking the spent match onto the table, he told Alvin, "Look here, you boys are going to ride through to Omaha, then change trains to the Missouri Pacific. I need to run in on someone tomorrow morning at Council Bluffs, so I won't be traveling with you after tonight. When you get to Icaria, there's a flophouse on Third Street owned by a fellow named Spud Farrell. He'll hire you a room for the week. Pay him cash-money. He's an old hellcat, so he'll give you the lowdown on the smart neighborhoods and where the best eats are. If you like, you and the midget can give the circus a once-over before I get there on Saturday. Just don't go till after dark. I'll be staying at the Belvedere Hotel. That's downtown on Main. I'll telephone to Spud when my train gets in. He'll let you know I arrived. All right?"

"Sure."

"Tell the midget if he does anything to put this job on the fritz, I'll pop him so hard he'll need Western Union to tell you good morning."

The farm boy coughed into his fist, then nodded. "I was out looking for him when I walked by your door and seen that girl sitting here. I ain't exactly sure where he is right now."

"I just saw him back there in the smoker playing cards with a flock of bond salesmen. What'll you bet he'll have 'em all busted by midnight?"

As the train passed another crossroad, Alvin heard the girl humming a few bars of jazz in the toilet. Her voice was wonderfully clear and lovely. Chester listened briefly, then took a drag off the cigarette and stood up. Somebody buzzed insistently to enter another drawing room back up the darkened aisle.

Chester told Alvin, "All right, you better scram now and get your sleep. You're not looking that fresh and there's a little song sparrow next door waiting for me to love her up." He led the farm boy to the compartment door. "So long, kid."

Leaving the drawing room, the farm boy bumped straight into the conductor who had blocked him back at the vestibule. One glance at Alvin and the conductor's face went sour. "You? Why, I shoulda — "

"Awww, keep your shirt on, pal," Alvin growled, squeezing past. "I'm beating it already!"

At Icaria, the train station was located in a section of town that had run down when the Singer Sewing Machine Company quit its thread mill contract and the labor turnover sent hundreds to public charity and pauper funds. Worn-out plank sidewalks led from the noisy Missouri Pacific locomotives and the crowded depot, past a potato warehouse and a grimy brickyard and a packing plant into the pathetic neighborhood of scratch houses and shiftlessness. A sudden cloudburst had descended upon Icaria earlier that week, drenching the old dirt roads to mud. Sewer drainage by the train district was dismal, too, the oily stench nauseating as the farm boy and the dwarf carried their suitcases past a row of shabby Negro residences and across the railroad tracks toward Third Street. They stopped for a few minutes to watch a freight train going back light to Kansas City. Sooty-eyed men stared at them from empty Illinois Central boxcars and sagging tarpaper cookshacks. Gray clouds were scattered about the late morning sky and the day was cool. A quarter mile past the tracks, a collection of broken-down flivvers crowded the yard of a squat framehouse on Clover Lane across the road from a blacksmith shop and a closed millinery. On a plank fence next to the elm-shrouded house, billposters had pasted a bright colorful notice for *Emmett J. Laswell's Traveling Circus Giganticus.* According to the advertisement, all the tent shows would open after the street parade on Friday. That meant this afternoon.

"I've never ridden a camel," remarked the dwarf, comparing the Arabian dromedary on the elaborately drawn poster to a notice in the morning paper he had purchased from a newsbutcher in the clubcar. "Have you?"

"Sure I did," Alvin lied. "It wasn't nothing special."

A black second-hand Chevrolet drove by in the rutted street. The farm boy put down his suitcase. He had slept better than he expected in the upper berth and woke just after dawn with the fever dissipated and his cough subdued. He was still tired, but not quite so enfeebled as he had been. The eggs he ate for breakfast in the buffet car had set him up just fine. Down behind the framehouse was a chilly creek hidden by dense cottonwoods and shagbark hickory trees where a pack of boys playing truant from school for the day rough-necked along the soggy embankment, voices chattering like nutty mockingbirds. Alvin expected to see hundreds of kids just like them at the circus by sundown.

Back near the depot, a steam whistle shrieked.

The dwarf asked, "Did Chester mention to you whether or not our flophouse puts up suppers? I'd rather save my card winnings for an emergency."

"I got pocket money enough for eats till the end of the week. If that don't do, he says we can wash dishes at a lunch counter."

Alvin picked up his tattered suitcase and started walking again. A cool breeze swept through the thick cottonwoods and brushed dust along the old board sidewalk.

"Actually, I'm quite good at dishwashing," said the dwarf, folding the newspaper under his arm. He rushed to keep up. "Auntie despised it, so she decided that doing them ought to be my after-supper chore.

I also directed Bessie's weekly marketing and regulated many of the household duties when Auntie went on holiday. Why, in less than a month I learned how to prepare cowheel jelly and sausage pudding and rummeled eggs, while Pleasance taught me to improve boiled starch by the addition of some salt or a little gum arabic dissolved. Isn't that fascinating?"

"You said it." Alvin suddenly felt a strong piss coming on and didn't see an outhouse.

"Oh, I doubt we'll have any trouble at all earning our way if need be."

"Gee, that's swell," the farm boy remarked, hurrying his pace along the wooden sidewalk. "Maybe you can buy your own pie tonight."

The boardinghouse at Third Street and Borton was three floors high and dingy with flaking paint and missing roof shingles. Virginia creeper draped the clapboard siding, and thick patches of milkweed clustered to the foundation. Old sycamores shrouded the upper floors. A steep cement staircase led up from the sidewalk to a dusty veranda littered with apple crates and soiled cushions and potato sacks filled with discards. The screen door was ajar and a single electric light was lit in the entry. A stink of fresh turpentine issued from somewhere indoors and faint voices echoed throughout. Parked at the curb out front was a black truck with an advertisement on both door panels for **Timothy Meyer & Co. Painting**. Scattered leaves blew about the dirt road. Alvin's stomach was going sour as he grew nervous again being in a strange town. What if he got sick here? Where would he go? The dwarf went indoors ahead of him, passing a small placard on the siding that read: **No Invalids!**

Upstairs, a radio set broadcast a jazzy dance program and the music echoed through the dark stairwell. The empty foyer for the big old house was gloomy and cool and smelled of linoleum and musty closets. Jade-green portières left of the entry hall across from the desk revealed a side parlor. A narrower hallway led to the dining room and kitchen at the back of the house. Overhead, the ceiling plaster showed cracks and water-blotches, and the brass light fixture had gone dark from years of tarnish. The front desk was unattended, so the dwarf set his suitcase next to a brass spittoon, then reached up from his tiptoes and rang the service bell. An office door behind the desk opened and a young blonde hardly older than Alvin came out. She was dressed plainly in a pale blue flower-print frock. Her hair was bobbed and curled and she had a darling face with brown calf-eyes. The farm boy's heart jumped when she smiled at him. "Good afternoon."

"Hello."

Her sweet face brightened further. "Why, you're with the circus, aren't you?"

Without hesitation, the dwarf nodded. "Dakota Bill, bareback riding and Indian knife tricks, at your service, ma'am." He bowed elegantly.

The girl smiled. "Pleased to meet you. My name is Clare." She looked across at Alvin. "You must be Melvin. Your telegraph arrived Wednesday evening."

"Yeah?"

"Of course, it's just lovely that you'll be staying here with us. Why, I adore the circus." Her brown eyes sparkled.

Alvin heard footsteps pounding down the stairwell from the second floor. A man's husky laughter echoed loudly out of the corner room above the parlor as a painter in lacquer-stained overalls came down the staircase into the foyer, look of distress on his face. He shouted to the blonde, "Honey, telephone Doc Evans, will you? I just swallowed some turpentine!"

"Oh, dear!"

"Tell him I'll be over his place in nothing flat!"

The painter hurried out of the boardinghouse and down to the sidewalk. The girl rushed back into the office and dialed for the operator. "Hello, Shirley? This is Clare." She nudged the door shut behind her.

Alvin walked to the front door and watched the painter running up the sidewalk. One block behind him, a postman strolled along with his mail sack while a delivery truck and a tan Hudson-Essex rattled past in the other direction. Tall shady elm trees blocked his sight farther on. A train whistle sounded in the distance.

The office door opened again and the blonde came out, shaking her head. "Would you believe that's the third call this week Doctor Evans has had for turpentine poisoning?"

Alvin walked back from the front door as a draft from the street swept up into the boardinghouse. A cough rattled out of his chest, making his eyes water.

"One cup of castor oil, two eggs, milk, flour, water and a little saccharate of lime," the dwarf announced, authoritatively.

"I beg your pardon?"

"It's a cure for turpentine poisoning, and quite effective, I should add." The dwarf beamed.

The blonde smiled. "Are you a doctor, too?"

Wiping his eyes, the farm boy spoke up ahead of the dwarf. "He ain't nothing but a mouth that walks. Don't trust him."

"My young companion is the skeptical sort," the dwarf explained, still smiling. "But, no, I am not a physician. Merely an interested bystander in humanity's welfare." Rascal bowed once more. "At your service."

Clare laughed. "Oh, I'm sure we'll have a wonderful time while you're here. Did you speak with Mr. Farrell about your room? I'm afraid he's gone to Perryville for the day."

"No, but we'll pay cash-money," said the farm boy, pulling a wad of small bills from his pants pocket. He felt like Rockefeller himself as he counted out ten dollars.

"Well, he's given you a corner room on the third floor with a fine view. I think it's adorable. Why, it even has its own plumbing." She took the payment from Alvin and put it into a metal box beneath the counter, then brought out a pair of keys. "These are for you. Don't forget, supper's prompt at six."

"What's that cost?" Alvin asked, gruffly. "Spud ought to know we ain't kings."

"Why, it's included with the room."

"Oh, that's swell."

She offered Alvin a lovely smile. "I'll just bet your circus is a peach!"

The farm boy blushed. He knew he resembled a crummy hobo, but she was treating him like gravy. What gives? Did she like him?

Clare asked, "Will I see you there tonight? I'm through at eight."

Because she was so pretty, he chose to go along with the gag. "Sure, we'll be there. We ain't set up regular yet with a tent like them other acts, so just look around for us. It's a pip of a show."

She gushed, "Oh, I'm excited already!"

The room was at the end of the hall by a window that looked down onto a grassy backyard of goldenrod and sawtooth sunflowers and bleached white laundry suspended on a wire from the kitchen porch to the slatted fence at Weaver Street. Only a few tenants were in the half-dozen rooms hired for the month, and the house was quiet. Alvin put down his suitcase, then unlocked the door and went in. The dwarf trailed behind, his own suitcase in hand. Morning light glowed behind drawn roller shades at the back and side windows, brightening a bare room that had a wood floor, two small iron beds covered in ratty quilts, an oak dresser and mirror, and a pair of spindle chairs. The dwarf went to the closet while Alvin tossed his old suitcase onto the bed nearest the wall. He was tired of lugging it around. Another small door led to a toilet with an old tub and washbasin and a porcelain commode, which Alvin used immediately. In the room across the hall, he heard a fellow walking about reciting aloud from the Holy Bible.

"This sure ain't the Ritz," Alvin remarked, as he came out of the toilet, buttoning his pants. He raised the shade above the backyard to watch a coal truck rumble down a wheel-rutted lane toward the railyard crossing and saw a pair of carpenters laboring on a wooden scaffold next door and a woman in an old hoop skirt across the road scattering corncobs among muddy hogs in a small wire-fenced pen. Frenchy once had a painting job until he got drunk at noon behind a lunch wagon and fell off the scaffold and landed on a cow, breaking her back. It cost him three days pay. Aunt Hattie like to boxed his ears.

Fastening the linen shade, Alvin said, "I'll bet you that painter fellow ain't drank no turpentine, neither. It smelled like kitchen brew to me. I seen drunkards at home tackle a bottle of overnight that knocks 'em flat sudden. Some doctor's probably using the stomach pump on him right now. What do you bet that Spud fellow hired us a room in a booze flat?"

The dwarf closed his suitcase and shut the closet. "Oh, I suspect there aren't a dozen establishments in this town unfriendly to the contentious fluid. Although I'm quite immune myself, drinking's become quite the thing to do, you know. Why, this past year even dear old Auntie refused to go to bed without enjoying a good-night toddy. Shall we go visit the circus this morning?"

"Nope, Chester said not till after dark." The farm boy sat on the mattress, testing its firmness. He felt tired again; he'd have a nap if he weren't so hungry. He sniffed the quilt, wrinkling his nose at a damp musty odor. "Ain't this a swell dump? I bet you we got bedbugs."

The dwarf went over to his own bed and climbed onto the mattress and bounced up and down squeaking the springs. Then he rolled over onto his stomach and sniffed the blue quilt. He slid off the bed and peeked underneath. When he stood up again, he announced, "Blue ointment and kerosene, mixed in equal proportions, then applied to the bedstead."

"Huh?"

"A very fine bedbug remedy," said the dwarf.

Alvin got up and went to the door. "How's about we get us some eats and watch the street parade? I'm awful hungry."

Spud Farrell's boardinghouse was closer to the grimy neighborhood of stovepipe shanties and truck gardens than to downtown. Here the narrow streets were unpaved, and motorcars had cut a thousand tracks in the dirt, and occasionally horse-drawn wagons still lumbered along under honey locust and sugar maples where tired men wearing overalls and denim walked to work at the railyard and sawmill each morning, metal buckets in hand.

Smelling wood smoke from old cook stoves, the farm boy and the dwarf strolled Third Street toward downtown. Wooden fences on both sides of the dirt street advertised the circus, and tall ironweed grew in thick patches between fence posts and gates. Up on the corner, a woman in pink cotton and a white apron swept her porch with a flurry of tiny children at her feet. Just ahead on Elm, a postman walking his morning route shouted to a fellow in a flashy new Buick parked at the curb of a blue stick Eastlake framehouse where two elderly women shoveled manure from a wheelbarrow into a freshly dug spinach patch. Two blocks from the boardinghouse, Alvin smelled crap-foul backhouses and chicken coops and livery stables on the breeze. Farther on, he saw scrawny apple and peach trees in weedy backyards whose tin garages, cluttered with rusty junk, stood doorless to the brisk wind. Auto horns sounded through the sun-warmed elms and willows, and Alvin thought he caught scent of a fresh-baked cherry pie on a window ledge somewhere closeby. Whistling a Sousa march, the dwarf led Alvin down an alley shortcut where chirping catbirds nested in wild grape, and crabapple branches and dogwoods scratched at the plank fences. They paused briefly to listen to phonograph music droning from a third-story attic and morning voices exchanging airy greetings across kitchen porches. They stepped back against the fence as an empty milktruck rumbled by, and covered their mouths from the dust and exhaust that roiled up in its wake. Emerging from the alley, they discovered shrieking children running about at recess beneath a black oak in a dusty schoolyard on South Main near the creek. A slatted fence separated the square lot from a white high-steepled Lutheran church next door. On the stoop of the gray weatherboarded schoolhouse, a plump older woman was busy scolding a trio of boys in brown knickers. Behind her, a small girl in a soiled petticoat stood by the doorway sobbing. Waiting for a delivery truck to pass, the dwarf rushed across the dirt street into a prickly ash thicket that separated the schoolyard from the Ford garage on the other lot. There he spied on the children trading turns swinging from a rubber tire and skipping rope, playing jacks on a flat patch of dirt, throwing a scruffy baseball back and forth, wrestling and riding each other about pick-a-back. Alvin was content to observe from the sidewalk across the street. He hated school. Teachers were ugly and mean and assigned lessons not a fellow on earth could figure out by himself. He preferred shoveling horse manure to reading books. If a kid had a decent egg on his shoulders and wasn't afraid of work, he could find a job that paid enough to buy a new suit of clothes when he needed it and a movie every Saturday night and pocket money for emergencies without busting himself up over spelling words nobody knew how to use and stacks of numbers on a blackboard that usually added up to a horsewhipping on his bare bottom in the woodshed out back. What did the world care, anyhow, if he slopped hogs and went fishing instead of learning about Abe Lincoln?

After a few minutes, Alvin whistled to the dwarf and crossed the street to the Ford garage where he nearly choked from the odor of gasoline engines. Just ahead, a short bridge spanned the ravine. Tall sycamores rose beside thick cottonwoods from the creek bottom and Alvin bent over the iron railing halfway across and spat and watched his spittle disappear into the cold swirling water. Walking on alone up the sloping road to Main Street, he counted nineteen swallows perched on telegraph wires between a Shell filling station and a Western Auto Supply store. He took a minute to study the ads for Goodyear tires and Mobil Oil on a barnsiding as three automobiles and a smelly fruit truck roared by. He watched a nurse in white guide an old woman up to a doctor's office in another clapboard framehouse where a hornet's nest was stuck under the corner eaves. Somebody yelled out his name and he looked behind him. Two blocks down the road, the dwarf was hurrying across the bridge. Alvin gave another whistle, and went on ahead downtown.

They sat at a small marble top table by the front window in Moore's Café next door to the Royale movie house on Main Street. Cigarette smoke and conversation filled the narrow dining room, dishes clanked, cooking grease hissed in the kitchen. Alvin sipped carefully at a cup of hot black coffee. It burned going down, but soothed his sore throat just the same. He was feeling better and better. The dwarf stirred ice about with a spoon in his glass of orangeade and watched the men and women passing by on the busy sidewalk outdoors. He remarked to the farm boy, "Those children are terribly excited over the circus. Why, it's all they could speak of."

"Nothing about arithmetic?"

"Oh, I'm sure most of them thoroughly enjoy schooldays. Incidentally, did I tell you that my father's Uncle Edgar taught moral philosophy at Virginia with William McGuffey himself? Much of my inspiration for learning came from the collection of *Eclectic Readers* my mother left me. Why, those books were among my very best friends at that time of my life."

The dwarf put his spoon on the table and drank from the glass of orangeade.

Alvin noticed several customers were staring now. Whether it was at him or the dwarf, he didn't care; he thought it was rude, so he stared back until they were forced to look elsewhere. When he was in the sanitarium, visitors occasionally wandered into the sick wards and every so often Alvin would awaken from a nap to find himself the object of somebody's nosy attention. It made him feel worse than ever. He learned to despise people who couldn't keep their eyes to themselves.

The waiter came to their table, carrying a plate of lamb and sweet potatoes and another with pickled beets and chicken fricassee. As he set the plates down, lamb for Alvin, chicken for Rascal, he asked, "Are you two fellows with the circus?"

"Sure we are," Alvin replied, already set for a swell fib. "I'm a lion tamer and my friend here does some juggling in a clown suit. It don't pay much, but we get by all right, I guess."

The waiter looked skeptical. "Sort of late in the season for the circus, ain't it? We don't usually see you folks much after Labor Day."

Alvin nodded. " 'Course it is, but business was scarce this summer. Come wintertime, even circus people got to eat like everyone else, ain't that so?"

"I suppose it is."

Downtown was filling up. Looking out through the window, the waiter said, "Got a swell parade today, do you?"

"Sure." Alvin stuck his fork into the lamb like he was starving. "Sells a flock of tickets."

A group of homely women dressed in black stopped at the window to peer in. One of them tapped on the glass and held up a placard upon which was written in thick black ink: **BOOZE**. The stocky woman next to her showed another placard reading: **Prisons, Insane Asylums, Condemned Cells!** Two more hatchet-faced women stepped forward and pressed tall placards to the glass: **Good Riddance to Bad Rubbish** and **DRY or DIE.** Their grim focus was directed toward the farm boy and the dwarf. The waiter tried shooing them away, "Go on! Beat it!"

Not one of them budged.

The dwarf offered a salute and a pickled beet.

Flustered by the unwanted attention, Alvin blurted out, "How come them ladies are doing that? Who the hell are they?"

"Temperance Union," replied the waiter, waving at them again to go away. "They don't care much for your sort."

The waiter put the bill on the table and left. Most of the customers were watching now with considerable amusement. Several laughed out loud. Alvin had lost some of his appetite. The dwarf, however, ate his chicken fricassee as if he were alone in his own kitchen and hadn't a care in the world. Soon, after tapping sharply once more on the window glass and displaying their placards, the temperance women moved on. A hearty round of applause from the restaurant patrons cheered their departure. Once they were gone, the farm boy drank his cup of coffee and ate half the plate of lamb and sweet potatoes without any idea at all why he had been given the bad eye.

Main Street was paved with bricks and its buildings were tall and dignified. Telephone wires crossed above motor traffic along six blocks of prominent enterprise. A loaded trolley ran up the center of the street, bell clanging at each intersection. People shouted and waved and dodged automobiles to reach F.W. Woolworth's five-and-dime or Piggly Wiggly and the postal telegraph office at Fifth Street. Businessmen in wing collars came and went from the First National Bank as sewer diggers labored to repair a broken water main next to a Rexall drugstore. The farm boy and the dwarf strolled in and out of the late-morning crowd from block to block, admiring show window displays under striped awnings, buying pears from a vendor on Sixth Street and a hot pretzel at a stand on Seventh, stopping briefly in front of a German bakery to enjoy the aroma of hot cinnamon buns, then watching a pack of scrawny dogs struggle over spoiled pork chops in the narrow alley between Clarke & Son's hardware and the butcher shop. Halfway up Main, the dwarf ducked into Oglethorpe's Boots while Alvin stared at a group of pretty secretaries and lady typewriters on midday lark by the wide cement steps of Schaick, Pilsner & Allyson - Attorneys at Law. The farm boy walked up the block to the pool hall next door to McKinney's barbershop and found it jammed with young men in shirtsleeves and suspenders, the odor of cigarette smoke and hair tonic and liquor stiff as a saloon. Earlier, at the Ford garage, Alvin had seen two boys with flasks in their hip pockets, and noticed a box of quart bottles in the passenger seat of a Dodge coupé parked out front of Vickers Apothecary next to the Family Welfare Association at Fifth and Main. He presumed that Icaria was ankle-deep in liquor like any other town. Who had stopped chasing booze when the saloons closed? Most fellows his age thought it was sporting to drink and take joyrides around the county and get a girl going with a bottle of hootch in the dark. He knew a youth named Henry Sullivan from Arcola not sixteen years old who drove a liquor truck for George Remus until a gang of hijackers stiff-armed him one night behind a Diamond gas station in Indiana and broke his jaw. Alvin decided he was allergic to booze himself because of how sick he got after hardly a swallow, worse yet since the consumption; but his cousins of both sexes were drunk on canned heat more than once behind the dance hall in downtown Farrington and none of the adults seemed to care much at all, themselves occupied day and night hiding hootch in the rubber collars of wagon horses or filling empty milk bottles with raw corn whiskey. Not more than a dozen arrests for liquor traffic had been made in Farrington since Christmas, yet each Sunday morning Reverend Whitehead of the United Methodist church and Dr. E.G. Fortune of the Episcopalians reminded their flocks how proud the Lord was of them for staying dry.

At the corner of Main and Seventh, Rascal stopped in front of a shoeshine shop to admire a pair of Gold Bond oxfords on the work counter. A hand-painted lithograph advertising the circus extravaganza was posted in the window. The farm boy studied a jewelry store across the street and thought about investigating a wrist-watch; he had seen a gold-filled Illinois watch back at Stantonsburg for forty dollars that he fancied quite a lot.

"Why, look," the dwarf remarked. "There's the Belvedere Hotel."

He directed Alvin's attention to an elegant four-story brick build-ing across the street in the next block where men in business suits crowded atop the cement steps to the front door and a pack of shiny automobiles were clustered out front. Rascal stepped back off the sidewalk to let a woman pushing a baby stroller get by. "Let's go scout the rooms. Perhaps we can improve our situation."

Watching a flock of pigeons silhouetted on the cloudy sky across the hotel's rooftop, Alvin shook his head. "Chester ain't checked in yet. He won't get here till tomorrow and he didn't say nothing about us dropping up to see him, neither. He told me that Spud fellow'd let us know when he got into town."

A column of black Ford sedans and a loaded melon truck and a blue delivery van roared by, trailing a cloud of smelly black exhaust. People along the sidewalk were staring at the dwarf. So, too, was a crowd across the street under the awning of Brown's clothing store. Just behind him were a couple of osteopath patients waiting to see Dr. Kessler, their faces pressed to the plate-glass. When the farm boy gave them his own evil eye, they turned away.

"Well, I still want to go have a look."

Alvin shrugged, preferring to remain out of doors in the sunlight. He was sick of hiding in the shadows. "Suit yourself, but I'm staying right here. Parade's coming any minute now."

"We wouldn't miss a trick."

"I ain't a-going with you."

"Well, so long, then."

The dwarf gave a farewell salute, and shot off the curb behind a loaded autobus.

"Hey!"

Alvin watched him dodge through traffic and disappear into a sidewalk crowd in front of the Lotus Café. Uptown, the trolley bell clanged. A new yellow Oldsmobile rolled by with two men balanced on the running boards smoking cigars. One of them held up a Republican placard. The driver honked the horn as he passed the I.O.O.F. building.

Alvin walked up the block to the Orient Theater on the corner of Eighth and Main where a freckled young newspaper boy in a flat cap and brown trousers leaned against the lamppost, a scrawny beagle at his feet. People stepped around him as they hurried past. A stack of unsold copies of the *Icarian Mercury-Gazette* sat on the dirty cement beside the curb. The boy was counting pennies into his front trouser pocket. Feeling a chill, Alvin walked under the marquee to get out of the draft. Framed-in glass next to the polished double doors held the theater program. Tonight, the Orient featured a beauty contest, a minstrel show, two Vitaphone melodramas, and a Western thriller. Beside the program in the glass case, a posted handbill promised wholesome recreation under the new ownership of the refurbished theater. Next week a series of lectures on current events would be sponsored by the Family Relief Society — Admission 10¢.

"Are you in the circus, mister?"

Alvin turned around and saw the newspaper boy standing next to the empty ticket booth, his beagle behind him. The boy's brown trousers were dusty and his old roundtoed shoes covered with mud.

For the third time since breakfast, Alvin told his new lie, "Sure I am."

The boy's face brightened. "Gee, that must be swell. Is that one of your clowns?" He pointed across the street to Rascal walking just then under a giant pair of spectacles that advertised an oculist near the Belvedere Hotel.

" 'Course it is."

"Why, I bet he's awful funny, ain't he?"

"So long as he ain't mooning up that ol' beer jug of his."

"Huh?"

"You never mind him," Alvin instructed the boy. "He woke with a grouch on today and ain't talking sense to no one. Say, how come you ain't in school? Waiting on the parade?"

The newspaper boy shook his head. "Naw, I got fleas from ol' Spike here, so Miss Othmar sent me home. My pop says I got to sell all my papers or I can't go to the circus tonight. We're busted, I guess."

Alvin watched the dwarf enter the Belvedere Hotel. A cold gust riffled the stack of newspapers at the curb. The boy bent down to scratch his dog's nose.

"Can't you dig up some dough nowhere?" Alvin asked him. "Why, I met a swell girl this morning at a flophouse where we hired a room that might let you do a basket of laundry for her. That'd be worth something, I'd bet."

The boy screwed up his face like he'd just swallowed a bottle of castor oil, then spat on the sidewalk. "Nothing doing! I ain't washin' for no dame. Momma whipped me last week 'cause Spike got mud on her clean sheets and made me scrub 'em all white again. No thanks!"

"Well, how come your daddy won't kick in a nickel or two? Is he a skinflint?"

The boy gave a shrug. "Pop's a crapshootin' fool and he got the craze again. Momma's fed up, but she don't want to be a joykiller, neither, so she don't say much." His expression changed to an eager grin. "Jeepers, it must be swell to ride all over in a circus wagon. You ain't got a sideshow for a kid whose dog eats tacks and razor blades, do you?"

"Naw, we ain't got nothing like that."

The newspaper boy lowered his head and kicked at the dirty pavement. "Aw, gee whiz, me and Spike never get a break."

"Tacks and razor blades?"

The newspaper boy nodded. "Pins, too!"

"Kid, you're almost as big a fibber as someone else I know."

The boy's face reddened. "If you got any tacks or pins on you, we can prove it." He rubbed his dog's neck. "And how!"

Alvin laughed out loud, and then coughed till his throat hurt.

The newspaper boy scowled and knelt down beside the scrawny old beagle and hugged him tightly. Alvin noticed a commotion across the street. A tall clown in greasepaint and blue polka dots encircled by shouting children was distributing heralds along the sidewalk by the Belvedere. Straightaway, Alvin heard the faint song of a steam calliope in the distance.

He looked back at the scruffy newspaper boy. "I guess a fresh kid like you'll probably never amount to nothing, huh?"

"Aw, phooey on you, too."

The farm boy took a fistful of dimes from his trouser pocket. "Here, kid." He put them into the boy's hand. "Go to the circus tonight. Take your folks with you. Have a swell time."

The newspaper boy shot to his feet. "Gee, mister! No kidding?"

"You said it." Alvin swatted the boy's cap. "See you later, kid."

Then he rushed across the street to join the crowd at the Belvedere Hotel. People were standing three or four deep now at the sidewalk and Alvin had to shove his way up the cement steps to the entrance. Next door, men and women leaned out from the upper floor windows of a radio and appliance store, shouting and waving to people on the street.

The lobby of the Belvedere was carpeted in Oriental rugs and rich with palms, stuffed easy chairs, gilded pier mirrors, and china cuspidors. A group of businessmen in black waistline coats stood at the registration desk, chatting with the clerk. Cigar smoke and conversation bloomed from the adjacent dining saloon. A pianist played "Shaking the Blues Away."

Alvin crossed the narrow lobby in search of the dwarf. The elevator opened and a young bellboy wearing a crimson monkeyjacket came out with a pair of Louis Vuitton bags. Alvin removed his cap and sneaked around a potted palm into the noisy dining saloon where thirty or forty well-dressed men and women sat enjoying lunch. He looked carefully table by table and past the end of the mahogany bar to where the downstairs toilets were located, but didn't see the dwarf anywhere, so he went back across the lobby to the registration desk and waited to speak to the clerk. When the gentlemen in waistcoats walked off, the clerk nodded for Alvin to step up to the desk.

"May I help you, son?"

"I'm looking for a friend of mine that come in here a few minutes ago, and I was wondering if you seen him at all, a little fellow with suspenders and blue trousers?"

"Is he a guest here?"

"No, sir. He ain't. We already got us a room across town." Briefly, the farm boy considered lending Chester's name to the discussion, but thought better of it.

After the clerk scribbled a series of names and numbers into the ledger, he said, "Describe your friend for me again, please."

"Well, like I said, he's about this high, with sort of — "

The clerk interrupted. "Is your friend with the circus?"

Alvin nodded. "Yes, sir."

Frowning, the clerk shut the ledger. "In that case, I can assure you he's not here. Our policy no longer permits circus people of any sort at this hotel. I suggest you look elsewhere. Good day."

The clerk walked off with the ledger.

Humiliated once again, Alvin slunk out of the Belvedere. He knew he'd made a fool of himself, but didn't care this time. He was sweaty and felt his fever rising. He coughed hard and wiped his mouth with his shirtsleeve. Atop the busy steps, he jostled for a decent view of upper Main Street. More painted clowns mingled along the downtown sidewalks, passing out handbills and distributing free admission tickets to pretty girls and small children. Just across the street, Alvin saw a rangy emerald clown with hair like a cotton candy rainbow seated at the curb by the Orient Theater, his elastic arms wrapped tightly about the newspaper boy and the scraggy beagle. Music from the circus band echoed on the wind. Uptown, the grand parade had begun.

The farm boy climbed up onto the stone balustrade and balanced against the building façade high above the crowded sidewalk. He held his breath when he saw the great Indian elephants lumbering down the street under black walnut trees three blocks away at Potter and Main. Astride each was a royal Nubian princess in peacock-blue silk and glittering sapphires. Marching ahead of the majestic pachyderms, flutists in green tricorn hats and scarlet plumes led a team of sixteen brown ponies from Lilliput drawing a gilded carriage wild with lavender roses and firebreathing dwarves. The crowd on Main roared with

234 | MONTE SCHULZ

delight as the circus band played *"Entry of the Gladiators."* Policemen
cleared the street ahead. A big bass drum boomed a martial rhythm as
imperial trumpets heralded the arrival of gold-turbanned equestrians
performing tumbling tricks atop prancing white stallions, while a curious menagerie of strange caged beasts and terrible human phenom-
ena in painted wagons were tugged along by plodding mule teams
and silver-collared draft-horses. From his stone perch, the farm boy
witnessed a euphonious parade of the fabulous and the bizarre, an
alchemistic history of the known world. No mere child's torpid dream
of Bengal tigers and gypsy sword swallowers: here, Caesar's grand war
chariot salvaged from those dusty storehouses of Leptis Magna rolled
again behind proud Arabian steeds under the hand of a dour Russian
Cossack as crimson pantalooned dwarves from Cairo and Bombay
flung knives and spun cartwheels between great dancing bears, and
a Sultan's rosy harem escorted a camel caravan of Iberian jugglers
and giraffe-necked giants and Chinese magicians and tattooed snake
charmers. Next came Gloucester's sea serpent swimming in a glass
turquoise tank wagon with three lovely mermaids rescued from a fisherman's net off Martinique, then Wellington's triumphant Waterloo
marching band in red dresscoat and gold braid with a rousing chorus
of *"Rule Brittania,"* and thirteen antiquarian bandwagons carved and
gilded by druidic gnomes recounting in painted mythological tableaux
wondrous stories of golden geese and fairy kings, enchanted nightingales and ancient jinnis, sleeping princesses and shipwrecked sailors. Block after windy block, midget clowns and fat clowns and giant
clowns juggled fiery torches and somersaulted off shoulder tops and
strode upon stilts and dove through flaming hoops and tossed bags of
warm peanuts and fresh Crackerjack to howling children until every
zebra, ostrich, llama, buffalo and gazelle had passed in revue, and the
Wild West bareback riders and rope dancers and spangled Prussian
acrobats had exhibited feats of daring and wonder, and the great thun-
dering steam calliope, *Seraphonium,* that deafening shriek of melodi-
ous pipe whistles, had summoned the brave and the curious to follow
the wagon parade of Emmett J. Laswell's Traveling Circus Giganticus
back to Icaria's showgrounds, and not one solitary child had been left

behind on Main Street.

The dining room was lit with oil lamps for supper. Nine dishes were set at the table and the portières drawn to keep out the hall draft. By six o'clock, all the boarders were seated and grace was spoken by Virgil Platt, a gaunt narrow man with gray whiskers on a weary face whose Bible reading Alvin had heard through the wall that morning. A hint of tears welled in the fellow's eyes when he thanked the Lord for such daily blessings as the living and penitent require. Seated across from Alvin were the oddest pair of middle-aged twins in Lord Fauntleroy dress: Eugene and Samuel Szopinski. Both wore pince-nez over powdered cheeks and smelled of fresh lilac water and talcum. Next to them was matronly Eva Chase from Vicksburg, dressed in pine-green cashmere and tortoise-shell eyeglasses. Beside the dwarf were two older fellows with slicked-back hair, black dinner jackets and smart linen collars: Percy Webster and Russell James. To Alvin's left on the parlor end opposite from Virgil Platt was silverhaired Mrs. Celia Burritt, overly elegant in a grenadine dress and satin mantel. Ox-tail soup and haricot mutton and sweet rice croquettes were on the table with hot coffee and a kettle of peppermint tea when Alvin sat down. He bowed his head with everyone else during grace, then listened to introductions by Mrs. Burritt, helped pass the serving plates around the table, and attended to a conversation begun by Eva Chase and the dwarf while Alvin was still upstairs napping after the parade. It was the strangest story he had ever heard.

"Now, those days," said Eva Chase in a reedy drawl, "my dear Carl had a marvelous gift for limerick which kept all the troupe in stitches when it rained and there was no show. He was the handsomest man I ever knew, yet so devoted to theater that only the feebleminded thought him capable of performing his tragic soliloquies in a fusty Barnum exhibit. And, oh, those dreadful drafty halls Mr. Forepaugh thought to hire for Carl's famous Gilbert & Sullivan stunts, quite unimaginable! I remember once in Nanty-Glo, the entire troupe went out after midnight and left free tickets on stoops all over town for the coal miners. Carl had such a fervid audience the next evening, he sent a telegraph to Jimmy Armstrong and another to the Manhattan Opera House. I was so hopeful for him back then."

Still drowsy from his nap, Alvin watched Virgil Platt scoop a warm helping of mutton and croquettes onto his plate and pass the silver platter to the Szopinski twins. Percy Webster slurped the ox-tail soup. Russell James examined his water glass for spots.

Mrs. Burritt remarked, "Love is deception's most potent elixir, darling. You see, few men truly intend anything remarkable in life. Distinction is much more the result of circumstance and good fortune than we've all been led to believe. Why, if Adam hadn't forgotten his breakfast that day, I'm quite certain none of us would've drawn our first wicked breath in the world."

"That's silly," said Eugene Szopinski.

"Entirely absurd," his brother Samuel added, cutting into the mutton.

Careful not to burn his fingers, Alvin took the serving plate of sweet rice croquettes while the dwarf poured himself a steaming cup of peppermint tea. He was starving to eat again, which meant he was sicker than ever.

Unbowed by Mrs. Burritt's needling observations, Eva Chase continued, "When I was still a girl of sixteen, Carl traveled down from Baltimore to see my performance of 'Evangeline' in a nickel tent show and he brought purple lilacs and champagne and offered to marry me once the show left Pearl River. He paid two dollars for a photographer to record my image on glass, and purchased a lovely old brass frame and a scented teakwood box to store it in. Later we had our fortunes told by a blind swamp gypsy who took Carl's hand by candlelight and traced upon it with a yellow fingernail a path of starry dreams and love priceless and pure."

"No such thing," Percy Webster interrupted. He set down his soup-spoon. "Dreams, that is. Why, I've been in love so often, quite naturally I know it like sunshine. But dreams are mere rumors, untrustworthy ones at that, scandalous and wretched insinuations that serenade our bed chambers with such fevered promises as only children and canaries ever endure."

"Eternal love is a figure of speech," said Mrs. Burritt. "If I'd been born mute, perhaps my girlhood room on Summer Avenue would yet host private teas and slumber parties for the fragile of heart."

"Oh, I just adore slumber parties," the dwarf interjected, stirring sugar into his tea. Alvin smothered a rising cough with his cotton napkin, far too intimidated to utter a word. He had never been around folks like these before and didn't want them to think he was a dumbbell.

Russell James said, "Well, of course, Percy is far too reckless a fellow to admit a fault, but nobody who has actually dismembered on Phineas Barnum's own stage a creature as delightful as May Wallace ought to expect his sleep to be blissful and unadorned."

The farm boy quit chewing.

"Such a tragedy," lamented Eugene Szopinski, as he cut apart the sweet rice croquette with his fork.

"Utterly grievous," Samuel Szopinski agreed, raising a stained napkin to his lips.

Virgil Platt ate supper vigorously with eyes locked firmly on his dinner plate.

After enjoying a sip of hot coffee, Eva Chase began again. "Once long ago, I traveled around the world with Father's old steamer trunk and my mother's lavender parasol and felt happy as a lark. In a hundred foreign cities from Rangoon to Constantinople, my sweet Carl was hailed as the greatest performer on earth. He danced in silver shoes with shiny green buckles and plucked emeralds and rubies out of thin air and sang like a nightingale, and one impossibly marvelous evening at the Maryinski Theater, he received a white rose bouquet and a private note of admiration from Empress Alexandra herself. When we left Paris to sail again for America, my desperate heart became so haunted by joy and fear, I counted every star fleeing heaven for the nightblack sea and scribbled secret wishes onto tiny scraps of paper and scattered each upon the cold waves. No girl ever born loved as I did then. By August, we'd traveled up the Mississippi to Memphis where Carl performed sixty-two lantern shows aboard a grand old Dixie paddle steamer that floated like a fancy wedding cake on the summer twilight river. There I was struck down by fever, pitifully bedridden two floors above a garden café of sweet blossoming honeysuckle and Spanish guitars. For half a month, I suffered that awful delirium alone lying prostrate beneath a frayed scrapquilt of calico rose petals, nibbling on overripe tangerines until juice stained my gown. Each night, flamenco melodies and mad fluttering moths tortured my dreams, those few that I recall because so wicked a fever inebriates the brain with rustling murmurs of unspoken desire, and once engaged these cruel phantasms fly about like ghosts. I remember rising from bed to stare into a beveled mirror on the chamber suite where I saw my reflection dressed smartly in diamonds and lace for a honeymoon trip somewhere, a wayward angel in waiting. Desolate with need, I called out for my precious Carl, but by then, you see, a vagabond circus had come down from Cairo toting flying-act rigging and tightwire, and he'd gone whispering across the water by moonlight."

"He'd met the pretty aerial ballerina," observed Eugene Szopinski, stabbing at another forkful of mutton.

"Miss Alice Vandermeer," Samuel Szopinski added, smiling wanly as he sipped his tea.

Mrs. Burritt put her rice plate aside and poured herself a cup of coffee. Somewhat theatrically, she remarked, "Who among us is not born to tragedy and sorrow? Love withers and our hearts dry up. Milk-white skin shrivels and goes gray. Disappointment hounds our every step. Who wakes each morning unaware of this?"

Quietly, the dwarf reached for the serving bowl of ox-tail soup, while Alvin listened to Virgil Platt chew his food, a most unpleasant noise like boot heels in mud.

Russell James said, "My beautiful daughter Lulu quit Ringling Brothers to go traipsing about with a vacuum cleaner salesman after her marriage to Mr. Zû had rotted away. She became so disagreeable I was forced to throw her wormy old chifforobe into the street and nail the back door shut."

Percy Webster lowered his fork. "Well, honey, you wrote her such nasty letters, what on earth did you expect?"

"Aggravation," said Eugene Szopinski.

"Impertinence," his brother Samuel suggested.

Eva Chase tasted a rice croquette, then dabbed her rosy lips delicately with a cloth napkin. She spoke in a voice sweet as ether: "Once when I was a girl, I slept for a whole year believing I'd been locked away in Mother's musty old cedar wedding chest, blessedly hidden from a grown woman's delicate powders and rouge and a gentleman's ardent correspondence. Instead, I'd drowned in leagues of sorrow more common than autumn rain, that awful solitude, and true hope no more than pale dewdrops. Too often I'd dreamed of a lovely white dove in a spangled cape dancing on the aerial rigging high in the big tent above a thousand delirious upturned faces, my dear Carl's adoring eyes among them. Then, one day, Mother hired a detective to poke about muddy carnival lots, eavesdropping at tent flaps for clues. He relayed news a month later from Louisville of a terrible accident at the matinee tightwire performance, a perfect swan dive to the sawdust, a mangled beauty. I rode the train all night guided by vaporish tea leaves and prayer. Arriving by dawn at a wet tent-littered fairgrounds, I worried that my memory of our journey around the world together was only a pierglass hallucination, a rhymeless delusion, for which a renowned artist such as he had no natural use. Hugo the Strong-Man sent me to a painted wagon by the Big Top where a plum-colored pygmy named Missus Bluebell guarded the door. Hearing my story, she shed a tear for both of us, then showed me inside. My belovéd Carl lay shrunken in the smoky shadows beside a burning oil lamp on a cot of embroidered pillows, dressed for theater footlights in green silk sashes and Chinese slippers, a chewed sprig of deadly nightshade and an ivory fan from Singapore on his red satin chest. A note in India ink waited for me atop his costume portmanteau, scribbled perhaps when I was still aboard the train. He wrote that love was ruthless, discordant, unworthy of our defenseless hearts. Be quick now and flee it. Forget its deceitful embrace. I buried him on a grassy hilltop in Vicksburg facing the summer Ferris wheels and the happy crowds."

A parlor clock chimed the half-hour as Alvin poured himself a cup of hot coffee to soothe his throat. Finished with his croquettes, the dwarf gingerly sipped peppermint tea. The spicy aroma of warm raisin pie under a checkered cloth on the walnut sideboard filled the narrow dining room.

Eugene Szopinski said, "We fell from the highwire at Buffalo when we were thirteen years old."

"Too young to appreciate the distance to earth," his brother Samuel explained as he cut up his last bite of mutton. "Now we're both scarred for life."

"Indeed," Russell James said, "one evening in my own youth, a passing mesmerist persuaded me that my heart had become a cold desiccated husk decaying within my chest, utterly devoid of normal human inclinations. Thus entranced, I toured for years with Sells-Floto as the Fossilized Man until Lulu's mother purchased me from the sideshow and brought me home with her."

"You see, my dear, that far perch eludes us all now and then," said Percy Webster, folding a napkin beside his supper plate, "yet blind-folded we proceed across heaven's great expanse determined to prove ourselves worthy of this brief moment."

Mrs. Burritt added, "I've always been grateful for those blessings that seem to come to us from far away."

Carefully, Virgil Platt put down his cup of coffee onto a polished china saucer. He rose from his chair at the head of the supper table and turned to Eva Chase. He said: "Only the empty-hearted lament those days of carnival and renown once they're gone. A man's gift maketh room for him, and bringeth him before great men. This, I believe, is the elation for which he was born."

The farm boy and the dwarf stalked through the damp woods four blocks from the rotten stink of old stockyards west of town. Lights burned yellow in the upstairs of houses behind them. A cold wind rustled early autumn leaves and Alvin felt a rising chill in the dark. He heard the lilting gaiety of a carousel somewhere up ahead as he followed the scurrying dwarf along a rutted path, sidestepping ripe clumps of poison ivy and fending off errant branches as he went. Lights from the circus glowed like will o' the wisps across the hidden wood. Up a short hill they went crouching Indian-fashion through patches of elderberry and silky dogwood. Alvin stopped to catch his breath at the top as the carnival wind gusted. The dwarf's chirping voice was senseless and joyful as he trampled tall stalks of grass toward the distant circus tents. Crowds of people from town swarmed the bright showgrounds entrance. Alvin, too, ran as best he could toward the sparkling galleries of merriment.

A hundred yards away he smelled hot roasted peanuts and fried onions on the evening wind. The greeter's call drew him closer still. Colorful flags and banners rippled and flapped. Pipe music shrieked. Two pairs of painted clowns clasping colored balloons danced a silly jig beside the ticket taker whose booming voice carried across the dark.

"STEP RIGHT UP! STEP RIGHT UP! WONDER OF WONDERS! MIRACLES, MYSTERY AND MAGIC!"

Burning ash from the fellow's cigar scattered on the wind as Alvin purchased tickets for himself and the dwarf and joined a line of people from town at the entry gate. He watched one of the green balloons escape a clown's idiot grasp in a gust of wind and rise drunkenly into the cold black sky. A plaintive cry rang out from a pack of children by the steaming popcorn stand as another clown on stilts attempted to catch the fugitive balloon, but already it had wafted up too far and soon vanished beyond the fancy circus lights and the fluttering banners high away into gray evening clouds. Wherever Alvin looked, people jammed exhibits and canvas tents. Pinwheels and Roman candles fizzed and sparkled in the night sky. A troupe of clowns on unicycles wheeled toward the Big Top. Jugglers in jester hats and Nubian sword swallowers performed feats of grand dexterity near the chariot cages and gilded Museum wagons. Bombastic sideshow talkers shouted above the crowds. Alvin stopped briefly to buy a fluffy stick of pink cotton candy next to a dart-throwing booth, then followed the dwarf past the Topsy-Turvy House toward the carousel where giggling children mounted high on regal steeds went round and round to a Strauss waltz while smiling mothers and fathers stood by in the sawdust admiring the painted wooden horses and the gilded poles under the electric canopy.

Wiping his sticky mouth on a shirtsleeve, Alvin watched a top-hatted midget in a painted sandwich board advertising a dog and pony show march past the carousel, yelling: "COME ONE! COME ALL! COME ONE! COME ALL!"

More skyrockets exploded over the tent circus.

Alvin felt a tug on his shirt.

"Look," the dwarf said, directing the farm boy's attention between tent exhibits to a collection of circus midgets fixed out in medieval silks: seven noblemen and a charming lady-in-waiting. They appeared to be gathering for a performance of some sort. One of them carried a lute and another held juggling pins.

"What of it?" He'd witnessed plenty of freaks acting up already. They made him jittery.

"My goodness," Rascal sighed. He crossed his legs oddly and bit his lip.

"Let's go see something," Alvin said, feeling impatient. He didn't know how long he had until fever wore him out or another coughing fit struck and he wanted to have some fun for once.

"You go along, if you like," the dwarf said, his roaming eyes stilled by the tiny maiden. "I believe I'll stay here awhile."

"Maybe we ought to have a look in that funhouse back there," Alvin suggested, reluctant to go off alone. What if he had a coughing fit like he did at that carnival in Galesburg last summer?

"Isn't she a knockout?" the dwarf remarked, as the darling midget performed a short melody on the penny flute while executing a dainty pirouette for her audience.

"Yeah, sure," Alvin replied, beginning to feel febrile and wobbly again. He watched one of the midgets breathe fire through a golden ring and another strummed the lute. "But what do you say we go have ourselves a good time? Why, I'll bet there's something doing in one of them big tents. Let's go have a look-see."

"No, thank you," the dwarf demurred, sounding moony now. "It's plenty wonderful right here." He sucked in his breath and folded his fingers together in a squirmy knot.

"Well, I ain't coming back for you," Alvin groused. "I'll be too busy hunting up some real fun."

A dreamy smile on his lips, the dwarf replied, "I'll look you up later on."

Disgusted, Alvin went off on his own, hoping to find the girl from Spud Farrell's boardinghouse. Without the dwarf to keep him company, nobody paid him any notice at all as he walked alone under the gusting banners and electric lights. The farm boy jostled and shoved with circus-goers at tent openings and game booths, and grew dizzy admiring the mechanical Whirly-Gig and the bright electric Ferris Wheel. He ate a steaming hotdog and a bag of popcorn while watching Tessie the Tassel Twirler perform for a noisy crowd of men in a 10¢ tent behind the marionette show *("She wiggles to the east, she wiggles to the west, she wiggles in the middle where the wiggling is best!")*. In the Topsy-Turvy House, he chased a gang of kids tossing half-chewed Crackerjack at each other through the dizzying Rolling Barrel and the Mad Tea Party in candlelit Upside-Down Room and out the slippery Shoe-Chute where Alvin tripped on the Crazy Stairs and skinned his knee. Outdoors again, more children ran past, screeching like wild animals. Fireworks boomed overhead. A cold wind blew across the sky, chasing the farm boy deeper yet into a glimmering sawdust land.

The citizens of Icaria swarmed the high-grass circus, clustering at Laswell's mysterious tent shows and cage wagons, awed by his Chinese magicians and Egyptian mummies and ferocious Bengal tigers, his wild black cannibals nine feet tall. A thousand tales of wonder in a single evening of blue fire and rolla bolla. For a nickel a head, the curious pack Charon's Tent of Sorcery to see a pale spook in a silken cloak grace Cleopatra's throne whose fragrant apparition roils from clouds of purple smoke by the bleak light of the sideshow conjurer's font. No sad angelfaced harlequin in pearls, but a proud Ptolemy rid at last of Antony and the asp. Tent flaps rustle as she strums a golden lyre: white doves fly forth: flower petals fall. Women faint and a few men yell "Cheat!" and "Humbug!" and half a dozen red-hot cigar butts are hurled across the amber haze of burning candle wax. A trio of fresh towheads who'd wriggled under the tattered canvas walls for a peek, crawl back out of the dusty shadows and race down the windy night to the elevated platforms under the square tent of Laswell's torch-lit Hall of Freaks where the gathered crowd is restless but timid.

"That's right, folks! Come in a little closer! She won't hurt you!"

At a rap of the sideshow talker's cane upon the podium, Sally Victoria, the Two-Headed Girl, dressed in a lavender and silver lamé tea gown, steps out from behind a woven brown curtain and begins to sing in harmonious duet a waltz lullaby called "Dreamy Moon." Her darling faces are dolled up with show-lashes and ruby-red lipstick and a fancy French hairdo. Harvey Allison from the hardware store on North Main falls in love by the second stanza and immediately begins composing a love sonnet to sweet Sally Victoria. When the song ends, the rural crowd hurries off to the growling Dog-Woman from Burma who swallows full-grown rats with shotglasses of Kentucky bourbon ("In her own land she is considered a great beauty, but she's a long way from home!"), and on to the next row of platforms where a mated pair of steely-clawed Stymphalian birds from the marshes of Arcadia squawk and hiss at photographs of President Hoover, and the recently unearthed Peking Man demonstrates his astonishing knowledge of algebraic equations, and the Human Pin Cushion from Iranistan receives one hundred forty-two needle punctures from audience volunteers while reciting "Ode on a Grecian Urn."

Then the bronze torches dim and the anxious crowd is invited to the platform draped in Oriental carpets at the back of Laswell's Hall of Freaks where a silken gold shroud is withdrawn from a glass aquarium revealing the Turtle Boy paddling in foamy brine and pink coral with the strange man-sized Bishop Fish: a queer pair, indeed.

A dark-bearded lecturer in black top-hat and tails steps out from backstage to address his audience: "Ladies and Gentlemen, listen to a tale of woe from distant maritimes, a fable for the ages. Here in this crystal tank a remnant of moral tragedy resides, for in truth these two sad creatures were once as human as you or I. Many years ago by the shores of an ancient sea dwelt a humble tinker of little means. Such was his station in life that even beggars took pity on him and shared what meager portions of bread and fish they had, knowing without such mercy the poor tinker would surely starve. By that same barren shore was a small chapel whose devout cleric ministered to all who sought comfort and delivery from the harshness of the world. He knew the tinker well and regarded him plainly as another child of God who had lost his way. Each morning the cleric watched the lowly tinker pass along the shore with his sack and his old nets. Each evening he watched the tinker return, his scant accumulations in tow. Perhaps he envied the tinker's perseverance. Perhaps he despised the tinker's disregard for pious fellowship. Who can say? From a nearby village the cleric had taken in a wayward youth to look after the chapel grounds and garden. Now, this youth, too, watched the tinker come and go and had little patience for hardship, believing that life was a blind drawing of lots and fortune simply a matter of will. One evening after vespers, the youth approached the cleric with a remarkable story. The meandering tinker, he claimed, had cast his ragged net upon the waters that morning and retrieved a treasure of uncommon degree. He had hidden it somewhere under the floor of his straw hovel, intending to tell no one, nor share even an ounce of his newfound prosperity. The cleric agreed that it was indeed characteristic of the selfish tinker to obscure so great a discovery and reminded the youth that all men are born stewards of this earth and that what belonged to one, belonged to all equally and without distinction. Therefore, the cleric determined that the tinker's vanity was in fact a sin whose absolution required the forsaking of his prize. Furthermore, he and the youth would go to the tinker that very night and remind him of this obligation. Now the cold sea was fitful and blustery as the cleric and the youth went along that ancient shore with lanterns to light their way in the dark. Few thieves from iniquitous Calcutta ever conspired so unmercifully as this cleric and the callous youth to plunder such a guileless mark. In his drafty hovel the tinker slept before a dull kindling fire while outside the cleric searched the sky for providential indications and saw instead a great black tempest rising off the sea. The youth stole into the straw hovel and shook the tinker awake and demanded he reveal the whereabouts of his treasure. The tinker replied that he no longer possessed it, that a dream he'd had persuaded him to cast it back into the sea, and he showed the youth an empty hole in the floor where the treasure had been hidden. Now the cleric, too, entered the bleak hovel and accused the tinker of deception and warned that blind avarice provoked a particularly harsh wrath from heaven. The poor tinker acknowledged that the greed of men was, indeed, insatiable, threatening of immorality and ruin. Better, he had decided, to be rid of wealth than remain its fearful servant. Furious, the youth stepped forward and bludgeoned the hapless tinker and dragged him from his sad hovel out into the storm and threw him to the raging sea. Then the youth returned to the straw hovel and began digging in the floor while the cleric sought guidance from heaven and the great dark tempest surged ashore with sea waves mighty and deep."

The top-hatted lecturer pauses to gaze briefly at the two curious creatures paddling lazily in the shallow coral water of the glass aquarium. A woman at the back of the tent who had fainted rises again to take her seat. The surrounding audience remains hushed by the lecturer's tale.

"At daybreak, a merchant passing along the barren shore caught sight of a fisherman's net half-buried in wet sand and straw. As he drew closer, the merchant spied a figure wriggling in the old net, a slimy fin, a long scaly cloak, a pair of drooping eyes shrouded in kelp: our pious Bishop Fish. Working to liberate this creature, the industrious merchant discovered another cowering beneath, this sad Turtle Boy, limpid and weak, limbless, wallowing in fear. Soon enough the merchant freed both from their entanglement in the old net, then seeing how curious was their appearance, how grotesque and godforsaken, he loaded both together atop his donkey cart and brought them along with him on his travels throughout the world. When he died, a good-hearted gypsy took possession of both creatures, and after many exhibitions in many carnivals in many lands, we present them here tonight. Legend has it that every creature on earth possesses its twin in the sea, a doppelgänger of the soul, a perfect likeness of its truest nature. Who knows? What is certain, however, is that the tinker and the cleric and the youth were never again seen on that distant shore, and if miracles are, indeed, indications of divine will, let no one leave this tent tonight unmoved."

The lecturer departs the stage as a pair of platform torches flare brightly, further illuminating the two strange creatures who paddle sluggishly about the aquarium, occasionally grazing each other, seemingly indifferent to the slackjawed audience. The pale Turtle Boy flops onto a flat stone perch and belches loudly enough to be heard at the back row. That trio of towheads who lie under the tent walls giggle while the plump Bishop Fish folds his fins together on a miry lap as if in prayer and shuts his eyes. The surrounding coral glistens in the flickering orange light. Eventually the platform torches dim once more and this tent crowd is shown to the rear exit in favor of another curious audience waiting out front. The show goes on.

Late in the evening, Alvin wandered through the Palace of Mirrors whose drafty corridors shimmered a pale winter blue and mocked his sorry reflection. The ceiling was hidden in black drapes that billowed like the wingéd shadows of great birds. Mechanical voices tittered laughter in the dark. Ticket stubs and dead cigarette butts littered the floor. A stink of bathtub gin and witch hazel and burning tobacco fouled the sparkling corridors. Alvin Pendergast strolled a crooked path and went nowhere while odd voices chattered here and there and the draft grew colder. In one mirror he resembled a pale blimp, in another a ridiculous string bean. He was elongated and squashed, his nose flattened, his smile wide as a pie, his eyes like saucers, his hands and feet swollen as if by a summer bee sting. His mouth looked sloppy and mean, his arms slithered like rubber snakes. Shadows of passersby darted from the corner of his eye. Soon he felt dizzy and stopped walking. Fever chilled his skin. He sat down and stared at a trio of reflections across the filthy corridor, each joyless and shriveled, sour with sweat. His head throbbed and his legs were numb and he felt faint. Alvin had expected to die in the sanitarium. He had seen blood in his sputum and imagined thousands of rancid tubercles growing like weeds beneath his ribs. For days on end he lay hushed in bed listening to the ashen wheezing of his own invalid lungs in hopeful anticipation of swan-winged angels descending to the gloom-gray ward. Doctors came and went, jotting notations on daily charts while muttering to themselves in Latin. Nurses spoke most cheerfully to the doomed. No more fishing under slants of drowsy sunlight. Alvin napped in septic clouds of waste and rude medications. Gurneys wheeled in and out. Homesickness for the farm persisted through numerous belladonna plasters and daily treatments of cod liver oil. A dozen series of X-ray photographs failed to reveal his despair. *These sanitarium corridors are dark and drafty, too, traveled by consumptive patients like himself whose bleak faces reflect malignancy and hemorrhage. The floor is cold on his feet and his gown flutters as he proceeds. No one speaks, but many faces seem familiar. Passing the children's ward he sees old schoolmates seated in a circle eating biscuits and custard pie, each exhibiting the scrofulous habit of watery eyes and translucent skin, glands swollen up like walnuts. Across the hallway, Mrs. Burritt and the Szopinski twins are taking the sun cure, bathing euphorically in a shower of bactericidal ultra-violet rays under bright tungsten lamps. They see his reflection in the mirror and wave as he passes. He pretends not to notice, so ashamed is he of being there. Why among all Pendergasts did he alone become infected? Aunt Hattie maintained his fate was sealed at birth. Uncle Henry argued in favor of invasive bacilli corrupting a glass of raw milk. What does it matter now? Down this dark angled corridor, the for-*

tunate expectorate lung stones and weave baskets for exercise while the ill-fated lie in tub-baths with cloths of black silk shrouding their eyes or endure the gruesome treatments of the artificial pneumothorax apparatus. Looking into a mirror ahead, he sees Rascal administering an injection to Clare from a hypodermic needle flooded with a solution of gold and sodium. Both are dressed in white sanitarium gowns. Quivering with fear, Clare calls to him for help, "Melvin!" while the draft in the corridor rises like a wintry spook. He feels as if he is suspended upside-down.

"Melvin?"

Wilted flower petals blown on the cold wind from the nearby woods showered the carnival darkness as Alvin lay on his back staring up at a poster of Jupiter the Balloon Horse nailed onto a two-by-four in front of an exhibit called Cirque Olympic. Clare knelt above him in a plain yellow print frock and cloche hat. She held a small beaded handbag at her side. A sudden gust riffled her dress, forcing her to cover herself from the scurrying sawdust. Across the way, a quartet of polka dot clowns and trained poodles turned cartwheels for a cheery group of children. Swarms of townspeople hurried by. High-arching skyrockets burst upon the cloudy night sky.

"Oh, Melvin, are you all right?" Clare asked, concern in her eyes. "I've been so worried."

Alvin's head swam as he sat up. He felt confused and had no idea where he was. He mumbled, "I was just having a nap."

"In the mirror house?"

"Huh?" Alvin's eyes watered and his head hurt. He thought he might be sick to his stomach.

"You were lying on the floor in the mirror house when Mr. Hughes from the radio shop found you. Are you sure you're all right? Maybe I should fetch a doctor. You look awfully pale."

"I got lost."

Clare giggled. "Why, you silly! You were only a few steps from the exit!"

"Oh yeah?" Alvin replied, still feeling bewildered. He looked back over his shoulder and saw the rear exit to the Palace of Mirrors. He hardly remembered a thing. "I guess it was dark."

"When Mr. Hughes and that other fellow carried you out of the mirror house, they said you felt light as a bird." Wind blew in her hair. "Have you been eating well?"

Alvin rose slowly, keeping his eyes focused on the poster of Jupiter the Balloon Horse. He was sorely feverish. "I got fixed up with a bad radish last week and it gave me a whopping bellyache. I suppose I was pretty sick for a couple days there."

He stood still for a moment to take his bearings. The Big Top was just ahead along the midway. Clare held him gently by the arm, close enough for Alvin to smell the fragrant Orange Blossom perfume she wore.

"Be careful," she said, keeping him steady.

"I'm all right now," Alvin lied, his dizziness easing. "I ain't sick no more."

"I'm awfully worried. You look so pasty and thin."

"Well, I guess I been working too much inside them tents," he told her, as a pair of gypsy swordsmen led a baby elephant past. He tried changing the subject. "This circus is pretty swell, ain't it?"

Clare's expression brightened. "Oh, it's so marvelous I'm just lost for words! It's absolutely grand! Why, I'll bet you've seen a million shows, haven't you? It must be wonderful to be in the circus."

"It's a panic, all right," he replied, watching the noisy crowds. "But see, we've got to put it over big every night and that ain't so easy, let me tell you. Some nights, well, even for those of us that got sawdust in our blood, it just ain't in the cards and whatever you do ain't half enough." The farm boy kicked at the dirt, uneasy with fibbing her.

Clare tugged at his arm. "Oh Melvin, let's go see the lions, can't we? Please?"

"Why, sure we can," he replied as the wind gusted, fanning up dry leaves and paper scraps. "If that's what you want." He knew he could honey her up if she gave him half a chance.

"Oh, it is!"

Alvin looked through the noisy crowds to the ticket booth at the opening to the Big Top. "Say, wait here, will you? Let me talk to that tooter over there."

"All right." Clare smiled sweetly. "Hurry!"

Alvin went across to the derbyhatted ticket taker. Keeping his back to Clare, he said, "I need two tickets."

"It's ten cents." The fellow's eyes were bloodshot and his teeth tobacco stained. He raised his eyes and nodded in Clare's direction. "Is she your sweetheart?"

Still feverish, the farm boy dug the change out of his pocket and handed it over on the sly. "Yeah, what of it?"

"She sure's a peach," said the ticket taker, his attention stuck on Clare. "I'll bet she's nice to smooch, too, ain't she?"

The farm boy scowled. "Say, maybe you ought to button up your face. I can scrap pretty good and I ain't afraid to, neither."

"Oh yeah?" The fellow snickered at Alvin.

"Yeah."

"Get on along, buster, I'm busy." Turning away from Alvin, he began his spiel again to the passing crowds. "STEP RIGHT UP! STEP RIGHT UP! NOW UNDER THE BIG TOP! FEROCIOUS LIONS TAMED BY THE INCOMPARABLE BALDINADO THE GREAT! WITNESS THE BEAUTIFUL JENNY DODGE PERFORMING THE MOST ASTOUNDING MID-AIR SOMERSAULTING EXPLOITS ON EARTH! WONDER OF WONDERS! STEP RIGHT UP! STEP RIGHT UP!"

The farm boy waved and Clare came over and he led her under the fluttering banners at the entrance to the Big Top, the ticket taker whistling rudely at Clare as she went by.

Once they were inside the tent, Alvin told her, "That fellow gives me the creeps."

She agreed, "He seems awfully fresh."

"That ain't the half of it."

By the crowded plankwood bleachers, Clare squealed, "Oh, Melvin, look at all the pretty ponies!"

The Wild West show had filled the big tent rings with Apache bareback riders and sturdy soldiers in blue cavalry outfits amid deafening gunfire. A frightful massacre! Siberian Cossacks and Arabian swordsmen emerged from the wings to join the fray. Wild horses stampeded over flaming hurdles. Guns boomed. Steel sabers flashed. The audience shrieked with delight at an Indian war cry and another round of booming cannon fire.

Alvin's ears were ringing when he felt Clare pinch his arm.

"Isn't it just wonderful?" she said.

"Sure," Alvin replied, "but I don't see nowhere to sit."

Since fainting in the mirror maze, he had become terrifically worried about getting stuck in a crowd. He guessed his fever hadn't reduced much at all and his stomach felt rotten. He watched a band of feathered Apaches riding bareback ponies away from the battle to a large cheer while a troupe of friendly clowns passed out sticks of cotton candy to eager children in the front row. More people shoved past. The ringmaster in red tails and black top-hat bounded into the center ring to a chorus of brass trumpets. High overhead a glittering troupe of blue-sequined aerialists crowded the lofty tightwire perches. Flaming torches flared. Smells of fresh popcorn and steaming horse manure and gun smoke filled the air. The ringmaster addressed his audience by megaphone: "LAD-IES AND GENTLEMEN! EMMETT J. LASWELL PRESENTS THE GRANDEST, MOST COLOSSAL, SPECTACULAR, SENSATIONAL SHOW OF THE AGE!"

"Didn't your little friend say he was with the Wild West show?" Clare asked, entwining her arm with Alvin's.

The farm boy shook his head as he coughed. "Naw, he laid an egg in Joplin with that fool knife trick of his and got canned. Now all they let him do is juggle apples on the midway for a kiddie show. I guess he'll be blowing the circus pretty soon now."

"Gee, that's too bad. But you'll still be performing tonight, won't you? I'm awfully anxious to watch. Remember, I'll be pulling for you."

Alvin cocked his head at her, feigning his best expression of puzzlement. "Ain't you seen my act? Why, I put it on an hour ago."

Clare's jaw dropped. "Oh dear!"

"It went over swell, too. First stunt of the night. Why, I never heard such a racket as when I gave them Bengal tigers the ol' whip. Laswell himself said it was just about the swellest performance he ever seen and he ain't usually that liberal with his compliments. Says he might even star me in the next show."

The farm boy looked off toward the prancing ringmaster. He scouted the bleachers again for somewhere they could have a better look at the string of gargantuan India elephants parading into the three-ring circus as the daring highwalkers balanced beneath silk parasols and formed pyramids across from the great trapeze. A huge cheer went up from the surrounding crowds. Tramp clowns danced and tumbled on the sawdust. A slim fellow in a silver suit was shot out of a giant black cannon and sailed across the tent into a rope net, saluting to the grandstand as he flew by. Zebras and camels and trained bears appeared in the wings with a family of Turkish acrobats. The ringmaster doffed his hat. When the farm boy turned back to Clare, she was gone. Alvin called her name and walked forward to the edge of the wooden bleachers and searched the audience there. When he didn't see her, he looked back toward the Big Top entrance and the flocks of people crowding around Zulu the Cannibal King who had come into the big canvas tent juggling six bleached human skulls.

"Melvin!"

Clare's voice, nearly drowned out by the commotion in the center ring, came from the musty darkness beneath the old bleachers. Crouching down under the fifth row planks, the farm boy saw Clare kneeling in the damp sawdust with a frilly bundle of white in her arms, a little girl dressed in Sunday lace wearing a cute baby bonnet on her head. When the child noticed Alvin staring at her, she cried out, "Mama! Mama! I want my mama!"

Clare smiled at the farm boy. "The poor dear's lost."

"How'd she get under there?" Alvin asked, crawling a few feet forward. A Phunny Phord clown car backfired over and over as a pile of midgets in police uniforms chased a pony-drawn firewagon around the outside of the rings and a trio of midget firemen parachuted down from the tent peak. The crowd roared with delight.

Alvin backed up as Clare guided the little girl out from under the bleachers. "She ain't hurt, is she?"

Clare shook her head. "No, but she's awfully frightened. And listen to her voice, it's so husky. I think she's caught a cold."

The child whimpered and buried her face in Clare's bosom.

"Well, where's her folks?" Alvin asked, searching the crowds near-by for a worried face. There were so many people jammed together under the tent, he wasn't surprised a little kid could get separated from her parents. Glancing up to the white canvas tent top, he watched a Chinese cyclist riding across the tightwire with a pair of squealing red-capped monkeys on his shoulders.

"Why, Melvin, I think she wants us to take her to her mother!"

The farm boy saw that Clare had let go of the child and was being tugged toward the tent exit. "What if her mama ain't left yet?" he asked. "What if she's still looking in the tent?"

The little girl pointed to the exit. "Mama! Mama!"

"You see?" Clare said. "I think she wants us to go with her, the poor dear. She seems to know where her mother went."

"Well, gee whiz, we ain't hardly seen nothing of the show yet," the farm boy complained, staring at the child who was about the homeliest kid he had ever laid eyes on. He wished she'd stop her sniveling. There were lots of worse places to get yourself lost than at a circus.

Instead, the little girl whimpered again, "I want my mama! I want my mama!"

Clare picked her up and gave her a hug. "Sweetheart, we'll find your mama, I promise." She looked up at Alvin. "Don't you see what I mean? Oh honey, I guess we'll just have to find her mother."

The crowd roared as the Great Baldinado strode into the lion cage and cracked his leather whip at the King of Beasts, inspiring the bandmaster to strike up a rousing chorus of "Cyrus the Great." A troupe of Egyptian contortionists emerged from a sequence of tiny drums. Gold-spangled acrobats soared on swaypoles high above as Clare led the little girl out of the Big Top with Alvin trailing reluctantly behind.

Wind blew across the busy midway, scattering wastepaper and errant balloons. Music from the carousel rang like distant choral bells. Alvin felt a chill and buttoned his shirt up to the collar. What a switch! An hour ago he had been alone and now he had himself a family. The thought crossed his mind that perhaps he might marry this girl one day if consumption didn't kill him. She was pretty and smelled like spring flowers. He thought he would go with her as often as she'd stand for it. They passed the musical Whirly-Gig as it discharged another group of breathless passengers. A roustabout in a flat cap winked at Clare as he took tickets for the next ride. On a platform a few feet away sat pasty-faced Minnie the Fat Lady eating a ripe watermelon. The little girl whined again for her mother and pointed Clare to the showgrounds entrance, crowded with newly arrived circus-goers. Alvin smelled steamed hotdogs and mustard and watched an old Negro in suspenders and a tarnished derby lead a pair of spotted ponies toward the lot of painted bandwagons. More boys from town hurried by, stuffing popcorn and Crackerjack into their mouths as they ran.

"Why, I think she wants us to take her home," Clare said to Alvin, as crimson skyrockets lit the black sky. "She's awfully insistent."

Across the midway, a skinny concessionaire's tiny white poodle rolled over and jumped up and did a backflip off an apple crate next to the soda pop stand. An audience of children clapped loudly.

The farm boy frowned. "Well, that just don't seem at all fair. You hardly been here yet and there's still lots to see."

"Oh, but there'll be other shows, and you said yourself that you're finished. Isn't that right? Meanwhile, this poor little tot's frightened half to death and can scarcely wait to get back to her mother." Clare knelt down to give the little girl a kiss on the nose and received a kiss on the lips in exchange. She giggled and the little girl pinched her cheek. Clare picked her up and hugged the smiling child to her bosom. "You see what I mean? Isn't she the cutest thing you ever saw? Oh Melvin, you're looking all blue. I suppose you've got your heart set on seeing the rest of the show tonight, don't you? Well, why don't I take her home myself? It's silly for both of us to leave so early and I'm sort of played out, anyhow, so I'm sure I wouldn't be good company."

Her dainty yellow frock fluttered in the wind. Somewhere across the dark showgrounds, a trumpet blew. A troupe of sequined acrobats marched out of the fluttering shadows beside the cage wagons.

His head hurting now, the farm boy shrugged. "If you say so."

Clare smiled. "Maybe we could go on an auto picnic tomorrow?" The child grabbed at Clare's breast. "Mama!"

"I ain't got a motor," Alvin answered, gazing down the dark windy midway where a familiar figure emerged from the belly-dancing sideshow, hat in hand. Chester Burke took a cigar from his breast pocket, lit it, then crushed the dead match in the dirty sawdust underfoot.

"Oh, we'll have a grand time," Clare promised, "but now I have to see this little dear home to her mother. You won't be sore at me, will you, Melvin?" She stared him in the eye, noticed his disappointment. "Oh, it's not as bad as all that, sweetie. I really do hope you'll look me up tomorrow, honest I do."

"Sure." The farm boy watched a pink-haired clown approach the gangster. They shook hands and the clown began speaking with Chester like they were pals.

Clare leaned forward and gave Alvin a soft peck on the cheek. "You're absolutely topping!" She hugged the little girl. "Say good night to Melvin, sweetheart. Bye-bye! Bye-bye!"

The child kicked and shrieked, "Mama! Mama!" and urged Clare toward the showgrounds gate. Clare waved back to Alvin as she passed under the rippling flags. A fresh gang of young people reeking of moonshine liquor bought tickets to the circus. The wind gusted hard as Clare vanished across the dark summer fields toward town. When the farm boy turned to look for Chester again, he found himself surrounded by half a dozen midget clowns dressed like Keystone Kops.

The circus wagons were parked trailer fashion in a large dirt lot behind the Big Top. Performers came and went, some dressed in costumes, others stripped down to workshirts, leotards and robes. A cookhouse next to one of the empty animal wagons drew plenty of attention with the circus so far from town, sideshow curiosities waiting in line with highwire artists and billposters and harness makers and sweaty roustabouts for a hot meal. Noise from clown alley echoed through the performers' painted wagons, lewd insults and elaborate gags traded back and forth for a laugh or a stiff jolt of booze. Inside the gilded wagon, *King of Lilliput*, a proud elderly midget dressed like Sir Lancelot and seated upon an overstuffed silk pillow under a shuttered window by a small cookstove offered his candid opinion of life with the circus to the farm boy and the dwarf.

"Now, if you were to have asked me thirty years ago how far I'd be willing to travel for riches and fame, why, I'd have said 'To the moon and back, my friend. To the moon and back!'"

He reached into a basket of fruit at his feet and drew out a ripe banana. Alvin sat on a narrow wood stool next to a cupboard full of old photographs and embroidered handkerchiefs and little knick-knacks. Still feeling feverish and wan, he ate from a bowl of Crackerjacks in his lap and tried to pretend he was all right, though his breathing was disturbingly labored. Rascal, dressed up as Napoleon at Waterloo and grinning like a sloppy drunk, reclined on a lavender fainting couch beside tiny Josephine who wore a pretty taffeta ballgown of her own and a powder-white pompadour. She was perhaps half a foot shorter than the dwarf with a grown woman's face and lovely opaline eyes. She and Rascal held Japanese fans and shared sips from a cloudy bottle of schnapps.

"But men are not trained seals," said Sir Lancelot, slowly peeling his banana. "We require more than a steady diet of fish and exercise to show our best. Yet how many exhibitors have ever appreciated this simple truth? Dan Rice died a drunkard when Spalding turned him out. Tom Thumb passed away rich but childless." He sniffed the banana. "Oh, how wonderful it once was to be young and hopeful."

Another dozen or so midgets wearing a variety of absurd theatrical costumes had stuffed themselves about the flowery interior of the painted wagon — Betty Boop with the Keystone Kops shoulder to shoulder on a feather bed, Emperor Nero on a footstool with a cup of tea, Billy the Kid dressed in chaps, six-guns, and a ten-gallon hat on a padded bench-seat beneath two flickering kerosene lamps with Merlin and Kaiser Wilhelm and Chief Crazy Horse — a scene utterly bewildering to the sick farm boy.

The dwarf remarked, "My companion and I have traveled quite a lot recently. Constitutionally speaking, it's been perilous, of course, but my Uncle Augustus always held to the opinion that getting out of bed every morning is well worth the risk."

Betty Boop giggled.

Alvin saw Merlin produce a silver hipflask from thin air and have a drink. The wagon was humid and smelled of fried onions and stale cigars. A bouquet of marigolds in a crystal vase on a carved bookshelf was already wilting in the heat from the stove. Alvin felt dizzy.

Smoothing his toga, Emperor Nero said, "I have led parades through countless hamlets whose populace imagines we exist only for the amusement of children. This is the harlequin's secret. He pretends to believe the audience adores his featherbrained antics, then weeps false tears of unhappiness when sentiment turns against him. Frivolity is bittersweet. It buys our meals, yet leaves the audience believing us fools: a dubious bargain, indeed."

Alvin listened to the wind gust through clown alley. He heard an angry row developing near one of the lion cages. Rascal hiccuped and sweet Josephine patted his back.

Merlin snapped his fingers and a miniature deck of playing cards appeared in his tiny hands.

"Do a trick," Kaiser Wilhelm requested, his spiked helmet tipped askew.

"Yes," agreed Chief Crazy Horse, "let's have some stunts. I'm feeling awfully low this evening."

Merlin addressed the farm boy: "Young man, are you clever at riddles?"

A titter of laughter swept through the Keystone Kops. Betty Boop clapped a hand across her mouth as a black eyelash sagged.

Too ill to appreciate the joke, Alvin shrugged. "I ain't heard one yet."

"He's rather slow on the uptake," said the dwarf, stifling a giggle of his own. "Better make it easy."

Alvin snapped back, "No, I ain't." He coughed harshly, muffled by his sleeve. The wagon was stifling and he began to feel faint once more. He wondered if the midgets kept a doctor handy.

"Go ahead, tell him your riddle," ordered Sir Lancelot, busy uncorking a bottle of wine. "Let's try to be gracious to our guests."

Merlin nodded while shuffling rapidly through the playing cards. He thought for a few moments, then quoted: *"A mighty black horse with gallant white wings, within his grand paunch bears many strange things."*

"Oh, that's so simple," said Billy the Kid, drawing his toy six-guns. He cocked both silver triggers with his thumbs.

"Don't tell, don't tell!" cried one of the Keystone Kops. "Let him guess!"

"He won't get it," Emperor Nero advised. "Ask him an easier one."

"Oh, let him try," said Josephine. She took another nip of schnapps and passed the bottle to the dwarf whose gray eyes lolled oddly.

"I ain't got any idea," Alvin growled, embarrassed by all these circus midgets staring at him like he was slow. Worse, he knew most of them were tipsy. It seemed all they did was drink once their act was over. He hated drunks, no matter what size they were.

"Don't be sore, honeypie," cooed Betty Boop. "Merlin's got a million snooty riddles and even we ain't heard 'em all. But here's the gag: If you guess one, the poor dope's finished."

"You're darned right he is," one the Keystone Kops put in gleefully.

"Go ahead, kill me," said Merlin, flourishing the deck of cards. "You're all a bunch of shallow-waisters, anyhow."

"I think Merlin needs a diet for his head," said Betty Boop. She blew him a kiss.

"I ought to give you a shiner for yours," Merlin shot back, riffling his playing cards like a loud ugly fart.

"Go ahead, rave on, you big horse. You can dish it out all right, but you sure can't take it."

"Oh, quit quarreling with him," Sir Lancelot told Betty Boop. "Can't you see he's tight?"

"It's a ship," Rascal proposed after imbibing another sip of schnapps. Josephine kissed him on the cheek. The dwarf smiled. "If I may help my young companion."

All eyes switched back to Merlin whose flamboyant posture drooped dramatically. The deck of cards vanished in the wink of an eye, replaced by a scowl and a muttered obscenity.

"Well, I'll be!" Emperor Nero laughed. "He got it!"

A boisterous cheer went up from the Keystone Kops. "HURRAH! HURRAH!"

"The little fellow's a credit to his race," declared Betty Boop.

"You said a mouthful!" Billy the Kid cackled. He tipped his ten-gallon hat to the dwarf. "Attaboy!"

Sir Lancelot lit a Cuban cigar.

Alvin heard the steam calliope roar to life across the windy show-grounds. Near clown alley, someone began practicing scales on an old violin. The farm boy ate a fistful of Crackerjacks and tried to forget how sick he felt. Why couldn't he go home? He was tired of all this nonsense.

Rascal burped, then remarked to no one in particular, "When my Uncle Augustus was just a boy before the Civil War, he was employed by a puppet show aboard the *Floating Palace* in the Gulf of Mexico, so I know all about boats. Once I determined the 'gallant white wings' were sails, it all made perfect sense. Also, Auntie and I played riddles quite often at supper, some of the cleverest you ever heard. Whoever guessed correctly won a glass of sherry, though I must tell you I preferred Coca-Cola, especially during the summer when the heat in our kitchen was simply dreadful. To be honest, I believe I won more often than not."

"Living straight keeps down the weight," Josephine remarked with a smile. She gave the dwarf another kiss on the cheek. "Aren't you precious?"

"Getting fresh, eh?" Billy the Kid snapped at her. He twirled a six-gun on one finger. "Maybe you better cut out wine tonics after the show, honey."

"She's after him, ain't she?" said Betty Boop. "Like mama and papa. I'll bet he's even got a decent stake somewhere."

Emboldened by nightfever, Alvin blurted, "Didn't he tell you he's a millionaire? Why sure, my little pal's got loads of dough. Just you ask him."

"Oh, I'll lay he doesn't," said Chief Crazy Horse. A yellow feather fell off his war bonnet. "Look at his patent leathers."

"What of it?" Josephine protested. "At least he ain't so nickel and dime! What's your aim in life besides getting a forkful of those dames you been chasing around with?"

Chief Crazy Horse laughed. "Josephine's motto is, 'Get 'em young, treat 'em rough, tell 'em nothing.'"

"Oh yeah? How about that skunk you dragged in here last week?" she snapped back. "All your taste is in your mouth!"

Sir Lancelot shushed her. "Aw, easy kid, easy."

Wind shook the circus wagon again. A pair of muleskinners walked past cursing Laswell. Alvin heard a flat ukulele join the practicing violinist across the dirt lot. Then he watched Merlin roll a silver dollar over his knuckles and remembered how Frenchy used to be able to do that before he got his hand caught in Uncle Henry's thresher.

"I guess you think the well-to-do got it all sewed up, don't you?" Kaiser Wilhelm cut in, finally. "Well, I was rich once, too. Like Midas, I tell you. Houses, boats, dames, swimming pools, you name it, and everything according to Hoyle. I played the market right out of school like a Morgan and nobody could say I wasn't liberal, neither. Why, they got plenty of orphanages and old folks homes these days in Philadelphia thanks to the charity bureaus I started up back then. Yessiree, it was all going so grand, and me the one that put it over. Well, when you pull down that kind of dough, you got to keep your eyes peeled for those that like to take it from you. In my case, I had my brother Frank who was always shooting off his head about how stingy I was towards my own flesh and blood once I'd made the grade. He earned a fair enough wage with United Cigar to keep his pretty wife Peggy in a new dress every month and those five kiddies of his rolling in toys, so I tell you he had nothing to kick about. Now, Peggy had a sister named Helen who wasn't hard to look at and seemed willing to give a short weight like me a tumble if I played my cards right. She smelled like lilies-of-the-valley, I tell you, and kissing her made me shiver, so I married her and built her a castle at Newport. That cost plenty all right, but I was sweet on Helen and we got on well together — or so I thought. Well, here's the pay-off: it was all a double-cross. Frank and Helen hired a detective to follow me around until he brought back pictures of me and some dame in a hotel room that proved I was a cheat. They got a judge to bust off the marriage and give everything I owned to Helen. Didn't matter that the dame from the hotel room worked in the steno pool at United Cigar and the judge played golf on Fridays with Helen's Uncle Bob. After that, everything went on the bum. I got so cockeyed sore, I started drinking. See, I had to take it out on someone, and there wasn't anybody left to put me wise to myself. Helen knew how to sell her stuff, all right, but she never did love me and I only got word the day her lawyer sent me the telegraph. Now, I don't hold with misery drinking anymore because I don't want to end up an old soak, and I don't take up any of the financial papers, either. I had a good enough nut on my shoulders when I was young to play the market for all it was worth. After Helen, though, I figured out that all a fellow really needs is some bread to dunk in his coffee and a sweetheart to tuck him in at night, and that's the straight of it."

Another cold gust of wind shook the wagon. Fiddling with her sagging eyelash, Betty Boop squeaked, "You're all set now, though, ain't you, honey?"

Kaiser Wilhelm smiled. "Sure I am."

"You bet he is," said Emperor Nero. "That's the Kaiser you're talking to."

Sir Lancelot puffed on his cigar as the Keystone Kops shared a bottle of wine and a plate of meat sandwiches brought over from the cookhouse. Billy the Kid played with his six-guns. Josephine stroked the dwarf's hand while the farm boy listened to the piping of the steam calliope near the Big Top and tried not to get sick all over himself.

The wagon door opened to the cold draft and Alvin saw a grimy fellow wearing a tattered brown derby stick his head inside. He growled at the Keystone Kops, "The boss wants to see y'all over to the office, and he don't mean maybe." He pointed a finger at Emperor Nero. "That means you, pipsqueak."

Then he slammed the door and left.

Nero wiped his mouth. "Ain't Johnny a scream?"

"Aw, raspberries," said Billy The Kid, getting to his feet. "Let's shove off."

Wind hissed through the upper branches of the old sycamore trees that flanked the boardinghouse where Alvin lay sweating under a ratty wool blanket in the dark. A side window was raised to the night air and a lilac scent of damp gardens carried past the storm screen. Ragged shadows from the streetlights below fluttered across the walls and ceiling. A hound dog tied to an iron stake in the lot next door barked off and on at ghostly intruders. The boardinghouse felt dead and empty.

Drumming his fingers on the iron bedpost, the dwarf rested under the sheets in his own bed, stripped to his union suit. It was hours past midnight. When the farm boy came back from the showgrounds, he had hoped to find Clare working at the front desk, but the light was out in the office and nobody answered when he called for her, and he went up to bed feeling feverish and lonesome. Meanwhile, the dwarf was full of stories from his night at the circus. He admitted running off to the showgrounds after the street parade. At North Street, he explained, a lion had escaped from its wagon cage and gone on a rampage through a widow's tomato patch until it was subdued by a pair of animal trainers in Pith helmets. One of Laswell's funnymen was horribly mauled trying to protect a crowd of children and had to be driven to a hospital in the next county. According to the dwarf, it was the most exciting thing he had ever seen — until he crossed paths with Josephine behind the Big Top.

"I introduced myself to her by the corner of the snake house where I was struck dumb by Cupid's arrow. I'd never been in love before. Isn't that remarkable? Auntie always cautioned me against passion, warning that my heart was born frail, susceptible to poisons of many sorts. Well, she needn't have worried. I feel lighter than air."

"I seen Chester at the circus tonight."

"Oh?"

Alvin rolled over in bed, shrugging off part of the blanket. The sheets beneath him were damp with sweat. "He was talking to one of them clowns. I don't know what for."

"They've traveled ten thousand miles this year," said the dwarf, shoving back his own covers. The bedsprings squeaked as he kicked at his blanket. "Josephine says she once performed with a royal Hungarian wire walker and rode in a gilded wagon that had its own sink and phonograph and marble tub from Savannah. That was years ago, of course, but did you know Mister Laswell still pays three hundred a week for many of the sideshow acts, more for the Big Top? It's fascinating, isn't it? Why, I believe a fellow could do a lot worse for himself than joining a circus."

Falling leaves blown free by the cold wind pattered the boarding-house roof like autumn rain. Alvin stared at the dark ceiling. Whenever he worried, his fever worsened. He thought about how far ten thousand miles was from home. He listened to the draft at the storm screen and the dusty leaves falling and the barking dog next door. The dwarf ruffled his sheets and sneezed. Alvin coughed into his pillow. He told Rascal, "You shouldn'ta gone there till dark."

"I found help."

"Beg your pardon?"

"We needn't be afraid now. While you were napping, my dear Josephine introduced me to the King of Lilliput who was quite gracious in showing me about the circus. You have no idea how many friends we've made here. I told them everything."

"Chester'll shoot you in the head."

The dwarf sat up in bed, casting his own odd shadow on the pale wallpaper behind him. He leveled his voice. "We were not made that we might live as brutes."

"I ain't fooling," Alvin warned.

"He has no hope who never had a fear."

"You're crazy."

Down on the front sidewalk below, a man whistled tunelessly walking Third Street toward the railyard. The dwarf sipped from the water glass he kept beside his bed. Once finished, he told Alvin, "You see, I'm done with Hadleyville forever. Auntie can keep my inheritance if she wishes. It is immaterial with me now. When Josephine was a tiny girl, her mother knew a witch who lived in a peach orchard just outside of town. She dallied with divination and brewed magic potions in her root cellar that amended one's stars in the heavens. Although Josephine was still no bigger than a cabbage at her thirteenth birthday, she was invited by Alice Roosevelt to dance a minuet on a tea table at Sagamore Hill for the President himself. Do you believe in destiny?"

A cold gust shook the storm screens. His fevered skin chilled by the draft, Alvin replied, "I believe it's a long walk home even if you don't get shot."

"I have faith in society." The dwarf leaned over onto his pillow. "We've never been alone. We've just imagined we were. When my mother gave birth to me, she intended that I belong to the world, not squander half my life hidden away from it. Auntie was cruel to tell those lies. I trusted her to know what was best for me and I was deceived. Tonight at the circus, Josephine and the King of Lilliput helped me discover a solution to the riddle of freedom. Would you care to hear it?"

The farm boy listened to the wind and thought about the wild pinewoods on the farm in Illinois, a distant call, indeed.

"'Tis true that we are in great danger," said the dwarf. "The greater therefore should our courage be."

"Don't joke me. I ain't in the mood."

The storm-shutters on the veranda downstairs rattled harshly as the dwarf told the farm boy, "Listen here: trust me, and I promise you that after tomorrow night, we won't have a worry in the world."

Morning light filled the lobby when Alvin came downstairs for breakfast. The dwarf had risen early and gone out on his own. All the windows in the lower boardinghouse were flung open to the morning air to let out the stink of turpentine fumes from the painters working on the second floor. The farm boy rang at the desk for Clare and another girl came out of the office and told him Clare would not be in until noon, so Alvin reluctantly left the boardinghouse and went downtown to eat. Trucks and automobiles rumbled along Third Street. The clouds were patchy now and blue sky shown through, warmer than yesterday. Alvin found a half-empty lunchroom two blocks from Main and bought himself hotcakes and ham and scrambled eggs and two cups of fresh coffee. He hadn't eaten much more than popcorn at the circus and woke with his fever gone but his stomach growling. The fainting spell he had suffered at the circus frightened him greatly. He knew he was sicker than last month and worried that sooner or later a relapse of his consumption might send him to the grave if he didn't watch out. He imagined the dwarf was back at the circus, honeying up his little sweetheart. Maybe he was busy working up a show of his own. Alvin had never seen so many half-pints at one place before in his entire life. The idea of them traveling around together wisecracking and putting on circus shows everyday didn't seem all that peculiar to him now after sitting in their wagon for an hour. He supposed it wasn't all that bad a life. The fact that a fellow doesn't come up much past another fellow's belt buckle shouldn't mean he doesn't deserve the best of what there is to be had.

When he finished with breakfast, the farm boy strolled around downtown for an hour or so, looking in store windows. The sidewalks were less crowded than yesterday and the trolley wasn't operating. A fresh bounce in his step from a full stomach, Alvin crossed the street to the jewelers where he bought a new wristwatch and stuck it in his pocket. Then he walked back to the boardinghouse. The painters were sitting out on the veranda drinking coffee and talking. One of them had a morning edition of the *Icarian Mercury-Gazette* spread apart on his lap and was reading a story to the others. A prominent businessman named Theodore Bowen had been robbed and badly beaten last night in his house on Cobb Avenue. His son had reported the matter to the police. Nobody had been arrested and no further details concerning the man's condition had been offered to the newspaper. When the farm boy came up the steps, the painters stepped back to let him by. He nodded and passed into the cool lobby. Behind him, the painter with the newspaper on his lap muttered a crude obscenity regarding circus people. Alvin checked at the desk for news of Clare again and received the same answer: she would be in for work at noon. A cabinet clock in the office chimed once. He went upstairs to wash his face.

In the third floor hallway, the farm boy listened to Virgil Platt reciting more Bible verses. Through the floor vents he thought he heard a woman performing "Beautiful Dreamer" a capella in a room somewhere downstairs. Maybe it was only the radio. A noisy delivery truck roared past the boardinghouse in the direction of the railyard. Alvin unlocked his room and went inside and found Chester standing by the raised window overlooking Third Street.

"Hiya, kid."

He had on the same charcoal-gray waistline suit and fedora from last night at circus. His face was drawn and tired. He held a white handkerchief to his mouth, dabbing a sore on his upper lip. The odor of turpentine had wafted up into the room through the vents, spoiling the sweet garden scent from the morning yard. Alvin smelled a trace of liquor, too.

"Sorry about this dump," Chester said, taking off his hat. He set it on one of the spindle chairs. His voice was cold and hoarse. "Spud's not the square shooter he used to be. When I knew him on the North Side before Prohibition, he drove a taxicab and wouldn't make a play on your sister for anything in the world. No cards or booze or dirty work with those switchboard girls, either. He led a clean life back then."

"I ain't got a sister," Alvin lied, trying to be funny. He was sick of Chester treating him like a hick. Besides, talking back didn't seem so risky anymore. They were all going to jail soon enough.

Shouts from the painters on the veranda to someone across the street echoed in the boardinghouse. Alvin closed the door behind him and sat on the dwarf's bed.

"I hear you boys were really whooping it up at the circus last night," Chester said, as he took out a cigarette and lit it. "Shooting the works."

He walked over to the sink and ran water over the smoldering match, washing it down the drain.

The bedsprings squeaked as the farm boy leaned forward. "You didn't leave off a message for us to pull out of going, did you? Nobody told us nothing about it, if you did."

Chester had a look in the closet. He nudged the dwarf's suitcase with his foot. "Hallie downstairs says you had a date to go out with her friend Clare last night."

The farm boy studied his shoe leather.

"Well, what's it all about?" Chester tapped hot ash off into the sink. "Is she sweet on you?"

"She says it's nobody's business."

Chester smiled. "I suppose that's so."

Alvin got up off the bed for a look outdoors. He wondered if Chester had in mind to call on her, too. "I ain't stuck on her or nothing. We talked about having a picnic this afternoon."

Chester exhaled smoke from his cigarette. "Did you meet her crowd? That'll tell you more about a girl than the hat she wears."

The farm boy coughed, then shook his head. "I ain't seen nobody yet but her."

Chester walked back over to the raised window. "It's a swell circus, isn't it?"

"We hardly seen half of it. There was a baby under the bleachers that wanted to go home with her. We missed the lions."

Chester laughed. "How's that again?"

Alvin kicked at the baseboard, and coughed again. "It was all a lot of nonsense."

"What a mob, though, eh? Why, I'll bet you Laswell was raking in the dough last night."

His expression blank, Chester watched a loaded fruit truck rumble by. The painters had gone back inside to work. A faint breeze rippled through the tall leafy honey locust next door.

The farm boy spoke up. "I seen a fellow without no arms or legs light his own cigar."

"He stood out, did he?"

"There was others, too. A fat lady with a flock of tattoos on her bosom and a monkey that played 'John Brown's Body' on a xylophone. Then they had a fellow from Indiana with a extra leg that kicked a football and danced a funny jig for us."

"I'll be damned."

The farm boy went over to examine the dwarf's water glass. There was a little puddle on the nightstand. He asked, "Did you hear about that fellow that got hisself knocked around last night?"

Chester blew smoke through the storm screen. "Sure I did. It was in the morning paper. That's rotten luck."

The farm boy rolled the water glass over in his hands. He was scared, but too sick anymore to worry about it. "You didn't have nothing to do about that, did you?"

"Are you asking if it was me that cracked him on the head and broke open his safe?" He chuckled. "I heard the cops found a clown wig under his desk and one of those phony red rubber clown noses in the backyard."

"So they think somebody from the circus did it?"

Chester nodded. "Sure, unless it's a frame-up."

"That'd work."

"Not for us. Brings too many cops to the circus, poking around, keeping their eyes peeled for any sort of funny business."

"I seen you talking with one of them clowns at the circus."

Chester snuffed out the cigarette on the worn rim of the window frame. He looked weary to Alvin, impatient. "Him? Fellow's name is Lester. He used to work in the Union Stock Yards before the War. He knew my pop from Market Street."

"Oh."

"Says he's finished with Laswell. Hates his guts. Wants to help us stick him up for a cut of the profit. Claims Laswell hasn't been to a bank since the show in Kirksville and Lester knows where he keeps the strong-box. The box office closes at midnight, so that's when Laswell collects the kale and stashes it. Well, tonight we'll be doing the collecting for him. Easy as pie."

"I don't know I'd trust a fellow I just met like that."

Chester walked back over to the toilet and flicked the burnt cigarette butt into the porcelain bowl and flushed. Then he washed his hands under the sink faucet and dried them on a rosy hand towel. When he finished, he told the farm boy, "My pop had the right dope about that. He didn't trust anybody he didn't owe. Lester's no brick, but he won't have the guts to pull out and he knows if he squeals he'll get what's coming to him. The fact is, you don't have to trust 'em if you know how to sell your stuff."

Chester wandered across the room and looked out to the house next door whose small attic window was propped open with a stick. A white fabric of some sort flapped across the shadowed frame like a ghost in the morning draft. The farm boy heard the boardinghouse telephone ring downstairs. Heavy footsteps tromped on the woodplank veranda. Somebody shouted.

Chester came away from the window with a bright smile. He told the farm boy, "I got a date to go out myself tonight, some gypsy dame who was giving me the once-over by the monkey show. I'd had a fair uplift already, but what a doll! I told her I'd drop over about ten. What I'll do is dope out the whole plan this afternoon and meet you at the ticket gate by half past nine. Get me?"

The farm boy nodded.

Chester looked him straight in the eye. "We're all set now?"

"Sure."

He broke a faint smile. "It's a cinch we'll knock it over. Tell the midget to pack his bags after supper."

Alvin nodded again. "All right."

Chester took his hat off the spindle chair. He had one more peek out over Third Street. As he left the room, he told the farm boy, "Our breaks is coming, kid."

The farm boy waited at the raised window overlooking Third Street until Chester came out of the boardinghouse and walked off under the green canopy of drooping willows toward downtown. Alvin watched a squirrel leap into the walnut tree from the rooftop next door and scramble down the trunk. He listened to one of the painters laughing downstairs. A pair of motorcars rattled past, one in either direction. Although Alvin felt tired enough to lie back down on the bed, he went to wash his face instead and use the toilet. He took the Illinois wristwatch out of his trouser pocket and saw that it was almost noon, so he decided to go back downstairs and wait for Clare on the shady veranda in the fresh air. He saw Percy Webster entering a bedroom at the front end of the upper hall as he locked his own door. Virgil Platt had quit his Bible recitations, but Alvin heard the floorboards creak as the old man continued to pace restlessly about his room. The farm boy took the rear staircase down to the lobby.

The door to the back porch was tied open to a draft against the painters' turpentine. Alvin glanced inside the kitchen and found it empty and looked into the dining room and saw Mrs. Burritt at the table with a cup of tea and a small book. Then he heard the painters carrying another ladder up the main staircase and Clare speaking to the postman. He had butterflies in his stomach when he walked into the lobby and saw her at the front desk. She was dressed in a pink apron frock with a cherry blossom print and dainty gold earrings. She looked swell. The postman left a brown package on the desk with Clare and went back outdoors. Upstairs, the painters struggled to maneuver the tall ladder across the second floor landing.

Alvin approached the desk. "Hello."

She raised her eyes, yet barely smiled. "Oh, hello there."

"I ain't seen you this morning."

"Mother kept me home to help with the wash," she said, hardly looking at him.

"Oh yeah?"

Clare took the package off the desk and put it into the office. When she came back out again, she told Alvin, "I'm afraid I also ate too much cotton candy last night. I had the awfulest indigestion before breakfast."

The office telephone rang and Clare went to answer it, closing the door behind her. Alvin heard Mrs. Burritt's voice in the parlor. Then the dog next door began barking as a pack of boys ran past on the sidewalk out front. When Clare hung up the telephone and came out, the farm boy asked, "Did you see that little girl home all right last night?"

Clare sat herself on a stool behind the desk. "Well, now that was the strangest thing. Do you know she never said a word to me about where she lived? Not one peep. Instead, she made me bring her to my house and fix her a cup of hot cocoa and a plate of sugar cookies."

"Is that so?"

"And the little dear insisted on sleeping in bed with me. I was so confused. She wouldn't tell me her name or where she lived or her mother's name or anything about herself at all. But when I woke up in the morning, she was gone."

"Just like that?"

Her face brightened somewhat. "Yes, isn't it peculiar?"

"You bet it is." Alvin hated youngsters, particularly ones who did nothing but moan and blubber for their mommas. Everyone in the family thought he'd have a big family one day, but Alvin didn't pay them any mind because he knew he would probably be dead before he ever got married.

"Well, that's not all. After breakfast, Mother came into the kitchen claiming that some of her silverware was missing and that she was sure the child was a thief. I said, 'Mother, you're absurd,' but she told Father and he's already informed the police. Then there was that beating with poor Mr. Bowen and the clown on Cobb Street last night, you know."

"Yeah, I heard about it."

"Well, it's all quite a mystery, don't you agree? First the child and where she came from, and then that circus clown attacking poor Mr. Bowen?"

"It sure is." He wondered if Spud told her about Chester. Wouldn't that be a surprise?

Clare lowered her eyes. "I can't go with you on a picnic today. I'm sorry."

"Huh?" The farm boy felt another swarm of butterflies fill up his gut. "How come?"

"Father says that since Mr. Bowen was attacked by circus people, he swears to tan me with a willow switch if I have anything more to do with their crowd so long as they're here in Icaria. So that's why I can't go to the circus tonight and I can't have a picnic with you."

"Well, I ain't in the circus."

"Pardon?" Clare's eyes narrowed.

What else could he do now but tell her the truth? "Fact is, I ain't never been in a circus, neither. That was just a made-up story."

"I don't understand."

Alvin shrugged. "It's how come you ain't seen my act last night, 'cause I ain't got one. I had to buy a ticket to get in just like everybody else."

Clare's expression darkened. "You mean, you lied to me?"

"No, I let my friend do the fibbing. I just didn't set him straight, is all."

"Is he in the circus?"

"Nope."

Her voice quivered, grew angry. "That's so deceitful."

"I know it," the farm boy admitted, suddenly realizing his confession might have been a mistake. Aunt Marie had always told him that honesty in love was the best tactic, but maybe she was wrong.

"I don't know what to say."

"Well, how about that picnic?"

Clare rushed into the office and slammed the door behind her.

Alvin gave her a minute or so, then rang the desk bell, hoping she would change her mind.

She yelled at him to go away.

Dejected and feverish, he went out onto the veranda. Avoiding the clutter of boxes and wicker and potted plants, he walked to the side porch and watched a woman in a calico skirt and cotton shawl carry a basketful of green apples up the street. Next door, a man in a white jacket and trousers lounged in a hammock chair smoking a pipe. One of the painters came out with a bucket of dirty gray water and poured it into the mulberry bushes beneath the veranda, then went back indoors again. Alvin heard the telephone ring. He considered trying to explain to Clare about the dwarf and Chester and how they had come to the circus. All he wanted to do was go on a picnic with her and tell her how pretty she was and let her know he'd write letters to her even if he got sent back to the sanitarium. He had worked it all out before breakfast. If she asked, he'd tell her everything. Of course, the trouble now was that she was too cross at him to listen.

Looking up, he saw Rascal scurry along the narrow alley beside the boardinghouse toward the rear garden. Alvin shouted after him, then hustled down the front steps and across the lawn and followed the dwarf's path through the scraggly ironweed and wilting sunflowers into the backyard where he found Rascal on his knees behind a damp patch of rhubarb by the rear garden fence.

"What're you doing there?" the farm boy asked, tiptoeing past a summer growth of sweetpea and moss roses. The tool shed in the back corner of the yard was open. The dwarf stirred cow dung into the soil with a trowel next to a squat terra-cotta pedestal. Bees swarmed in the gooseberry nearby.

Without interrupting his labor, Rascal replied, "I'm planting red tulips as a declaration of my love for sweet Josephine, and blue hyacinths as a foreswearing of constancy."

"Do you remember this ain't your yard?"

"I've already obtained permission from Mr. Farrell this morning. In fact, he was pleased to grant me the favor."

"You seen Spud?" Alvin liked that name. He thought maybe one day he'd go by Spud Pendergast.

"Of course."

"Well, what's the big idea? We ain't stayin' past tonight."

"Home is where we hang our hat, don't you agree?"

The farm boy walked over to the back fence. Across the road in a poultry yard, chickens squawked at a small brown terrier chasing about in the dirt. After studying the surroundings to be sure no one was listening, Alvin told the dwarf, "Chester's got a plan doped out for tonight. He was just upstairs."

Rascal planted his autumn flowers and took up a tin watering pot and sprinkled the black soil. After that, he washed off his hands with the garden hose and wiped them dry on his shirt and got up. "Isn't it pitiable?"

"How's that?"

"To be at once a tee-total failure and utterly malign."

The dwarf stared at his planting ground with undisguised satisfaction. He emptied the watering pot, then collected the trowel and a muddy tan-fork and dropped them both into it.

"You ought to watch out what you say."

"I'm not at all worried."

"What're you so high-hatted about?" asked Alvin, irritation rising with his fever. What made the dwarf think he was all that brave? He hadn't stood up since Hadleyville. He was nobody's hero.

"Consider whether thou art not, thyself, the cause of thy misfortunes; if so, be more prudent for the future."

Alvin smiled. "Yes, we have no bananas."

He chuckled at his own joke.

The dwarf glared back at him. "This is quite serious! I've had a reading this morning and discovered how close is the link between jeopardy and fortune. Indeed, our very fates are defined through the subtlest of actions by ourselves and those with whom we've chosen to associate."

"Aw, go on."

"Associate not thyself with wicked companions, and thy journey will be accomplished in safety."

Alvin raised an eyebrow. "You seen a fortune teller today?"

The dwarf nodded gravely. "The preternaturally gifted Madame Zelincka, as peculiarly constituted an individual as I've ever encountered. She's invited us to a sitting in her parlor this evening. I assured her we'd both attend."

"Well, I ain't a-going. That's nothing but a humbug."

Rascal smiled. "Despair not; thy love will meet its due return."

"Beg pardon?"

"You see, I took the liberty of inquiring on your behalf. Through Madame Zelincka's reading, those incorporeal intelligences on the other side of the veil communicated a message of joy and confidence to your sorrowing soul. She counsels patience."

"She knew about Clare?" the farm boy asked, somewhat incredulously. Aunt Hattie swore by palmistry and spiritistic divinations, while Uncle Henry always maintained it was bunk.

The dwarf nodded. "Madame Zelincka interprets emanations from all brains, near and far. In fact, she says I may be able to speak with my mother this evening if the atmospheric conditions in her spirit-room remain constant. I'm very excited. Madame Zelincka met my mother several years ago during a mesmeric trance and says she is more than willing to remove the veil between our world and the ethereal plane to reunite a loving son with his mother. She's obviously quite experienced with spirit-communions."

"You mean, conjuring ghosts?"

"Spiritual intercourse," the dwarf corrected. "My friend, such manifestations have not been banished by the electric light. There's an unseen world that surrounds us, awaiting a purifying flood of influence from the spirits, radiant fore-gleams of our future informed by our past. Even Buster Brown says ghosts can't do us any harm. Nobody can do you as much harm as yourself. All that glitters is not gold and all that's mysterious is not ghosts in this world of wonders. I've decided I'm going to be good and find out all about it on the other side of Jordan."

The farm boy watched a scrawny goat chewing on tufts of grass in a pen next to the poultry yard. He shook his head. "That's a lot of hooey. If you ask me, there ain't no such thing as ghosts."

"Oh? How would you know that?"

"Well, I ain't never seen one," Alvin replied, giving the garden fence a shake. He guessed if there were any real ghosts, he and the dwarf would've been paid a visit by at least one of those unfortunate souls Chester had murdered this summer. Down the road, the post-man emerged from an old framehouse. Alvin watched a woman in curlpapers wave to him from the second-story window.

"Have you ever seen the Queen of England?"

"No, but I seen pictures."

"Well, Madame Zelincka has a grand collection of spirit photo-graphs atop the secretary in her office. I'm sure she'll be happy to show them to you this evening."

Fatigued enough for a nap, Alvin shrugged. "What's the use?"

Taking up the tin watering pot, the dwarf looked him straight in the eye. "Listen here: in Hadleyville last March I hired a tarot reading in my bedroom that predicted, *'If thou goest to a far country, thy lot will be to undergo many perils.'* Isn't that remarkable? Actually, I thought I'd never leave that house alive, yet look how distant I've traveled since then, how many miles from that grave Auntie named my home. Has this all been hallucination? Although there are mechanisms in place at the circus tonight that will free us from the quagmire we've blundered into, what about tomorrow? What then? I've never been more determined in my life to see beyond the horizon. This evening, Madame Zelincka has promised to offer those of us seated in her spirit circle a vision of Jordan and immortal truth. When I hear my dear mother's voice, I'll be assured that there are, indeed, other lives and other purposes than this."

The farm boy swatted at a passing bee. "Talking ghosts?"

Walking over to the tool shed, the dwarf replied: "There are more things in heaven and earth, Horatio, than are dreamt of in your philosophy."

At twilight on Beecher Street, dried summer leaves blew uphill along the old plank sidewalk. Lamps glowed behind curtained windows of the tall elegant homes obscured under magnolia and sugar maples and flowering oak. Cats hid in poison moonseed and peeked out through iron gates. Bluestreaking meteors raced across the cold black sky. Near the top of the street, the dwarf climbed the narrow stairs of a dark Victorian and rang the brass doorbell. Alvin waited by a garden urn on the brick walkway below. A shadow clouded the stained glass side panel as a young man in denim and suspenders came to answer the door. Summoned by the dwarf, the farm boy followed up the wooden steps and past the young man into the house.

Effluvium of incense and amber-lit gasoliers filled the entry hall. Turkish carpet runners of indigo and crimson ran the length of the house and up a dark-wood staircase to the second floor. All the walls were decorated in olivegreen anaglypta and Morris floral patterns, and the ceiling overhead was painted with golden sunbursts and wild roses. The scratchy phonograph recording of a nocturne by Chopin played in the front parlor to the left where the dwarf hurried straight off upon entering the house. Welcomed by the young man, Madame Zelincka's son Albert, the farm boy was shown through a knotted rope portière into a formal parlor illuminated by electric tulip sconces and oil table lamps. Seated next to the phonograph cabinet on a rosewood chesterfield in the bay window were an earnest little man and his wife, both in elegant evening dress as if out for a night at the opera. Across the room, the dwarf occupied a velvet easy-chair by the fireplace whose mantelpiece of carved marble resembled the entablature of a Greek temple. Behind him, the double doors leading to another room were closed. Mahogany bookshelves and potted palms flanked the arching doorframe.

"So, this is Alvin," said the woman, her blue silver-beaded gown sparkling in the reflected light. "What a fine-looking boy." She offered a warm smile. "Dear, my name is Edith, and this is my husband, Oscar Elliotsen."

Oscar rose from his seat to greet the farm boy. His oiled-hair and thin-waxed moustache glistened as he crossed the carpet to shake hands. "Good to know you, son."

"Yes, sir." Alvin felt himself blush. They were treating him like a king. How come?

"I heard quite a lot about you this morning," his wife added, leaning over to remove the needle from the phonograph as her husband returned to the chesterfield. "It's so extraordinary."

"Thanks."

Wondering what all Rascal had told them, Alvin took off his cap and sat down on a rose tufted sofa near the dwarf. It had been a long hike from Third Street and he was glad to be off his feet. Fresh gardenias in a crystal vase on the side table beside him gave off a delightful scent. He decided this was one of the swellest houses he had ever been in. But who were these people?

"Although my dear friend here is a confirmed materialist," the dwarf remarked, putting his feet upon a stitched hassock, "I'm convinced he is more than fit for our kindred purposes."

Edith smiled at Alvin. "Well, doesn't that sound familiar? Oscar was quite the skeptic himself, weren't you, dear?" She patted him on the knee. "Why, for years he was utterly persuaded that spiritism was jugglery of the commonest sort."

"Pure imposture," her husband confirmed, crossing his arms. "Pabulum for crack-brained lunatics."

Edith added, "He believed that claims of spiritualist miracles were less violations of the laws of God and nature than fraudulent trickery."

Oscar nodded, sternly. "Ingenious deception."

"Well, ain't it the truth?" the farm boy blurted, maybe not so facetiously. He still considered this whole business of setting up a pow-wow with the spirit world a lot of hooey.

Edith gasped. "My heavens, no! Those of us still in the flesh may well be persuaded that our side of the veil is all there is, that our lasting purpose is merely seed for soil, yet how can that be when a living gate such as Madame Zelincka informs us how strong our ethereal link is to those who've already passed over?"

"Our departed loved ones grieve for us in the idyllic realm," the dwarf explained, "longing to demonstrate the divine knowledge that death is not the end — "

"That light of perfect understanding," Edith interjected.

"Whose message," the dwarf continued, "brings comfort to the living and joy to the disincarnate spirit, finally unburdened of all regret and sorrow."

"Mental telegraphy is no humbug," said Oscar, straightening up. He gave Alvin a fearsome look. "Why, Thomas Edison himself knew more about etheric forces than all the sensitives in America. Indeed, I've been told he performed experiments at Menlo Park which proved that electricity is itself simply the manifestation of disembodied spirits."

Edith remarked, "Just last spring, my husband witnessed the use of an Ediphone to record spirit voices."

"It is our own vital electricity," Oscar explained, "our electrical emanations, that initiates the spiritual telegraph through which these trance mediums perform. There's no longer any recondite mystery about it. The science behind celestial guidance has become clear as day. In fact, I'm inclined to believe that anyone with the proper mental physiology should be able to achieve spiritual rapport."

Edith agreed. "It's true, of course. I've communicated clairaudiently with my sister Sara for years. She passed over with typhus when she was just nine and I missed her terribly before I learned what a lovely purpose she has now among the spirit spheres and how beautiful everything is over there."

The double doors parted behind Alvin, and he heard a woman's lilting voice issue from the back parlor: "Flowers whose fragrance lingers, whose bloom fades not, a summer's day of joyous youth."

Oscar Elliotsen and the dwarf got up and Alvin looked over his shoulder to where Madame Zelincka stood under the mahogany archway dressed in a flowing lavender robe.

Edith grinned and clapped her hands. "Oh dear, I had a crystal vision of you just yesterday evening, materializing for me like this in gossamer silk, spirit-spun!"

Quickly, Alvin stood, too, having decided to keep any further opinions under his hat. He didn't want these folks to hate him. People were being friendly for once and he didn't want to foul it up. Besides which, he knew he had good reason to make friends with the dearly departed.

Madame Zelincka smiled as she strolled into the parlor. "Then it would have been infelicitous of the spirits not to have called us together this evening." She surveyed the room. Her face was pale and lovely, her eyes blue as the sky. She was sober and statuesque, taller than her guests, and her brown hair, a graceful chignon of dark curls, hung down her back. "I'm so pleased you're all here."

Alvin smelled a scent of sweet verbena as the medium drew near. She winked at him and he blushed. Why hadn't he worn a suit? He felt like a hick.

Oscar Elliotsen said, "I've been waiting all week to tell you that Mrs. Tingley's temple dome at Point Loma was even more beautiful than you promised."

Edith said, "My husband's favorite shade is amethyst."

Oscar added, "We joined a harmonial circle on our final evening with Dr. de Purucker that got over to Madame Blavatsky herself. As she spoke to us of her celestial life now, we were inundated by a wonderful sprinkling of fresh violets from the summerland."

The dwarf remarked, "Oh, I've read that the pure dry air of California inspires the most startling manifestations."

Madame Zelincka's eyes sparkled in the golden light from the shaded oil lamps. She nodded. "That's quite true. Contrary to our original theories of vibration and mental regions, spirit magnetism appears to be invigorated by atmospheric conditions that most closely resemble the radiant fountains of sunlight those exalted souls enjoy in the seventh sphere."

"Madame Zelincka?"

A dainty older woman dressed in a white lace gown with a garland of pearls and a crystal pendant appeared under the archway. Alvin saw she had been crying lately, her powdered face drawn with tears of sadness.

The medium greeted her with a warm smile. "Lillian, come meet our friends." To the others in the parlor, she explained, "The disembodied spirit of Lillian's late husband Joseph has survived in an etheric body for three years now without knowing he's passed to a life beyond our own. Because he's still able to see and hear his loved ones, he thinks he's dreaming, a not uncommon spiritual infirmity for those whose physical lives were crippled somehow by disease or discontent. Tonight, this mental agony of Joseph's, shared faithfully by his dear Lillian, will be addressed by our psychic circle and the purpose of his life in spheres above, revealed to him at last."

Lillian remained in the doorway, her fingers knotted tightly together. "Can't we begin now?"

Madame Zelincka polled her guests. When each nodded a willingness to proceed with the séance, she smiled. "Well then, perhaps we should retire to the spirit room."

Edith agreed, rising from the chesterfield. "Indeed! There is no artifice to the odic flame. Mysteries will be revealed, enlightenment gained only when we commence our sitting."

"That light of heaven beaming through to us," the dwarf said, starting for the back parlor.

"The great truth," Oscar Elliotsen added, crossing the carpet arm-in-arm with his wife.

"There is no death," Edith affirmed.

The farm boy waited briefly by a potted palm on the side of the doorway where several unshelved books were stacked casually atop the flanking bookcase: *Scientific Basis of Spiritualism, Thirty Years Among the Dead, Gleams of Light and Glimpses Thro' the Rift, Somnolism and Psycheism, Proofs of the Truths of Spiritualism,* and a thick blue volume with the odd title *OAHSPE.* He hadn't seen any ghost pictures yet.

As Madame Zelincka entered the back parlor, her son Albert increased the illumination in order for everybody to see where they needed to go. The spirit room was a perfect octagon draped in burgundy silk at each wall, divided by bracket gas lamps with tulip shades tinted pale heliotrope, yet barren of furniture except for the round spirit table and six mackintosh chairs. Persian rugs covered the floor while the entire ceiling above shimmered with golden stars on an indigo sky.

The sitters took their places at the table with the dwarf seated between Lillian and Madame Zelincka, the farm boy to Lillian's right, Edith next to Alvin, and Oscar Elliotsen between his wife and the medium: a proper balance of men and women around the spirit circle. Once everyone was comfortable, Madame Zelincka placed a fountain pen and a stack of blank message cards on the table, then motioned to Albert who departed through the front parlor, drawing the mahogany doors shut behind him. Tulip-shaded gaslights were reduced to a faint purple glow and the sitters became still. The darkened spirit room was cool and the air dry and clean. Alvin remembered how his sisters had played with a Ouija board planchette and automatic writing when they were younger. For half a year, Mary Ann claimed to be clairvoyant and told everyone in the family she had received personal messages on a slate hidden in her closet from a ghost named Agatha. Both Amy and Mary Ann learned how to crack their toes like the Fox sisters and imitate spirit rappings under the dining room table. Only Grandma Louise was fooled. No one in Alvin's family had ever mentioned attending a genuine séance.

He heard Madame Zelincka's melodic voice speak out of the gloom: "Please place your hands on the table, palms down."

She waited a few moments for the sitters to comply, then began, "By the constitution of our universe, each of us exists in the all-pervading ether as pure spirit until we are born into the material world, which is itself the beginning of our individuality that persists after physical death when the spirit quits the body once more to join celestial spheres. Those of us who remain earthbound give off thought-rays that attract beings of an ethereal order to the gates between life and death. Because even the long-departed remember earthly pleasures, many would gladly forsake the highest realms of eternal glory for the joy of seeing families gathered together again for Sunday dinner or watching a belovéd child at play once more. This insistence upon revisiting the earth-plane is achieved by the attracting odylic energies of a sympathetic medium, which permit direct communication with spirits across the veil much like electricity is filtered through a galvanic battery. These spirits experience a séance like a blissful afternoon dream, a pleasant interlude. They yearn to be called."

Madame Zelincka became silent.

After a few minutes, the farm boy felt a strange chill in the air, not unlike the dark draft in the Palace of Mirrors. His fellow sitters were barely visible across the spirit table, but the ceiling sky of stars seemed luminescent, floating gently in the gloom high overhead. He heard a faint tinkling nearby like the ringing of a tiny bell. A brief vibration rattled the table. Lillian drew a sudden breath. Alvin felt a mild breeze pass through the darkness behind him while the jingling increased to a delicate melody from a music box some garden fairy might possess. The spirit table shuddered and tipped. He heard Edith whisper to her husband. The table shook hard and the farm boy's arms tingled as if stung by electricity and the spirit table trembled and began to rise ever so slightly from the floor. Lillian squealed and briefly pulled her hands away. Strange knocking sounds circled the room. Raising his eyes, the farm boy saw an apparition of fireflies mingling with the stars. It sent a cold shiver up his back.

"Spirit lights," Edith murmured.

The table rose to a foot above the floor and hovered silently. Higher in the dark, the spirit lights glowed blue and flew about the room like burning phosphorous on a spectral draft. Alvin heard the ticking of a metronome somewhere and the beat of a snare drum. He held his breath as the table tipped precipitously toward Oscar Elliotsen who grunted but stayed in his chair. Then the music faded away and the spirit table descended slowly to the floor.

A violet aura formed about Madame Zelincka.

She spoke aloud, "Ethan?"

The spirit lights suddenly fled and the farm boy felt his hair ruffled by another chilly breeze. A single bird feather wafted out of the darkness overhead, drifting and spinning slowly downward toward the sitters.

It alighted precisely in the center of the spirit table.

Madame Zelincka spoke again. "Ethan?"

A minute of silence.

Another feather.

Then, like a distant tinny voice over the radio, *"I want my milk and johnnycake."*

The medium asked, "Are you hungry, Ethan?"

"Yes, ma'am. I sit by the river everyday without catching so much as a tadpole. The fishing is very poor in the spirit land."

Changing slightly the timbre of her voice, Madame Zelincka told the sitters, "Poor Ethan is an orphan child who drowned in the Potomac the night our great President Lincoln was murdered, so his physical remains went unsought, his passing disregarded. As Ethan waits to be claimed, his tragic predicament summons other desperate souls to the gate."

Madame Zelincka reached under her own chair and brought up a small paraffin lamp that she lit with a lucifer match and placed on the spirit table. Then she passed one of the blank cards to the dwarf, one to Lillian, and one to Edith. By now, Alvin had forgotten he ever had a fever.

Her violet aura dimmed by the lamplight, Madame Zelincka said, "I must tell you now that there are tramp spirits who infiltrate many sittings hoping to impersonate a familiar loved one for the purpose of instituting mischief. The messages from such beings only confuse true spirit teachings, like a ray of light deflected at its source. They can be hurtful and dangerous. Therefore, determining proof of a spirit's identity is essential. What I would like each of you to do now is to compose a thought or a question on your card that might only be addressed through direct writing by one who knows you best. When you've done so, place the card beneath your chair and leave it there until I ask for it."

Madame Zelincka took the fountain pen and handed it to Edith. "Mrs. Elliotsen, would you please begin?"

"Surely."

The medium raised her voice. "Ethan?"

"Yes, ma'am."

"Are the others here?"

"Yes, ma'am. They each wish to speak. Shall I let them?"

"Soon, dear."

"I learned a song by the river this morning. Would you care to hear it?"

"Of course."

"Ta-ra-ra-boom-dee-ay. Ta-ra-ra-boom-dee-ay."

The farm boy heard a faint giggling echo race about the spirit room. He watched Edith pass the fountain pen to Lillian, who began scribbling onto her card. The flame within the paraffin lamp flickered. Alvin squinted nervously into the dark, but saw nothing. His legs felt numb.

Madame Zelincka said, "That's very nice, Ethan. Can you sing another?"

"No, ma'am. The water's very cold today. I watched three squirrels fight over a walnut. I think it may snow soon."

"Ethan, may I please speak with Joseph Cheney?"

"Yes, ma'am."

Lillian handed the pen to the dwarf, and hid her message card. Oscar stifled a cough. The dwarf rapidly scrawled something and gave the fountain pen back to Madame Zelincka.

The medium extinguished the flame in the paraffin lamp, darkening the spirit room once again. She spoke softly, "Joseph?"

The sitters were each silent.

Alvin felt the barest prickling over his skin, but held his attention on the medium. For perhaps half a minute, Madame Zelincka gazed dimly into the purple shadows beyond the table.

Then, slowly, a green luminous effluence emerged from her eyes and ears and mouth, like a radiant fluid passing into the atmosphere.

"Emanations of ectoplastic strings," the dwarf murmured in the gloom, his own eyes wide with wonder.

"Ghost serpents," said Oscar Elliotsen.

"Pure etherium from across the veil," Edith said, with a smile. "Essence of the divine."

Alvin watched in awe as the glowing ectoplasm curled and floated about the spirit table, briefly caressing the stack of message cards, then winding in and out of the sitters, trailing away from Madame Zelincka like plumes of faint green smoke.

The medium spoke up, "Joseph?"

A man's husky voice echoed out of the darkness across the room. *"Yes, ma'am."*

Alvin searched quickly about for the source while Madame Zelincka said, "Lillian, please ask your question."

Lillian brought her card out from under the table. She spoke sweetly: "My husband Joseph was always quite a deuce with the girls. We first met during college at the Junior Promenade when I was on Reception Committee. Norris Webster introduced us to each other next to the coat closet where Joseph told a particularly clever joke."

"Which three members of our esteemed faculty most resemble a camp breakfast? Bacon, Dunn, Browne!"

The dwarf laughed aloud.

Oscar Elliotsen stifled a cough.

Nodding, Lillian passed her card to Madame Zelincka who glanced at it briefly with a smile. Then the medium inquired, "Are you feeling well, Joseph?"

"I'm not sure. My wife believes I ought to take more exercise. When I was a student at the university, I threw the hammer on Field Day and never lost."

Madame Zelincka smiled. "Joseph, do you know where you are now?"

"I see a table with chairs and a circle of people I've never met. Are you having a party? Was I invited? I suppose I must've been because I'm here, aren't I? Really, I can't quite remember."

The medium asked, "Do you feel lost, Joseph?"

"I've had peculiar forebodings recently. I've been confused and I haven't slept

well. There's a strange darkness all about. Is this the Mohonk Mountain House? Lillian and I were married in the Parlor Wing twenty-three years ago. It was my wife's idea to return for our anniversary."

"Joseph insisted we make the same walk up to Sky Top cliff as we had when we were young," Lillian told Madame Zelincka. "The trail was awfully cold in the evening, black as pitch, and quite treacherous coming down. I should have known there would be an accident. My husband suffered terrible ulcerations after his fall, yet refused a physical examination until he was unable to rise from bed at the end of the week."

"I had an accident?"

"Don't you recall?" Madame Zelincka asked.

The husky spirit voice crossed the room. *"I have no memory. I can't think."*

Lillian said, "I prayed by your bedside and mopped your brow for thirteen days, my darling. I held you to the very end."

Softening her voice, the medium told Lillian, "Your husband is gradually losing his earth memories. His mental life now occurs in spiritual darkness which he's experiencing as a form of wakeful delirium." She spoke up. "Joseph?"

"Yes, ma'am?"

"Do you know what year it is?"

"Of course I do. It's 1926."

"No, it isn't," the medium replied. "This is now 1929."

"That's impossible!"

"Yet it's true."

"Where have I been? Am I insane?"

The medium asked, "Do you believe you are?"

"As a man thinketh in his heart, so is he."

"This is no mental derangement or dementia. Three years ago, you passed over to the spirit side of life. You've lost your mortal body, Joseph. Your earthly life is finished."

"I don't believe you. Why, it's utter nonsense. Now I'm sure this is all a silly dream."

"You've been wandering in a twilight state for quite some time now, unconscious of the truth. Do you still need to eat? Do you feel the chill of autumn? We've gathered here in our circle tonight to wake you from this sleep of death that has blocked the spiritual progression which is your natural destiny."

Alvin watched the tulip lamps briefly flicker across the dark. A slight breeze passed by the spirit table bearing a musky odor of shaving soap and cologne, but he saw no one. Were the other sitters not so calm, he'd have been utterly petrified with fright.

"Oh dear! Lillian, is this not some hideous nightmare? Am I really dead?"

"Darling, I've missed you so!"

Madame Zelincka said, "Joseph, nobody ever really dies. We simply pass on to an invisible world of higher mental spheres. The grave is not our final goal."

Alvin heard the voice shift again to another corner of the spirit room. *"If I've died, why am I not in heaven?"*

"Heaven is within you, Joseph, as it is with all of us. You're drawn here to the magnetic aura of the living perhaps because of a conscience stricken with discomfort over mistakes you made during your life on earth, or bothersome worries that should no longer concern you."

"Have you considered the wisdom of disturbing the dead? Perhaps I'm an evil spirit. When I was a boy, I always thought I'd like to be a pickpocket or a highwayman. Perhaps I'm unfit for heaven of any sort."

"Rubbish!" Lillian scolded. "Why, darling, you're the most decent, kindhearted man I've ever known."

Madame Zelincka said, "Don't be downhearted, Joseph. This outer darkness you're experiencing is only the tomorrow of death from which each of us rises, sphere to sphere, in our spiritual progression to immortal realms."

"I seem to have forgotten everything I ever knew about life. I feel so blue. I just want to sleep. Perhaps I'm better off dead, after all."

"Joseph, a spirit never dies. These sorrows you've known on the earth plane will all pass away while the flowers you once discarded will bloom again in the summerland. The hour for sleep is done."

"Will I go sit up in a tree somewhere with Jesus and eat figs?"

Madame Zelincka answered simply, "Where your treasure is,

Joseph, there will your heart be also."

"I hope to be with my dear Lillian again one day."

"You will. Do you see the spirit guides waiting for you beyond the veil?"

"Oh, yes! Now I do! Great Scott, I hadn't noticed before."

"You've awakened at last," Madame Zelincka said. "Joseph, it's time for you to go."

"Is there sympathy beyond the grave?"

"Yes, indeed."

"Thank you."

"Good-bye, darling," Lillian said, her soft eyes bright in the green ectoplasmic glow. "Good-bye."

"Good-bye."

The husky voice faded away.

A chilly gust of air raced through the darkened spirit room and was gone.

Alvin fixed his gaze on the medium who seemed to be drowsing in her chair, both eyes shut, her lovely aura shimmering beneath errant strands of luminous ectoplasm. Was she done now? He was already frazzled and worn out. How long was this sitting supposed to last?

The tulip lamps appeared dimmer still.

Madame Zelincka spoke again, "Ethan?"

"Yes, ma'am?"

"Is Dena Elliotsen willing to speak with us?"

"Yes, ma'am. She's right here."

"Please let her do so."

The sitters waited.

Soon the farm boy felt a peculiar disquiet in the violet darkness. He heard a rustling of petticoats somewhere close by, and thought he smelled a scent of rosewater wafting through the spirit circle. Again he searched the dark and saw no one. He almost coughed, but stifled it quickly.

"Mother?"

A girl's dulcet voice.

Edith Elliotsen straightened in her chair. "Sweetheart, is that you?"

"*Mother?*"

Madame Zelincka spoke to Edith, "Take the card, dear, from under your chair and read to us now the question you chose, then confirm the answer written beneath it."

"*Mother?*"

The phantom voice rose in pitch, a strange inflection of urgency. Under a pale glow of writhing ectoplasm, Edith retrieved her message card and stared at it through her reading glasses, then gasped.

The girl's voice echoed across the spirit room. "*Mother, are you there?*"

Edith spoke aloud: "Is kitten in the closet, dear?"

"*No, ma'am, she's in father's drawer.*"

"Oh, dear me!" Edith cried, "It's her! My little darling!"

Alvin watched Oscar Elliotsen take the card from his wife and read the ghost script beneath Edith's handwriting. When his chest heaved forth a sob, Edith gently placed a hand on her husband's coat sleeve.

Madame Zelincka spoke into the gloom: "Dena Elliotsen?"

"*Yes, ma'am.*"

"Can you see your mother here across the gate?"

"*No, ma'am, it's still so very dark.*"

Edith explained, "My daughter was blinded by typhoid fever the week of her fourteenth birthday. The poor little dear. It broke our hearts."

"*Yet it was I, Mother, who bore the burden of sightlessness thereafter, confined to the downstairs of the house on Porter Street like a helpless infant when my soul so desperately sought the ardor other girls my age already knew.*"

"That deceiver of tender youth," Edith cautioned, "from which our only wish was to protect you."

"*By hiding me away from that most beautiful sorrow? Oh, Mother dear, have you never learned? Desire is the blood of life! Alone at night with my knitting, I hungered for the glow of youthful love and plotted my flight to Boston with no fear that I recall. How often these long years I've wondered if the courage I found to board that train came unexpectedly from my blindness, apart from which I might not have dared enter that vile garment factory on Lincoln Street nor the cold flat I took alone.*"

Yet now I see how the remnants I sorted morning till night all that winter long were woven scrap by scrap into a tawdry lace that came to be my own design."

"You're being cruel," Edith said, her voice quivering. Oscar Elliotsen took his wife's hand.

"No more so than the vain echo of dreams that murmur hope when life promises none. That light of day I felt from my window facing the eastern sky brought sanctuary from unanswered prayers and led me to Robert Watkins in whose arms my heart at last took flight."

"I've always refused to speak his name aloud," said Edith, dabbing one eye with a handkerchief. Alvin heard a faint breeze ripple the burgundy drapes about the room. He thought of those birds in the dark rafters of Uncle Henry's barn.

"A woman loves at her own peril. I hold no bitterness, no remorse. Denying myself that sweet flowering of love for which each of us is born would have been far more shameful. Suppose he had not been destitute of character, and marriage his aspiration, do you imagine me in a pleasant cottage somewhere, belovéd of my own children and content? But that was not my fate. Mother dear, I never shared your unwavering faith in the mercy of the world. When Robert withdrew his love, my sorrow was complete. Alone and bed-ridden with grief, I refused to treat a simple cold until the pneumonia that grew one night out of a sudden fever swept me away from that wretched circumstance."

"Darling, we prayed so hard that you'd come back to us," Edith said, weeping now. "When your father brought me the letter from St. Elizabeth's Hospital, I believe my heart stopped beating altogether."

Alvin noticed a dim gray light in the darkness above the spirit table behind Madame Zelincka. He held his breath as it became a gleam of white that drew nearer the circle.

"Mother, these quiet meadows sustain all my memories of life: the pretty orchard blossoms and sweet clover, that shady brook in the dell, the larks that sang for us each morning, and you and Father whispering beside my cradle and my casket by twilight. Awakening here, I found my blindness merely a fading dream. I walked all day without need of instinct and saw the wind pass through the catalpa trees by the river. I know now, Mother, the soul is like the perfume of the flower, its splendid bloom rising unseen, its essence lovingly savored, its worth beyond beauty."

Dumbfounded, Alvin watched the white luminance descend over

the table by the Elliotsens like a cloud of light. Within the heart of that silver radiance, a hazy shadow emerged in the form of a graceful spirit hand that reached down to Edith and gave her a wild rose, still damp with dew.

"I'll always be with you, Mother."

Then the luminous cloud faded away to darkness while Edith and Oscar Elliotsen huddled together, weeping. Across the table, Alvin heard the dwarf whisper something to Lillian about teleplasmic arms and spectral phosphorescence after which the spirit room was quiet once more.

Another couple of minutes passed.

Alvin's heart quit drumming. He let out a breath, shifted his shoes on the carpet, hoping to leave. Then he heard Madame Zelincka speak firmly into the gloom, "Ophelia, are you here?"

Rascal sat up on the parlor cushion he had brought for his chair.

"Your son has come a long way to speak with you," said the medium. A light breeze passed across the room, fluttering through Madame Zelincka's robe. The spirit table trembled and thumped.

The dwarf spoke aloud, "Mother?"

A harmony of whispered voices, nearly inaudible, entered the dark and Alvin thought he heard the faint strains of a piano hymn like those Aunt Hattie played after Sunday dinner on the farm.

Madame Zelincka asked, "Ophelia? Are you here?"

The dim tulip lights flickered and a rhythmic knocking chased along the walls as the spirit table slid half a foot sideways while Edith's white rose and the stack of message cards briefly levitated.

The dwarf called into the dark, "Mother? Is that you?"

A warm draft fragrant with sweet honeysuckle swept into the spirit room and the knocking ceased and the table became still once again.

A pleasant female voice spoke from the shadows. *"Arthur?"*

Madame Zelincka indicated for the dwarf to remove his message card from beneath the chair. Doing so, he read aloud, "We seek at the end of life's rainbow, a treasure we hope to find there — "

"And wealth we do find, but not of the kind we expected, no, something more rare."

Across the room stood a woman dressed in white, her features indistinct as if bathed in morning mist.

"Ophelia Glynn Burtnett?" the medium inquired.

"My mother," confirmed the dwarf, handing his message card to Madame Zelincka.

"Your father wrote that poem in our wedding album a long while ago when we were very young. Do you know he was the handsomest man I ever saw? I felt so proud to sit in his carriage. When I was a girl, I dreamed of white peonies and bridesmaids all in a row and beautiful oaths of love and duty foresworn. To be blessed throughout my life with the endearment of those nearest my heart gave me such joy. Yet good fortune so often leads to forgetfulness. The road is always best on the other side. What I cherished most, your father held in disregard, and what he sought, I never wanted. Do you believe we can know our destiny before the evidence of it becomes clear? You were my only child, Arthur, born on a summer evening beneath the nursery Grandfather Burtnett built. I needed three days and a wealth of prayer to bring you into this world, and I remember worrying that if I didn't hurry you along, your aunts and uncles would all give up and go home. I wasn't afraid for myself. Augustus said I had a true mother's fight in me and would surely prevail in that good struggle. Early in the season, a family of bluejays had nested in the walnut tree outside my bedroom window and I listened to their chattering all the while. I waited for you longer than anyone thought I could and only when you came forth and drew your first breath as my wonderful child, did I pass on to a life and a purpose that still seems mysterious to me."

"I grew up without you, Mother, all these years," the dwarf said in a trembling voice, "only a photograph of you and a poem on my bedstand."

"You've been very brave."

"I've tried to be a decent and faithful son, though I admit I've had my trials."

"Arthur, human nature hasn't changed a particle since I passed. All we know of morals, high and holy, we find in our own hearts. There is no aristocracy of merit on earth or in heaven absent of that goodness. You've walked in a state of grace all your life, and I've been proud to call you mine."

The farm boy held his gaze on the woman in white across the room whose shimmering spirit garments seemed translucent in the violet dark, her lovely face and slender hands paler than alabaster. Despite the clear white fire of her ghostly countenance, somehow she appeared to Alvin as substantial as anyone else in the spirit room.

The dwarf lowered his eyes. "I've always worried that you'd have been greatly disappointed at seeing me, how I was born to this stature — my deformity. It seems no one in the family had ever in memory … well, I'm told I was quite unexpected."

"Shame on you, Arthur. Your birth was my greatest joy, my love for you more perfect than heaven's gleam. If all your life were a breath of honey, and heartache left to others, would you have had the courage to come seek me here? One day years from now when your morning room is quiet and the blanket that warms your legs has become thread-worn and faded, you'll know that our truest blessings can never be soiled by vain utterances and that in the eyes of those who love us well, our spirit suffers no lasting stain."

The dwarf hesitated, his voice fractured by emotion. Then, like a child seeking favor, he asked, "Will I marry?"

Alvin saw the tulip lights flicker while the manifestation appeared to ripple like pond water under a passing breeze.

"That heart which is penetrated by love for thee will indeed prove true."

Madame Zelincka lightly squeezed the hand of the teary-eyed dwarf who hesitated over his next question, brow furrowed with consternation. What did a loving son require most of his mother's eternal spirit? The farm boy watched intently as the dwarf asked the apparition across the room, "Will my life prove worthy of your sacrifice?"

The woman in white raised her hands toward the spirit table and answered with a radiant smile, *"Arthur, my dear, your life's greatest glory is yet to be revealed."*

With those words, she began to recede into the dark, her lambent spirit form evaporating to a pale translucence like a bright light extinguishing from within.

The dwarf cried out and rose from his chair and stood with his knees at the table as the glowing apparition gradually faded back into the darkness and disappeared. A draft redolent of honeysuckle ruffled the silk curtains and the spirit room fell silent, each of the sitters mute in the wake of the strange spiritistic occurrences.

Alvin heard a creak overhead as somebody walked the floor upstairs.

The dwarf sat back down on his pillow.

After another minute or so, Madame Zelincka spoke up: "Ethan?"

"*Yes, ma'am?*"

Her lovely violet aura diminishing, Madame Zelincka collected her stack of message cards together and glanced at her guests around the spirit circle. Then she said, "Ethan, may we ask you one more question?"

"*Yes, ma'am.*"

The farm boy stared at the medium.

Lillian Cheney shut her eyes.

"Is this world of strife to end in dust at last?"

Edith Elliotsen squeezed her husband's hand. The dwarf looked toward the curtained shadows where that perfect reflection of his mother had vanished. Alvin noticed a faint odor waft past his face like a child's breath of sour milk.

"Ethan?"

A songbird warbled from a distant tree.

"*No, ma'am,*" a small boy's voice echoed in reply. "*Life is everlasting.*"

Alvin Pendergast waited near the ticket booth at the showgrounds entrance in a dusty wind. By the hour on his new wristwatch, half past nine had come and gone and Chester hadn't yet appeared. Circusgoers passed through the gate flushed with glee as the ringing song of the carousel swept across the early autumn dark. A flurry of gold Roman candles boomed among the stars to the cheers of small children, but tonight the farm boy disregarded the hot popcorn and the bellowing barkers. He had seen the elephant and now he wanted to go back home to the Pendergast farm. In the sanitarium, Alvin had witnessed a slight woman named Anna Cates pass away so beset with chronic phthisis that gangrene had developed in one lung, which alternately hissed and gurgled when she spoke. The doctors pronounced her ghastly infections unmistakably hopeless and left her in the consumption ward to die. Rumor had it she owned a house in

Ohio tended to by a trusted neighbor, and two calico cats who slept beside her pillow at night, but no surviving family in the world. Her discharge from the sanitarium back to Oberlin was implacably denied by the administrator, so she retired to bed that last week of her miserable life, refusing to rise day or night until she was called to heaven, *"half to forget the wandering and the pain, half to remember days that have gone by, and dream and dream that I am home again."*

Feeling light-headed, Alvin watched a stocky marshal ride past on horseback wearing a white ten-gallon hat and shiny six-guns on his belt. Deputies from Icaria wandered in and out of the showgrounds, trailed by painted clowns holding seltzer bottles and nickel balloons. He watched two schoolboys in blue denim overalls light a thick firecracker and toss it over the fence into the wagon circle. When it went off with a noisy bang, both ran away to hide in the grassy meadow. Another quarter of an hour went by without Chester showing up and the farm boy grew cold and anxious. He feared both the known and the unknown. His fever rose steadily with a hacking cough he fought to subdue. Windblown grit stung his eyes and drew tears. Buttoning up his jacket, Alvin turned away from the ticket booth and the flapping banners and stared out across the wooded meadow toward Icaria, lit yellow beneath the evening clouds.

Soon, Chester waltzed out of the dark, looking dapper in a striped gray suit with a white carnation on his lapel. He was whistling a smart "I'll Say She Does," with a hint of satisfaction on his lips. Circus-going kiddies from downtown dodged around him like he was a king. He lit a cigarette and tossed the match into the damp grass. Alvin gave him a short wave, then regretted it when Chester frowned. The gangster angled away from the main gate and Alvin followed him, trying to act more casual now.

Once they were in the grassy shadows away from the big crowds, Chester stopped and gave the farm boy a once-over. "Say, kid, you're looking a little giddy around the gills. You just get off the Whirly-Gig or something?"

"I ain't been nowhere at all," Alvin answered, wondering how pasty he really looked. Was it so clear? He tried to stiffen up, act ace high like he knew Chester expected.

"Well, don't worry. We won't be here much longer." Putting his back to the crowds at the showgrounds entrance, Chester told Alvin, "I got it all taken care of after supper. I doped out the plan with Lester over a couple of steaks, and paid a visit to Spud Farrell. He's got an office in the icehouse out by the trainyards. Not half bad for a dump like this. Back in Cicero, he was selling rock candy under a crumb box at the Starvation Army. Of course, now that he's a big wheel out here in hickville, well, some fellows seem to have it in mind these days to turn every square racket into a shakedown, I don't know why." He stared Alvin straight in the eye. "Do I look like sucker bait to you, kid?"

"No."

Chester smiled, then took a drag off the cigarette and exhaled into the cold breeze. "I guess good ol' Spud thought he could fry the fat out of us once we tipped over the joint, like he'd nabbed us jaywalking and was going to blow off to our mommies. I don't mind sharing the gravy train, but we haven't been dough-heavy all summer and every-one knows it. When I offered to kick in a third and he wouldn't give, I figured it was time to knock off the song and dance and tell him the bad news. He made a lousy choice. I'm letting you and Lester divvy up his cut."

The farm boy's limbs went numb. "You killed Spud?"

"He was a menace to my peace of mind. Now he's out of the game. Soon as we're through here tonight, I want you and the midget to get your bags and beat it out of that flea trap. I'll be waiting for you in a motor over on Ash Street. Just don't shout it to the world when you're leaving. Get me?"

Alvin felt petrified. "Sure."

Chester flashed a grin. "I tell you, kid, this circus is the softest touch I've ever seen. When the tents close at midnight, Lester'll kick in the box, and we'll take our split and do a Houdini. Laswell won't know up from down."

"Nope."

"All I need you to do is keep an eye on his trailer for me until I do the honors with my little hotsy. She's expecting me any minute now and a smart fellow doesn't keep a sexy dame waiting. Just keep track of the comings and goings at Laswell's trailer so nothing queers the deal before we pop him."

"Which one's his?" Alvin asked, utterly confused about his role in all this. Did Lester know about him and the dwarf?

"Did you see those old firewagons back of the Big Top?"

Alvin nodded. "Yeah, I guess so."

"Well, Laswell's trailer is right behind them. It's painted up orange and blue top to bottom like a French whore, with a crocodile eating a naked Chinaman on the side. You can't miss it."

"All right."

"Just keep your eyes peeled for anything fishy going on there. Think you can handle that?"

"Sure."

Chester took a drag off his cigarette. "Where's the midget?"

The farm boy shrugged. "Fooling around somewhere, I suppose."

"All right, well, just make sure you two are there when it's time to bug out. I'd hate to leave you behind. If the cops get hold of you, they'll break your guts before breakfast and pretty soon they'll turn on the heat for me, and that'd make us both a couple of very unhappy fellows."

"Don't worry," Alvin said, scared to death now. "We'll be there."

"I believe you. Just be on time."

Chester took another puff off his cigarette, then flicked it away and went into the circus. Alvin waited a couple of minutes, then followed through the main gate. Sawdust blew everywhere in the cold wind. Confetti spun up out of Clown Alley as a piping steam fiddle played a rambunctious melody. Alvin crossed the showgrounds toward the Big Top, oblivious to the costumed apes on camelback, golden-horned satyrs trailing black-eyed hermaphrodites, the glint of ancient wares in a makeshift Pantechnicon. All he could think about was whether or not his disease would kill him before Chester did. He guessed now that he ought to have gone back to the sanitarium, after all. Truth was, Doc Hartley had always been kind to him. It wasn't his fault Alvin had a relapse. Lots of folks did. Some got better and others died. That was just how life played out. It wasn't anybody's fault. Not like the deliberate killings of Rosa Jean and her daddy, that bank clerk at Stantonsburg, the preacher at Allenville, and that poor kid he and Rascal buried in the muddy stall last month. Now Spud, too. How many others as well? For shame, for shame! Frenchy would tell Alvin he was caught between a shit and a sweat, all for having crossed the river with Chester that night. Frenchy also used to say there's no use in sticking your neck out till you know what the score is, but Alvin hadn't paid any notice to that and now he was on the run with a cruel stonehearted killer who would likely shoot him over a hamburger roll.

When Alvin reached the Big Top, he felt two jumps ahead of a fit. His legs were wobbly and his head was swimming. He was afraid if he sat down he wouldn't get back up again. Inside, the three-ring circus was at mid-performance. Trumpeters announced the arrival of Egyptian war chariots and a side-saddled Persian princess. Exotic birds fluttered across the smoke. High above the strutting ringmaster, diminutive elves and fairies mingled in an aerial ballet, while outside, the tent barker roared again to a swelling crowd, "STEP RIGHT UP! STEP RIGHT UP! NOW UNDER THE BIG TOP! ROPEWALK-ERS AND COSSACKS! LIONS AND UNICORNS! KINGS AND QUEENS! COME ONE! COME ALL! STEP RIGHT UP! STEP RIGHT UP!

A tiny hand tugged at the farm boy's right sleeve.

Turning about, Alvin found the diminutive Emperor Nero just behind him, white toga splotched with burgundy wine stains, laurel wreath tipped slightly askew.

Suppressing a burp, the clown midget told the farm boy, "Your presence is requested at the wagon of Mademoiselle Estralada."

"Pardon?"

"It's dreadfully important."

"I ain't supposed to go nowhere but here. I got an appointment I can't pull out of."

"It's been called off."

Alvin frowned. "Says who?"

"Says I, but it ain't just my opinion. Let's go."

Another harsh gust kicked up, further soiling Emperor Nero's white toga with grime. A pair of African elephants wailed under the Big Top. Circus cannons thundered.

Emperor Nero whistled to Alvin from beside the ticket booth. "What in thunder are you waiting for? You're not afraid, are you?"

The farm boy walked closer. In fact, he was quite a bit afraid. "Maybe. I ain't seen nobody put one over on him yet."

Emperor Nero sneered. "Aw, there's nothing to it! We'll fix that big stiff, all right. You just wait. If he starts any trouble, I tell you, I used to be pretty handy myself. What do you say?"

The farm boy shrugged. Why not? Any choice he made now was the same as another. Besides, he had already taken plenty of orders from Chester and what good had it done him?

Banners flapped loudly in the wind. A fresh crowd of towners lined up at the ticket booth. On the other side, Emperor Nero stepped back to let Alvin pass, and then kicked the bottom of the booth to draw the barker's attention. "Say, hatchet-face, what's the dope? I hear you got bitched by Little Flora last night. Ain't that a shame?"

The fellow handed out a pair of tickets, refusing to look at the circus midget. "You ought to scram before I push your face in."

Emperor Nero gave the ticket booth another hard kick. "She says getting familiar with you scared the life half out of her."

Someone in the crowd heard that and laughed aloud.

The fellow threw aside the ticket punch and slid off his stool. "Say, who do you think you are, shooting off your head? I'll poke you in the nose!"

Emperor Nero put up his fists. "Oh, you want to rough it up a bit, do you? Why, that'd be swell by me. I'll be laughing myself sick in nothing flat."

The barker started away from the ticket booth. "You'll start squealing when you get what's coming to you. Just stay right there. I'll fix you, you little pop."

"Aw, go sit on a tack, Nellie!" Emperor Nero kicked a cloud of dust up toward the barker, then ran past the farm boy, shouting, "Come on, kid, let's beat it!"

The midget rushed off through the scattered crowds, Alvin hurrying right behind him. People in line at the soda pop concession laughed as they went by. More rockets fizzed and boomed and schoolchildren ran toward the sparkling lights of the ringing carousel. Emperor Nero led Alvin between twin tents of the giraffe-necked Negresses, Zira and Lot, and a snaggle-toothed sorceress named Fatima who wore smoke-dark glasses and blew green fire off her fingertips at passersby. A stink of trained pigs and filthy pony punks overwhelmed the warm roasted peanuts and popcorn as the farm boy chased Emperor Nero behind the cage wagons where a lion tamer in safari suit and Pith helmet smoked a fat cigar and recited his spiel for a later performance while the jungle cats paced and growled amid swarms of black flies.

Crawling under a rope line behind the museum wagons and elephant tubs, Emperor Nero chortled, "Oh, that companion of yours is a very wicked fellow."

"Huh?"

"I tell you, he's got all the angles."

The farm boy banged his foot on a tent stake next to the Apple Family's dog and pony show. He heard drum taps inside the tent and a clash of cymbals. Emperor Nero crossed a narrow alley of manure and sawdust toward a painted gypsy wagon parked beneath a leafy cottonwood tree at the north boundary of the showgrounds. Lilac bushes curled under the rear iron wheels. Oil lamps glowed behind linen shades within. On the wagon steps, Josephine sat beside Chief Crazy Horse, and Alvin thought he saw a couple more circus midgets lurking in the shadows by the fenceline. The carved front door was shut.

"You're late," said Crazy Horse, getting up. His great feathered war bonnet drooped onto the wooden step above him.

"You're darned right I am!" Emperor Nero replied, fixing his laurel wreath. "That big horse Johnny Mills tried to kill me back there. Ain't it so, kid?"

The farm boy nodded. "Sure it is."

Tiny Josephine spoke up, "Mademoiselle Estralada invited the gangster to call on her at half past the hour. Merlin says they're still with Billy the Kid and a bottle of Scotch behind the Big Top. What if he figures out it's a stall to get him pickled? Just thinking about it gives me the cold shivers. I believe this is very dangerous."

"Aw, you're imagining things," said Chief Crazy Horse. "We're all set now, ain't we? What's the trouble?" He straightened his war bonnet. "We'll put it over, all right. Don't you worry."

"I ain't following any of this," Alvin remarked, more nervous by the minute now. Going back on Chester scared the hell out of him. He coughed as the wind gusted. "What's it all about?"

"Beg your pardon, dear?" said Josephine, smoothing her blue satin gown as she rose from the wagon step. Her tiny feet were pinched into gold satin mules with silver nightingales painted on the toes.

"Well, nobody's told me nothing yet," the farm boy growled. "Chester ain't no dumbbell. Try to cross him, he'll shoot the whole lot of us in the head."

"Maybe so," said Chief Crazy Horse, "but we can't poop out on a pal. Why, if you fellows don't do nothing, sooner or later you're both liable to get pinched, and Ol' Sparkie'll be the finish of that."

Josephine added, "I wouldn't see my little sweetheart hurt for anything in the world."

"Oh, he's got a marvelous plan," said Emperor Nero, knotting the wine-stained toga into his fist. "I just know we'll knock it over."

Chief Crazy Horse told Alvin, "Don't forget, kid, these thicknecks ain't so tough they can't get remunerated like the rest of us."

Alvin saw a pair of Keystone Kops crawl out from beneath the painted wagon. One of them with an oddly familiar babyface gave him a grand stage salute. When Alvin waved back, the midget blew lightly on his police whistle and chased after his partner through the thick sumac and prickly ash that cluttered the fenceline.

Kaiser Wilhelm hurried out from the alleyway behind the cage wagons, waving his tiny arms. "They're coming! They're coming!" The spiked helmet fell off the Kaiser's head into the dirt and he stooped to pick it up.

Josephine stole a quick look at her gold watch pendant. "Oh, dear!

It's time!"

"I tell you, we'll panic 'em," Chief Crazy Horse told Alvin, jumping down off the wagon steps. "Just you wait and see."

Emperor Nero grabbed the farm boy by the sleeve. "Come on, kid. The show's starting."

"Where're we going?"

"The best damned seat in the house," he said, shoving Alvin underneath the painted wagon where the farm boy saw a trapdoor hanging open. "Go on, climb in."

"What?"

Emperor Nero gave Alvin a stiff kick in the pants. "Make it snappy!"

"Ain't you coming, too?"

"Nope, I got to shove off. The gypsy ain't so liberal with the rest of us."

The farm boy crawled next to the trap door and had a peek up into the shadowy interior of the gypsy wagon. "There ain't room enough!"

Alvin looked behind him and saw the circus midget had already gone. Scared of Chester finding him where he didn't belong, he reached through the opening, grabbed for a handhold, and pulled himself upward into the dark. As he rolled clear, someone jerked the trap door closed.

A match flared briefly, illuminating the dwarf who giggled and blew the match out again.

"What the hell is this?" the farm boy grunted, shifting his knees to get comfortable. It was so dark he couldn't tell up from down. He smelled a peppery odor of incense and burning kerosene, and when he leaned backward he felt the brush of clothes hanging on a rack behind him.

"Shhh! We're in a costume closet," Rascal murmured. "Will you please be quiet? They'll be here any minute."

"Well, I can't see nothing. It's dark as pitch."

"Shhh!" The dwarf crept forward and slid open a thin foot-wide rectangular slot in the closet wall that revealed the wagon's lamp-lit interior. "Here," he whispered, "have a look."

Peeking through the narrow slot, Alvin saw a cozy boudoir draped in paisley textiles and bamboo like a Turkish harem, a pillow-heaped divan, Chinese lilies in cut glass flower vases, hand mirrors and Japanese fans on a tea table, muslin curtained windows, and a beaded portière concealing the front of the wagon.

"It's lovely, isn't it?" the dwarf remarked. "Why, I could easily imagine myself — "

"Shhh!"

Alvin heard voices from the wagon steps, an iron key turning in the door lock. He shrank back from the slot as the floorboards trembled under the heavy footfall. The dwarf shoved by for a look.

Chester Burke spoke as the door swung shut. "Go ahead, sweetheart, argue me out of it."

The farm boy pushed the dwarf away from the slot as Mademoiselle Estralada slipped through the beaded portière, her blue glass-crystal earrings and silver bracelets jingling. She was dressed head to foot in shiny indigo and gold silk sashes, her skin coffee-brown, eyes brighter than wet pearls. She spoke to Chester while unlocking the bottom drawer of a teak cabinet. "I just knew you were thirsty."

"Maybe I should get a haircut instead." Chester lit a cigarette as he came into the boudoir. "I ought to cut out getting drunk, start leading a clean life, and all that."

"It's not healthy to deny oneself pleasure," the gypsy remarked, reaching down into the cabinet. Alvin watched her draw out a pale blue decanter of ice water and a pair of tall heavy fluted glasses. "I've always believed intoxications to be borrowed dreams."

Chester exhaled a plume of smoke. "Sweetheart, I can see you and me are going to get on swell together. What do you say we take a hootch bottle and go hire a car for a joyride, just the two of us?"

"Oh, there's no need to go anywhere," the gypsy said, sliding open a drawer in the upper cabinet for a china saucer and a pair of silver vented spoons. "I'm sure I have everything you could ever want right here in this wagon."

"Oh yeah?" Chester cracked a grin.

"Be contented with thy present fortune," said Mademoiselle Estralada as she opened a tiny porcelain bowl atop the cabinet. "Constancy on thy part will meet a due return."

She placed a handful of sugar lumps on the china saucer with the vented spoons. Alvin muffled a cough with his sleeve, and the dwarf dug an elbow angrily into his ribs. It was stifling in the closet and Alvin wasn't sure how long he could remain crowded into there without getting sick.

"Say, didn't I hop into my best suit to date you up tonight?" Chester asked, picking up a scratched glass daguerreotype in a faded green plush frame. He examined it intently for a few moments. "I tell you, I'm a dandy fine fellow, once you get to know me."

Mademoiselle Estralada smiled. "You're a very pretty man."

Chester replaced the daguerreotype, and tapped ash into a silver ashtray. "Well, it's not all that often I get taken in hand by a sweet peach like you, too. Maybe tomorrow night you'll let me blow you to dinner, what do you say?"

"Why, that would be wonderful." Among the stuffed satin pillows on the divan were beaded pincushions embroidered with fancy chenille and pearls. Mademoiselle Estralada made room among these for Chester. "I hope this is comfortable."

"Oh, sure it is." He brought the ashtray with him as he sat down, then eased back onto one of the stuffed pillows. "It's swell."

Wiping sweat from his forehead, Alvin watched the gypsy take a round wicker basket from behind the divan and draw out a cloudy green bottle which she placed on the teak cabinet with the water decanter and fluted glasses, the vented spoons and sugar lumps.

Chester had a drag off his cigarette. "What're we drinking, honey?"

Mademoiselle Estralada smiled. "La Fée Verte."

"Beg your pardon?"

She showed him the bottle whose label read *Pernod Fils - 60°*.

"I'll be damned, that's 120 proof."

"Too strong for you?"

"Hell no, I've been drinking alcorub all week. I'll be all right. I'm full of pep. You like this hightoned liquor, do you?"

The gypsy smiled again. *"Avec les Fleurs, avec les Femmes, avec L'Absinthe, avec le Feu, on peut se divertir un peu, jouer son rôle en quelque drame."*

Chester laughed. "Gee, I ain't parley-voo'd fran-say with a dame since the war." He tapped his cigarette over the ashtray.

"Oh, were you in France?" the gypsy asked, pulling the cork from the bottle of Swiss absinthe.

"Me and 'Black Jack' Pershing himself at Saint-Mihiel with the Austrian 88's." Chester sung, *"It's the wrong way to tickle Mary, it's the wrong place to go."*

He laughed.

Mademoiselle Estralada said, "That's very nice."

She poured the absinthe into the first glass, filling about a third of it with a lovely emerald liquid that glimmered in the lamplight.

Chester smiled. "Thanks a million. I tell you, that war was the graft of the century. All I got out of it was a drink habit and some cheap chromos for a souvenir." He winked. "Don't worry, honey. I came back clean."

"Did you kill anyone?" the gypsy asked, pouring an inch less absinthe into the other glass. A sweet scent of licorice filtered into the sweltering closet. Alvin had never seen such pretty liquor in his life. Just looking at the green drink made him thirsty.

"Naw, I'm a pacifist. I didn't hold much for shooting scrapes. I preferred bourbon and dice with my pals in the drinkeries. It was a hell of a lot safer."

"That's very sensible."

Mademoiselle Estralada put a lump of sugar in one of the vented spoons, then took the pale blue decanter, placed the spoon over the fluted glass, and dribbled ice water onto the sugar, gradually dissolving it through the spoon into the emerald absinthe below.

Chester took one last drag off the cigarette butt, and snuffed it out in the silver ashtray. "Say, that reminds me, this beauty pageant you were telling me about, that wouldn't have been at the Navy Pier, would it? See, I went out to a speakie on the South Side one evening to shake a hoof with a dame from Halstead Street. You know, the sort a fellow wants to slick up for even if he's just taking her downtown to a ping-pong parlor."

The gypsy lightly stirred the mixture, her spoon making a pleasant tinkling sound as the swirling green liquid became a cloudy opalescent. Then she gave the glass to Chester. "À votre santé."

"Thanks." He sniffed it, and took a sip. "Say, that's not half bad."

"It's sweet, no?"

He took a longer sip and licked his lips. "Yeah, sort of minty."

"I'm happy you like it."

"Sure I do." Chester took a long swig, draining half the glass. "Anyhow, trouble was, this dame's pop was one of those old-timers who thinks nobody younger than himself'll ever amount to anything. If a fellow dating his little girl wasn't rubbing elbows with the well-to-do, he thought she'd laid an egg for letting the fellow pay a call on her in the first place."

Chester took another drink of absinthe while the gypsy stirred her own glass. "Well, she wasn't exactly a society dame herself, but when I bought her a fox neckpiece, he acted like I hadn't done anything more than have her down to a sweetshop for a couple of chocolate drops. Told her I was a missing link! Well, that made me pretty sore, so I fibbed to the cops that his alleydog'd bitten me in the back of the leg and they came and took it to the pound. I tell you, that old goat cried like a dame when he found out."

Chester finished the glass of absinthe. He studied it briefly, and gave the glass back to Mademoiselle Estralada. "Gee, that was swell. How about another?"

"Certainly."

Alvin watched the gypsy set her own glass aside and fill Chester's half up with absinthe. She took another lump of sugar with the vented spoon and slowly dissolved more ice water into the gangster's glass.

"At any rate," Chester said, settling back on the divan, "I got nothing to kick about tonight."

"You seem very happy."

"Sure I am."

The dwarf scuttled away from Alvin into the wardrobe of dresses where he covered his face with one of the gypsy's gowns and sneezed. Then he crawled back to the slot just as Mademoiselle Estralada returned Chester's glass to him. "Here you are."

"Thanks." He drank half of it down in one long gulp and broke a grin afterward. "Gee, that's refreshing."

The gypsy sipped her own absinthe, then sat down next to Chester on the puffy divan. A wind gust outside shook the wagon windows. Lamps flickered. She remarked, "Lester says you're from the Big Town."

Chester took another drink. "Not lately. I had a run-in last spring with some mental defectives mucking around Lauterbach's saloon in Cicero. They were pretending to be snoopers in their Sunday blacks while hijacking two dozen barrels of rum a month out of the storehouses in Skaggs grocery trucks. Too bad none of 'em were any too good at it."

Alvin watched Chester finish off his second glass of absinthe, and wipe his lips with the back of one hand. Madamoiselle Estralada asked, "You were a watchman?"

He shook his head. "Naw, I worked for a messenger service Lauterbach hired to send these sports a notice about how unhappy he was with the job they were doing. After me and some of the boys delivered them a valentine to a garage at North Clark Street, I decided I ought to get away from the liquor traffic for a while, maybe buy a secondhand motor, go see some of the country."

The gypsy smiled. "What a marvelous idea. Would you care for another drink?"

Chester gave her the empty glass. His eyes had drooped a fair amount since entering the painted wagon, his speech deteriorated to a mild slur. "Don't mind if I do."

Mademoiselle Estralada filled his fluted glass more than half full with absinthe. Once again she performed her ritual with the sugar lumps and the vented spoon and the dribbling ice water. Alvin began to feel closed in and worried that Chester had a cast-iron stomach and could probably drink arsenate of lead without getting knocked flat.

Chester picked up one of her Japanese fans and waved it about. "Say, I thought you were gonna tell my fortune."

Mademoiselle Estralada stirred the drink. "Would you still like me to?"

She tapped the spoon clean on the rim of the absinthe glass and set it aside. Her painted eyelashes glittered in the kerosene shadows.

"Why sure, it'd be swell."

The pretty gypsy gave Chester his third glass of absinthe, then sat down again beside him on the divan and took his free hand in her own and gently traced the map of his palm with her fingertips while he drank two-thirds of the sweet liquor. "Let not distrust mar thy happiness."

Chester kept his eyes on her as he took another drink. He waited for her to speak again. When she didn't, he frowned. "Is that all? Nothing about me and Sunshine Charlie and a basement full of mazuma? I thought you were a fortune teller. You sure ain't no Evangeline Adams, honey. Go on, try again, but this time tell me how big my fortune's going to be."

He drank the rest of his absinthe and let the fluted glass roll off his fingers onto the divan. In the closet, the dwarf started to whisper something until Alvin hushed him.

Mademoiselle Estralada frowned. "Please don't scold me. When I was a child, I tamed lions for the circus in Budapest and charmed the king cobra."

"Sister, I don't know that I'd hire you to train a flock of seals if you weren't any better at it than you are at telling a fellow's fortune."

Narrowing her eyes, the gypsy took his other hand and rapidly re-traced the lines across his palm. Then she advised, "If thou payest attention to all the departments of thy calling, a fortune awaits thee, greater than any treasure within the country in which thou residest."

Chester cracked a sloppy grin. "Gee, now that's more like it, sweetheart. Sounds like I ought to break into the foreign oil game, what do you think?"

The dark-skinned gypsy leaned over and retrieved Chester's empty glass from the divan, then stood up, her jewelry tinkling in the shadowy boudoir. She told him, "As the seasons vary, so will thy fortune."

Chester laughed. "Oh yeah? Well, here's one for you, sweetheart:

As long as dandelions bloom, as long as fruit ripens, as long as grain grows, just so long will men drink! Now, go ahead and fill 'er up again. I'm getting thirsty."

"If you like," the gypsy replied, taking Chester's glass back to the bottle of Pernod Fils.

"I sure do."

Alvin watched Madamoiselle Estralada sip briefly from her own drink, then pour more absinthe from the green bottle into Chester's glass. Black wisps of burning kerosene diffused the lamplight throughout the boudoir.

Chester spoke up from the liquor trance he had been lapsing into for the past quarter hour. "What do you say you come over here and we tell each other some smutty stories?"

The gypsy stirred the absinthe into another milky green cloud. She arched an eyebrow. "You wish to be naughty?" The spoon clinked on the inside of Chester's glass.

"You bet I do."

Mademoiselle Estralada put down the vented spoon, brought him the glass of absinthe, and kissed him on the cheek. He grabbed her by the elbow and kissed her on the lips.

"Sweetheart," he murmured as he let go, "you just drain me up."

The gypsy smiled.

Chester drank half the glass, then burped. "Say, what do you got in this liquor of yours? Gasoline?"

"Elixir of wormwood," Mademoiselle Estralada replied, "grown in the Val-de-Travers."

"You don't say." Chester drank another gulp, his mouth smeared crimson with the gypsy's evening lipstick. "Well, it's got one hell of a wallop, whatever it is."

"I'm so glad you enjoy it."

"A good cocktail sure makes the evening go, don't it?" Chester poured more absinthe down his throat, then stared cockeyed at the gypsy. "How come you ain't sitting here beside me, honey? Got a tummy ache?"

He giggled like he was daffy.

Mademoiselle Estralada reached behind her to the tea table between the closet door and the divan and drew out a Chinese lily from the cut glass vase.

Chester said, "Make love to me, honey, and I promise I'll take you to Jelly Roll Morton's show at the Cotton Club next week. Cross my heart." He gulped more absinthe and started blinking strangely. "You see if I don't."

The gypsy sniffed the delicate lily as she swayed in front of Chester. "Darling, I'm afraid I'm awfully done in tonight."

Alvin watched Chester drink to the bottom of his fourth glass of absinthe. The gangster groused, "Aw, so that's how it is, sweetheart, you don't love me, do you?" His voice had degenerated now to a sad drunkard's slur.

"Of course, I do, you pretty man. You know I do."

Chester dropped his empty glass onto the Persian rug in front of the divan. "I'm not a bad sort," he mumbled. "I tell you, we'll have packs of fun, won't we?"

"Sure we will, darling," Mademoiselle Estralada murmured in a soothing tone as Chester passed out. "Beautiful fun."

The farm boy and dwarf waited silently behind the hidden closet slot, hardly breathing in the dark. Wind rattled the wagon as they watched Mademoiselle Estralada stroke Chester's forehead with her fingertips. After a few minutes she quit and whispered something into his ear. Then she turned toward the closet and nodded.

"Let's go," the dwarf said, nudging Alvin away from the trapdoor.

"Huh?"

The wagon's front door opened and Alvin heard a flurry of footsteps. One of the Keystone Kops poked his head through the beaded curtain. He held a cotton cloth and a red rubber clown nose, which he handed wordlessly to the gypsy. The farm boy watched bug-eyed as Mademoiselle Estralada went back to the divan and stuffed the fat clown nose into Chester's mouth and tied a fierce gag around the back of his head with the cotton cloth. Both Kaiser Wilhelm and another Keystone Kop slipped into the boudoir.

"Are they going to kill him?" Alvin whispered to the dwarf who had already dropped down through the trap door.

"Oh, heavens no! That would be murder. Hurry up!"

The farm boy heard the circus midgets dragging something into the gypsy's boudoir, then the dwarf tugged on his ankle and Alvin wriggled his way back down out of the closet and dropped onto his knees in the sawdust beneath the painted wagon. As he crawled out into the cold wind, the farm boy told the dwarf, "When he sees what we done to him, he'll shoot us all in the head."

"No, he won't."

Across the showgrounds, the shrill music of the grand calliope, *Seraphonium,* piped into the night air with the noise of the gleeful crowds. By the front stairs, Emperor Nero and Chief Crazy Horse and Merlin and Sir Lancelot and Billy the Kid had gathered with more Keystone Kops, all bearing grave expressions. A wild animal cage had been rolled up next to the gypsy's wagon, its iron door swung open.

The dwarf took Alvin by the arm. "Come on now, we have to leave."

A chill ran through the farm boy, fear needling his spine. He said, "I tell you, this is all a lot of nonsense. He'll kill us for sure."

"Let's go."

They left the painted wagon to head off in the direction of the noisy midway. Nearby, a great cheer went up as someone rang the big steel gong atop the Strongman Pole. After Alvin's confinement in the dark closet, the glittering lights of Laswell's Circus Giganticus seemed wildly incandescent, a dazzling barrage of electric merriment. The farm boy's head swam, his legs tingled, as he chased the dwarf past the Palace of Mirrors and Laswell's shivery Hall of Freaks toward the whirling Ferris Wheel where lovely little Josephine sat waiting for them atop an apple crate between the dart throw and the shooting gallery. The hot roseate lights dyed her powdered pompadour a glittery pink like cotton candy and she held a paper fan at her chin to protect her show makeup from the windblown grime of the evening midway. When she saw the dwarf emerging from the crowd by the penny pitch, she shot to her feet with a squeal. The dwarf rushed forward to receive an embrace.

Josephine kissed him on the cheek. "My darling, you were so brave!"

Catching his breath as he came up behind her, the farm boy remarked, "Aw, he ain't done nothin' but watch."

The pretty circus midget smiled. "You were both very brave."

"Well, I guess that's so."

With a solemn voice, the dwarf told Josephine, "This is the beginning of the end."

She nodded. "Then we ought to be very careful."

Behind them, the glittering Ferris Wheel stopped briefly to discharge a load of rowdy passengers, mostly young people anxious to rejoin the midway crowds. Perhaps a hundred yards away, just beyond the nickel games and the hootchy-kootchy tent, a big roar went up in the direction of the animal cages. Alvin heard a round of applause amid the buzzing "oohs" and "aahs" of delighted children. The fresh tide of strolling circus-goers along the midway shifted immediately toward the excitement. Even the sideshow talkers and pitchmen paused in mid-spiel, looking somewhat quizzical.

"Let's all wait here," Josephine advised, her hand on the dwarf.

He shook his head. "No, dear. My friend and I must see this through to its conclusion, but perhaps you should stay. It'll certainly be perilous."

"What're you cooking up now?" Alvin asked as he watched a pack of panting schoolboys rush up the circus midway toward the commotion. His own head was buzzing with fever and excitement.

"You and I have one last duty to perform," replied the dwarf. "I'm afraid it's unavoidable."

"If I stay here," Josephine asked, "will you promise to come back safely?"

"You have my word."

"Then I won't go. Please be careful, darling."

She leaned forward and kissed the dwarf and hugged him tightly. Once they broke apart, the dwarf turned to the farm boy. "We mustn't be cowards."

"I ain't saying nothing till you feed me the dope on where we're going."

"This way," the dwarf said, directing Alvin into the weltering crowds up the midway, which resembled a street parade of circus-goers and roughnecks and curious tent performers in silken capes and silver spangles. Half the distance to the furor, a bearded albino magician stood high on a gilded stool, casting white doves into the night sky. Here and there, somersaulting clowns zigzagged toward the hubbub. Farther ahead, the farm boy saw a mob of people jamming together near the Topsy-Turvy House. The dwarf cut a path closer yet until he and the farm boy drew at last within sight of the ballyhoo — a hulking caged gorilla hauled out from the menagerie onto the crowded midway for all to see. Atop the iron cage, a sign read:

CONGO THE GREAT!
FEROCIOUS MAN-EATING BEAST FROM DARKEST AFRICA!!!

A gang of boys had already encircled the exhibit, banging on the bars and taunting the creature with sticks. No trainer showed his face. The burly gorilla lolled in one squalid corner of the wild animal cage, heedless of the clamor. People shouted filthy curses and hurled garbage. Arriving from the Big Top, the Dixie Jubilee Minstrels played a stirring "Invictus" to exuberant cheers. Then Alvin saw a boy with a hefty firecracker light it with a safety match and toss the firecracker into the cage beside the gorilla. When it exploded with an ear-jarring bang, the monster awoke with a vicious roar, sweeping most of the crowd back from the iron cage. A tall boy carrying a long stout stick jabbed the gorilla from behind. Two deputies from Icaria emerged from the crowd to chase the boy away, but another youth tossed a second burning firecracker at the gorilla. It detonated an instant after hitting the beast, driving the creature into a frenzy. Howling with rage, the huge gorilla threw itself at the bars, side to side, then leaped for the front of the cage whose iron door, when struck by the angry beast, simply swung open to the riotous midway. A red-haired fellow in a plaid tam o'shanter standing next to Alvin and the dwarf fainted dead away as the gorilla climbed down from the iron cage and bellowed at its tormentors. Women screamed. Children ran. The gorilla moved toward those too frightened to escape as a strident voice from the gallery behind the Topsy-Turvy House shouted, "SHOOT HIM! SHOOT HIM!"

Which the deputies certainly did, emptying both their revolvers into the crazed beast from a dozen feet away, firing and firing and firing, until the gorilla toppled over backward.

When the echo of gunshots had fled across the dark, a strange hush permeated the midway.

Not a soul moved.

Only the colored flags and banners flapping in the cold wind over the Big Top disturbed the quiet.

Then one of the deputies approached the fallen gorilla and poked the carcass with the toe of his boot. He holstered his revolver and walked carefully around the perimeter of the beast whose blood soaked the dirt. He paused at the gorilla's head, then bent down for a closer look. He frowned. "Well, I'll be damned."

He leaned forward and undid two buttons poorly hidden in the fur at the neckline.

"Looky-here, Tom!" he called to his partner.

Then the deputy slipped off the head of the fallen beast, exposing the ashen lifeless face of Chester Burke. "Why, this ain't no gorilla. It's just some fellow in a monkey suit."

One morning in early October, Alvin Pendergast sat in a prairie grass meadow watching the old trucks and painted wagons of Emmett J. Laswell's Traveling Circus Giganticus load up along a narrow dirt road that led west beyond the woods to a farther country. He had packed his own suitcase in the upper dark of the boardinghouse and left by the back door without saying a word. He brought three apples and a handful of crackers in the pockets of his coat and ate one of the apples while he sat there. His brown Montgomery Ward suitcase lay beside him in the damp switchgrass. Except for the spare cash-money Chester had neglected to collect from the dwarf, the farm boy believed it contained all he owned in the world.

Half a year ago he had left home for fear of being put in the grave, woefully ignorant of life. He had thought to escape somehow the relapse of consumption that raced through his blood by going away where nobody he laid eyes upon would judge him according to the prognosis of his decay, where each day would be a clean slate upon which brave new adventures would be written. Instead, some secret corner of his heart longed for familiarities unaffected by disease: a bee-swarmed path behind Culbertson's lumber shanties, goodnight melodies from his daddy's radio set, that old signalman on the Burlington railway staggering along the tracks at six o'clock each evening with a load of hootch in him, the damp Illinois corn wind in autumn. Guarded mercies too numerous to evade. Six months of sneaking in and out of these strange towns had left him lonely and tired, reconciled to worsening nightsweats and a malignant guilt. On the wooded path back to the boardinghouse after Chester's death at the circus, Alvin had asked the dwarf about the disposition of the gangster's departed spirit, if he knew where such sinners reside in the afterlife. The dwarf explained that their late companion was a moral imbecile whose criminal passions had consigned him forever to a lightless Hades, incapable of inflicting further pain and misery on fellow souls yet held slave by his habitual desire to do so. He would thirst but never drink, complicit in his own agony. There is no peace for the wicked and the damned, the dwarf assured Alvin, and left it at that. They were free now, their torment resolved, and that would have to be enough. He refused to utter another word on the subject. What he had failed to clarify was what Chester's fate meant for Alvin, to where the farm boy's own spirit was tending, shamed as he was by unforgivable behavior all this past summer long. Contrition was meaningless; what's done was done. How was he supposed to live out what days remained him now, infected body and soul? That secret corner of his heart provided the answer: He would go back home to the farm where he belonged, after all. He would take up a tin pail and fling oats to Mama's chickens and sweep potato bugs off the porch after supper and help old Uncle Boyd dig that ditch along his driveway and repair Uncle Henry's barn floor and fill a bushel peach basket for Aunt Hattie and another for Auntie Emma and learn to whistle a dandy ragtime jig outside Granny Chamberlain's window where autumn's shadows are thatched with maple branches and moonlight, for it was she who told him once that the answers to all life's riddles are found within a box of tricks hidden up in this good earth, God alone knows where, and nothing of truth is revealed until all our days here have run their course. Some tomorrow he would put on his work-clothes at dawn and breathe the field smoke of burning corn stubble and share another dinner plate of fried catfish with Cousin Frenchy and tell his sisters a pretty swell bedtime story; and when his own time came, be it sooner or later, he would go to his rest, safe at last in the bosom of his family.

Alvin left the chewed-over apple core in the thick grass and wiped his hands on the back of his trousers. Most of the circus wagons were loaded. Rumbling truck engines spewed exhaust into the cold morning air. He saw the dwarf on the road by the great steam calliope, a black derby hat on his misshapen head. Rascal carried a flat wooden box under one arm as he left the circus caravan and crossed the road down into the grassy meadow toward the farm boy. A chilly breeze rippled through the autumn maples, scattering old dried leaves all about. The farm boy smelled burning ash on the morning air. He picked up the cheap matting suitcase and began walking toward the wagons. The first couple of trucks started rolling forward. Fifty yards from the road, he met the dwarf who told him, earnestly, "They were quite disappointed."

The farm boy set his old suitcase back down in the wet switchgrass. "You know I didn't promise nothing."

"Of course I do."

"I ain't got an act like you. I'd be shoveling manure like some hick."

The farm boy kicked at a muddy clump of grass. His fever was gone for now, but he still felt tired. Up on the road, another truck engine roared to life.

"Why should our endeavor be so loved, and the performance so loathed?"

"Beg your pardon?"

Rascal smiled. "My dear Josephine asked me to give you this."

He handed Alvin the wooden box.

"What is it?"

"See for yourself."

Alvin undid the brass latch that held it shut. Inside the box he found a polished steel throwing-knife with a leather handle.

The dwarf told him, "It's a souvenir from Buffalo Bill Cody's Wild West show where my very own Josephine performed the treacherous

Wheel of Death on two continents. She risked her mortal life for six dollars a day and meals, and when the show closed, a Pawnee warrior by the name of Gideon White Cloud gave it to her in celebration of her extraordinary courage. Josephine wishes you to have it in appreciation of your own."

The farm boy took the knife out of the wooden box and rolled it over in his fingers. "Ain't you ascared no more?"

"Of course I am," replied the dwarf, "but when there's no peril in the fight, there's no glory in the triumph. Fear is bravery's stepchild. Hiding under the floorboards of my bedroom last spring, I'd resigned myself to the sorry prospect of scavenging and disrepute because I was ignorant of the steadfastness of hope. Auntie always imagined me incapable of sorting out my own affairs and too weak of heart to seek my way in the world without her constant guidance. She mistook my natural hesitancy for cowardice, and perhaps her stingy opinion informed my own ridiculous behavior these past few years. Well, no matter, because, you see, what I've learned since crawling out from under that tacky old house is that we needn't be children to fix our sights past tomorrow, or the day afterward, and be brave enough to call that our rightful place."

A dark flock of sparrows sailed over the meadow toward the morning woods as the farm boy thought about Hadleyville and how big the sky looked west of the Mississippi. "We seen a lot."

The dwarf grinned. "Oh, but there's so much more."

Up on the road, the pipes of the gilded calliope shrieked and steam rose into the hazy morning sky. Flanked by a few last scrambling roustabouts loading on, the painted circus caravan had begun moving.

"You won't change your mind?"

The farm boy shook his head. "There ain't much sense in it."

He squeezed the knife handle tightly, kicked harder at the clump of grass. What's done was done. Somebody rang an iron ship's bell mounted atop one of the circus wagons. The clanging echo shot out across the autumn meadow.

"My friend, you've been a wonderful traveling companion. Perhaps one day we'll find each other in another circumstance more fitting our best ambitions. You know, Uncle Augustus always told me the journey provides its own possibilities."

"I hope so."

The dwarf reached into his back pocket and took out a small shiny-black arrowhead. "This is a token of my own admiration. I dug it out of a beaver dam on the Belle Fourche River on my first excursion out West and have held it for luck ever since. I want you to have it." He handed the arrowhead to the farm boy. "Thou art now the favorite of fortune."

Alvin smiled, deeply touched by both gifts. "Thanks."

"Well, good-bye, my friend."

"Good-bye."

They shook hands, the farm boy and the dwarf, then parted as the autumn wind swept out of the east, chasing fallen leaves across the meadow.

Alvin Pendergast watched Rascal hurry away through the damp switchgrass, watched until the dwarf joined the long caravan of rolling circus wagons heading to another horizon.

Then he, too, started for home.

THE AUTHOR WOULD LIKE TO THANK THOSE WHO WALKED WITH HIM, THESE MANY YEARS.

STEVEN ALLABACK, MATTHEW J. BRUCCOLI, WYLENE DUNBAR, KAREN FORD, BILL HOTCHKISS, STERLING LORD, SHELLY LOWENKOPF, DENNIS LYNDS, GARDNER MEIN, DAVID MICHAELIS, STUART MILLER, JODY MILLWARD, JANE ST. CLAIR, PHILIP SPITZER, DAVID STANFORD, SID STEBEL, GINGER SWANSON, GEETS VINCENT, BARBARA ZITWER.

AND GARY GROTH, WHO SAW IN MY WORK WHAT I HAD HOPED WAS THERE ALL ALONG.

LASTLY, MY WIFE AND FAMILY, IN WHOM THE MEANING OF THIS BOOK IS FOUND.